RAGGED DICK

MARK, THE MATCH BOY

Ragged Dick
and
Mark, the Match Boy

HORATIO ALGER, JR.

WITH A NEW INTRODUCTION BY RYCHARD FINK

SCRIBNER PAPERBACK FICTION
Published by Simon & Schuster

SCRIBNER PAPERBACK FICTION
Simon & Schuster Inc.
Rockefeller Center
1230 Avenue of the Americas
New York, NY 10020

Introduction copyright © 1962 by Macmillan Publishing Company

First Scribner Paperback Fiction Edition 1998

SCRIBNER PAPERBACK FICTION and colophon are
registered trademarks of Simon & Schuster Inc.

Manufactured in the United States of America

3 5 7 9 10 8 6 4 2

Library of Congress Cataloging-in-Publication Data is available.

ISBN 0-684-84290-4

Horatio Alger as a Social Philosopher

TWO KINDS of general literature are available to the student of American society: on one hand, studies that examine the influences of "great," "thoughtful," "artistic," and "sober" men, and on the other hand, studies of popular culture in which ideas and attitudes that have a strange paternity are brought into focus. In many instances a student can read a great deal of American history before he becomes acquainted with the latter, and there is a danger that if he delays too long he will not really understand his heritage.

But in this far from best of all possible worlds, the virtuous often go unrewarded, truth is usually honored in the breach, joy is generally unrefined, crime often pays a lot, and national taste and sensitivity, look for them where you will, are typically deplorable. Is it the thinking of John Dewey that best explains our age—or the witless perversions of his arguments by uninspired school administrators? Is it the great novelists or poets like Thomas Wolfe or Robert Frost who represent our literary ideals—or the best-selling writers like Lloyd C. Douglas and Edgar Guest? Which newspaper reflects the opinions of the majority of Americans—the *New York Times* or the New York *Daily News*? Do the architectural ideas of Frank Lloyd Wright dot our landscape—or those of designers of look-alike split-level traps? Are more people satisfied by *I Love Lucy* than by *Death of a Salesman*?

Thus, to be valid a sample of a nation's values must be broad. It must include nonsense as well as sense, the vulgar as well as the tasteful, and the parochial as well as the universal. The great statement of an inspired thinker most often reaches the people through the work of a lesser breed. After all, many voices announce the dedications of a people, croakers along with warblers, and the heritage of Americans is tangled and diffuse. Until we understand that our creed is carried by a sad and glorious mixture of men who must be understood as we find them, it is not likely that we will acquire the reasons and the strength to sift out the tawdry in favor of the humane and the generous.

On this basis, a student of American culture should give far more attention to the novels and ideas of Horatio Alger than is usually the case. There is no doubt that what he wrote was bilge, but it was inspired. His novels, it can be argued, wove a far firmer strand in the American character than the work of men with sounder intellectual credentials.

Even today Alger remains a standard measuring rod for American life. For example, a 1962 *New York Times* obituary on Benjamin Fairless, ex-chairman of the board of U. S. Steel, began with a reference to his "Horatio Alger climb" to fame and fortune. A few days after that news item, Charles Luckman, former head of Lever Brothers, and presently a prominent architect, explained the alphabet of success in a New York *Herald-Tribune* article. He said, "A is for ability, B is for breaks, and C is for courage. Without any of these, no man can be continuously, truly successful." Mr. Luckman spoke almost one hundred years after the publication of Alger's first great success, *Ragged Dick,* and his advice supplemented that offered by a character in the novel: " ' I hope, my lad,' Mr. Whitney said, 'you will prosper and rise in the world. You know in this free country poverty is no bar to a man's advancement.' " In January 1962, James Reston wrote in a *New York Times* column that the Republican party wanted candidates with "an Horatio Alger image."

Alger elaborated on the theme of the self-made man in about one hundred twenty books that sold at least seventeen million copies, and perhaps more.[1] Countless boys read him during a period that stretched from the Reconstruction to World War I. Among them were Joyce Kilmer, Christy Mathewson, John Drew, William Wrigley, Jr., and John Dewey. There are many testimonials on Alger's influence. While Walter Lippmann reported that he was neither amused nor edified by Alger's message (which suggests that Lippmann's sobriety has a very long history), Edward W. Bok, the famous editor of the *Ladies' Home Journal,* claimed that the same ideas made his life productive. "They can laugh all they like at Alger now," Bok wrote, "but he pulled his weight in the world when he was with us."

Alger was both popular and enormously influential. A majority of the men who were adults during the 1930's probably were more familiar with his name than those of Tolstoy, Balzac, and Melville. Although he is barely read today, American culture still carries his message, and most men seem to find it true, good, and reasonable. In treating Alger seriously, we do justice to part of our living conviction.

Horatio Alger was born January 13, 1832, in Revere, Massachusetts.[2] He was named after his father, a Unitarian minister of that righteous breed who knew himself and God, and usually spoke for both. The father was determined that his own purposes would live on in the boy, and set about shaping him into another holy vessel. Like Samuel Butler's Mr. Pontifex, he thrust stupidity from the boy, even at the expense of boxing his ears, and the child was raised within a rigid pattern of unfeeling expectations. Only when the Reverend was away on church business did Mrs. Alger dare show affection to Horatio. He grew up, grave and solemn, dubbed Holy Horatio by the other children. When his father ordered him to tell what he was going to be when he reached manhood, Horatio answered, "A teacher of God's ways and a preacher of His Will." But to his mother, he confessed that he did not want to be anything, not anything at all.

When Horatio was fourteen he went away to Gates Academy, a secondary boarding school, and two years later he entered Harvard. There he started a diary the day he was enrolled and for the first entry wrote, "I promise to do my best in every subject and uphold the learning of this place." Horatio never had many academic problems as an undergraduate. He loved foreign languages, becoming proficient in French, Greek, Latin, and Italian. At graduation he ranked tenth in a class of sixty-two.

But finding a home away from home was not easy. First he roomed at Mrs. Curran's. The good woman baked him a chocolate cake each Sunday, but unfortunately moved too swiftly to serve up other of the sweets of life. As he noted in his diary, "She stood in the doorway as I passed to my room and had on very little and I might have seen her bare but I did not look. I shall move to where there is greater respect for decency." Horatio then moved to the home of a Miss Mullins, but left after three days with the ambiguous comment, "I must be more careful where I go." He finally settled in the home of Lloyd Thurstone, an elderly gentleman with whom he ate cookies and talked of philosophy.

It was here that Horatio lived part of the basic plot he was to use in his books. There was a large mortgage on the Thurstone house; because of a bad investment, Mr. Thurstone fell behind in his payments and was threatened with foreclosure proceedings. Aware of the problem, Horatio entered an essay, "Athens at the Time of Socrates," in a contest sponsored by the college, won the first prize of $40, and gave it to Mr. Thurstone. In 1860, as Horatio was completing his work at Harvard Divinity School, Mr. Thurstone died and bequeathed him two thousand dollars.

At college Horatio fell in love with Patience Stires when he was only seventeen. The Reverend Alger acted quickly when he received his son's letter announcing an impending wedding. He made a hurried trip to Harvard and put the stamp of his iron will on the matter, and Horatio turned away from his love. However, it had been first and best love for the young man, and he never forgot the girl. Thirty years later, he raced to her bedside as she was dying. But it was the first loss that did the damage. Because he lacked the courage to choose love when it was at hand, Horatio never found the strength in later life to search and choose again. The emotions of childhood and of youth were stunted; as a man he was a case of arrested development, unhappy despite success and fame.

Horatio tried to break free of his father when he graduated from Harvard in 1852. He had already considered a literary career, and he thought over its possibilities when he first read *Moby Dick*. "What a thrilling life the literary must be!" he wrote in his diary. "Imagination and observation—these I take to be the important requisites. Would it be desirable for me to take up writing as a life work?" Instead of entering divinity school, he worked for a while on a magazine. But it failed, and Horatio lost the first flush of his rebellious spirit. He finally entered Harvard Divinity School and worked well during the first few years. But the closer he came to graduation—to becoming the person his father wished for—the harder it was to swallow his fate. ". . . I will receive my degree as something to carry through the years to remind me of my folly," he wrote in his diary. However, when his parents arrived for the graduation ceremonies, Horatio was not there. The famous Alger plot was at work; two devil-may-care school friends, on their way to Europe, had dropped in just after Horatio received his two-thousand-dollar legacy. And Horatio had gone off with them to Paris to learn about Literature and Life.

Anyone called Holy Horatio who goes to Paris as a rebel is bound to meet that city on its own terms. What happened to Horatio was bound to happen, a triumph of circumstances and coincidence. He met a singer in a cafe,

Elise Monselet, who had grown bored with Frenchmen. No one can or should say more about the inevitable seduction than Horatio did in his diary.

Feb. 4th. I was a fool to have waited so long. It is not vile as I thought. Without question I will be better off physically, anyhow I have sometimes thought so. She is more passionate than me. . . .

Feb. 6th. I ought to know more. Elise makes fun of me. She says she knows I wanted to. . . . I am learning things from her.

Feb. 7th. Should I go on and is it right? What makes it wrong? She doesn't think it is wrong and nobody else does, only I.

Feb. 10th. I won't do it again. If nothing else, from now on I will be clean. I *shall*. They may laugh but I will leave if anything they say to me. I want to be alone and I don't want to see Elise. She must leave me alone. I want to get away somewhere anywhere. My head aches.

Horatio thought it over. But he thought it over as someone who had come to Paris to learn about Literature and Life. What else could he conclude? A few days later he wrote:

I want to live to be great. Suppose it is vain—all great men are vain. What have they got that I need to be like them? Whatever it is I will see. If I insist with myself why shouldn't I be, as well as the rest of them? It is just something that grows inside and I can feel it just as surely as I am writing. It seems to depend on doing what you want because all of them are that way. I will do *what I want* hereafter, least I can do is try. They say true genius has no bounds as to conventions. Genius has prerogatives. Then I will have prerogatives too.

Horatio went back to Elise that day. Shortly after, with genius and prerogatives in full bloom, he allowed himself to be stolen from her by Charlotte Evans, an English girl studying art in Paris. That relationship did not go well. Charlotte was a bit of a shrew and enough of a nag to make Horatio pay attention to a letter from his mother begging him to return home. He went as quietly as he could, but Charlotte chased him onto the boat. They landed in New York, Horatio excused himself for a moment to buy a newspaper, and ducked for home without her.

After the outbreak of the Civil War, Horatio made several unsuccessful attempts to enlist in the army. First he broke his arm, then he was in a train accident, and finally he came down with pneumonia. In 1864, he was ordained pastor of the Unitarian Church in Brewster, Massachusetts, but in early 1866 he left there for New York with the outline of *Ragged Dick* in his luggage.

The man responsible for this move was William T. Adams, editor of a children's monthly, *Student & Schoolmate,* and the author of many juvenile books under the pseudonym of Oliver Optic. He had attended a service at Alger's church and invited the pastor to send him a manuscript. The mail brought, first, "Squire Pitman's Peaches," and then, "Deacon Baxter's Cow," and both were published in the magazine. Adams asked for more, and when the first chapters of *Ragged Dick* were submitted, he urged Alger to commit himself more fully to writing. Alger's dream of a life of letters could not be rejected.

Adams introduced Alger to New York, and pointed out to him the literary possibilities in the adventures and problems of boys who came to the city to make their way. When A. K. Loring, a Boston publisher, offered to issue *Ragged Dick* as a novel, Alger signed a contract for six books. Like his own creation, Ragged Dick, Alger was on his way to Fame and Fortune.

As the Ragged Dick episodes began to appear, they came to the attention of Charles O'Connor, superintendent of the Newsboys' Lodging House. Founded in 1853, the lodging house was a haven for many of the boys who had left home during and immediately after the Civil War. Here, newsboys, bootblacks, and messengers could live decently for only a few pennies a day, and be protected from many of the temptations and dangers of the city. O'Connor found the values in Alger's stories made-to-order for his purposes. searched the author out, and introduced himself. The lodging house, he said, could be an unending source of inspiration for Alger's writing, which, in turn, would continue to encourage struggling and ambitious boys. This was the beginning of a lifelong association between the two men, and between Alger and the Newsboys' Lodging House.

Now the pattern of Alger's life was set. His books catapulted him into fame and success. He haunted the streets of New York, coming to know them well, and used them for much of the background description and incident in his books. Various mayors, as early as 1871, appointed him to numerous commissions and committees on vice, the elimination of crime, and other urban problems.

One of Alger's crusades is worth noting, for it places him within the humanitarian tradition. While exploring New York, Alger stumbled across one of the most vicious practices of the time. This was the padrone or contract labor system, one aspect of which involved young street musicians from Calabria who were imported and sent out to beg. The boys were treated brutally, many of them dying because of privation, cruelty, and disease. In 1871, Alger depicted their plight in *Phil, the Fiddler,* and began a public campaign to free them, during which period his life was threatened many times. Failing to secure help from the Children's Aid Society, which was fighting for child labor laws in industry, Alger and several other people organized meetings in parks and rented halls. The commotion they stirred up was given broad coverage in the press. Finally, when a particularly brutal example of mistreatment came to light, a court case on behalf of the injured child was filed by the Society for the Prevention of Cruelty to Animals. An explosion of public indignation followed and in 1874 the state legislature passed a law for the prevention of cruelty to children, the first of its kind in the nation. A major part of that triumph belonged to Horatio Alger.

Three to five books a year poured from Alger's pen, and the more he wrote for boys the stronger became his desire to write at least one serious book—"One Great Book," as he called it in his diary—one that would merit critical acclaim. Although Alger was hurt by those who mocked his juvenile prose, he was under no illusions at this time of his life about its literary value. He knew that he stood for decency, for the best that was in the idea of America and for his version of Protestant ethics. The boys who read his books and took their preachments seriously would be much the better for what he had to say. But he believed there was another kind of book in him, and thought more soberly as time went on of trying to bring it to life. However, nothing seemed to come of the matter.

Toward the end of the 1880's Alger's publisher suggested that he take an extended trip to California. Alger's newest books were not selling as well as the earlier ones, and Loring believed it would be wise for his most successful author to put his plot into Midwestern and Far Western settings. The journey brought Alger eventually to San Francisco, where he was lionized by a pair of literary sisters from the Friday Afternoon Club, until he was dispossessed by the club's next speaker, who happened to be Bret Harte.

Back East again, ill and unhappy, Alger settled temporarily in Peekskill, N.Y. A particularly brutal murder occurred shortly after he arrived, and the victim's widow muttered something about seeing a prowler in the vicinity. Alger, a stranger in town, was picked up as a suspect and jailed despite his protests that he was the famous writer. By the time the mess was untangled, the widow had made profuse apologies to Alger and sent a pleading cablegram to a married sister in Europe to come and help her. During the following weeks Alger and the widow had tea together almost every day, and he listened with growing eagerness to the descriptions of the sister, Una Garth, who was to arrive. She came, and in a matter of days Alger was courting her. The presence of Mr. Garth, a foreign sales representative for a Chicago concern, did not deter Alger. Mr. Garth, a bit taken aback by this unconventional situation, soon moved his family to New York. Alger followed, and in order to be alone with Una during her husband's many business trips, Alger bought a farm outside the city. Una helped him furnish it, even chiding him for wanting to buy two beds. There is no doubt that a scandal was brewing, but Mr. Garth saved the day by whisking Una back to Paris.

Alger was miserable. He wanted to follow, but did not have enough money. As he calmed down, he saw his plight clearly; he wanted to be with Una and only his pen could take him to her. He was still too disturbed by the whole chain of events to write, and only managed at first to get off a daily letter to Una. He paid little attention to her replies which indicated quite plainly that distance had bred disenchantment. Slowly he regained control of himself and then exploded with energy. Within a month he wrote *Frank and Fearless* and *Walter Sherwood's Probation*, and received a large advance from his delighted publisher. It was a prosperous and eager Alger who took off for Paris.

Alger did everything he could to rekindle a flame in Una, but she was too circumspect and Mr. Garth too watchful. She was flooded with messengers, sometimes as many as three a day, and it was out of sheer self-protection that she agreed to visit Alger occasionally. On these occasions they talked only of literature. Once more Alger was dreaming of writing "One Great Book." He had a title, *Tomorrow*, and told Una that all he needed was a story good enough to go with it. At one point he thought he had the idea he had been waiting for, but under Una's questioning soon discovered he had lifted the plot from *A Tale of Two Cities*. Then, while reading *The Three Musketeers*, Alger considered writing a version that would follow a group of American boys to fame and fortune. Next he thought of outlining the history of the world in a style that ordinary men could understand. His work would be in three volumes, *Yesterday, Today,* and *Tomorrow*. When he finally started writing again, he read the first pages of a novel to Una. Noting the event in her diary, she prayed that the Lord would spare Horatio a knowledge of his incapacity. The book became *Struggling Upward,* another Alger triumph. Shortly after finishing it, Alger suffered a physical and mental collapse and, under restraint, was carried away to a hospital.

Alger returned to New York a broken man. He went back to O'Connor, his dearest friend, who took him in and for six years cared for him in quarters in the Newsboys' Lodging House. Despite recurring illnesses, Alger's capacity for work reappeared. Books flowed from the office of the lodging house, and honors poured in once again. Now, however, more aware of criticism than ever and less able to accept it, Alger took to writing long introductions to his novels. Some were more than 5,000 words long, but his publisher always managed to find an excuse not to print them. Six years after Alger's return, O'Connor died. Alger stayed on in the lodging house, but it was no longer the same without his old friend. In early spring, 1898, he went back to New England, to South Natick, Massachusetts. There he read, and talked, and thought. He had visitors from New York, but more and more he wished to be alone. At first he had copies of all his books on shelves in his rooms, but when the latest of his novels arrived, *A New York Boy,* he read it, and had all the other books removed. One of the last items in his diary suggests what was on his mind as he was dying: "Wait for me, world, and I will tell you a story." He died July 18, 1899.

His favorite epitaph, one that O'Connor had thought was "slick," did not seem appropriate to his family:

> Six feet underground reposes Horatio Alger, *Helping Himself* to a part of the earth, not *Digging for Gold* or *In Search of Treasure,* but *Struggling Upward* and *Bound to Rise* at last *In a New World* where it shall be said he is *Risen from the Ranks.*

Horatio Alger's novels can be considered in two ways: as literature and as vehicles for the expression of social values. As literature, the less said of his books the better.

A poet can command attention if he has written one good sonnet, but a novelist cannot be salvaged because of a few good lines.

Herbert R. Mayes, Alger's only biographer, argues rather briefly that Alger represents the beginnings of realism in American fiction. A. K. Loring, his publisher, insisted that Alger was the first to record accurately a large part of American city life in fiction. Such claims are hard to accept. True, there are hundreds of portraits and situations in Alger's novels that are accurate and realistic, but they are drops of water in an otherwise arid desert. One can also find caricature and irony, but neither are sustained enough to represent a clear literary posture. The best of Alger's jibes, for all the impact they undoubtedly had on the boys who read and chuckled over them, lapse into preachments or reflect the author's innocence. A good deal of Alger is funny, but only because we read him out of familiarity with a language whose meanings have shifted a good deal since his day. He is filled with unwitting double-meanings, as, for example, in this passage from *Ragged Dick*: the snob says to Dick, " 'I've seen you before.' 'Oh, have you?' asks Dick wheeling around. 'Then p'r'aps you'd like to see me behind.' "

Alger is a monument to bad taste. He comes to us from the world of Victorian furniture and architecture. Like them, he is terrible; however, he is such a special instance of the terrible that he exercises a fatal fascination. As long as any reader has the slightest touch of artistic masochism, an hour with an Alger novel will bring to life a bit of agonized fondness for him. Reading him, there will quite likely cross one's face what Mencken described as the expression of a physician contemplating an eczema.

Although we cannot admit Alger's fiction as literature, his prescription for the good life has to be treated seriously. However, no student of American life and manners has ever investigated him at length. When one considers the number of doctoral candidates in universities who are searching for acceptable dissertation topics, it is a miracle that no one has staked Alger out for an exploration in depth.

With few exceptions. the discussions of Alger that do exist are all quite brief. and the commentators show considerable variety in their judgments. Stewart H. Holbrook wrote of him at some length in *Lost Men of American History,* and claimed that he was responsible for teaching the common man the *laissez faire* philosophy of Herbert Spencer. To Holbrook, it was Alger's thesis ". . . that in the United States a boy. no matter how patched his pants, could rise from the slums or from the farms. to become a capitalist. complete with plug hat and gold-headed cane. . . ."[3] Beyond even Fiske, Youmans, and Sumner, Holbrook continues. Alger ". . . was the man who put free and untrammeled competition on the side of the angels, and kept it there until well into the next century."[4]

Most other comments on Alger are far more modest than this. They range from the point that his novels brought heroes to sudden success. thus reinforcing the myth that the good life could be had by all, to the assertion that he preached Protestant piety and virtue, sometimes in a vulgar way.[5] Although there is some measure of agreement among the commentators, there is a broad enough variation to warrant a closer look at Alger's social values.

What were the obvious meanings in Alger's novels? His plot, which recurred with minor variations, depicted a poor boy eager for financial success who. through luck, pluck, and virtue, achieved his goal. Here is the idea of worldly success as it can come to the self-made common man.

None of this was invented by Alger. As a matter of fact, his social values do not derive from any creative thinking on his part. As George C. Homans, a brilliant contemporary social scientist. has remarked, one of the basic tasks of an age that is striving to understand itself is to raise the obvious to its highest level of generality. This is exactly what Alger did. He patterned a commitment to life that underscored the dominant myths, hopes. and prejudices of a majority of Americans. He echoed some of the most important ideas of the most complex revolution in modern social development—the movement in which ordinary men put themselves in the center of the universe. His books told American boys what they already half-believed and wanted to go on believing. Wish and faith fed upon themselves in Alger's novels, and it is doubtful that we will escape the consequences for some time to come. Before that can be discussed, however, the major sources of his inspiration need to be clarified.

The glowing heart of the matter in Alger's novels was the idea of success. Its clearest measure was material prosperity: the possession of commercial, industrial, and farming property, cash, an attractive, well-furnished home, and numerous personal effects. Success meant having a share of the good things of life. Here was the product of the age of geographical expansion and the ideas of Protestantism. Together, these historic events turned man's ancient longing for material well-being into an active program of achievement.

The notion of success was well-founded enough at the beginning of the seventeenth century to make the Reverend William Perkins' *A Treatise of Vocations* (1603) a self-help handbook that many New England colonists brought with them to America. Later that century William Penn wrote a series of pamphlets in which he hammered away at the theme of success as he advertised the material benefits awaiting immigrants in Pennsylvania. This land, he said, "lies 600 miles nearer the sun than England." Men who cannot marry in Europe can marry in Pennsylvania "and bestow thrice more in all necessaries and conveniences (and not a little in ornamental things too) for themselves, their wives, and children, both as to apparel and household stuff." In this new world, Penn advised, "the air is sweet and clear . . . like the south parts of France," grapes will produce "as good wine as any European countries . . . ," animals of profit and pleasure abound, shrubs have great curative value, and families have "some six, seven, and eight sons." As for Philadelphia: "The improvement of the place is best measured by the advance of value upon every man's lot. I will venture to say that the worst lot in town, without any improvement upon it, is worth four times more than it was when it was laid out, and the best forty." For people with capital, £100 would purchase five thousand acres of farmland, and hard-working, honest men without capital could rent two-hundred-acre farms for a shilling an acre.[6] No wonder so many hungered for the new world when such a bill of particulars outlined the successful life there.

The first and greatest native-born American spokesman for the idea of success was, of course, Benjamin Franklin. In *Poor Richard's Almanack* (1732-1757), he trumpeted the slogans of the movement. The doctrine could be reduced to a simple formula: "In short, the way to wealth, if you desire it, is as plain as the way to market. It depends chiefly on two words, industry and frugality. . . ."[7] The single work by Franklin that received the greatest circulation was *The Speech of Father Abraham*, better known as *The Way to Wealth*. Franklin made his position quite clear here. The prudential virtues became sobriety, industry (diligence), and frugality (thrift), but Franklin never suggested for a moment that the accumulation of wealth in any of its forms was a proper end in itself or that it depended only upon these virtues. "This doctrine, my friends, is reason and wisdom; but after all, do not depend too much upon your own industry, and frugality, and prudence. though excellent things; for they may all be blasted without the blessing of Heaven; and therefore, ask that blessing humbly, and be not uncharitable to those that at present seem to want it, but comfort and help them."[8]

"Reason and wisdom . . . ." Far too often nineteenth-century spokesmen for the cult of success stressed environmental opportunities, the physical and human resources that awaited exploitation. and the more obvious, crude, secular ways of handling one's self and others that could produce material affluence. As Louis B. Wright pointed out, those who wrote many of the best-selling success manuals before and after the Civil War took Franklin and "stripped him of his urbanity, his humor, his understanding of intellectual values, and his genuine wisdom."[9]

"Reason and wisdom . . . ." And, Franklin had added, without the blessing of Heaven, all may be blasted. From this standpoint, the main chance, as it was presented by the incredible opportunities in America, was best acted upon by the man who had in his character a proper feeling for the gifts of God and a willingness to act out His ethical strictures, particularly charity.

This was the version of success that Alger preached. Holbrook's claim that Alger taught Spencerian individualism fails to take account of the absolute sincerity of the Protestant ethic in Alger. An Alger hero not only sought, found, and made the best use of opportunities, but he also possessed traits of character that kept him on the path of righteousness. Alger's image of the self-made man demanded more than the chance to be just lucky or shrewd. A self-made man also had to be deserving of good fortune, to be the kind of man whom the Lord could favor. If he were not on His side, he could still succeed, but the flaw in his manhood would be there for all to see. He would be a cheap, crafty, malicious wretch, a brewer of trouble for others and himself.

Quite typically, an Alger villain was often a well-to-do man who was "bad" in the simple moral sense of the word. For example, in *The Young Adventurer*, the hero's mother, when she was a girl, had received a marriage proposal from Squire Hudson, the wealthiest man in the village. Since she knew that he was "cold and selfish," she had married a far poorer man. Squire Hudson's ambition is to get the hero's father to over-extend his mortgage so he will be destroyed. Alger has the squire soliloquize about an additional loan that "will give me an extra hold on Nelson, and hasten the day when the farm will come into my hands. When Mary Nelson refused my hand I resolved some day to have my revenge. I have waited long, but it will come at last. When she and her children are paupers, she may regret the slight she put upon me."[10] These Alger villains were self-made men, but their sobriety, industry, and frugality could not hide the fact that they were evil in spirit.

On the other hand, an Alger hero used the fruits of success with compassion and loving kindness. In *Making His Way*, Frank Courtney unmasks his stepfather as the forger of a will that cheated Frank of his inheritance. Rich once more, Frank, who is to become a lawyer, helps his dearest friend, Herbert Grant, become a doctor, and the two young men, waiting for patients and clients, "will live together, and their common expenses will be defrayed by Frank." The book ends with the following dialogue:

> "If I didn't like you so well, Frank," said Herbert, "I would not accept this great favor at your hands ____"
>
> "But since we are dear friends," interrupts Frank, with a smile.
>
> "I know that you enjoy giving even more than I do the receiving."

The concept of individualism expressed by Alger's successful, self-made, common man can be better understood if the diverse strands in the notion of individualism are made clear. In a searching analysis, Ralph Henry Gabriel has argued that the philosophy of individualism, as it finally emerged in the nineteenth century, involved four different positions: first, the religious version of the gospel of wealth and the accompanying doctrine of stewardship; second, the straightforward proposition that the prizes in the race of life went to the swiftest of foot; third, the economic and social implications of the classical *laissez-faire* arguments of Adam Smith and company; and fourth, the support given the second and third positions by the concept of the evolutionary struggle for existence.[11] To set Alger's social values in their proper niche, we will examine the last three positions first.

The belief that success came to those who moved the fastest was based on the old adage, "Every man for himself and the devil take the hindmost." In practice, this was often an amoral, secular, rugged individualism that approved of cunning, sharp dealings, and unrestricted self-aggrandizement. Here was dog-eat-dog in the school of hard knocks. The man who failed did not have the stuff it took to make a go of things. Any good that resulted from the machinations of those who were on their way to success was unintended. This was the approach to life behind Mark Hanna's declaration that "no man in public office owes the public anything."[12] Henry Ford was another who saw no way around the dehumanization that was in the race of life: "Great business is really too big to be human," he said.[13]

To understand classical *laissez-faire* individualism, one must begin with the social unity of medieval life and the conviction that religion was the only fit measure of experience. This social unity was maintained as long as men remained within the generally static time and space allotted by pre-Renaissance European custom and geography; it ended once the boundaries of life were pierced by the rediscovery of Greek and Roman ideals, and by the challenge of exploration. In the modernism that grew out of the fifteenth, sixteenth, and seventeenth centuries, secularism with its new images of man became a concrete dedication in political and social thinking.

This secularization came particularly swiftly in England. In British politics, the idea of the divine right of kings was contradicted by John Locke's contention, "The great and chief end therefore of men's uniting into commonwealths and putting themselves under government is the preservation of their property."[14] In British social thought, the justice and compassion of a personal God were, in everyday practice, overshadowed by the vast, impersonal forces of a nature whose demands bore a startling resemblance to the desires of commercial traders and manufacturers.

The rising middle class needed a rationale that could help it abandon the traditional ideology of management —the theory of dependence—in which the poor, as John Stuart Mill explained, had their lives regulated for them, not by them. By 1750, the idea of independence had been recognized as the intellectual device that could change the nature of social responsibility. The task of social leadership became that of helping each man become independent, responsible for himself and for his adherence to the rules and demands of his place in life. If men were responsible for themselves, they could be treated as if they were independent beings needing no assistance from their betters. Then the entrepreneur could, in good conscience, deny having any obligation toward the poor. He could conceive of the worker as an independent entity whose labor might be handled impersonally. It was Adam Smith, Edmund Burke, and Thomas R. Malthus, among others, who ultimately clarified this position.

The arguments of these men, from which they built what has been called "an edifice of gloomy error," had three steps: first, the State is unable to protect the laborer; second, the employer is actually unable to injure him; third, he alone can help or hinder himself.

Smith argued that the laws of nature made preference and restraint unnecessary:

> . . . The obvious and simple system of natural liberty establishes itself of its own accord. Every man, as long as he does not violate the laws of justice, is left perfectly free to pursue his own interests his own way, and to bring both his industry and capital into competition with those of any other man, or order of men.[15]

Burke confirmed this argument with a doctrine of self-interest:

> The proposition is self-evident, and nothing but the malignity, perverseness, and ill-governed passions of mankind, and particularly the envy they bear to each other's prosperity, could prevent their seeing and acknowledging it, with thankfulness to the benign and wise Disposer of all things, who obliges men, whether they will or not, in pursuing their own selfish interests, to connect the general good with their own individual success.[16]

Malthus disclosed the persistent pressure of population upon subsistence. The miseries of the poor are most often ended by wars of extermination and sickness; but the laborer himself may prevent the full recurrence of misery by exercising moral restraint in the establishment of a family, and by learning certain necessary truths that flow from the principle of population.

In the *laissez-faire* orientation, the laws of nature, as they apply to business, must remain untouched by any agency of government. They operate and adjust automatically because they are emanations of the majestic design of the universe itself. Self-interest guarantees that the best conditions will appear as each man works for himself. Charity and poor relief will not abolish poverty, but self-imposed moral restraints and learning may do so.

By 1813, in England, the industrial class had secured the new ideologies of management that allowed the dominance of the cash nexus. In post-Civil War America, during the age of boodle and the great barbecue, the arguments of Spencer were available for the support of the idea of economic individualism. Government, Spencer said, fulfills its function when it retains men in the circumstances to which they are to be adapted, and the moment it does any more than protect, it becomes an aggressor.[17]

A free society was at last at hand: a theory of independence absolved the businessman and industrialist from any responsibility for the ultimate welfare of the working class; a theory of statistical efficiency allowed human effort to be impersonally priced and purchased in an open market; a theory of subordination continued to maintain a rank-order society in which the rich commanded, and the poor and the ignorant had to accept responsibility for their lack of virtue. From this summit, the businessmen and industrialists swore loyalty to private rights and interests which they made superior to all other social and political realities.

Social Darwinism extended the *laissez-faire* position and validated it in a new way. It supplied a simple argument to those who owned and controlled the good things of life. Their defense took this form: only the fittest survive to hold power; we hold power; therefore, we are the fittest. Life was a competitive struggle that weeded out the incapable and gave control of the nation to those who had the cleverness and determination to make the most of opportunities. In the victory that comes to such men they express their peculiar fitness to command, exercise broad social control, and enjoy prosperity. "Successful business entrepreneurs," Richard Hofstadter concluded in his study of social Darwinism, "seemed to have accepted almost by instinct the Darwinian terminology which had emerged from the conditions of their existence."[18]

Alger's heroes did not express the individualism of these three positions. The arithmetic of success for them was pluck and luck plus the Protestant ethic. As has been pointed out, this stemmed directly from Franklin's formula, but in Alger's calculations, the old printer-diplomat's deism was replaced by Alger's Unitarian faith. Not only was the Alger hero in the right place at the right time, but he was there with a wholesomeness of spirit. Emerson made the point well when he wrote, "There is always a reason, *in the man,* for his good or bad fortune, and so in making money."[19] Such inwardness was many things, particularly an ability to recognize that material success was not a solitary and self-contained end. In the dialectic of living, it was also a beginning of social responsibility.

Here is the reason why there is considerable confusion about Alger's social values. Alger accepted the doctrine of stewardship, but so did many businessmen and industrialists, and their spokesmen—men who in addition had allegiances to the individualisms of *laissez faire* and social Darwinism. For instance, even Spencer accepted the idea of responsibility. You cannot exercise sympathy, charity, or benevolence through the mechanisms of government, he argued, without turning these warm human virtues into impersonal attitudes. The misery that pervades society is real, and must be faced, but only through the voluntary actions of those who care enough to want to do good. Distress must be assuaged by the expression of sympathy. When men willingly present themselves as benefactors, "not only do they remedy the particular evils to be met, but they help to mould humanity into a form by which such evils will one day be precluded."[20]

Andrew Carnegie was another who expressed all the aspects of individualism that have been discussed. His life, from poor boy to millionaire, was an Alger story come alive. Born in Scotland in 1835, he migrated to Pennsylvania in 1848. Carnegie spotted every main chance that came his way; few men of his generation ever ran any harder for success. He cultivated and expressed all the virtues of the self-made man that have been noted, and added others. His exuberance, compounded of self-confidence and drive, made the *laissez-faire* position completely meaningful to him. An omnivorous reader, he knew the historical, philosophical, political, economic, and scientific voices of his age, including social Darwinism. He said, "While the law [of competition] may be sometimes hard for the individual, it is best for the race, because it insures the survival of the fittest in every department."[21] Poverty was always "honest poverty" to him, the soil in which all virtues grew. Here was where men trained for the contests of the business world, and developed resolute and indomitable wills. Carnegie accepted the "gospel of wealth" (one of his books had this title) and the idea of stewardship without reservation. Certainly the free libraries he spent millions to establish are monuments to his acceptance of social responsibility. He believed that the community was always a partner in the creation of wealth, and that wealth should be returned to it. No man should die and leave his heirs anything. However, none of his ideas rested upon any assumed relationship between business and religion, for Carnegie was a free-thinker.

Thus, although Alger's social philosophy had some operational reference to Carnegie's, the two were not identical. Similarly Alger's social philosophy differed from that of Spencer or the unctuous Daniel Drew. Alger offered a purer and more naive strain of the success theme than any of the men with whom commentators usually link him.

It is not enough, however, to label Alger's novels as self-help books that preached success to aspiring boys. They carry other messages as well. If one looks closely at them, one sees that they also expressed a fascinating mixture of democratic equalitarianism and social criticism. Although no one has ever commented on it, Alger's influence on this level undoubtedly must have been great. There is no evidence that Alger intended this. Once again, all he did was express the obvious.

Alger did far more than push success upon his poor and honest heroes. He gave them dignity and planted it in their natures in such a way that it had the status of a natural right. He was far less kind to the sons of many of his rich villains. The self-seeking, dishonest, and conniving squires, businessmen, and lawyers he described spawned wretched little snobs. As Alger sketched them, they lacked all dignity and seldom picked up any along the way.

An Alger hero "was a bright-looking boy, with brown hair, a ruddy complexion, and dark-blue eyes, who looked, and was, frank and manly." Sometimes he turned up "with a face not handsome, but frank and good-humored, and an expression indicating an energetic and hopeful temperament" or with "a bright, attractive face, strong and resolute," but he was still the same.

An Alger son of the rich was equally unmistakable. For example, "He was a boy of sixteen, of slender form and sallow complexion, dressed with more pretension than taste. . . . His mean and insignificant features were far from rendering him attractive. . . ." Other young villains had more precise faults:

Mark Manning was slender and dark, with a soft voice and rather effeminate ways. He didn't care for the rough sports in which most boys delight; he never played baseball or took part in athletic exercises, but liked to walk about sprucely dressed, and had even been seen on the campus on a Saturday afternoon with his hands incased in kid gloves.

Kid gloves were the sign of depravity in all young Alger villains. They were always being put on, taken off, or waved in the faces of Alger heroes. The heart of the conflict between the two types was always the same: according to the villain, the Alger hero simply did not "know his place." *Brave and Bold* presents as good a sample of the problem as any of his novels. In this book, the hero, Robert Ruston, asks Hester Paine, the daughter of a rich lawyer, to walk home from a graduation exercise before the young villain, Halbert Davies ("smoothing his kid gloves"), could make the same request. Halbert is "mortified and angry" and swears that Robert will "be sorry for his impudence." The boys meet the next day (Halbert was "swinging his cane in his gloved hand"), and Robert is charged with "putting on airs for a factory boy."

"You mustn't regard yourself as Miss Paine's equal because she condescended to walk with you," Halbert said. "You had better associate with those of your own class hereafter, and not push yourself in where your company is not agreeable."

"Keep your advice to yourself, Halbert Davies," said Robert, hotly, for he felt the insult conveyed in these words. "If I am a factory boy I don't intend to submit to your impertinence; and I advise you to be careful what you say."

Using such scenes, Alger restated the case for democratic equalitarianism in the spirit of an unreconstructed Jacksonian. He underlined the American attitude that any common man, pauper or what have you, was the salt of the earth. The young villains always charged that the hero "puts on as many airs as if he were a prince instead of a beggar," or said, smugly, "Oh, you know, he is much below us in a social point of view." The Alger hero always defended his intrinsic worth as a free-born American who was as good as any other man. He never would back away from any defense of wounded self-esteem. Robert Ruston tells Halbert Davies' father, "It will be a serious thing for me if I lose my place here, for my mother and I are poor, and my wages make the greatest part of our income. But I cannot make this apology you require. I will sooner lose my place."

In *Do and Dare*, the hero's father, the village postmaster, has died, and the squire has managed to get the job for one of his own relatives. The hero argues that his mother deserves the position and states baldly that without it "we shall have a hard time." A brief exchange follows:

"I am surprised that in your father's long tenure of office he did not save something," said the squire, in a tone which indicated not only surprise but reproof.

"There was not much chance to save on a salary of four hundred dollars a year," said Herbert, "after supporting a family of three."

"Ahem," said the squire sagely; "where there's a will there's a way. Improvidence is the great fault of the lower classes."

"We don't belong to the lower classes," said Herbert, flushing with indignation.

Squire Walsingham was secretly ambitious of representing his district some day in Congress, and he felt that he had made a mistake. It won't do for an aspirant to office to speak of the lower classes—and the squire hastened to repair his error.

Alger was after more than fair treatment for his heroes. Little people of all kinds stood up for their rights in his pages: "You are very impertinent. You forget that you are nothing but a servant." "A servant has the right to be treated decently, Mr. Mark."

What was Alger after? On one side were many of the rich, mean and dishonest, willing to use power and position to hurt people. Their sons were not a bit better. On the other side were those on the way up, people with courage, good judgment, a feeling of responsibility—and the vote. The two forces must clash, and the victory must go to those whose strength is welded to virtue. Is this a morality tale? A fable? Or a proposition men must make come true?

There is evidence in over one hundred novels that Alger pleaded the case of the common man and doubted the morality of many of those who owned and managed society. Each novel, of course, had balance: some common men were thieves and jackals, and some rich men were honorable and wise. Yet Alger's readers could learn a lesson whose meaning was not too difficult from the social criticism of people like Wendell Phillips. Perhaps some of the men who made the years after the Civil War an age of dissent learned part of their rebelliousness and doubt from Horatio Alger. In our own day, comic books were treated as juvenile nonsense until men like Frederic Wertham exposed the violence they preached. It is more than possible that the parents, teachers, and ministers who approved of Alger's preachments might also have missed part of his message.

The last big idea taught by Alger was the most obvious. He always included luck and good fortune in the pattern of success. Let Alger state the case: "His plan [was] a doubtful one, requiring for success not only pluck and persistency, but good health and luck. Not many boys can expect an uninterrupted course of prosperity when thrown upon their own exertions." Call it Providence or the breaks, Alger made it the real key to success.

His books had other messages. They supported the importance of education, deplored smoking and drinking, and insisted on truthfulness, cleanliness, and honesty. Alger joined McGuffey and the rest of the middle class in these matters, and they need no amplification.

Alger was a major pump station on the pipe line that carried the American dream. There was not an idea in anything he wrote that was not already in the thought and feelings of Americans. But Alger affirmed the obvious in his claptrap prose with such conviction and energy that the big ideas he transmitted became even more credible.

Today, Dale Carnegie and Norman Vincent Peale are his direct descendants. The Lloyd C. Douglas school of fiction follows his propositions. People live his plot and find it good and reasonable. He helped make success a quasi-religious moral idea that leaves people who fail (whether in spelling or in something bigger) with the conviction they are unloved. He stands for trying harder, wanting more, and contributing to the community chest. The people who want to distribute Sears, Roebuck catalogs to Russians to persuade them of America's superiority are his disciples, too.

Any person who wants to know his country should get acquainted with Horatio Alger. It is dangerous to ignore a man whose ideas hang on so stubbornly. The novels that follow are as good as any he wrote. Step inside his world—and a larger part of you than you may care to admit will be at home.

RYCHARD FINK

Professor of Philosophy
Newark State College
Union, New Jersey

NOTES

[1] This is the considered judgment of Frank Luther Mott, *Golden Multitudes* (New York: The Macmillan Co., 1947), pp. 158-159. Mott's arithmetic casts doubt upon the accuracy of circulation figures that have gone as high as two hundred million copies.

[2] See Herbert R. Mayes, *Alger: A Biography Without A Hero* (New York: Macy-Masius, 1928).

[3] Stewart H. Holbrook, *Lost Men of American History* (New York: The Macmillan Company, 1948), p. 237.

[4] *Ibid.*, p. 228.

[5] Among representative books that comment on Alger are: Irvin G. Wyllie, *The Self-Made Man in America*, Arthur M. Schlesinger, *The Rise of the City*, Harold J. Laski, *The American Democracy*, Harvey Wish, *Society and Thought in Modern America*, Henry Steele Commager, *The American Mind*, and Marle Curti, *The Growth of American Thought*.

[6] Quoted by Louis B. Wright, *The Atlantic Frontier* (New York: Alfred A. Knopf, 1947), pp. 219-222. The Penn pamphlets were published during the period 1681-1685.

[7] Benjamin Franklin, "Advice To A Young Tradesman," in Harry R. Warfels and others, editors, title, *Rhapsodist, and Other Uncollected Writings* (New York: American Book Company, 1947), p. 121.

[8] ———, "The Way to Wealth," *Ibid.*, p. 125.

[9] Louis B. Wright, "Franklin's Legacy," *Virginia Quarterly Review*, XXII, 1946, p. 279.

[10] In view of Alger's repetition, it seems useless to quote from more than one of his novels in order to support any particular point. It should be noted that thirty-two of his novels were read by way of preparation for this introduction—certainly a labor of love!

[11] See Ralph Henry Gabriel, *The Course of American Democratic Thought* (New York: The Ronald Press Company, 1940), p. 158.

[12] Quoted by Matthew Josephson, *The Robber Barons* (New York: Harcourt, Brace and Company, 1934), p. 353.

[13] Henry Ford, *My Life and Work* (Garden City: Doubleday, Page and Company, 1923), p. 263.

[14] John Locke, *Selections* (New York: Charles Scribner's Sons, 1928), p. 75.

[15] Adam Smith, *Wealth of Nations* (London: Methuen, 1920), p. 44.

[16] Edmund Burke, "Thoughts and Details on Scarcity," in *Burke's Works* (Boston: Little, Brown and Company, 1869), volume seven, p. 383.

[17] See Herbert Spencer, *Social Statics* (New York: D. Appleton and Company, 1913), p. 127.

[18] Richard Hofstadter, *Social Darwinism in American Thought* (Philadelphia: University of Pennsylvania Press, 1944), p. 30.

[19] Ralph Waldo Emerson, *The Conduct of Life* (Boston: Houghton, Mifflin and Company, 1888), p. 99.

[20] Spencer, *op. cit.*, p. 178.

[21] Quoted by Harvey Wish, *op. cit.*, p. 178.

Contents

MARK, THE MATCH BOY

RAGGED DICK

Chapter 1

Ragged Dick Is Introduced to the Reader

"WAKE UP there, youngster," said a rough voice.

Ragged Dick opened his eyes slowly, and stared stupidly in the face of the speaker, but did not offer to get up.

"Wake up, you young vagabond!" said the man, a little impatiently; "I suppose you'd lay there all day, if I hadn't called you."

"What time is it?" asked Dick.

"Seven o'clock."

"Seven o'clock! I oughter 've been up an hour ago. I know what 'twas made me so precious sleepy. I went to the Old Bowery last night, and didn't turn in till past twelve."

"You went to the Old Bowery? Where'd you get your money?" asked the man, who was a porter in the employ of a firm doing business on Spruce Street.

"Made it by shines, in course. My guardian don't allow me no money for theatres, so I have to earn it."

"Some boys get it easier than that," said the porter significantly.

"You don't catch me stealin', if that's what you mean," said Dick.

"Don't you ever steal, then?"

"No, and I wouldn't. Lots of boys does it, but I wouldn't."

"Well, I'm glad to hear you say that. I believe there's some good in you, Dick, after all."

"Oh, I'm a rough customer!" said Dick. "But I wouldn't steal. It's mean."

"I'm glad you think so, Dick," and the rough voice sounded gentler than at first. "Have you got any money to buy your breakfast?"

"No, but I'll soon get some."

While this conversation had been going on, Dick had got up. His bedchamber had been a wooden box half full of straw, on which the young bootblack had reposed his weary limbs, and slept as soundly as if it had been a bed of down. He dumped down into the straw without taking the trouble of undressing. Getting up too was an equally short process. He jumped out of the box, shook himself, picked out one or two straws that had found their way into the rents of his clothes, and, drawing a well-worn cap over his uncombed locks, he was all ready for the business of the day.

Dick's appearance as he stood beside the box was rather peculiar. His pants were torn in several places, and had apparently belonged in the first instance to a boy two sizes larger than himself. He wore a vest, all the bottons of which were gone except two, out of which peeped a shirt which looked as if it had been worn a month. To complete his costume he wore a coat too long for him; dating back, if one might judge from its general appearance, to a remote antiquity.

Washing the face and hands is usually considered proper in commencing the day, but Dick was above such refinement. He had no particular dislike to dirt, and did not think it necessary to remove several dark streaks on his face and hands. But in spite of his dirt and rags there was something about Dick that was attractive. It was easy to see that if he had been clean and well dressed he would have been decidedly good-looking. Some of his companions were sly, and their faces inspired distrust; but Dick had a frank, straight-forward manner that made him a favorite.

Dick's business hours had commenced. He had no

office to open. His little blacking-box was ready for use, and he looked sharply in the faces of all who passed, addressing each with, "Shine yer boots, sir?"

"How much?" asked a gentleman on his way to his office.

"Ten cents," said Dick, dropping his box, and sinking upon his knees on the sidewalk, flourishing his brush with the air of one skilled in his profession.

"Ten cents! Isn't that a little steep?"

"Well, you know 'taint all clear profit," said Dick, who had already set to work. "There's the *blacking* costs something, and I have to get a new brush pretty often."

"And you have a large rent too," said the gentleman quizzically, with a glance at a large hole in Dick's coat.

"Yes, sir," said Dick, always ready to joke; "I have to pay such a big rent for my manshun up on Fifth Avenoo, that I can't afford to take less than ten cents a shine. I'll give you a bully shine, sir."

"Be quick about it, for I am in a hurry. So your house is on Fifth Avenue, is it?"

"It isn't anywhere else," said Dick, and Dick spoke the truth there.

"What tailor do you patronize?" asked the gentleman, surveying Dick's attire.

"Would you like to go to the same one?" asked Dick, shrewdly.

"Well, no; it strikes me that he didn't give you a very good fit."

"This coat once belonged to General Washington," said Dick comically. "He wore it all through the Revolution, and it got torn some, 'cause he fit so hard. When he died he told his widder to give it to some smart young feller that hadn't got none of his own; so she gave it to me. But if you'd like it, sir, to remember General Washington by, I'll let you have it reasonable."

"Thank you, but I wouldn't want to deprive you of it. And did your pants come from General Washington too?"

"No, they was a gift from Lewis Napoleon. Lewis had outgrown 'em and sent 'em to me,—he's bigger than me, and that's why they don't fit."

fault

"It seems you have distinguished friends. Now, my lad, I suppose you would like your money."

"I shouldn't have any objection," said Dick.

"I believe," said the gentleman, examining his pocket-book, "I haven't got anything short of twenty-five cents. Have you got any change?"

"Not a cent," said Dick. "All my money's invested in the Erie Railroad."

"That's unfortunate."

"Shall I get the money changed, sir?"

"I can't wait; I've got to meet an appointment immediately. I'll hand you twenty-five cents, and you can leave the change at my office any time during the day."

"All right, sir. Where is it?"

"No. 125 Fulton Street. Shall you remember?"

"Yes, sir. What name?"

"Greyson,—office on second floor."

"All right, sir; I'll bring it."

"I wonder whether the little scamp will prove honest," said Mr. Greyson to himself, as he walked away. "If he does, I'll give him my custom regularly. If he don't, as is most likely, I shan't mind the loss of fifteen cents."

Mr. Greyson didn't understand Dick. Our ragged hero wasn't a model boy in all respects. I am afraid he swore sometimes, and now and then he played tricks upon unsophisticated boys from the country or gave a wrong direction to honest old gentlemen unused to the city. A clergyman in search of the Cooper Institute he once directed to the Tombs Prison, and, following him unobserved, was highly delighted when the unsuspicious stranger walked up the front steps of the great stone building on Centre Street, and tried to obtain admission.

"I guess he wouldn't want to stay long if he did get in," thought Ragged Dick, hitching up his pants. "Leastways I shouldn't. They're so precious glad to see you that they won't let you go, but board you gratooitous, and never send in no bills."

Another of Dick's faults was his extravagance. Being always wide-awake and re. dy for business, he earned enough to have supported him comfortably and respect-

ably. There were not a few young clerks who employed
Dick from time to time in his professional capacity, who
scarcely earned as much as he, greatly as their style and
dress exceeded his. Dick was careless of his earnings.
Where they went he could hardly have told himself.
However much he managed to earn during the day, all
was generally spent before morning. He was fond of
going to the Old Bowery Theatre, and to Tony Pastor's,
and if he had any money left afterwards, he would invite
some of his friends in somewhere to have an oyster stew;
so it seldom happened that he commenced the day with
a penny.

Then I am sorry to add that Dick had formed the habit
of smoking. This cost him considerable, for Dick was
rather fastidious about his cigars, and wouldn't smoke the
cheapest. Besides, having a liberal nature, he was generally ready to treat his companions. But of course the
expense was the smallest objection. No boy of fourteen
can smoke without being affected injuriously. Men are
frequently injured by smoking, and boys always. But
large numbers of the newsboys and boot-blacks form the
habit. Exposed to the cold and wet they find that it warms
them up, and the self-indulgence grows upon them. It is
not uncommon to see a little boy, too young to be out of
his mother's sight, smoking with all the apparent satisfaction of a veteran smoker.

There was another way in which Dick sometimes lost
money. There was a noted gambling-house on Baxter
Street, which in the evening was sometimes crowded with
these juvenile gamesters, who staked their hard earnings,
generally losing of course, and refreshing themselves from
time to time with a vile mixture of liquor at two cents a
glass. Sometimes Dick strayed in here, and played with
the rest.

I have mentioned Dick's faults and defects, because I
want it understood, to begin with, that I don't consider
him a model boy. But there were some good points about
him nevertheless. He was above doing anything mean or
dishonorable. He would not steal, or cheat, or impose
upon younger boys, but was frank and straight-forward,

manly and self-reliant. His nature was a noble one, and had saved him from all mean faults. I hope my young readers will like him as I do, without being blind to his faults. Perhaps, although he was only a bootblack, they may find something in him to imitate.

And now, having fairly introduced Ragged Dick to my young readers, I must refer them to the next chapter for his further adventures.

Chapter 2

Johnny Nolan

AFTER DICK had finished polishing Mr. Greyson's boots he was fortunate enough to secure three other customers, two of them reporters in the Tribune establishment, which occupies the corner of Spruce Street and Printing House Square.

When Dick had got through with his last customer the City Hall clock indicated eight o'clock. He had been up an hour, and hard at work, and naturally began to think of breakfast. He went up to the head of Spruce Street, and turned into Nassau. Two blocks further, and he reached Ann Street. On this street was a small, cheap restaurant, where for five cents Dick could get a cup of coffee, and for ten cents more, a plate of beef-steak with a plate of bread thrown in. These Dick ordered, and sat down at a table.

It was a small apartment with a few plain tables unprovided with cloths, for the class of customers who patronized it were not very particular. Our hero's breakfast was soon before him. Neither the coffee nor the steak were as good as can be bought at Delmonico's; but then it is very doubtful whether, in the present state of his wardrobe, Dick would have been received at that aristocratic restaurant, even if his means had admitted of paying the high prices there charged.

Dick had scarcely been served when he espied a boy about his own size standing at the door, looking wistfully into the restaurant. This was Johnny Nolan, a boy of fourteen, who was engaged in the same profession as Ragged Dick. His wardrobe was in very much the same condition as Dick's.

"Had your breakfast, Johnny?" inquired Dick, cutting off a piece of steak.

"No."

"Come in, then. Here's room for you."

"I ain't got no money," said Johnny, looking a little enviously at his more fortunate friend.

"Haven't you had any shines?"

"Yes, I had one, but I shan't get any pay till to-morrow."

"Are you hungry?"

"Try me, and see."

"Come in. I'll stand treat this morning."

Johnny Nolan was nowise slow to accept this invitation, and was soon seated beside Dick.

"What'll you have, Johnny?"

"Same as you."

"Cup o' coffee and beefsteak," ordered Dick.

These were promptly brought, and Johnny attacked them vigorously.

Now, in the boot-blacking business, as well as in higher avocations, the same rule prevails, that energy and industry are rewarded, and indolence suffers. Dick was energetic and on the alert for business, but Johnny was the reverse. The consequence was that Dick earned probably three times as much as the other.

"How do you like it?" asked Dick, surveying Johnny's attacks upon the steak with evident complacency.

"It's hunky."

I don't believe "hunky" is to be found in either Webster's or Worcester's big dictionary; but boys will readily understand what it means.

"Do you come here often?" asked Johnny.

"Most every day. You'd better come too."

"I can't afford it."

"Well, you'd ought to, then," said Dick. "What do you do with your money, I'd like to know?"

"I don't get near as much as you, Dick."

"Well, you might if you tried. I keep my eyes open,—that's the way I get jobs. You're lazy, that's what's the matter."

Johnny did not see fit to reply to this charge. Probably he felt the justice of it, and preferred to proceed with the breakfast, which he enjoyed the more as it cost him nothing.

Breakfast over, Dick walked up to the desk, and settled the bill. Then, followed by Johnny, he went out into the street.

"Where are you going, Johnny?"

"Up to Mr. Taylor's, on Spruce Street, to see if he don't want a shine."

"Do you work for him reg'lar?"

"Yes. Him and his partner wants a shine most every day. Where are you goin'?"

"Down front of the Astor House. I guess I'll find some customers there."

At this moment Johnny started, and, dodging into an entry way, hid behind the door, considerably to Dick's surprise.

"What's the matter now?" asked our hero.

"Has he gone?" asked Johnny, his voice betraying anxiety.

"Who gone, I'd like to know?"

"That man in the brown coat."

"What of him. You aint scared of him, are you?"

"Yes, he got me a place once."

"Where?"

"Ever so far off."

"What if he did?"

"I ran away."

"Didn't you like it?"

"No, I had to get up too early. It was on a farm, and I had to get up at five to take care of the cows. I like New York best."

"Didn't they give you enough to eat?"

"Oh, yes, plenty."

"And you had a good bed?"

"Yes."

"Then you'd better have stayed. You don't get either of them here. Where'd you sleep last night?"

"Up an alley in an old wagon."

"You had a better bed than that in the country, didn't you?"

"Yes, it was as soft as—as cotton."

Johnny had once slept on a bale of cotton, the recollection supplying him with a comparison.

"Why didn't you stay?"

"I felt lonely," said Johnny.

Johnny could not exactly explain his feelings, but it is often the case that the young vagabond of the streets, though his food is uncertain, and his bed may be any old wagon or barrel that he is lucky enough to find unoccupied when night sets in, gets so attached to his precarious but independent mode of life, that he feels discontented in any other. He is accustomed to the noise and bustle and ever-varied life of the streets, and in the quiet scenes of the country misses the excitement in the midst of which he has always dwelt.

Johnny had but one tie to bind him to the city. He had a father living, but he might as well have been without one. Mr. Nolan was a confirmed drunkard, and spent the greater part of his wages for liquor. His potations made him ugly, and inflamed a temper never very sweet, working him up sometimes to such a pitch of rage that Johnny's life was in danger. Some months before, he had thrown a flat-iron at his son's head with such terrific force that unless Johnny had dodged he would not have lived long enough to obtain a place in our story. He fled the house, and from that time had not dared to re-enter it. Somebody had given him a brush and box of blacking, and he had set up in business on his own account. But he had not energy enough to succeed, as has already been stated, and I am afraid the poor boy had met with many hardships, and suffered more than once from cold and hunger. Dick had befriended him more than once, and often given him a breakfast or dinner, as the case might be.

"How'd you get away?" asked Dick, with some curiosity. "Did you walk?"

"No, I rode on the cars."

"Where'd you get your money. I hope you didn't steal it."

"I didn't have none."

"What did you do, then?"

"I got up about three o'clock, and walked to Albany."

"Where's that?" asked Dick, whose ideas on the subject of geography were rather vague.

"Up the river."

"How far?"

"About a thousand miles," said Johnny, whose conceptions of distance were equally vague.

"Go ahead. What did you do then?"

"I hid on top of a freight car, and came all the way without their seeing me.* That man in the brown coat was the man that got me the place, and I'm afraid he'd want to send me back."

"Well," said Dick, reflectively, "I dunno as I'd like to live in the country. I couldn't go to Tony Pastor's, or the Old Bowery. There wouldn't be no place to spend my evenings. But I say, it's tough in winter, Johnny, 'specially when your overcoat's at the tailor's, an' likely to stay there."

"That's so, Dick. But I must be goin', or Mr. Taylor'll get somebody else to shine his boots."

Johnny walked back to Nassau Street, while Dick kept on his way to Broadway.

"That boy," soliloquized Dick, as Johnny took his departure, "ain't got no ambition. I'll bet he won't get five shines today. I'm glad I aint like him. I couldn't go to the theatre, nor buy no cigars, nor get half as much as I wanted to eat.—Shine yer boots, sir?"

Dick always had an eye to business, and this remark was addressed to a young man, dressed in a stylish manner, who was swinging a jaunty cane.

* A fact.

"I've had my boots blacked once already this morning, but this confounded mud has spoiled the shine."

"I'll make 'em all right, sir, in a minute."

"Go ahead, then."

The boots were soon polished in Dick's best style, which proved very satisfactory, our hero being a proficient in the art.

"I haven't got any change," said the young man, fumbling in his pocket, "but here's a bill you may run somewhere and get changed. I'll pay you five cents extra for your trouble."

He handed Dick a two-dollar bill, which our hero took into a store close by.

"Will you please change that, sir?" said Dick walking up to the counter.

The salesman to whom he proffered it took the bill, and, slightly glancing at it, exclaimed angrily, "Be off, you young vagabond, or I'll have you arrested."

"What's the row?"

"You've offered me a counterfeit bill."

"I didn't know it," said Dick.

"Don't tell me. Be off, or I'll have you arrested."

Chapter 3

Dick Makes a Proposition

THOUGH DICK was somewhat startled at discovering that the bill he had offered was counterfeit, he stood his ground bravely.

"Clear out of this shop, you young vagabond," repeated the clerk.

"Then give me back my bill."

"That you may pass it again? No sir, I shall do no such thing."

"It doesn't belong to me," said Dick. "A gentleman that owes me for a shine gave it to me to change."

"A likely story," said the clerk, but he seemed a little uneasy.

"I'll go and call him," said Dick.

He went out, and found his late customer standing on the Astor House steps.

"Well, youngster, have you brought back my change? You were a precious long time about it. I began to think you had cleared out with the money."

"That aint my style," said Dick proudly.

"Then where's the change?"

"I haven't got it."

"Where's the bill then?"

"I haven't got that either."

"You young rascal!"

"Hold on a minute, mister," said Dick, "and I'll tell you all about it. The man what took the bill said it wasn't good, and kept it."

"The bill was perfectly good. So he kept it, did he? I'll go with you to the store, and see whether he won't give it back to me."

Dick led the way, and the gentleman followed him into the store. At the reappearance of Dick in such company, the clerk flushed a little, and looked nervous. He fancied that he could browbeat a ragged boot-black, but with a gentleman he saw that it would be a different matter. He did not seem to notice the new-comers, but began to replace some goods on the shelves.

"Now," said the young man, "point out the clerk that has my money."

"That's him," said Dick, pointing out the clerk.

The gentleman walked up to the counter.

"I will trouble you," he said a little haughtily, "for that bill which that boy offered you, and which you still hold in your possession."

"It was a bad bill," said the clerk, his cheek flushing, and his manner nervous.

"It was no such thing. I require you to produce it, and let the matter be decided."

The clerk fumbled in his vest-pocket, and drew out a bad-looking bill.

"This is a bad bill, but it is not the one I gave the boy."

"It is the one he gave me."

The young man looked doubtful.

"Boy," he said to Dick, "is this the bill you gave to be changed?"

"No, it isn't."

"You lie, you young rascal!" exclaimed the clerk, who began to find himself in a tight place, and could not see the way out.

This scene naturally attracted the attention of all in the store, and the proprietor walked up from the lower end, where he had been busy.

"What's all this, Mr. Hatch?" he demanded.

"That boy," said the clerk, "came in and asked change for a bad bill. I kept the bill, and told him to clear out. Now he wants it again to pass on somebody else."

"Show the bill."

The merchant looked at it. "Yes, that's a bad bill," he said. "There is no doubt about that."

"But it is not the one the boy offered," said Dick's patron. "It is one of the same denomination, but on a different bank."

"Do you remember what bank it was on?"

"It was on the Merchants' Bank of Boston."

"Are you sure of it?"

"I am."

"Perhaps the boy kept it and offered the other."

"You may search me if you want to," said Dick, indignantly.

"He doesn't look as if he was likely to have any extra bills. I suspect that your clerk pocketed the good bill, and has substituted the counterfeit note. It is a nice little scheme of his for making money."

"I haven't seen any bill on the Merchants' Bank," said the clerk, doggedly.

"You had better feel in your pockets."

"This matter must be investigated," said the merchant, firmly. "If you have the bill, produce it."

"I haven't got it," said the clerk; but he looked guilty notwithstanding.

"I demand that he be searched," said Dick's patron.

"I tell you I haven't got it."

"Shall I send for a police officer, Mr. Hatch, or will you allow yourself to be searched quietly?" said the merchant.

Alarmed at the threat implied in these words, the clerk put his hand into his vest-pocket, and drew out a two-dollar bill on the Merchants' Bank.

"Is this your note?" asked the shopkeeper, showing it to the young man.

"It is."

"I must have made a mistake," faltered the clerk.

"I shall not give you a chance to make such another mistake in my employ," said the merchant sternly. "You may go up to the desk and ask for what wages are due you. I shall have no further occasion for your services."

"Now, youngster," said Dick's patron, as they went out of the store, after he had finally got the bill changed, "I must pay you something extra for your trouble. Here's fifty cents."

"Thank you, sir," said Dick. "You're very kind. Don't you want some more bills changed?"

"Not to-day," said he with a smile. "It's too expensive."

"I'm in luck," thought our hero complacently. "I guess I'll go to Barnum's tonight, and see the bearded lady, the eight-foot giant, the two-foot dwarf, and the other curiosities, too numerous to mention."

Dick shouldered his box and walked up as far as the Astor House. He took his station on the sidewalk, and began to look about him.

Just behind him were two persons,—one, a gentleman of fifty; the other, a boy of thirteen or fourteen. They were speaking together, and Dick had no difficulty in hearing what was said.

"I am sorry, Frank, that I can't go about, and show you some of the sights of New York, but I shall be full of business to-day. It is your first visit to the city too."

"Yes, sir."

"There's a good deal worth seeing here. But I'm afraid you'll have to wait till next time. You can go out and walk by yourself, but don't venture too far, or you may get lost."

Frank looked disappointed.

"I wish Tom Miles knew I was here," he said. "He would go around with me."

"Where does he live?"

"Somewhere up town, I believe."

"Then, unfortunately, he is not available. If you would rather go with me than stay here, you can, but as I shall be most of the time in merchants' countingrooms, I am afraid it would not be very interesting."

"I think," said Frank, after a little hesitation, "that I will go off by myself. I won't go very far, and if I lose my way, I will inquire for the Astor House."

"Yes, anybody will direct you here."

"Very well, Frank, I am sorry I can't do better for you."

"Oh, never mind, uncle, I shall be amused in walking around, and looking at the shop-windows. There will be a great deal to see."

Now Dick had listened to all this conversation. Being an enterprising young man, he thought he saw a chance for a speculation, and determined to avail himself of it.

Accordingly he stepped up to the two just as Frank's uncle was about leaving, and said, "I know all about the city, sir; I'll show him around, if you want me to."

The gentleman looked a little curiously at the ragged figure before him.

"So you are a city boy, are you?"

"Yes, sir," said Dick, "I've lived here ever since I was a baby."

"And you know all about the public buildings, I suppose?"

"Yes, sir."

"And the Central Park?"

"Yes, sir. I know my way all round."

The gentleman looked thoughtful.

"I don't know what to say, Frank," he remarked after a while. "It is rather a novel proposal. He isn't exactly the sort of guide I would have picked out for you. Still he looks honest. He has an open face, and I think can be depended upon."

"I wish he wasn't so ragged and dirty," said Frank, who felt a little shy about being seen with such a companion.

"I'm afraid you haven't washed your face this morning," said Mr. Whitney, for that was the gentleman's name.

"They didn't have no wash-bowls at the hotel where I stopped," said Dick.

"What hotel did you stop at?"

"The Box Hotel."

"The Box Hotel?"

"Yes, sir, I slept in a box on Spruce Street."

Frank surveyed Dick curiously.

"How did you like it?" he asked.

"I slept bully."

"Suppose it had rained?"

"Then I'd have wet my best clothes," said Dick.

"Are these all the clothes you have?"

"Yes, sir."

Mr. Whitney spoke a few words to Frank, who seemed pleased with the suggestion.

"Follow me, my lad," he said.

Dick in some surprise obeyed orders, following Mr. Whitney and Frank into the hotel, past the office, to the foot of the staircase. Here a servant of the hotel stopped Dick, but Mr. Whitney explained that he had something for him to do, and he was allowed to proceed.

They entered a long entry, and finally paused before a door. This being opened a pleasant chamber was disclosed.

"Come in, my lad," said Mr. Whitney.

Dick and Frank entered.

Chapter 4

Dick's New Suit

"Now," said Mr. Whitney to Dick, "my nephew here is on his way to a boarding-school. He had a suit of clothes in his trunk about half worn. He is willing to give them to you. I think they will look better than those you have on."

Dick was so astonished that he hardly knew what to say. Presents were something that he knew very little about, never having received any to his knowledge. That so large a gift should be made to him by a stranger seemed very wonderful.

The clothes were brought out, and turned out to be a neat gray suit.

"Before you put them on, my lad, you must wash yourself. Clean clothes and a dirty skin don't go very well together. Frank, you may attend to him. I am obliged to go at once. Have you got as much money as you require?"

"Yes, uncle."

"One more word, my lad," said Mr. Whitney, addressing Dick; "I may be rash in trusting a boy of whom I know nothing, but I like your looks, and I think you will prove a proper guide for my nephew."

"Yes, I will, sir," said Dick, earnestly. "Honor bright!"

"Very well. A pleasant time to you."

The process of cleansing commenced. To tell the truth Dick needed it, and the sensation of cleanliness he found both new and pleasant. Frank added to his gift a shirt, stockings, and an old pair of shoes. "I am sorry I haven't any cap," he said.

"I've got one," said Dick.

"It isn't so new as it might be," said Frank, surveying an old felt hat, which had once been black, but was now dingy, with a large hole in the top and a portion of the rim torn off.

"No," said Dick; "my grandfather used to wear it when he was a boy, and I've kep' it ever since out of respect for his memory. But I'll get a new one now. I can buy one cheap on Chatham Street."

"Is that near here?"

"Only five minutes' walk."

"Then we can get one on the way."

When Dick was dressed in his new attire, with his face and hands clean, and his hair brushed, it was difficult to imagine that he was the same boy.

He now looked quite handsome, and might readily have been taken for a young gentleman, except that his hands were red and grimy.

"Look at yourself," said Frank, leading him before the mirror.

"By gracious!" said Dick, staring back in astonishment, "that isn't me, is it?"

"Don't you know yourself?" asked Frank, smiling.

"It reminds me of Cinderella," said Dick, "when she was changed into a fairy princess. I see it one night at Barnum's. What'll Johnny Nolan say when he sees me? He won't dare to speak to such a young swell as I be now. Aint it rich?" and Dick burst into a loud laugh. His fancy was tickled by the anticipation of his friend's surprise. Then the thought of the valuable gifts he had received occurred to him, and he looked gratefully at Frank.

"You're a brick," he said.

"A what?"

"A brick! You're a jolly good fellow to give me such a present."

"You're quite welcome, Dick," said Frank, kindly. "I'm better off than you are, and I can spare the clothes just as well as not. You must have a new hat though. But that we can get when we go out. The old clothes you can make into a bundle."

"Wait a minute till I get my handkercher," and Dick pulled from the pocket of the pants a dirty rag, which might have been white once, though it did not look like it, and had apparently once formed a part of a sheet or shirt.

"You mustn't carry that," said Frank.

"But I've got a cold," said Dick.

"Oh, I don't mean you to go without a handkerchief. I'll give you one."

Frank opened his trunk and pulled out two, which he gave to Dick.

"I wonder if I aint dreamin'," said Dick, once more surveying himself doubtfully in the glass. "I'm afraid I'm dreamin', and shall wake up in a barrel, as I did night afore last."

"Shall I pinch you so you can wake here?" asked Frank, playfully.

"Yes," said Dick, seriously, "I wish you would."

He pulled up the sleeve of his jacket, and Frank pinched him pretty hard, so that Dick winced.

"Yes, I guess I'm awake," said Dick; "you've got a pair of nippers, you have.

"But what shall I do with my brush and blacking?" he asked.

"You can leave them here till we come back," said Frank. "They will be safe."

"Hold on a minute," said Dick, surveying Frank's boots with a professional eye, "you ain't got a good shine on them boots. I'll make 'em shine so you can see your face in 'em."

And he was as good as his word.

"Thank you," said Frank; "now you had better brush your own shoes."

This had not occurred to Dick, for in general the professional boot-black considers his blacking too valuable to expend on his own shoes or boots, if he is fortunate enough to possess a pair.

The two boys now went downstairs together. They met the same servant who had spoken to Dick a few minutes before, but there was no recognition.

"He don't know me," said Dick. "He thinks I'm a young swell like you."

"What's a swell?"

"Oh, a feller that wears nobby clothes like you."

"And you, too, Dick."

"Yes," said Dick, "who'd ever have thought as I should have turned into a swell?"

They had now got out on Broadway, and were slowly walking along the west side by the Park, when who should Dick see in front of him, but Johnny Nolan?

Instantly Dick was seized with a fancy for witnessing Johnny's amazement at his change in appearance. He stole up behind him, and struck him on the back.

"Hallo, Johnny, how many shines have you had?"

Johnny turned round expecting to see Dick, whose voice he recognized, but his astonished eyes rested on a nicely dressed boy (the hat alone excepted) who looked indeed like Dick, but so transformed in dress that it was difficult to be sure of his identity.

"What luck, Johnny?" repeated Dick.

Johnny surveyed him from head to foot in great bewilderment.

"Who be you?" he said.

"Well, that's a good one," laughed Dick; "so you don't know Dick?"

"Where'd you get all them clothes?" asked Johnny. "Have you been stealin'?"

"Say that again, and I'll lick you. No, I've lent my clothes to a young feller as was goin' to a party, and didn't have none fit to wear, and so I put on my second-best for a change."

Without deigning any further explanation, Dick went off, followed by the astonished gaze of Johnny Nolan, who could not quite make up his mind whether the neat-looking boy he had been talking with was really Ragged Dick or not.

In order to reach Chatham Street it was necessary to

cross Broadway. This was easier proposed than done. There is always such a throng of omnibuses, drays, carriages, and vehicles of all kinds in the neighborhood of the Astor House, that the crossing is formidable to one who is not used to it. Dick made nothing of it, dodging in and out among the horses and wagons with perfect self-possession. Reaching the opposite sidewalk, he looked back, and found that Frank had retreated in dismay, and that the width of the street was between them.

"Come across!" called out Dick.

"I don't see any chance," said Frank, looking anxiously at the prospect before him. "I'm afraid of being run over."

"If you are, you can sue 'em for damages," said Dick.

Finally Frank got safely over after several narrow escapes, as he considered them.

"Is it always so crowded?" he asked.

"A good deal worse sometimes," said Dick. "I knowed a young man once who waited six hours for a chance to cross, and at last got run over by an omnibus, leaving a widder and a large family of orphan children. His widder, a beautiful young woman, was obliged to start a peanut and apple stand. There she is now."

"Where?"

Dick pointed to a hideous old woman, of large proportions, wearing a bonnet of immense size, who presided over an apple-stand close by.

Frank laughed.

"If that is the case," he said, "I think I will patronize her."

"Leave it to me," said Dick, winking.

He advanced gravely to the apple-stand, and said, "Old lady, have you paid your taxes?"

The astonished woman opened her eyes.

"I'm a gov'ment officer," said Dick, "sent by the mayor to collect your taxes. I'll take it in apples just to oblige. That big red one will about pay what you're owin' to the gov'ment."

"I don't know nothing about no taxes," said the old woman, in bewilderment.

"Then," said Dick, "I'll let you off this time. Give us two of your best apples, and my friend here, the President of the Common Council, will pay you."

Frank, smiling, paid three cents apiece for the apples, and they sauntered on, Dick remarking, "If these apples aint good, old lady, we'll return 'em and get our money back." This would have been rather difficult in his case, as the apple was already half consumed.

Chatham Street, where they wished to go, being on the East side, the two boys crossed the Park. This is an enclosure of about ten acres, which years ago was covered with a green sward, but is now a great thoroughfare for pedestrians and contains several important public buildings. Dick pointed out the City Hall, the Hall of Records, and the Rotunda. The former is a white building of large size, and surmounted by a cupola.

"That's where the mayor's office is," said Dick. "Him and me are very good friends. I once blacked his boots by particular appointment. That's the way I pay my city taxes."

Chapter 5

Chatham Street and Broadway

THEY WERE soon in Chatham Street, walking between rows of ready-made clothing shops, many of which had half of their stock in trade exposed on the sidewalk. The proprietors of these establishments stood at the doors, watching attentively the passers-by, extending urgent invitations to any who even glanced at the goods, to enter.

"Walk in, young gentlemen," said a stout man, at the entrance of one shop.

"No, I thank you," replied Dick, "as the fly said to the spider."

"We're selling off at less than cost."

"Of course you be. That's where you makes your money," said Dick. "There aint nobody of any enterprise that pretends to make any profit on his goods."

The Chatham Street trader looked after our hero as if he didn't quite comprehend him; but Dick, without waiting for a reply, passed on with his companion.

In some of the shops auctions seemed to be going on.

"I am only offered two dollars, gentlemen, for this elegant pair of doeskin pants, made of the very best of cloth. It's a frightful sacrifice. Who'll give an eighth? Thank you, sir. Only seventeen shillings! Why the cloth cost more by the yard!"

This speaker was standing on a little platform haranguing to three men, holding in his hand meanwhile a pair of pants very loose in the legs, and presenting a cheap Bowery look.

Frank and Dick paused before the shop door, and finally saw them knocked down to rather a verdant-looking individual at three dollars.

"Clothes seem to be pretty cheap here," said Frank.

"Yes, but Baxter Street is the cheapest place."

"Is it?"

"Yes. Johnny Nolan got a whole rig-out there last week, for a dollar,—coat, cap, vest, pants, and shoes. They was very good measure, too, like my best clothes that I took off to oblige you."

"I shall know where to come for clothes next time," said Frank, laughing. "I had no idea the city was so much cheaper than the country. I suppose the Baxter Street tailors are fashionable?"

"In course they are. Me and Horace Greeley always go there for clothes. When Horace gets a new suit, I always have one made just like it; but I can't go the white hat. It aint becomin' to my style of beauty."

A little farther on a man was standing out on the sidewalk, distributing small printed handbills. One was handed to Frank, which he read as follows,—

"GRAND CLOSING-OUT SALE!—A variety of Beautiful and Costly Articles for Sale, at a Dollar apiece. Unparalleled Inducements! Walk in, Gentlemen!"

"Whereabouts is this sale?" asked Frank.

"In here, young gentlemen," said a black-whiskered individual, who appeared suddenly on the scene. "Walk in."

"Shall we go in, Dick?"

"It's a swindlin' shop," said Dick, in a low voice. "I've been there. That man's a reg'lar cheat. He's seen me before, but he don't know me coz of my clothes."

"Step in and see the articles," said the man, persuasively, "You needn't buy, you know."

"Are all the articles worth more'n a dollar?" asked Dick.

"Yes," said the other, "and some worth a great deal more."

ambitious

"Such as what?"

"Well, there's a silver pitcher worth twenty dollars."

"And you sell it for a dollar. That's very kind of you," said Dick, innocently.

"Walk in, and you'll understand it."

"No, I guess not," said Dick. "My servants is so dishonest that I wouldn't like to trust 'em with a silver pitcher. Come along, Frank. I hope you'll succeed in your charitable enterprise of supplyin' the public with silver pitchers at nineteen dollars less than they are worth."

"How does he manage, Dick?" asked Frank, as they went on.

"All his articles are numbered, and he makes you pay a dollar, and then shakes some dice, and whatever the figgers come to, is the number of the article you draw. Most of 'em aint worth sixpence."

A hat and cap store being close at hand, Dick and Frank went in. For seventy-five cents, which Frank insisted on paying, Dick succeeded in getting quite a neat-looking cap, which corresponded much better with his appearance than the one he had on. The last, not being considered worth keeping, Dick dropped on the sidewalk, from which, on looking back, he saw it picked up by a brother boot-black who appeared to consider it better than his own.

They retraced their steps and went up Chambers Street to Broadway. At the corner of Broadway and Chambers Street is a large white marble warehouse, which attracted Frank's attention.

"What building is that?" he asked, with interest.

"That belongs to my friend A. T. Stewart," said Dick. "It's the biggest store on Broadway.* If I ever retire from boot-blackin', and go into mercantile pursuits, I may buy him out, or build another store that'll take the shine off this one."

"Were you ever in the store?" asked Frank.

"No," said Dick; "but I'm intimate with one of Stew-

---

* Mr. Stewart's Tenth Street store was not open at the time Dick spoke.

art's partners. He is a cash boy, and does nothing but take money all day."

"A very agreeable employment," said Frank laughing.

"Yes," said Dick, "I'd like to be in it."

The boys crossed to the West side of Broadway, and walked slowly up the street. To Frank it was a very interesting spectacle. Accustomed to the quiet of the country, there was something fascinating in the crowds of people thronging the sidewalks, and the great variety of vehicles constantly passing and repassing in the street. Then again the shop-windows with their multifarious contents interested and amused him, and he was constantly checking Dick to look in at some well-stocked window.

"I don't see how so many shopkeepers can find people enough to buy of them," he said. "We haven't got but two stores in our village, and Broadway seems to be full of them."

"Yes," said Dick; "and its pretty much the same in the avenoos, 'specially the Third, Sixth, and Eighth avenoos. The Bowery, too, is a great place for shoppin'. There everybody sells cheaper'n anybody else, and nobody pretends to make no profit on their goods."

"Where's Barnum's Museum?" asked Frank.

"Oh, that's down nearly opposite the Astor House," said Dick. "Didn't you see a great building with lots of flags?"

"Yes."

"Well, that's Barnum's.* That's where the Happy Family live, and the lions, and bears, and curiosities generally. It's a tip-top place. Haven't you ever been there? It's most as good as the Old Bowery, only the plays isn't quite so excitin'."

"I'll go if I get time," said Frank. "There is a boy at home who came to New York a month ago, and went to Barnum's, and has been talking about it ever since, so I suppose it must be worth seeing."

"They've got a great play at the Old Bowery now,"

---

* Since destroyed by fire, and rebuilt farther up Broadway, and again burned down in February.

pursued Dick. " 'Tis called the 'Demon of the Danube.' The Demon falls in love with a young woman, and drags her by the hair up to the top of a steep rock where his castle stands."

"That's a queer way of showing his love," said Frank, laughing.

"She didn't want to go with him, you know, but was in love with another chap. When he heard about his girl bein' carried off, he felt awful, and swore an oath not to rest till he had got her free. Well, at last he got into the castle by some underground passage, and he and the Demon had a fight. Oh, it was bully seein' 'em roll round the stage, cuttin' and slashin' at each other."

"And which got the best of it?"

"At first the Demon seemed to be ahead, but at last the young Baron got him down, and struck a dagger into his heart, sayin', 'Die, false and perjured villain! The dogs shall feast upon thy carcass!' and then the Demon give an awful howl and died. Then the Baron seized his body, and threw it over the precipice."

"It seems to me the actor who plays the Demon ought to get extra pay, if he has to be treated that way."

"That's so," said Dick; "but I guess he's used to it. It seems to agree with his constitution."

"What building is that?" asked Frank, pointing to a structure several rods back from the street, with a large yard in front. It was an unusual sight for Broadway, all the other buildings in that neighborhood being even with the street.

"That is the New York Hospital," said Dick. "They're a rich institution, and take care of sick people on very reasonable terms."

"Did you ever go in there?"

"Yes," said Dick; "there was a friend of mine, Johnny Mullen, he was a newsboy, got run over by a omnibus as he was crossin' Broadway down near Park Place. He was carried to the Hospital, and me and some of his friends paid his board while he was there. It was only three dollars a week, which was very cheap, considerin' all the care they took of him. I got leave to come and see him while he was here. Everything looked so nice and comfortable, that I thought a little of coaxin' a omnibus driver to run over me, so I might go there too."

"Did your friend have to have his leg cut off?" asked Frank, interested.

"No," said Dick; "though there was a young student there that was very anxious to have it cut off; but it wasn't done, and Johnny is around the streets as well as ever."

While this conversation was going on they reached No. 365, at the corner of Franklin Street.*

"That's Taylor's Saloon," said Dick. "When I come into a fortun' I shall take my meals there reg'lar."

"I have heard of it very often," said Frank. "It is said to be very elegant. Suppose we go in and take an ice-cream. It will give us a chance to see it to better advantage."

"Thank you," said Dick; "I think that's the most agreeable way of seein' the place myself."

The boys entered, and found themselves in a spacious and elegant saloon, resplendent with gilding, and adorned on all sides by costly mirrors. They sat down to a small table with a marble top, and Frank gave the order.

"It reminds me of Aladdin's palace," said Frank, looking about him.

"Does it?" said Dick; "he must have had plenty of money."

"He had an old lamp, which he had only to rub, when the Slave of the Lamp would appear, and do whatever he wanted."

"That must have been a valooable lamp. I'd be willin' to give all my Erie shares for it."

There was a tall, gaunt individual at the next table, who apparently heard this last remark of Dick's. Turning towards our hero, he said, "May I inquire, young man, whether you are largely interested in this Erie Railroad?"

"I haven't got no property except what's invested in Erie," said Dick, with a comical side-glance at Frank.

---

* Now the office of the Merchant's Union Express Company.

"Indeed! I suppose the investment was made by your guardian."

"No," said Dick; "I manage my property myself."

"And I presume your dividends have not been large?"

"Why, no," said Dick; "you're about right there. They haven't."

"As I supposed. It's poor stock. Now, my young friend, I can recommend a much better investment, which will yield you a large annual income. I am agent of the Excelsior Copper Mining Company, which possesses one of the most productive mines in the world. It's sure to yield fifty per cent on the investment. Now, all you have to do is to sell out your Erie shares, and invest in our stock, and I'll insure you a fortune in three years. How many shares did you say you had?"

"I didn't say, that I remember," said Dick. "Your offer is very kind and obligin', and as soon as I get time I'll see about it."

"I hope you will," said the stranger. "Permit me to give you my card. 'Samuel Snap, No. — Wall Street.' I shall be most happy to receive a call from you, and exhibit the maps of our mine. I should be glad to have you mention the matter also to your friends. I am confident you could do no greater service than to induce them to embark in our enterprise."

"Very good," said Dick.

Here the stranger left the table, and walked up to the desk to settle his bill.

"You see what it is to be a man of fortune, Frank," said Dick, "and wear good clothes. I wonder what that chap'll say when he sees me blackin' boots to-morrow in the street?"

"Perhaps you earn your money more honorably than he does, after all," said Frank. "Some of these mining companies are nothing but swindles, got up to cheat people out of their money."

"He's welcome to all he gets out of me," said Dick.

Chapter 6

Up Broadway to Madison Square

As the boys pursued their way up Broadway, Dick pointed out the prominent hotels and places of amusement. Frank was particularly struck with the imposing fronts of the St. Nicholas and Metropolitan Hotels, the former of white marble, the latter of a subdued brown hue, but not less elegant in its internal appointments. He was not surprised to be informed that each of these splendid structures cost with the furnishing not far from a million dollars.

At Eighth Street Dick turned to the right, and pointed out the Clinton Hall Building now occupied by the Mercantile Library, comprising at that time over fifty thousand volumes.*

A little farther on they came to a large building standing by itself just at the opening of Third and Fourth Avenues, and with one side on each.

"What is that building?" asked Frank.

"That's the Cooper Institute," said Dick; "built by Mr. Cooper, a particular friend of mine. Me and Peter Cooper used to go to school together."

"What is there inside?" asked Frank.

"There's a hall for public meetin's and lectures in the basement, and a readin' room and a picture gallery up above," said Dick.

Directly opposite Cooper Institute, Frank saw a very

---

* Now not far from one hundred thousand.

large building of brick, covering about an acre of ground.

"Is that a hotel?" he asked.

"No," said Dick; "that's the Bible House. It's the place where they make Bibles. I was in there once,—saw a big pile of 'em."

"Did you ever read the Bible?" asked Frank, who had some idea of the neglected state of Dick's education.

"No," said Dick; "I've heard it's a good book, but I never read one. I aint much on readin'. It makes my head ache."

"I suppose you can't read very fast."

"I can read the little words pretty well, but the big ones is what stick me."

"If I lived in the city, you might come every evening to me, and I would teach you."

"Would you take so much trouble about me?" asked Dick, earnestly.

"Certainly; I should like to see you getting on. There isn't much chance of that if you don't know how to read and write."

"You're a good feller," said Dick, gratefully. "I wish you did live in New York. I'd like to know somethin'. Whereabouts do you live?"

"About fifty miles off, in a town on the left bank of the Hudson. I wish you'd come up and see me sometime. I would like to have you come and stop two or three days."

"Honor bright?"

"I don't understand."

"Do you mean it?" asked Dick, incredulously.

"Of course I do. Why shouldn't I?"

"What would your folks say if they knowed you asked a boot-black to visit you?"

"You are none the worse for being a boot-black, Dick."

"I aint used to genteel society," said Dick. "I shouldn't know how to behave."

"Then I could show you. You won't be a boot-black all your life, you know."

"No," said Dick; "I'm goin' to knock off when I get to be ninety."

"Before that, I hope," said Frank, smiling.

"I really wish I could get somethin' else to do," said Dick, soberly. "I'd like to be a office boy, and learn business, and grow up 'spectable."

"Why don't you try, and see if you can't get a place, Dick?"

"Who'd take Ragged Dick?"

"But you aint ragged now, Dick."

"No," said Dick; "I look a little better than I did in my Washington coat and Louis Napoleon pants. But if I got in a office, they wouldn't give me more'n three dollars a week, and I couldn't live 'spectable on that."

"No, I suppose not," said Frank, thoughtfully. "But you would get more at the end of the first year."

"Yes," said Dick; "but by that time I'd be nothin' but skin and bones."

Frank laughed. "That reminds me," he said, "of the story of an Irishman, who, out of economy, thought he would teach his horse to feed on shavings. So he provided the horse with a pair of green spectacles which made the shavings look eatable. But unfortunately, just as the horse got learned, he up and died."

"The hoss must have been a fine specimen of architectur' by the time he got through," remarked Dick.

"Whereabouts are we now?" asked Frank, as they emerged from Fourth Avenue into Union Square.

"That is Union Park," said Dick, pointing to a beautiful enclosure, in the centre of which was a pond, with a fountain playing.

"Is that the statue of General Washington?" asked Frank, pointing to a bronze equestrian statue, on a granite pedestal.

"Yes," said Dick; "he's growed some since he was President. If he'd been as tall as that when he fit in the Revolution, he'd have walloped the British some, I reckon."

Frank looked up at the statue, which is fourteen and a half feet high, and acknowledged the justice of Dick's remark.

sense of humor

"How about the coat, Dick?" he asked. "Would it fit you?"

"Well, it might be rather loose," said Dick, "I aint much more'n ten feet high with my boots off."

"No, I should think not," said Frank, smiling. "You're a queer boy, Dick."

"Well, I've been brought up queer. Some boys is born with a silver spoon in their mouth. Victoria's boys is born with a gold spoon, set with di'monds; but gold and silver was scarce when I was born, and mine was pewter."

"Perhaps the gold and silver will come by and by, Dick. Did you ever hear of Dick Whittington?"

"Never did. Was he a Ragged Dick?"

"I shouldn't wonder if he was. At any rate he was very poor when he was a boy, but he didn't stay so. Before he died, he became Lord Mayor of London."

"Did he?" asked Dick, looking interested. "How did he do it?"

"Why, you see, a rich merchant took pity on him, and gave him a home in his own house, where he used to stay with the servants, being employed in little errands. One day the merchant noticed Dick picking up pins and needles that had been dropped, and asked him why he did it. Dick told him he was going to sell them when he got enough. The merchant was pleased with his saving disposition, and when soon after, he was going to send a vessel to foreign parts, he told Dick he might send anything he pleased in it, and it should be sold to his advantage. Now Dick had nothing in the world but a kitten which had been given him a short time before."

"How much taxes did he have to pay for it?" asked Dick.

"Not very high, probably. But having only the kitten, he concluded to send it along. After sailing a good many months, during which the kitten grew up to be a strong cat, the ship touched at an island never before known, which happened to be infested with rats and mice to such an extent that they worried everybody's life out, and even ransacked the king's palace. To make a long story short, the captain, seeing how matters stood, brought Dick's cat ashore, and she soon made the rats and mice scatter. The king was highly delighted when he saw what havoc she made among the rats and mice, and resolved to have her at any price. So he offered a great quantity of gold for her, which, of course, the captain was glad to accept. It was faithfully carried back to Dick, and laid the foundation of his fortune. He prospered as he grew up, and in time became a very rich merchant, respected by all, and before he died was elected Lord Mayor of London."

"That's a pretty good story," said Dick; "but I don't believe all the cats in New York will ever make me mayor."

"No, probably not, but you may rise in some other way. A good many distinguished men have once been poor boys. There's hope for you, Dick, if you'll try."

"Nobody ever talked to me so before," said Dick. "They just called me Ragged Dick, and told me I'd grow up to be a vagabone (boys who are better educated need not be surprised at Dick's blunders) and come to the gallows."

"Telling you so won't make it turn out so, Dick. If you'll try to be somebody, and grow up into a respectable member of society, you will. You may not become rich,—it isn't everybody that becomes rich, you know,—but you can obtain a good position, and be respected."

"I'll try," said Dick, earnestly. "I needn't have been Ragged Dick so long if I hadn't spent my money in goin' to the theatre, and treatin' boys to oyster-stews, and bettin' money on cards, and such like."

"Have you lost money that way?"

"Lots of it. One time I saved up five dollars to buy me a new rig-out, cos my best suit was all in rags, when Limpy Jim wanted me to play a game with him."

"Limpy Jim?" said Frank, interrogatively.

"Yes, he's lame; that's what makes us call him Limpy Jim."

"I suppose you lost?"

"Yes, I lost every penny, and had to sleep out, cos I hadn't a cent to pay for lodgin'. 'Twas a awful cold night, and I got most froze."

"Wouldn't Jim let you have any of the money he had won to pay for a lodging?"

"No; I axed him for five cents, but he wouldn't let me have it."

"Can you get lodging for five cents?" asked Frank, in surprise.

"Yes," said Dick, "but not at the Fifth Avenue Hotel. That's it right out there."

Chapter 7

The Pocket-Book

THEY HAD reached the junction of Broadway and of Fifth Avenue. Before them was a beautiful park of ten acres. On the left-hand side was a large marble building, presenting a fine appearance with its extensive white front. This was the building at which Dick pointed.

"Is that the Fifth Avenue Hotel?" asked Frank. "I've heard of it often. My Uncle William always stops there when he comes to New York."

"I once slept on the outside of it," said Dick. "They was very reasonable in their charges, and told me I might come again."

"Perhaps sometime you'll be able to sleep inside," said Frank.

"I guess that'll be when Queen Victoria goes to the Five Points to live."

"It looks like a palace," said Frank. "The queen needn't be ashamed to live in such a beautiful building as that."

Though Frank did not know it, one of the queen's palaces is far from being as fine a looking building as the Fifth Avenue Hotel. St. James' Palace is a very ugly-looking brick structure, and appears much more like a factory than like the home of royalty. There are few hotels in the world as fine-looking as this democratic institution.

At that moment a gentleman passed them on the sidewalk, who looked back at Dick, as if his face seemed familiar.

"I know that man," said Dick, after he had passed. "He's one of my customers."

"What is his name?"

"I don't know."

"He looked back as if he thought he knew you."

"He would have knowed me at once if it hadn't been for my new clothes," said Dick. "I don't look much like Ragged Dick now."

"I suppose your face looked familiar."

"All but the dirt," said Dick, laughing. "I don't always have the chance of washing my face and hands in the Astor House."

"You told me," said Frank, "that there was a place where you could get lodging for five cents. Where's that?"

"It's the Newsboys' Lodgin' House, on Fulton Street," said Dick, "up over the 'Sun' office. It's a good place. I don't know what us boys would do without it. They give you supper for six cents, and a bed for five cents more."

"I suppose some boys don't even have the five cents to pay,—do they?"

"They'll trust the boys," said Dick. "But I don't like to get trusted. I'd be ashamed to get trusted for five cents, or ten either. One night I was comin' down Chatham Street, with fifty cents in my pocket. I was goin' to get a good oyster-stew, and then go to the lodgin' house; but somehow it slipped through a hole in my trowses-pocket, and I hadn't a cent left. If it had been summer I shouldn't have cared, but it's rather tough stayin' out winter nights."

Frank, who had always possessed a good home of his own, found it hard to realize that the boy who was walking at his side had actually walked the streets in the cold without a home, or money to procure the common comfort of a bed.

"What did you do?" he asked, his voice full of sympathy.

"I went to the 'Times' office. I knowed one of the pressmen, and he let me set down in a corner, where I was warm, and I soon got fast asleep."

"Why don't you get a room somewhere, and so always have a home to go to?"

"I dunno," said Dick. "I never thought of it. P'rhaps I may hire a furnished house on Madison Square."

"That's where Flora McFlimsey lived."

"I don't know her," said Dick, who had never read the popular poem of which she is the heroine.

While this conversation was going on, they had turned into Twenty-fifth Street, and had by this time reached Third Avenue.

Just before entering it, their attention was drawn to the rather singular conduct of an individual in front of them. Stopping suddenly, he appeared to pick up something from the sidewalk, and then looked about him in rather a confused way.

"I know his game," whispered Dick. "Come along and you'll see what it is."

He hurried Frank forward until they overtook the man, who had come to a stand-still.

"Have you found anything?" asked Dick.

"Yes," said the man, "I've found this."

He exhibited a wallet which seemed stuffed with bills, to judge from its plethoric appearance.

"Whew!" exclaimed Dick; "you're in luck."

"I suppose somebody has lost it," said the man, "and will offer a handsome reward."

"Which you'll get."

"Unfortunately I am obliged to take the next train to Boston. That's where I live. I haven't time to hunt up the owner."

"Then I suppose you'll take the pocket-book with you," said Dick, with assumed simplicity.

"I should like to leave it with some honest fellow who would see it returned to the owner," said the man, glancing at the boys.

"I'm honest," said Dick.

"I've no doubt of it," said the other. "Well, young

man, I'll make you an offer. You take the pocket-book——"

"All right. Hand it over, then."

"Wait a minute. There must be a large sum inside. I shouldn't wonder if there might be a thousand dollars. The owner will probably give you a hundred dollars reward."

"Why don't you stay and get it?" asked Frank.

"I would, only there is sickness in my family, and I must get home as soon as possible. Just give me twenty dollars, and I'll hand you the pocket-book, and let you make whatever you can out of it. Come, that's a good offer. What do you say?"

Dick was well dressed, so that the other did not regard it as at all improbable that he might possess that sum. He was prepared, however, to let him have it for less, if necessary.

"Twenty dollars is a good deal of money," said Dick, appearing to hesitate.

"You'll get it back, and a good deal more," said the stranger, persuasively.

"I don't know but I shall. What would you do, Frank?"

"I don't know but I would," said Frank, "if you've got the money." He was not a little surprised to think that Dick had so much by him.

"I don't know but I will," said Dick, after some irresolution. "I guess I won't lose much."

"You can't lose anything," said the stranger briskly. "Only be quick, for I must be on my way to the cars. I am afraid I shall miss them now."

Dick pulled out a bill from his pocket, and handed it to the stranger, receiving the pocket-book in return. At that moment a policeman turned the corner, and the stranger, hurriedly thrusting the bill into his pocket, without looking at it, made off with rapid steps.

"What is there in the pocket-book, Dick?" asked Frank in some excitement. "I hope there's enough to pay you for the money you gave him."

Dick laughed.

"I'll risk that," said he.

cheater

"But you gave him twenty dollars. That's a good deal of money."

"If I had given him as much as that, I should deserve to be cheated out of it."

"But you did,—didn't you?"

"He thought so."

"What was it, then?"

"It was nothing but a dry-goods circular got up to imitate a bank-bill."

Frank looked sober.

"You ought not to have cheated him, Dick," he said, reproachfully.

"Didn't he want to cheat me?"

"I don't know."

"What do you s'pose there is in that pocket-book?" asked Dick, holding it up.

Frank surveyed its ample proportions, and answered sincerely enough, "Money, and a good deal of it."

"There aint stamps enough in it to buy an oyster-stew," said Dick. "If you don't believe it, just look while I open it."

So saying he opened the pocket-book, and showed Frank that it was stuffed out with pieces of blank paper, carefully folded up in the shape of bills. Frank, who was unused to city life, and had never heard anything of the "drop-game," looked amazed at this unexpected development.

"I knowed how it was all the time," said Dick. "I guess I got the best of him there. This wallet's worth somethin'. I shall use it to keep my stiffkit's of Erie stock in, and all my other papers what aint of no use to anybody but the owner."

"That's the kind of papers it's got in it now," said Frank, smiling.

"That's so!" said Dick.

"By hokey!" he exclaimed suddenly, "if there aint the old chap comin' back ag'in. He looks as if he'd heard bad news from his sick family."

By this time the pocket-book dropper had come up. Approaching the boys, he said in an undertone to

Dick, "Give me back that pocket-book, you young rascal!"

"Beg your pardon, mister," said Dick, "but was you addressin' me?"

"Yes, I was."

" 'Cause you called me by the wrong name. I've knowed some rascals, but I aint the honor to belong to the family."

He looked significantly at the other as he spoke, which didn't improve the man's temper. Accustomed to swindle others, he did not fancy being practised upon in return.

"Give me back that pocket-book," he repeated in a threatening voice.

"Couldn't do it," said Dick, coolly. "I'm go'n' to restore it to the owner. The contents is so valooable that most likely the loss has made him sick, and he'll be likely to come down liberal to the honest finder."

"You gave me a bogus bill," said the man.

"It's what I use myself," said Dick.

"You've swindled me."

"I thought it was the other way."

"None of your nonsense," said the man angrily. "If you don't give up that pocket-book, I'll call a policeman."

"I wish you would," said Dick. "They'll know most likely whether it's Stewart or Astor that's lost the pocket-book, and I can get 'em to return it."

The "dropper," whose object it was to recover the pocket-book, in order to try the same game on a more satisfactory customer, was irritated by Dick's refusal, and above all by the coolness he displayed. He resolved to make one more attempt.

"Do you want to pass the night in the Tombs?" he asked.

"Thank you for your very obligin' proposal," said Dick; "but it aint convenient to-day. Any other time, when you'd like to have me come and stop with you, I'm agreeable; but my two youngest children is down with the measles, and I expect I'll have to set up all night to take care of 'em. Is the Tombs, in gineral, a pleasant place of residence?"

Dick asked this question with an air of so much earnestness that Frank could scarcely forbear laughing, though it is hardly necessary to say that the dropper was by no means so inclined.

"You'll know sometime," he said, scowling.

"I'll make you a fair offer," said Dick. "If I get more'n fifty dollars as a reward for my honesty, I'll divide with you. But I say, aint it most time to go back to your sick family in Boston?"

Finding that nothing was to be made out of Dick, the man strode away with a muttered curse.

"You were too smart for him, Dick," said Frank.

"Yes," said Dick, "I aint knocked round the city streets all my life for nothin'."

independent

Chapter 8

Dick's Early History

"HAVE YOU always lived in New York, Dick?" asked Frank, after a pause.

"Ever since I can remember."

"I wish you'd tell me a little about yourself. Have you got any father or mother?"

"I aint got no mother. She died when I wasn't but three years old. My father went to sea; but he went off before mother died, and nothin' was ever heard of him. I expect he got wrecked, or died at sea."

"And what became of you when your mother died?"

"The folks she boarded with took care of me, but they was poor, and they couldn't do much. When I was seven the woman died, and her husband went out West, and then I had to scratch for myself."

"At seven years old!" exclaimed Frank, in amazement.

"Yes," said Dick, "I was a little feller to take care of myself, but," he continued with pardonable pride, "I did it."

"What could you do?"

"Sometimes one thing, and sometimes another," said Dick. "I changed my business accordin' as I had to. Sometimes I was a newsboy, and diffused intelligence among the masses, as I heard somebody say once in a big speech he made in the Park. Them was the times when Horace Greeley and James Gordon Bennett made money."

"Through your enterprise?" suggested Frank.

"Yes," said Dick; "but I give it up after a while."

"What for?"

"Well, they didn't always put news enough in their papers, and people wouldn't buy 'em as fast as I wanted 'em to. So one mornin' I was stuck on a lot of Heralds, and I thought I'd make a sensation. So I called out 'GREAT NEWS! QUEEN VICTORIA ASSASSINATED!' All my Heralds went off like hot cakes, and I went off, too, but one of the gentlemen what got sold remembered me, and said he'd have me took up, and that's what made me change my business."

"That wasn't right, Dick," said Frank.

"I know it," said Dick; "but lots of boys does it."

"That don't make it any better."

"No," said Dick, "I was sort of ashamed at the time, 'specially about one poor old gentleman,—a Englishman he was. He couldn't help cryin' to think the queen was dead, and his hands shook when he handed me the money for the paper."

"What did you do next?"

"I went into the match business," said Dick; "but it was small sales and small profits. Most of the people I called on had just laid in a stock, and didn't want to buy. So one cold night, when I hadn't money enough to pay for a lodgin', I burned the last of my matches to keep me from freezin'. But it cost too much to get warm that way, and I couldn't keep it up."

"You've seen hard times, Dick," said Frank, compassionately.

"Yes," said Dick, "I've knowed what it was to be hungry and cold, with nothin' to eat or to warm me; but there's one thing I never could do," he added, proudly.

"What's that?"

"I never stole," said Dick. "It's mean and I wouldn't do it."

"Were you ever tempted to?"

"Lots of times. Once I had been goin round all day, and hadn't sold any matches, except three cents' worth early in the mornin'. With that I bought an apple, thinkin'

I should get some more bimeby. When evenin' come I was awful hungry. I went into a baker's just to look at the bread. It made me feel kind o' good just to look at the bread and cakes, and I thought maybe they would give me some. I asked 'em wouldn't they give me a loaf, and take their pay in matches. But they said they'd got enough matches to last three months; so there wasn't any chance for a trade. While I was standin' at the stove warmin' me, the baker went into the back room, and I felt so hungry I thought I would take just one loaf, and go off with it. There was such a big pile I don't think he'd have known it."

"But you didn't do it?"

"No, I didn't, and I was glad of it, for when the man came in ag'in, he said he wanted some one to carry some cake to a lady in St. Mark's Place. His boy was sick, and he hadn't no one to send; so he told me he'd give me ten cents if I would go. My business wasn't very pressin' just then, so I went, and when I come back, I took my pay in bread and cakes. Didn't they taste good, though?"

"So you didn't stay long in the match business, Dick?"

"No, I couldn't sell enough to make it pay. Then there was some folks that wanted me to sell cheaper to them; so I couldn't make any profit. There was one old lady— she was rich, too, for she lived in a big brick house—beat me down so, that I didn't make no profit at all; but she wouldn't buy without, and I hadn't sold none that day; so I let her have them. I don't see why rich folks should be so hard upon a poor boy that wants to make a livin'."

"There's a good deal of meanness in the world, I'm afraid, Dick."

"If everybody was like you and your uncle," said Dick, "there would be some chance for poor people. If I was rich I'd try to help 'em along."

"Perhaps you will be rich sometime, Dick."

Dick shook his head.

"I'm afraid all my wallets will be like this," said Dick, indicating the one he had received from the dropper, "and will be full of papers what aint of no use to anybody except the owner."

"That depends very much on yourself, Dick," said Frank. "Stewart wasn't always rich, you know."

"Wasn't he?"

"When he first came to New York as a young man he was a teacher, and teachers are not generally very rich. At last he went into business, starting in a small way, and worked his way up by degrees. But there was one thing he determined in the beginning: that he would be strictly honorable in all his dealings, and never overreach any one for the sake of making money. If there was a chance for him, Dick, there is a chance for you."

"He knowed enough to be a teacher, and I'm awful ignorant," said Dick.

"But you needn't stay so."

"How can I help it?"

"Can't you learn at school?"

"I can't go to school 'cause I've got my livin' to earn. It wouldn't do me much good if I learned to read and write, and just as I'd got learned I starved to death."

"But are there no night-schools?"

"Yes."

"Why don't you go? I suppose you don't work in the evenings."

"I never cared much about it," said Dick, "and that's the truth. But since I've got to talkin' with you, I think more about it. I guess I'll begin to go."

"I wish you would, Dick. You'll make a smart man if you only get a little education."

"Do you think so?" asked Dick, doubtfully.

"I know so. A boy who has earned his own living ever since he was seven years old must have something in him. I feel very much interested in you, Dick. You've had a hard time of it so far in life, but I think better times are in store. I want you to do well, and I feel sure you can if you only try."

"You're a good fellow," said Dick, gratefully. "I'm afraid I'm a pretty rough customer, but I aint as bad as some. I mean to turn over a new leaf, and try to grow up 'spectable."

"There've been a great many boys begin as low down

as you, Dick, that have grown up respectable and honored. But they had to work pretty hard for it."

"I'm willin' to work hard," said Dick.

"And you must not only work hard, but work in the
right way."

"What's the right way?"

"You began in the right way when you determined
never to steal, or do anything mean or dishonorable,
however strongly tempted to do so. That will make people have confidence in you when they come to know you.
But, in order to succeed well, you must manage to get as
good an education as you can. Until you do, you cannot
get a position in an office or counting-room, even to run
errands."

"That's so," said Dick, soberly. "I never thought how
awful ignorant I was till now."

"That can be remedied with perseverance," said Frank.
"A year will do a great deal for you."

"I'll go to work and see what I can do," said Dick,
energetically.

Chapter 9

A Scene in a Third Avenue Car

THE BOYS had turned into Third Avenue, a long street, which, commencing just below the Cooper Institute, runs out to Harlem. A man came out of a side street, uttering at intervals a monotonous cry which sounded like "glass puddin'."

"Glass pudding!" repeated Frank, looking in surprised wonder at Dick. "What does he mean?"

"Perhaps you'd like some," said Dick.

"I never heard of it before."

"Suppose you ask him what he charges for his puddin'."

Frank looked more narrowly at the man, and soon concluded that he was a glazier.

"Oh, I understand," he said. "He means 'glass put in.' "

Frank's mistake was not a singular one. The monotonous cry of these men certainly sounds more like "glass puddin'," than the words they intend to utter.

"Now," said Dick, "where shall we go?"

"I should like to see Central Park," said Frank. "Is it far off?"

"It is about a mile and a half from here," said Dick. "This is Twenty-ninth Street, and the Park begins at Fifty-ninth Street."

It may be explained, for the benefit of readers who have never visited New York, that about a mile from the City Hall the cross-streets begin to be numbered in regular order. There is a continuous line of houses as far as One Hundred and Thirtieth Street, where may be found the terminus of the Harlem line of horse-cars. When the entire island is laid out and settled, probably the numbers will reach two hundred or more. Central Park, which lies between Fifty-ninth Street on the South and One Hundred and Tenth Street on the north, is true to its name, occupying about the centre of the island. The distance between two parallel streets is called a block, and twenty blocks make a mile. It will therefore be seen that Dick was exactly right, when he said they were a mile and a half from Central Park.

"That is too far to walk," said Frank.

" 'Twon't cost but six cents to ride," said Dick.

"You mean in the horse-cars?"

"Yes."

"All right then. We'll jump aboard the next car."

The Third Avenue and Harlem line of horse-cars is better patronized than any other in New York, though not much can be said for the cars, which are usually dirty and overcrowded. Still, when it is considered that only seven cents are charged for the entire distance to Harlem, about seven miles from the City Hall, the fare can hardly be complained of. But of course most of the profit is made from the way-passengers who only ride a short distance.

A car was at that moment approaching, but it seemed pretty crowded.

"Shall we take that, or wait for another?" asked Frank.

"The next'll most likely be as bad," said Dick.

The boys accordingly signalled to the conductor to stop, and got on the front platform. They were obliged to stand up till the car reached Fortieth Street, when so many of the passengers had got off that they obtained seats.

Frank sat down beside a middle-aged woman, or lady, as she probably called herself, whose sharp visage and thin lips did not seem to promise a very pleasant disposition. When the two gentlemen who sat beside her arose, she spread her skirts in the endeavor to fill two seats. Disregarding this, the boys sat down.

"There aint room for two," she said looking sourly at Frank.

"There were two here before."

"Well, there ought not to have been. Some people like to crowd in where they're not wanted."

"And some like to take up a double allowance of room," thought Frank; but he did not say so. He saw that the woman had a bad temper, and thought it wisest to say nothing.

Frank had never ridden up the city as far as this, and it was with much interest that he looked out of the car windows at the stores on either side. Third Avenue is a broad street, but in the character of its houses and stores it is quite inferior to Broadway, though better than some of the avenues further east. Fifth Avenue, as most of my readers already know, is the finest street in the city, being lined with splendid private residences, occupied by the wealthier classes. Many of the cross streets also boast houses which may be considered palaces, so elegant are they externally and internally. Frank caught glimpses of some of these as he was carried towards the Park.

After the first conversation, already mentioned, with the lady at his side, he supposed he should have nothing further to do with her. But in this he was mistaken. While he was busy looking out of the car window, she plunged her hand into her pocket in search of her purse, which she was unable to find. Instantly she jumped to the conclusion that it had been stolen, and her suspicions fastened upon Frank, with whom she was already provoked for "crowding her," as she termed it.

"Conductor!" she exclaimed in a sharp voice.

"What's wanted, ma'am?" returned the functionary.

"I want you to come here right off."

"What's the matter?"

"My purse has been stolen. There was four dollars and eighty cents in it. I know, because I counted it when I paid my fare."

"Who stole it?"

"That boy," she said pointing to Frank, who listened to the charge in the most intense astonishment. "He crowded in here on purpose to rob me, and I want you to search him right off."

"That's a lie!" exclaimed Dick, indignantly.

"Oh, you're in league with him, I dare say," said the woman spitefully. "You're as bad as he is, I'll be bound."

"You're a nice female, you be!" said Dick, ironically.

"Don't you dare to call me a female, sir," said the lady, furiously.

"Why, you aint a man in disguise, be you?" said Dick.

"You are very much mistaken, madam," said Frank quietly. "The conductor may search me, if you desire it."

A charge of theft, made in a crowded car, of course made quite a sensation. Cautious passengers instinctively put their hands on their pockets, to make sure that they, too, had not been robbed. As for Frank, his face flushed, and he felt very indignant that he should even be suspected of so mean a crime. He had been carefully brought up, and been taught to regard stealing as low and wicked.

Dick, on the contrary, thought it a capital joke that such a charge should have been made against his companion. Though he had brought himself up, and known plenty of boys and men, too, who would steal, he had never done so himself. He thought it mean. But he could not be expected to regard it as Frank did. He had been too familiar with it in others to look upon it with horror.

Meanwhile the passengers rather sided with the boys. Appearances go a great ways, and Frank did not look like a thief.

"I think you must be mistaken, madam," said a gentleman sitting opposite. "The lad does not look as if he would steal."

"You can't tell by looks," said the lady, sourly. "They're deceitful; villains are generally well dressed."

"Be they?" said Dick. "You'd ought to see me with my Washington coat on. You'd think I was the biggest villain ever you saw."

"I've no doubt you are," said the lady, scowling in the direction of our hero.

"Thank you, ma'am," said Dick. " 'Tisn't often I get such fine compliments."

"None of your impudence," said the lady, wrathfully. "I believe you're the worst of the two."

Meanwhile the car had been stopped.

"How long are we going to stop here?" demanded a passenger, impatiently. "I'm in a hurry, if none of the rest of you are."

"I want my pocket-book," said the lady, defiantly.

"Well, ma'am, I haven't got it, and I don't see as it's doing you any good detaining us all here."

"Conductor, will you call a policeman to search that young scamp?" continued the aggrieved lady. "You don't expect I'm going to lose my money, and do nothing about it."

"I'll turn my pockets inside out if you want me to," said Frank, proudly. "There's no need of a policeman. The conductor, or any one else, may search me."

"Well, youngster," said the conductor, "if the lady agrees, I'll search you."

The lady signified her assent.

Frank accordingly turned his pockets inside out; but nothing was revealed except his own porte-monnaie and a penknife.

"Well, ma'am, are you satisfied?" asked the conductor.

"No, I aint," said she, decidedly.

"You don't think he's got it still?"

"No, but he's passed it over to his confederate, that boy there that's so full of impudence."

"That's me," said Dick, comically.

"He confesses it," said the lady; "I want him searched."

"All right," said Dick, "I'm ready for the operation, only, as I've got valooable property about me, be careful not to drop any of my Erie Bonds."

The conductor's hand forthwith dove into Dick's pocket, and drew out a rusty jack-knife, a battered cent, about fifty cents in change, and the capacious pocket-book which he had received from the swindler who was anxious to get back to his sick family in Boston.

"Is that yours, ma'am?" asked the conductor, holding up the wallet which excited some amazement, by its size, among the other passengers.

"It seems to me you carry a large pocket-book for a young man of your age," said the conductor.

"That's what I carry my cash and valooable papers in," said Dick.

"I suppose that isn't yours, ma'am," said the conductor, turning to the lady.

"No," said she, scornfully. "I wouldn't carry round such a great wallet as that. Most likely he's stolen it from somebody else."

"What a prime detective you'd be!" said Dick. "P'rhaps you know who I took it from."

"I don't know but my money's in it," said the lady, sharply. "Conductor, will you open that wallet, and see what there is in it?"

"Don't disturb the valooable papers," said Dick, in a tone of pretended anxiety.

The contents of the wallet excited some amusement among the passengers.

"There don't seem to be much money here," said the conductor, taking out a roll of tissue paper cut out in the shape of bills, and rolled up.

"No," said Dick. "Didn't I tell you them were papers of no valoo to anybody but the owner? If the lady'd like to borrow, I won't charge no interest."

"Where is my money, then?" said the lady, in some discomfiture. "I shouldn't wonder if one of the young scamps had thrown it out of the window."

"You'd better search your pocket once more," said the gentleman opposite. "I don't believe either of the boys is in fault. They don't look to me as if they would steal."

"Thank you, sir," said Frank.

The lady followed out the suggestion, and plunging her hand once more into her pocket, drew out a small porte-monnaie. She hardly knew whether to be glad or sorry at this discovery. It placed her in rather an awkward position after the fuss she had made, and the detention to which she had subjected the passengers, now, as it proved, for nothing.

"Is that the pocket-book you thought stolen?" asked the conductor.

"Yes," said she, rather confusedly.

"Then you've been keeping me waiting all this time

for nothing," he said, sharply. "I wish you'd take care to be sure next time before you make such a disturbance for nothing. I've lost five minutes, and shall not be on time."

"I can't help it," was the cross reply; "I didn't know it was in my pocket."

"It seems to me you owe an apology to the boys you accused of a theft which they have not committed," said the gentleman opposite.

"I shan't apologize to anybody," said the lady, whose temper was not of the best; "least of all to such whipper-snappers as they are."

"Thank you, ma'am," said Dick, comically; "your handsome apology is accepted. It aint of no consequence, only I didn't like to expose the contents of my valooable pocket-book, for fear it might excite the envy of some of my poor neighbors."

"You're a character," said the gentleman who had already spoken, with a smile.

"A bad character!" muttered the lady.

But it was quite evident that the sympathies of those present were against the lady, and on the side of the boys who had been falsely accused, while Dick's drollery had created considerable amusement.

The cars had now reached Fifty-ninth Street, the southern boundary of the Park, and here our hero and his companion got off.

"You'd better look out for pickpockets, my lad," said the conductor, pleasantly. "That big wallet of yours might prove a great temptation."

"That's so," said Dick. "That's the misfortin' of being rich. Astor and me don't sleep much for fear of burglars breakin' in and robbin' us of our valooable treasures. Sometimes I think I'll give all my money to an Orphan Asylum, and take it out in board. I guess I'd make money by the operation."

While Dick was speaking, the car rolled away, and the boys turned up Fifty-ninth Street, for two long blocks yet separated them from the Park.

Chapter 10

Introduces a Victim of Misplaced Confidence

"WHAT A queer chap you are, Dick!" said Frank laughing. "You always seem to be in good spirits."

"No, I aint always. Sometimes I have the blues."

"When?"

"Well, once last winter it was awful cold, and there was big holes in my shoes, and my gloves and all my warm clothes was at the tailor's. I felt as if life was sort of tough, and I'd like it if some rich man would adopt me, and give me plenty to eat and drink and wear, without my havin' to look so sharp after it. Then agin' when I've seen boys with good homes, and fathers, and mothers, I've thought I'd like to have somebody to care for me."

Dick's tone changed as he said this, from his usual levity, and there was a touch of sadness in it. Frank, blessed with a good home and indulgent parents, could not help pitying the friendless boy who had found life such up-hill work.

"Don't say you have no one to care for you, Dick," he said, lightly laying his hand on Dick's shoulder. "I will care for you."

"Will you?"

"If you will let me."

"I wish you would," said Dick, earnestly. "I'd like to feel that I have one friend who cares for me."

Central Park was now before them, but it was far from presenting the appearance which it now exhibits. It had not been long since work had been commenced upon it, and it was still very rough and unfinished. A rough tract of land, two miles and a half from north to south, and a half a mile broad, very rocky in parts, was the material from which the Park Commissioners have made the present beautiful enclosure. There were no houses of good appearance near it, buildings being limited mainly to rude temporary huts used by the workmen who were employed in improving it. The time will undoubtedly come when the Park will be surrounded by elegant residences, and compare favorably in this respect with the most attractive parts of any city in the world. But at the time when Frank and Dick visited it, not much could be said in favor either of the Park or its neighborhood.

"If this is Central Park," said Frank, who naturally felt disappointed, "I don't think much of it. My father's got a large pasture that is much nicer."

"It'll look better some time," said Dick. "There aint much to see now but rocks. We will take a walk over it if you want to."

"No," said Frank, "I've seen as much of it as I want to. Besides, I feel tired."

"Then we'll go back. We can take the Sixth Avenue cars. They will bring us out at Vesey Street, just beside the Astor House."

"All right," said Frank. "That will be the best course. I hope," he added, laughing, "our agreeable lady friend won't be there. I don't care about being accused of *stealing* again."

"She was a tough one," said Dick. "Wouldn't she make a nice wife for a man that likes to live in hot water, and didn't mind bein' scalded two or three times a day?"

"Yes, I think she'd just suit him. Is that the right car, Dick?"

"Yes, jump in, and I'll follow."

The Sixth Avenue is lined with stores, many of them of very good appearance, and would make a very respectable principal street for a good-sized city. But it is only one of several long business streets which run up the island, and illustrate the extent and importance of the city to which they belong.

No incidents worth mentioning took place during their ride down town. In about three-quarters of an hour the boys got out of the car beside the Astor House.

"Are you goin' in now, Frank?" asked Dick.

"That depends upon whether you have anything else to show me."

"Wouldn't you like to go to Wall Street?"

"That's the street where there are so many bankers and brokers,—isn't it?"

"Yes, I s'pose you aint afraid of bulls and bears,—are you?"

"Bulls and bears?" repeated Frank, puzzled.

"Yes."

"What are they?"

"The bulls is what tries to make the stock go up, and the bears is what try to growl 'em down."

"Oh, I see. Yes, I'd like to go."

Accordingly they walked down on the west side of Broadway as far as Trinity Church, and then, crossing, entered a street not very wide or very long, but of very great importance. The reader would be astonished if he could know the amount of money involved in the transactions which take place in a single day in this street. It would be found that although Broadway is much greater in length, and lined with stores, it stands second to Wall Street in this respect.

"What is that large marble building?" asked Frank, pointing to a massive structure on the corner of Wall and Nassau Streets. It was in the form of a parallelogram, two hundred feet long by ninety wide, and about eighty feet in height, the ascent to the entrance being by eighteen granite steps.

"That's the Custom House," said Dick.

"It looks like pictures I've seen of the Parthenon at Athens," said Frank, meditatively.

"Where's Athens?" asked Dick. "It aint in New York State,—is it?"

"Not the Athens I mean, at any rate. It is in Greece, and was a famous city two thousand years ago."

"That's longer than I can remember," said Dick. "I can't remember distinctly more'n about a thousand years."

"What a chap you are, Dick! Do you know if we can go in?"

The boys ascertained, after a little inquiry, that they would be allowed to do so. They accordingly entered the Custom House and made their way up to the roof, from which they had a fine view of the harbor, the wharves crowded with shipping, and the neighboring shores of Long Island and New Jersey. Towards the north they looked down for many miles upon continuous lines of streets, and thousands of roofs, with here and there a church-spire rising above its neighbors. Dick had never before been up there, and he, as well as Frank, was interested in the grand view spread before them.

At length they descended, and were going down the granite steps on the outside of the building, when they were addressed by a young man, whose appearance is worth describing.

He was tall, and rather loosely put together, with small eyes and a rather prominent nose. His clothing had evidently not been furnished by a city tailor. He wore a blue coat with brass buttons, and pantaloons of rather scanty dimensions, which were several inches too short to cover his lower limbs. He held in his hand a piece of paper, and his countenance wore a look of mingled bewilderment and anxiety.

"Be they a-payin' out money inside there?" he asked, indicating the interior by a motion of his hand.

"I guess so," said Dick. "Are you a goin' in for some?"

"Wal, yes. I've got an order here for sixty dollars,— made a kind of speculation this morning."

"How was it?" asked Frank.

"Wal, you see I brought down some money to put in the bank, fifty dollars it was, and I hadn't justly made up my mind what bank to put it into, when a chap came up in a terrible hurry, and said it was very unfortunate, but the bank wasn't open, and he must have some money right off. He was obliged to go out of the city by the next train. I asked him how much he wanted. He said fifty dollars. I told him I'd got that, and he offered me a check on the bank for sixty, and I let him have it. I thought that was a pretty easy way to earn ten dollars, so I counted out the money and he went off. He told me I'd hear a bell ring when they began to pay out money. But I've waited most two hours, and I haint heard it yet. I'd ought to be goin', for I told dad I'd be home to-night. Do you think I can get the money now?"

"Will you show me the check?" asked Frank, who had listened attentively to the countryman's story, and suspected that he had been made the victim of a swindler. It was made out upon the "Washington Bank," in the sum of sixty dollars, and was signed "Ephraim Smith."

"Washington Bank!" repeated Frank. "Dick, is there such a bank in the city?"

"Not as I knows on," said Dick. "Leastways I don't own any shares in it."

"Aint this the Washington Bank?" asked the countryman, pointing to the building on the steps of which the three were now standing.

"No, it's the Custom House."

"And won't they give me any money for this?" asked the young man, the perspiration standing on his brow.

"I am afraid the man who gave it to you was a swindler," said Frank, gently.

"And won't I ever see my fifty dollars again?" asked the youth in agony.

"I am afraid not."

"What'll dad say?" ejaculated the miserable youth. "It makes me feel sick to think of it. I wish I had the feller here. I'd shake him out of his boots."

"What did he look like? I'll call a policeman and you shall describe him. Perhaps in that way you can get track of your money."

Dick called a policeman, who listened to the description, and recognized the operator as an experienced swindler. He assured the countryman that there was very little chance of his ever seeing his money again. The boys left the miserable youth loudly bewailing his bad luck, and proceeded on their way down the street.

"He's a baby," said Dick, contemptuously. "He'd ought to know how to take care of himself and his money. A feller has to look sharp in this city, or he'll lose his eye-teeth before he knows it."

"I suppose you never got swindled out of fifty dollars, Dick?"

"No, I don't carry no such small bills. I wish I did," he added.

"So do I, Dick. What's that building at the end of the street?"

"That's the Wall-Street Ferry to Brooklyn."

"How long does it take to go across?"

"Not more'n five minutes."

"Suppose we just ride over and back."

"All right!" said Dick. "It's rather expensive; but if you don't mind, I don't."

"Why, how much does it cost?"

"Two cents apiece."

"I guess I can stand that. Let us go."

They passed the gate, paying the fare to a man who stood at the entrance, and were soon on the ferry-boat, bound for Brooklyn.

They had scarcely entered the boat, when Dick, grasping Frank by the arm, pointed to a man just outside of the gentlemen's cabin.

"Do you see that man, Frank?" he inquired.

"Yes, what of him?"

"He's the man that cheated the country chap out of his fifty dollars."

Chapter 11

Dick as a Detective

Dɪᴄᴋ's ready indentification of the rogue who had cheated the countryman, surprised Frank.

"What makes you think it is he?" he asked.

"Because I've seen him before, and I know he's up to them kind of tricks. When I heard how he looked, I was sure I knowed him."

"Our recognizing him won't be of much use," said Frank. "It won't give back the countryman his money."

"I don't know," said Dick, thoughtfully. "May be I can get it."

"How?" asked Frank, incredulously.

"Wait a minute, and you'll see."

Dick left his companion, and went up to the man whom he suspected.

"Ephraim Smith," said Dick, in a low voice.

The man turned suddenly, and looked at Dick uneasily.

"What did you say?" he asked.

"I believe your name is Ephraim Smith," continued Dick.

"You're mistaken," said the man, and was about to move off.

"Stop a minute," said Dick. "Don't you keep your money in the Washington Bank?"

"I don't know any such bank. I'm in a hurry, young man, and I can't stop to answer any foolish questions."

The boat had by this time reached the Brooklyn pier, and Mr. Ephraim Smith seemed in a hurry to land.

"Look here," said Dick, significantly; "you'd better not go on shore unless you want to jump into the arms of a policeman."

"What do you mean?" asked the man, startled.

"That little affair of yours is known to the police," said Dick; "about how you got fifty dollars out of a greenhorn on a false check, and it mayn't be safe for you to go ashore."

"I don't know what you're talking about," said the swindler with affected boldness, though Dick could see that he was ill at ease.

"Yes you do," said Dick. "There isn't but one thing to do. Just give me back that money, and I'll see that you're not touched. If you don't, I'll give you up to the first p'liceman we meet."

Dick looked so determined, and spoke so confidently, that the other, overcome by his fears, no longer hesitated, but passed a roll of bills to Dick and hastily left the boat.

All this Frank witnessed with great amazement, not understanding what influence Dick could have obtained over the swindler sufficient to compel restitution.

"How did you do it?" he asked eagerly.

"I told him I'd exert my influence with the president to have him tried by *habeas corpus*," said Dick.

"And of course that frightened him. But tell me, without joking, how you managed."

Dick gave a truthful account of what occurred, and then said, "Now we'll go back and carry the money."

"Suppose we don't find the poor countryman?"

"Then the p'lice will take care of it."

They remained on board the boat, and in five minutes were again in New York. Going up Wall Street, they met the countryman a little distance from the Custom House. His face was marked with the traces of deep anguish; but in his case even grief could not subdue the cravings of appetite. He had purchased some cakes of one of the old women who spread out for the benefit of passers-by an array of apples and seed-cakes, and was munching them with melancholy satisfaction.

"Hilloa!" said Dick. "Have you found your money?"

"No," ejaculated the young man, with a convulsive gasp. "I shan't ever see it again. The mean skunk's cheated me out of it. Consarn his picter! It took me most six months to save it up. I was workin' for Deacon Pinkham in our place. Oh, I wish I'd never come to New York! The deacon, he told me he'd keep it for me; but I wanted to put in in the bank, and now it's all gone, boo hoo!"

And the miserable youth, having despatched his cakes, was so overcome by the thought of his loss that he burst into tears.

"I say," said Dick, "dry up, and see what I've got here."

The youth no sooner saw the roll of bills, and comprehended that it was indeed his lost treasure, than from the depths of anguish he was exalted to the most ecstatic joy. He seized Dick's hand, and shook it with so much energy that our hero began to feel rather alarmed for its safety.

"'Pears to me you take my arm for a pump-handle," he said. "Couldn't you show your gratitood some other way? It's just possible I may want to use my arm ag'in some time."

The young man desisted, but invited Dick most cordially to come up and stop a week with him at his country home, assuring him that he wouldn't charge him anything for board.

"All right!" said Dick. "If you don't mind I'll bring my wife along, too. She's delicate, and the country air might do her good."

Jonathan stared at him in amazement, uncertain whether to credit the fact of his marriage. Dick walked on with Frank, leaving him in an apparent state of stupefaction, and it is possible that he has not yet settled the affair to his satisfaction.

"Now," said Frank, "I think I'll go back to the Astor House. Uncle has probably got through his business and returned."

"All right," said Dick.

The two boys walked up to Broadway, just where the tall steeple of Trinity faces the street of bankers and brokers, and walked leisurely to the hotel. When they arrived at the Astor House, Dick said, "Good-by, Frank."

"Not yet," said Frank; "I want you to come in with me."

Dick followed his young patron up the steps. Frank went into the reading-room, where, as he had thought probable, he found his uncle already arrived, and reading a copy of "The Evening Post," which he had just purchased outside.

"Well, boys," he said, looking up, "have you had a pleasant jaunt?"

"Yes, sir," said Frank. "Dick's a capital guide."

"So this is Dick," said Mr. Whitney, surveying him with a smile. "Upon my word, I should hardly have known him. I must congratulate him on his improved appearance."

"Frank's been very kind to me," said Dick, who, rough street-boy as he was, had a heart easily touched by kindness, of which he had never experienced much. "He's a tip-top fellow."

"I believe he is a good boy," said Mr. Whitney. "I hope, my lad, you will prosper and rise in the world. You know in this free country poverty in early life is no bar to a man's advancement. I haven't risen very high myself," he added, with a smile, "but have met with moderate success in life; yet there was a time when I was as poor as you."

"Were you, sir?" asked Dick, eagerly.

"Yes, my boy, I have known the time when I have been obliged to go without my dinner because I didn't have enough money to pay for it."

"How did you get up in the world?" asked Dick, anxiously.

"I entered a printing-office as an apprentice, and worked for some years. Then my eyes gave out and I was obliged to give that up. Not knowing what else to do, I went into the country, and worked on a farm. After a while I was lucky enough to invent a machine, which has brought me in a great deal of money. But there was one thing I got while I was in the printing-office which I value more than money."

"What was that, sir?"

"A taste for reading and study. During my leisure hours I improved myself by study, and acquired a large part of the knowledge which I now possess. Indeed, it was one of my books that first put me on the track of the invention, which I afterwards made. So you see, my lad, that my studious habits paid me in money, as well as in another way.

"I'm awful ignorant," said Dick, soberly.

"But you are young, and, I judge, a smart boy. If you try to learn, you can, and if you ever expect to do any-thing in the world, you must know something of books."

"I will," said Dick, resolutely. "I aint always goin' to black boots for a livin'."

"All labor is respectable, my lad, and you have no cause to be ashamed of any honest business; yet when you can get something to do that promises better for your future prospects, I advise you to do so. Till then earn your living in the way you are accustomed to, avoid ex-travagance, and save up a little money if you can."

"Thank you for your advice," said our hero. "There aint many that takes an interest in Ragged Dick."

"So that's your name," said Mr. Whitney. "If I judge you rightly, it won't be long before you change it. Save your money, my lad, buy books, and determine to be somebody, and you may yet fill an honorable position."

"I'll try," said Dick. "Good-night, sir."

"Wait a minute, Dick," said Frank. "Your blacking-box and old clothes are upstairs. You may want them."

"In course," said Dick. "I couldn't get along without my best clothes, and my stock in trade."

"You may go up to the room with him, Frank," said Mr. Whitney. "The clerk will give you the key. I want to see you, Dick, before you go."

"Yes, sir," said Dick.

"Where are you going to sleep to-night, Dick?" asked Frank, as they went upstairs together.

"P'r'aps at the Fifth Avenue Hotel—on the outside," said Dick.

"Haven't you any place to sleep, then?"

"I slept in a box, last night."

"In a box?"

"Yes, on Spruce Street."

"Poor fellow!" said Frank, compassionately.

"Oh, 'twas a bully bed—full of straw! I slept like a top."

"Don't you earn enough to pay for a room, Dick?"

"Yes," said Dick; "only I spend my money foolish, goin' to the Old Bowery, and Tony Pastor's, and sometimes gamblin' in Baxter Street."

"You won't gamble any more,—will you, Dick?" said Frank, laying his hand persuasively on his companion's shoulder.

"No, I won't," said Dick.

"You'll promise?"

"Yes, and I'll keep it. You're a good feller. I wish you was goin' to be in New York."

"I am going to a boarding-school in Connecticut. The name of the town is Barnton. Will you write to me, Dick?"

"My writing would look like hens' tracks," said our hero.

"Never mind. I want you to write. When you write you can tell me how to direct, and I will send you a letter."

"I wish you would," said Dick. "I wish I was more like you."

"I hope you will make a much better boy, Dick. Now we'll go in to my uncle. He wishes to see you before you go."

They went into the reading-room. Dick had wrapped up his blacking-brush in a newspaper with which Frank had supplied him, feeling that a guest of the Astor House should hardly be seen coming out of the hotel displaying such a professional sign.

"Uncle, Dick's ready to go," said Frank.

"Good-by, my lad," said Mr. Whitney. "I hope to hear good accounts of you sometime. Don't forget what I have told you. Remember that your future position depends mainly upon yourself, and that it will be high or low as you choose to make it."

He held out his hand, in which was a five-dollar bill. Dick shrunk back.

"I don't like to take it," he said. "I haven't earned it."

"Perhaps not," said Mr. Whitney; "but I give it to you because I remember my own friendless youth. I hope it may be of service to you. Sometime when you are a prosperous man, you can repay it in the form of aid to some poor boy, who is struggling upward as you are now."

"I will, sir," said Dick, manfully.

He no longer refused the money, but took it gratefully, and, bidding Frank and his uncle good-by, went out into the street. A feeling of loneliness came over him as he left the presence of Frank, for whom he had formed a strong attachment in the few hours he had known him.

Chapter 12

Dick Hires a Room on Mott Street

GOING OUT into the fresh air Dick felt the pangs of hunger. He accordingly went to a restaurant and got a substantial supper. Perhaps it was the new clothes he wore, which made him feel a little more aristocratic. At all events, instead of patronizing the cheap restaurant where he usually procured his meals, he went into the refectory attached to Lovejoy's Hotel, where the prices were higher and the company more select. In his ordinary dress, Dick would have been excluded, but now he had the appearance of a very respectable, gentlemanly boy, whose presence would not discredit any establishment. His orders were therefore received with attention by the waiter, and in due time a good supper was placed before him.

"I wish I could come here every day," thought Dick. "It seems kind o' nice and 'spectable, side of the other place. There's a gent at that other table that I've shined boots for more'n once. He don't know me in my new clothes. Guess he don't know his boot-black patronizes the same establishment."

His supper over, Dick went up to the desk, and, presenting his check, tendered in payment his five-dollar bill, as if it were one of a large number which he possessed. Receiving back his change he went out into the street.

Two questions now arose: How should he spend the

evening, and where should he pass the night? Yesterday, with such a sum of money in his possession, he would have answered both questions readily. For the evening, he would have passed it at the Old Bowery, and gone to sleep in any out-of-the-way place that offered. But he had turned over a new leaf, or resolved to do so. He meant to save his money for some useful purpose,—to aid his advancement in the world. So he could not afford the theatre. Besides, with his new clothes, he was unwilling to pass the night out of doors.

"I should spile 'em," he thought, "and that wouldn't pay."

So he determined to hunt up a room which he could occupy regularly, and consider as his own, where he could sleep nights, instead of depending on boxes and old wagons for a chance shelter. This would be the first step towards respectability, and Dick determined to take it.

He accordingly passed through the City Hall Park, and walked leisurely up Centre Street.

He decided that it would hardly be advisable for him to seek lodgings in Fifth Avenue, although his present cash capital consisted of nearly five dollars in money, besides the valuable papers contained in his wallet. Besides, he had reason to doubt whether any of his line of business lived on that aristocratic street. He took his way to Mott Street, which is considerably less pretentious, and halted in front of a shabby brick lodging-house kept by a Mrs. Mooney, with whose son Tom, Dick was acquainted.

Dick rang the bell, which sent back a shrill metallic response.

The door was opened by a slatternly servant, who looked at him inquiringly, and not without curiosity. It must be remembered that Dick was well dressed, and that nothing in his appearance bespoke his occupation. Being naturally a good-looking boy, he might readily be mistaken for a gentleman's son.

"Well, Queen Victoria," said Dick, "is your missus at home?"

"My name's Bridget," said the girl.

"Oh, indeed!" said Dick. "You looked so much like the queen's picter what she gave me last Christmas in exchange for mine, that I couldn't help calling you by her name."

"Oh, go along wid ye!" said Bridget. "It's makin' fun ye are."

"If you don't believe me," said Dick, gravely "all you've got to do is to ask my partic'lar friend, the Duke of Newcastle."

"Bridget!" called a shrill voice from the basement.

"The missus is calling me," said Bridget, hurriedly. "I'll tell her ye want her."

"All right!" said Dick.

The servant descended into the lower regions, and in a short time a stout, red-faced woman appeared on the scene.

"Well, sir, what's your wish?" she asked.

"Have you got a room to let?" asked Dick.

"Is it for yourself you ask?" questioned the woman, in some surprise.

Dick answered in the affirmative.

"I haven't got any very good rooms vacant. There's a small room in the third story."

"I'd like to see it," said Dick.

"I don't know as it would be good enough for you," said the woman, with a glance at Dick's clothes.

"I ain't very partic'lar about accommodations," said our hero. "I guess I'll look at it."

Dick followed the landlady up two narrow staircases, uncarpeted and dirty, to the third landing, where he was ushered into a room about ten feet square. It could not be considered a very desirable apartment. It had once been covered with an oilcloth carpet, but this was now very ragged, and looked worse than none. There was a single bed in the corner, covered with an indiscriminate heap of bedclothing, rumpled and not over-clean. There was a bureau, with the veneering scratched and in some parts stripped off, and a small glass, eight inches by ten, cracked across the middle; also two chairs in rather a disjointed condition. Judging from Dick's appearance, Mrs. Mooney thought he would turn from it in disdain.

But it must be remembered that Dick's past experience had not been of a character to make him fastidious. In comparison with a box. or an empty wagon, even this little room seemed comfortable. He decided to hire it if the rent proved reasonable.

"Well, what's the tax?" asked Dick.

"I ought to have a dollar a week," said Mrs. Mooney, hesitatingly.

"Say seventy-five cents, and I'll take it," said Dick.

"Every week in advance?"

"Yes."

"Well, as times is hard, and I can't afford to keep it empty, you may have it. When will you come?"

"To-night," said Dick.

"It aint lookin' very neat. I don't know as I can fix it up to-night."

"Well, I'll sleep here to-night, and you can fix it up to-morrow."

"I hope you'll excuse the looks. I'm a lone woman, and my help is so shiftless, I have to look after everything myself; so I can't keep things as straight as I want to."

"All right!" said Dick.

"Can you pay me the first week in advance?" asked the landlady, cautiously.

Dick responded by drawing seventy-five cents from his pocket, and placing it in her hand.

"What's your business, sir, if I may inquire?" said Mrs. Mooney.

"Oh, I'm professional!" said Dick.

"Indeed!" said the landlady, who did not feel much enlightened by this answer.

"How's Tom?" asked Dick.

"Do you know my Tom?" said Mrs. Mooney in surprise. "He's gone to sea,—to Californy. He went last week."

"Did he?" said Dick. "Yes, I knew him."

Mrs. Mooney looked upon her new lodger with increased favor, in finding that he was acquainted with her son, who, by the way, was one of the worst young scamps in Mott Street, which is saying considerable.

"I'll bring over my baggage from the Astor House this evening," said Dick in a tone of importance.

"From the Astor House!" repeated Mrs. Mooney, in fresh amazement.

"Yes, I've been stoppin' there a short time with some friends," said Dick.

Mrs. Mooney might be excused for a little amazement at finding that a guest from the Astor House was about to become one of her lodgers—such transfers not being common.

"Did you say you was purfessional?" she asked.

"Yes, ma'am," said Dick, politely.

"You aint a—a—" Mrs. Mooney paused, uncertain what conjecture to hazard.

"Oh, no, nothing of the sort," said Dick, promptly. "How could you think so, Mrs. Mooney?"

"No offense, sir," said the landlady, more perplexed than ever.

"Certainly not," said our hero. "But you must excuse me now, Mrs. Mooney, as I have business of great importance to attend to."

"You'll come round this evening?"

Dick answered in the affirmative, and turned away.

"I wonder what he is!" thought the landlady, following him with her eyes as he crossed the street. "He's got good clothes on, but he don't seem very particular about his room. Well; I've got all my rooms full now. That's one comfort."

Dick felt more comfortable now that he had taken the decisive step of hiring a lodging, and paying a week's rent in advance. For seven nights he was sure of a shelter and a bed to sleep in. The thought was a pleasant one to our young vagrant, who hitherto had seldom known when he rose in the morning where he should find a resting-place at night.

"I must bring my traps round," said Dick to himself. "I guess I'll go to bed early to-night. It'll feel kinder good to sleep in a reg'lar bed. Boxes is rather hard to the back, and aint comfortable in case of rain. I wonder what Johnny Nolan would say if he knew I'd got a room of my own."

Chapter 13

Micky Maguire

ABOUT nine o'clock Dick sought his new lodgings. In his hands he carried his professional wardrobe, namely, the clothes which he had worn at the commencement of the day, and the implements of his business. These he stowed away in the bureau drawers, and by the light of a flickering candle took off his clothes and went to bed. Dick had a good digestion and a reasonably good conscience; consequently he was a good sleeper. Perhaps, too, the soft feather bed conduced to slumber. At any rate his eyes were soon closed. and he did not awake until half-past six the next morning.

He lifted himself on his elbow, and stared around him in transient bewilderment.

"Blest if I hadn't forgot where I was," he said to himself. "So this is my room, is it? Well, it seems kind of 'spectable to have a room and a bed to sleep in. I'd orter be able to afford seventy-five cents a week. I've throwed away more money than that in one evenin'. There aint no reason why I shouldn't live 'spectable. I wish I knowed as much as Frank. He's a tip-top feller. Nobody ever cared enough for me before to give me good advice. It was kicks, and cuffs, and swearin' at me all the time. I'd like to show him I can do something."

While Dick was indulging in these reflections, he had risen from bed, and, finding an accession to the furniture of his room, in the shape of an ancient wash-stand bearing a cracked bowl and broken pitcher, indulged himself in the rather unusual ceremony of a good wash. On the whole, Dick preferred to be clean, but it was not always easy to gratify his desire. Lodging in the street as he had been accustomed to do, he had had no opportunity to perform his toilet in the customary manner. Even now he found himself unable to arrange his dishevelled locks, having neither comb nor brush. He determined to purchase a comb, at least, as soon as possible, and a brush too, if he could get one cheap. Meanwhile he combed his hair with his fingers as well as he could, though the result was not quite so satisfactory as it might have been.

A question now came up for consideration. For the first time in his life Dick possessed two suits of clothes. Should he put on the clothes Frank had given him, or resume his old rags?

Now, twenty-four hours before, at the time Dick was introduced to the reader's notice, no one could have been less fastidious as to his clothing than he. Indeed, he had rather a contempt for good clothes, or at least he thought so. But now, as he surveyed the ragged and dirty coat and the patched pants, Dick felt ashamed of them. He was unwilling to appear in the streets with them. Yet, if he went to work in his new suit, he was in danger of spoiling it, and he might not have it in his power to purchase a new one. Economy dictated a return to the old garments. Dick tried them on, and surveyed himself in the cracked glass; but the reflection did not please him.

"They don't look 'spectable," he decided; and, forthwith taking them off again, he put on the new suit of the day before.

"I must try to earn a little more," he thought, "to pay for my room, and to buy some new clo'es when these is wore out."

He opened the door of his chamber, and went downstairs and into the street, carrying his blacking-box with him.

It was Dick's custom to commence his business before breakfast; generally it must be owned, because he began the day penniless and must earn his meal before he ate it. To-day it was different. He had four dollars left in his pocket-book; but this he had previously determined not to touch. In fact he had formed the ambitious design of starting an account at a savings' bank, in order to have something to fall back upon in case of sickness or any other emergency, or at any rate as a reserve fund to expend in clothing or other necessary articles when he required them. Hitherto he had been content to live on from day to day without a penny ahead; but the new vision of respectability which now floated before Dick's mind, owing to his recent acquaintance with Frank, was beginning to exercise a powerful effect upon him.

In Dick's profession as in others there are lucky days, when everything seems to flow prosperously. As if to encourage him in his new-born resolution, our hero obtained no less than six jobs in the course of an hour and a half. This gave him sixty cents, quite abundant to purchase his breakfast, and a comb besides. His exertions made him hungry, and, entering a small eating-house he ordered a cup of coffee and a beefsteak. To this he added a couple of rolls. This was quite a luxurious breakfast for Dick, and more expensive than he was accustomed to indulge himself with. To gratify the curiosity of my young readers, I will put down the items with their cost,—

Coffee,	....	5 cts.
Beefsteak,	....	15 cts.
A couple of rolls,	....	5 cts.
		——25 cts.

It will thus be seen that our hero had expended nearly one-half of his morning's earnings. Some days he had been compelled to breakfast on five cents, and then he was forced to content himself with a couple of apples, or cakes. But a good breakfast is a good preparation for a busy day, and Dick sallied forth from the restaurant lively and alert, ready to do a good stroke of business.

Dick's change of costume was liable to lead to one result of which he had not thought. His brother boot-

blacks might think he had grown aristocratic, and was
putting on airs,—that, in fact, he was getting above his
business, and desirous to outshine his associates. Dick
had not dreamed of this, because in fact, in spite of his
new-born ambition, he entertained no such feelings. There
was nothing of what boys call "big-feeling" about him.
He was a thorough democrat, using the word not politi-
cally, but in its proper sense, and was disposed to frater-
nize with all whom he styled "good fellows," without
regard to their position. It may seem a little unnecessary
to some of my readers to make this explanation; but
they must remember that pride and "big feeling" are
confined to no age or class, but may be found in boys as
well as men, and in boot-blacks as well as those of a
higher rank.

The morning being a busy time with the boot-blacks,
Dick's changed appearance had not as yet attracted much
attention. But when business slackened a little, our hero
was destined to be reminded of it.

Among the down-town boot-blacks was one hailing
from the Five Points,—a stout, red-haired, freckled-
faced boy of fourteen, bearing the name of Micky
Maguire. This boy, by his boldness and recklessness, as
well as by his personal strength, which was considerable,
had acquired an ascendency among his fellow profes-
sionals, and had a gang of subservient followers, whom he
led on to acts of ruffianism, not unfrequently terminating
in a month or two at Blackwell's Island. Micky himself
had served two terms there; but the confinement appeared
to have had very little effect in amending his conduct,
except, perhaps, in making him a little more cautious
about an encounter with the "copps," as the members of
the city police, are, for some unknown reason, styled
among the Five-Point boys.

Now Micky was proud of his strength, and of the
position of leader which it had secured him. Moreover
he was democratic in his tastes, and had a jealous hatred
of those who wore good clothes and kept their faces clean.
He called it putting on airs, and resented the implied
superiority. If he had been fifteen years older, and had

a trifle more education, he would have interested himself in politics, and been prominent at ward meetings, and a terror to respectable voters on election day. As it was, he contented himself with being the leader of a gang of young ruffians, over whom he wielded a despotic power.

Now it is only justice to Dick to say that, so far as wearing good clothes was concerned, he had never hitherto offended the eyes of Micky Maguire. Indeed, they generally looked as if they patronized the same clothing establishment. On this particular morning it chanced that Micky had not been very fortunate in a business way, and, as a natural consequence, his temper, never very amiable, was somewhat ruffled by the fact. He had had a very frugal breakfast,—not because he felt abstemious, but owing to the low state of his finances. He was walking along with one of his particular friends, a boy nicknamed Limpy Jim, so called from a slight peculiarity in his walk, when all at once he espied our friend Dick in his new suit.

"My eyes!" he exclaimed, in astonishment; "Jim, just look at Ragged Dick. He's come into a fortun', and turned gentleman. See his new clothes."

"So he has," said Jim. "Where'd he get 'em, I wonder?"

"Hooked 'em, p'r'aps. Let's go and stir him up a little. We don't want no gentlemen on our beat. So he's puttin' on airs,—is he? I'll give him a lesson."

So saying the two boys walked up to our hero, who had not observed them, his back being turned, and Micky Maguire gave him a smart slap on the shoulder.

Dick turned round quickly.

Chapter 14

A Battle and a Victory

"WHAT'S that for?" demanded Dick, turning round to see who had struck him.

"You're gettin' mighty fine!" said Micky Maguire, surveying Dick's new clothes with a scornful air.

There was something in his words and tone, which Dick, who was disposed to stand up for his dignity, did not at all relish.

"Well, what's the odds if I am?" he retorted. "Does it hurt you any?"

"See him put on airs, Jim," said Micky, turning to his companion. "Where'd you get them clo'es?"

"Never mind where I got 'em. Maybe the Prince of Wales gave 'em to me."

"Hear him, now, Jim," said Micky. "Most likely he stole 'em."

"Stealin' aint in *my* line."

It might have been unconscious the emphasis which Dick placed on the word "my." At any rate Micky chose to take offence.

"Do you mean to say that *I* steal?" he demanded, doubling up his fist, and advancing towards Dick in a threatening manner.

"I don't say anything about it," answered Dick, by no means alarmed at this hostile demonstration. "I know you've been to the island twice. P'r'aps 'twas to make a visit along of the Mayor and Aldermen. Maybe you was a innocent victim of oppression. I aint a goin' to say."

Micky's freckled face grew red with wrath, for Dick had only stated the truth.

"Do you mean to insult me?" he demanded, shaking his fist already doubled up in Dick's face. "Maybe you want a lickin'?"

"I aint partic'larly anxious to get one," said Dick, coolly. "They don't agree with my constitution which is nat'rally delicate. I'd rather have a good dinner than a lickin' any time."

"You're afraid," sneered Micky. "Isn't he, Jim?"

"In course he is."

"P'r'aps I am," said Dick, composedly, "but it don't trouble me much."

"Do you want to fight?" demanded Micky, encouraged by Dick's quietness, fancying he was afraid to encounter him.

"No, I don't," said Dick. "I aint fond of fightin'. It's a very poor amusement, and very bad for the complexion, 'specially for the eyes and nose, which is apt to turn red, white, and blue."

Micky misunderstood Dick, and judged from the tenor of his speech that he would be an easy victim. As he knew, Dick very seldom was concerned in any street fight,—not from cowardice, as he imagined, but because he had too much good sense to do so. Being quarrelsome, like all bullies, and supposing that he was more than a match for our hero, being about two inches taller, he could no longer resist an inclination to assault him, and tried to plant a blow in Dick's face which would have hurt him considerably if he had not drawn back just in time.

Now, though Dick was far from quarrelsome, he was ready to defend himself on all occasions, and it was too much to expect that he would stand quiet and allow himself to be beaten.

He dropped his blacking-box on the instant, and returned Micky's blow with such good effect that the young bully staggered back, and would have fallen, if he had not been propped up by his confederate, Limpy Jim.

"Go in, Micky!" shouted the latter, who was rather a

forgiving

coward on his own account, but liked to see others fight. "Polish him off, that's a good feller."

Micky was now boiling over with rage and fury, and required no urging. He was fully determined to make a terrible example of poor Dick. He threw himself upon him, and strove to bear him to the ground; but Dick, avoiding a close hug, in which he might possibly have got the worst of it, by an adroit movement, tripped up his antagonist, and stretched him on the sidewalk.

"Hit him, Jim!" exclaimed Micky, furiously.

Limpy Jim did not seem inclined to obey orders. There was a quiet strength and coolness about Dick, which alarmed him. He preferred that Micky should incur all the risks of battle, and accordingly set himself to raising his fallen comrade.

"Come, Micky," said Dick, quietly, "you'd better give it up. I wouldn't have touched you if you hadn't hit me first. I don't want to fight. It's low business."

"You're afraid of hurtin' your clo'es," said Micky, with a sneer.

"Maybe I am," said Dick. "I hope I haven't hurt yours."

Micky's answer to this was another attack, as violent and impetuous as the first. But his fury was in the way. He struck wildly, not measuring his blows, and Dick had no difficulty in turning aside so that his antagonist's blow fell upon the empty air, and his momentum was such that he nearly fell forward headlong. Dick might readily have taken advantage of his unsteadiness, and knocked him down; but he was not vindictive, and chose to act on the defensive, except when he could not avoid it.

Recovering himself, Micky saw that Dick was a more formidable antagonist than he had supposed, and was meditating another assault, better planned, which by its impetuosity might bear our hero to the ground. But there was an unlooked-for interference.

"Look out for the 'copp,' " said Jim, in a low voice.

Micky turned round and saw a tall policeman heading towards him, and thought it might be prudent to suspend hostilities. He accordingly picked up his blacking-box, and, hitching up his pants, walked off, attended by Limpy Jim.

"What's that chap been doing?" asked the policeman of Dick.

"He was amoosin' himself by pitchin' into me," replied Dick.

"What for?"

"He didn't like it 'cause I patronize a different tailor from him."

"Well, it seems to me you *are* dressed pretty smart for a boot-black," said the policeman.

"I wish I wasn't a boot-black," said Dick.

"Never mind, my lad. It's an honest business," said the policeman, who was a sensible man and a worthy citizen. "It's an honest business. Stick to it till you get something better."

"I mean to," said Dick. "It aint easy to get out of it, as the prisoner remarked, when he was asked how he liked his residence."

"I hope you don't speak from experience."

"No," said Dick; "I don't mean to get into prison if I can help it."

"Do you see that gentleman over there?" asked the officer, pointing to a well-dressed man who was walking on the other side of the street.

"Yes."

"Well, he was once a newsboy."

"And what is he now?"

"He keeps a bookstore, and is quite prosperous."

Dick looked at the gentleman with interest, wondering if he should look as respectable when he was a grown man.

It will be seen that Dick was getting ambitious. Hitherto he had thought very little of the future, but was content to get along as he could, dining as well as his means would allow, and spending the evenings in the pit of the Old Bowery, eating peanuts between the acts if he was prosperous, and if unlucky supping on dry bread or an apple, and sleeping in an old box or a wagon. Now, for the first time, he began to reflect that he could not black boots all his life. In seven years he would be a man, and, since his meeting with Frank, he felt that he would like to be a respectable man. He could see and appreciate the difference between Frank and such a boy as Micky Maguire, and it was not strange that he preferred the society of the former.

In the course of the next morning, in pursuance of his new resolutions for the future, he called at a savings bank, and held out four dollars in bills besides another dollar in change. There was a high railing, and a number of clerks busily writing at desks behind it. Dick, never having been in a bank before, did not know where to go. He went, by mistake, to the desk where money was paid out.

"Where's your book?" asked the clerk.

"I haven't got any."

"Have you any money deposited here?"

"No sir, I want to leave some here."

"Then go to the next desk."

Dick followed directions, and presented himself before an elderly man with gray hair, who looked at him over the rims of his spectacles.

"I want you to keep that for me," said Dick, awkwardly emptying his money out on the desk.

"How much is there?"

"Five dollars."

"Have you got an account here?"

"No, sir."

"Of course you can write?"

The "of course" was said on account of Dick's neat dress.

"Have I got to do any writing?" asked our hero, a little embarrassed.

"We want you to sign your name in this book," and the old gentleman shoved round a large folio volume containing the names of depositors.

Dick surveyed the book with some awe.

"I aint much on writin'," he said.

"Very well; write as well as you can."

The pen was put into Dick's hand, and, after dipping it in the inkstand, he succeeded after a hard effort, accompanied by many contortions of the face, in inscribing upon the book of the bank the name

DICK HUNTER.

"Dick!—that means Richard, I suppose," said the bank officer, who had some difficulty in making out the signature.

"No; Ragged Dick is what folks call me."

"You don't look very ragged."

"No, I've left my rags at home. They might get wore out if I used 'em too common."

"Well, my lad, I'll make out a book in the name of Dick Hunter, since you seem to prefer Dick to Richard. I hope you will save up your money and deposit more with us."

Our hero took his bank-book, and gazed on the entry "Five Dollars" with a new sense of importance. He had been accustomed to joke about Erie shares; but now, for the first time, he felt himself a capitalist; on a small scale, to be sure, but still it was no small thing for Dick to have five dollars which he could call his own. He firmly determined that he would lay by every cent he could spare from his earnings towards the fund he hoped to accumulate.

But Dick was too sensible not to know that there was something more than money needed to win a respectable position in the world. He felt that he was very ignorant. Of reading and writing he only knew the rudiments, and that, with a slight acquaintance with arithmetic, was all he did know of books. Dick knew he must study hard, and he dreaded it. He looked upon learning as attended with greater difficulties than it really possesses. But Dick had good pluck. He meant to learn, nevertheless, and resolved to buy a book with his first spare earnings.

When Dick went home at night he locked up his bank-book in one of the drawers of the bureau. It was wonderful how much more independent he felt whenever he reflected upon the contents of that drawer, and with what an important air of joint ownership he regarded the bank building in which his small savings were deposited.

Chapter 15

Dick Secures a Tutor

THE NEXT MORNING Dick was unusually successful, having plenty to do, and receiving for one job twenty-five cents,—the gentleman refusing to take change. Then flashed upon Dick's mind the thought that he had not yet returned the change due to the gentleman whose boots he had blacked on the morning of his introduction to the reader.

"What'll he think of me?" said Dick to himself. "I hope he won't think I'm mean enough to keep the money."

Now Dick was scrupulously honest, and though the temptation to be otherwise had often been strong, he had always resisted it. He was not willing on any account to keep money which did not belong to him, and he immediately started for 125 Fulton Street (the address which had been given him) where he found Mr. Greyson's name on the door of an office on the first floor.

The door being open, Dick walked in.

"Is Mr. Greyson in?" he asked of a clerk who sat on a high stool before a desk.

"Not just now. He'll be in soon. Will you wait?"

"Yes," said Dick.

"Very well; take a seat then."

Dick sat down and took up the morning "Tribune," but presently came to a word of four syllables, which he pronounced to himself a "sticker," and laid it down. But

131

he had not long to wait, for five minutes later Mr. Greyson entered.

"Did you wish to speak to me, my lad?" said he to Dick, whom in his new clothes he did not recognize.

"Yes, sir," said Dick. "I owe you some money."

"Indeed!" said Mr. Greyson, pleasantly; "that's an agreeable surprise. I didn't know but you had come for some. So you are a debtor of mine, and not a creditor?"

"I b'lieve that's right," said Dick, drawing fifteen cents from his pocket, and placing in Mr. Greyson's hand.

"Fifteen cents!" repeated he, in some surprise. "How do you happen to be indebted to me in that amount?"

"You gave me a quarter for a-shinin' your boots, yesterday mornin', and couldn't wait for the change. I meant to have brought it before, but I forgot all about it till this mornin'."

"It had quite slipped my mind also. But you don't look like the boy I employed. If I remember rightly he wasn't as well dressed as you."

"No," said Dick. "I was dressed for a party, then, but the clo'es was too well ventilated to be comfortable in cold weather."

"You're an honest boy," said Mr. Greyson. "Who taught you to be honest?"

"Nobody," said Dick. "But it's mean to cheat and steal. I've always knowed that."

"Then you've got ahead of some of our business men. Do you read the Bible?"

"No," said Dick. "I've heard it's a good book, but I don't know much about it."

"You ought to go to some Sunday School. Would you be willing?"

"Yes," said Dick, promptly. "I want to grow up 'spectable. But I don't know where to go."

"Then I'll tell you. The church I attend is at the corner of Fifth Avenue and Twenty-first Street."

"I've seen it," said Dick.

"I have a class in the Sunday School there. If you'll come next Sunday, I'll take you into my class, and do what I can to help you."

friendly, generous

"Thank you," said Dick, "but p'r'aps you'll get tired of teaching me. I'm awful ignorant."

"No, my lad," said Mr. Greyson, kindly. "You evidently have some good principles to start with, as you have shown by your scorn for dishonesty. I shall hope good things of you in the future."

"Well, Dick," said our hero, apostrophizing himself, as he left the office; "you're gettin' up in the world. You've got money invested, and are goin' to attend church, by partic'lar invitation, on Fifth Avenue. I shouldn't wonder much if you should find cards, when you get home, from the Mayor, requestin' the honor of your company to dinner, along with other distinguished guests."

Dick felt in very good spirits. He seemed to be emerging from the world in which he had hitherto lived, into a new atmosphere of respectability, and the change seemed very pleasant to him.

At six o'clock Dick went into a restaurant on Chatham Street, and got a comfortable supper. He had been so successful during that day that, after paying for this, he still had ninety cents left. While he was despatching his supper, another boy came in, smaller and slighter than Dick, and sat down beside him. Dick recognized him as a boy who three months before had entered the ranks of the boot-blacks, but who, from a natural timidity, had not been able to earn much. He was ill-fitted for the coarse companionship of the street boys, and shrank from the rude jokes of his present associates. Dick had never troubled him; for our hero had a certain chivalrous feeling which would not allow him to bully or disturb a younger and weaker boy than himself.

"How are you, Fosdick?" said Dick, as the other seated himself.

"Pretty well," said Fosdick. "I suppose you're all right."

"Oh, yes, I'm right side up with care. I've been havin' a bully supper. What are you goin' to have?"

"Some bread and butter."

"Why don't you get a cup o' coffee?"

"Why," said Fosdick, reluctantly, "I haven't got money enough to-night."

"Never mind," said Dick; "I'm in luck to-day. I'll stand treat."

"That's kind in you," said Fosdick, gratefully.

"Oh, never mind that," said Dick.

Accordingly he ordered a cup of coffee, and a plate of beef-steak, and was gratified to see that his young companion partook of both with evident relish. When the repast was over, the boys went out into the street together, Dick pausing at the desk to settle for both suppers.

"Where are you going to sleep to-night, Fosdick?" asked Dick, as they stood on the sidewalk.

"I don't know," said Fosdick, a little sadly. "In some door-way, I expect. But I'm afraid the police will find me out, and make me move on."

"I'll tell you what," said Dick, "you must go home with me. I guess my bed will hold two."

"Have you got a room?" asked the other, in surprise.

"Yes," said Dick, rather proudly, and with a little excusable exultation. "I've got a room over in Mott Street; there I can receive my friends. That'll be better than sleepin' in a door-way,—won't it?"

"Yes, indeed it will," said Fosdick. "How lucky I was to come across you! It comes hard to me living as I do. When my father was alive I had every comfort."

"That's more'n I ever had," said Dick. "But I'm goin' to try to live comfortable now. Is your father dead?"

"Yes," said Fosdick, sadly. "He was a printer; but he was drowned one dark night from a Fulton ferry-boat, and, as I had no relations in the city, and no money, I was obliged to go to work as quick as I could. But I don't get on very well."

"Didn't you have no brothers nor sisters?" asked Dick.

"No," said Fosdick; "father and I used to live alone. He was always so much company to me that I feel very lonesome without him. There's a man out West somewhere that owes him two thousand dollars. He used to live in the city, and father lent him all his money to help him go into business; but he failed, or pretended to, and went off. If father hadn't lost that money he would have left me well off; but no money would have made up his loss to me."

"What's the man's name that went off with your father's money?"

"His name is Hiram Bates."

"P'r'aps you'll get the money again, sometime."

"There isn't much chance of it," said Fosdick. "I'd sell out my chances of that for five dollars."

"Maybe I'll buy you out some time," said Dick. "Now, come round and see what sort of a room I've got. I used to go to the theatre evenings, when I had money; but now I'd rather go to bed early, and have a good sleep."

"I don't care much about theatres," said Fosdick. "Father didn't use to let me go very often. He said it wasn't good for boys."

"I like to go to the Old Bowery sometimes. They have tip-top plays there. Can you read and write well?" he asked, as a sudden thought came to him.

"Yes," said Fosdick. "Father always kept me at school when he was alive, and I stood pretty well in my classes. I was expecting to enter at the Free Academy* next year."

"Then I'll tell you what," said Dick; "I'll make a bargain with you. I can't read much more'n a pig; and my writin' looks like hens' tracks. I don't want to grow up knowin' no more'n a four-year-old boy. If you'll teach me readin' and writin' evenin's, you shall sleep in my room every night. That'll be better'n door-steps or old boxes, where I've slept many a time."

"Are you in earnest?" said Fosdick, his face lighting up hopefully.

"In course I am," said Dick. "It's fashionable for young gentlemen to have private tootors to introduce 'em into the flower-beds of literatoor and science, and why shouldn't I foller the fashion? You shall be my perfessor; only you must promise not to be very hard if my writin' looks like a rail-fence on a bender."

"I'll try not to be too severe," said Fosdick, laughing.

*Now the College of the City of New York.

"I shall be thankful for such a chance to get a place to sleep. Have you got anything to read out of?"

"No," said Dick. "My extensive and well-selected library was lost overboard in a storm, when I was sailin' from the Sandwich Islands to the desert of Sahara. But I'll buy a paper. That'll do me a long time."

Accordingly Dick stopped at a paper-stand, and bought a copy of a weekly paper, filled with the usual variety of reading matter,—stories, sketches, poems, etc.

They soon arrived at Dick's lodging-house. Our hero, procuring a lamp from the landlady, led the way into his apartment, which he entered with the proud air of a proprietor.

"Well, how do you like it, Fosdick?" he asked, complacently.

The time was when Fosdick would have thought it untidy and not particularly attractive. But he had served a severe apprenticeship in the streets, and it was pleasant to feel himself under shelter, and he was not disposed to be critical.

"It looks very comfortable, Dick," he said.

"The bed aint very large," said Dick; "but I guess we can get along."

"Oh, yes," said Fosdick, cheerfully. "I don't take up much room."

"Then that's all right. There's two chairs, you see, one for you and one for me. In case the mayor comes in to spend the evenin' socially, he can sit on the bed."

The boys seated themselves, and five minutes later, under the guidance of his young tutor, Dick had commenced his studies.

Chapter 16

The First Lesson

FORTUNATELY for Dick, his young tutor was well qualified to instruct him. Henry Fosdick, though only twelve years old, knew as much as many boys of fourteen. He had always been studious and ambitious to excel. His father, being a printer, employed in an office where books were printed, often brought home new books in sheets, which Henry was always glad to read. Mr. Fosdick had been, besides, a subscriber to the Mechanics' Apprentices' Library, which contains many thousands of well-selected and instructive books. Thus Henry had acquired an amount of general information, unusual in a boy of his age. Perhaps he had devoted too much time to study, for he was not naturally robust. All this, however, fitted him admirably for the office to which Dick had appointed him,—that of his private instructor.

The two boys drew up their chairs to the rickety table, and spread out the paper before them.

"The exercises generally commence with ringin' the bell," said Dick; "but as I aint got none, we'll have to do without."

"And the teacher is generally provided with a rod," said Fosdick. "Isn't there a poker handy, that I can use in case my scholar doesn't behave well?"

" 'Taint lawful to use fire-arms," said Dick.

"Now, Dick," said Fosdick, "before we begin, I must find out how much you already know. Can you read any?"

"Not enough to hurt me," said Dick. "All I know about readin' you could put in a nutshell, and there'd be room left for a small family."

"I suppose you know your letters?"

"Yes," said Dick, "I know 'em all, but not intimately. I guess I can call 'em all by name."

"Where did you learn them? Did you ever go to school?"

"Yes; I went two days."

"Why did you stop?"

"It didn't agree with my constitution."

"You don't look very delicate," said Fosdick.

"No," said Dick, "I aint troubled much that way, but I found lickins didn't agree with me."

"Did you get punished?"

"Awful," said Dick.

"What for?"

"For indulgin' in a little harmless amoosement," said Dick. "You see the boy that was sittin' next to me fell asleep, which I considered improper in school-time; so I thought I'd help the teacher a little by wakin' him up. So I took a pin and stuck into him; but I guess it went a little too far, for he screeched awful. The teacher found out what it was that made him holler, and whipped me with a ruler till I was black and blue. I thought 'twas about time to take a vacation; so that's the last time I went to school."

"You didn't learn to read in that time, of course?"

"No," said Dick; "but I was a newsboy a little while; so I learned a little, just so's to find out what the news was. Sometimes I didn't read straight, and called the wrong news. One mornin' I asked another boy what the paper said, and he told me the King of Africa was dead. I thought it was all right till folks began to laugh."

"Well, Dick, if you'll only study well, you won't be liable to make such mistakes."

"I hope so," said Dick. "My friend Horace Greeley told me the other day that he'd get me to take his place now and then when he was off makin' speeches if my edication hadn't been neglected."

"I must find a good piece for you to begin on," said Fosdick, looking over the paper.

"Find an easy one," said Dick, "with words of one story."

Fosdick at length found a piece which he thought would answer. He discovered on trial that Dick had not exaggerated his deficiencies. Words of two syllables he seldom pronounced right, and was much surprised when he was told how "through" was sounded.

"Seems to me it's throwin' away letters to use all them," he said.

"How would you spell it?" asked his young teacher.

"T-h-r-u," said Dick.

"Well," said Fosdick, "there's a good many other words that are spelt with more letters than they need to have. But it's the fashion, and we must follow it."

But if Dick was ignorant, he was quick, and had an excellent capacity. Moreover he had perseverance, and was not easily discouraged. He had made up his mind he must know more, and was not disposed to complain of the difficulty of his task. Fosdick had occasion to laugh more than once at his ludicrous mistakes; but Dick laughed too, and on the whole both were quite interested in the lesson.

At the end of an hour and a half the boys stopped for the evening.

"You're learning fast, Dick," said Fosdick. "At this rate you will soon learn to read well."

"Will I?" asked Dick with an expression of satisfaction. "I'm glad of that. I don't want to be ignorant. I didn't use to care, but I do now. I want to grow up 'spectable."

"So do I, Dick. We will both help each other, and I am sure we can accomplish something. But I am beginning to feel sleepy."

"So am I," said Dick. "Them hard words make my head ache. I wonder who made 'em all?"

"That's more than I can tell. I suppose you've seen a dictionary."

"That's another of 'em. No, I can't say I have, though

I may have seen him in the street without knowin' him."

"A dictionary is a book containing all the words in the language."

"How many are there?"

"I don't rightly know; but I think there are about fifty thousand."

"It's a pretty large family," said Dick. "Have I got to learn 'em all?"

"That will not be necessary. There are a large number which you would never find occasion to use."

"I'm glad of that," said Dick; "for I don't expect to live to be more'n a hundred, and by that time I wouldn't be more'n half through."

By this time the flickering lamp gave a decided hint to the boys that unless they made haste they would have to undress in the dark. They accordingly drew off their clothes, and Dick jumped into bed. But Fosdick, before doing so, knelt down by the side of the bed, and said a short prayer.

"What's that for?" asked Dick curiously.

"I was saying my prayers," said Fosdick, as he rose from his knees. "Don't you ever do it?"

"No," said Dick. "Nobody ever taught me."

"Then I'll teach you. Shall I?"

"I don't know," said Dick, dubiously. "What's the good?"

Fosdick explained as well as he could, and perhaps his simple explanation was better adapted to Dick's comprehension than one from an older person would have been. Dick felt more free to ask questions, and the example of his new friend, for whom he was beginning to feel a warm attachment, had considerable effect upon him. When, therefore, Fosdick asked again if he should teach him a prayer, Dick consented, and his young bedfellow did so. Dick was not naturally irreligious. If he had lived without a knowledge of God and of religious things, it was scarcely to be wondered at in a lad who, from an early age, had been thrown upon his own exertions for the means of living, with no one to care for him or give him good advice. But he was so far good that he could ap-

resourceful

preciate goodness in others, and this it was that had drawn him to Frank in the first place, and now to Henry Fosdick. He did not, therefore, attempt to ridicule his companion, as some boys better brought up might have done, but was willing to follow his example in what something told him was right. Our young hero had taken an important step towards securing that genuine respectability which he was ambitious to attain.

Weary with the day's work, and Dick perhaps still more fatigued by the unusual mental effort he had made, the boys soon sank into a deep and peaceful slumber, from which they did not awaken till six o'clock the next morning. Before going out Dick sought Mrs. Mooney, and spoke to her on the subject of taking Fosdick as a room-mate. He found that she had no objection, provided he would allow her twenty-five cents a week extra, in consideration of the extra trouble which his companion might be expected to make. To this Dick assented, and the arrangement was definitely concluded.

This over, the two boys went out and took stations near each other. Dick had more of a business turn than Henry, and less shrinking from publicity, so that his earnings were greater. But he had undertaken to pay the entire expenses of the room, and needed to earn more. Sometimes, when two customers presented themselves at the same time, he was able to direct one to his friend. So at the end of the week both boys found themselves with surplus earnings. Dick had the satisfaction of adding two dollars and a half to his deposits in the Savings Bank, and Fosdick commenced an account by depositing seventy-five cents.

On Sunday morning Dick bethought himself of his promise to Mr. Greyson to come to the church on Fifth Avenue. To tell the truth, Dick recalled it with some regret. He had never been inside a church since he could remember, and he was not much attracted by the invitation he had received. But Henry, finding him wavering, urged him to go, and offered to go with him. Dick gladly accepted the offer, feeling that he required some one to lend him countenance under such unusual circumstances.

Dick dressed himself with scrupulous care, giving his shoes a "shine" so brilliant that it did him great credit in a professional point of view, and endeavored to clean his hands thoroughly; but, in spite of all he could do, they were not so white as if his business had been of a different character.

Having fully completed his preparations, he descended into the street, and, with Henry by his side, crossed over to Broadway.

The boys pursued their way up Broadway, which on Sunday presents a striking contrast in its quietness to the noise and confusion of ordinary weekdays, as far as Union Square, then turned down Fourteenth Street, which brought them to Fifth Avenue.

"Suppose we dine at Delmonico's," said Fosdick, looking towards that famous restaurant.

"I'd have to sell some of my Erie shares," said Dick.

A short walk now brought them to the church of which mention has already been made. They stood outside, a little abashed, watching the fashionably attired people who were entering, and were feeling a little undecided as to whether they had better enter also, when Dick felt a light touch upon his shoulder.

Turning round, he met the smiling glance of Mr. Greyson.

"So, my young friend, you have kept your promise," he said. "And whom have you brought with you?"

"A friend of mine," said Dick. "His name is Henry Fosdick."

"I am glad you have brought him. Now follow me, and I will give you seats."

Chapter 17

Dick's First Appearance in Society

IT WAS the hour for morning service. The boys followed Mr. Greyson into the handsome church, and were assigned seats in his own pew.

There were two persons already seated in it,—a good-looking lady of middle age, and a pretty little girl of nine. They were Mrs. Greyson and her only daughter Ida. They looked pleasantly at the boys as they entered, smiling a welcome to them.

The morning service commenced. It must be acknowledged that Dick felt rather awkward. It was an unusual place for him, and it need not be wondered at that he felt like a cat in a strange garret. He would not have known when to rise if he had not taken notice of what the rest of the audience did, and followed their example. He was sitting next to Ida, and as it was the first time he had ever been near so well-dressed a young lady, he naturally felt bashful. When the hymns were announced, Ida found the place, and offered a hymn-book to our hero. Dick took it awkwardly, but his studies had not yet been pursued far enough for him to read the words readily. However, he resolved to keep up appearances, and kept his eyes fixed steadily on the hymn-book.

At length the service was over. The people began to file slowly out of church, and among them, of course, Mr. Greyson's family and the two boys. It seemed very

strange to Dick to find himself in such different companionship from what he had been accustomed, and he could
not help thinking, "Wonder what Johnny Nolan 'ould say
if he could see me now!"

But Johnny's business engagements did not often sum-
mon him to Fifth Avenue, and Dick was not likely to be
seen by any of his friends in the lower part of the city.

"We have our Sunday school in the afternoon," said
Mr. Greyson. "I suppose you live at some distance from
here?"

"In Mott Street, sir," answered Dick.

"That is too far to go and return. Suppose you and
your friend come and dine with us, and then we can come
here together in the afternoon."

Dick was as much astonished at this invitation as if he
had really been invited by the Mayor to dine with him
and the Board of Aldermen. Mr. Greyson was evidently
a rich man, and yet he had actually invited two boot-
blacks to dine with him.

"I guess we'd better go home, sir," said Dick, hesitating.

"I don't think you can have any very pressing engagements to interfere with your accepting my invitation,"
said Mr. Greyson, good-humoredly, for he understood
the reason of Dick's hesitation. "So I take it for granted
that you both accept."

Before Dick fairly knew what he intended to do, he
was walking down Fifth Avenue with his new friends.

Now, our young hero was not naturally bashful; but
her certainly felt so now, especially as Miss Ida Greyson
chose to walk by his side, leaving Henry Fosdick to walk
with her father and mother.

"What is your name?" asked Ida, pleasantly.

Our hero was about to answer "Ragged Dick," when it
occurred to him that in the present company he had better forget his old nickname.

"Dick Hunter," he answered.

"Dick!" repeated Ida. "That means Richard, doesn't
it?"

"Everybody calls me Dick."

"I have a cousin Dick," said the young lady, sociably. "His name is Dick Wilson. I suppose you don't know him?"

"No," said Dick.

"I like the name of Dick," said the young lady, with charming frankness.

Without being able to tell why, Dick felt rather glad she did. He plucked up courage to ask her name.

"My name is Ida," answered the young lady. "Do you like it?"

"Yes," said Dick. "It's a bully name."

Dick turned red as soon as he had said it, for he felt that he had not used the right expression.

The little girl broke into a silvery laugh.

"What a funny boy you are!" she said.

"I didn't mean it," said Dick, stammering. "I meant it's a tip-top name."

Here Ida laughed again, and Dick wished himself back in Mott Street.

"How old are you?" inquired Ida, continuing her examination.

"I'm fourteen,—goin' on fifteen," said Dick.

"You're a big boy of your age," said Ida. "My cousin Dick is a year older than you, but he isn't as large."

Dick looked pleased. Boys generally like to be told that they are large of their age.

"How old be you?" asked Dick, beginning to feel more at his ease.

"I'm nine years old," said Ida. "I go to Miss Jarvis's school. I've just begun to learn French. Do you know French?"

"Not enough to hurt me," said Dick.

Ida laughed again, and told him that he was a droll boy.

"Do you like it?" asked Dick.

"I like it pretty well, except the verbs. I can't remember them well. Do you go to school?"

"I'm studying with a private tutor," said Dick.

"Are you? So is my cousin Dick. He's going to college this year. Are you going to college?"

"Not this year."

"Because, if you did, you know you'd be in the same class with my cousin. It would be funny to have two Dicks in one class."

They turned down Twenty-fourth Street, passing the Fifth Avenue Hotel on the left, and stopped before an elegant house with a brown stone front. The bell was rung, and the door being opened, the boys, somewhat abashed, followed Mr. Greyson into a handsome hall. They were told where to hang their hats, and a moment afterwards were ushered into a comfortable dining-room, where a table was spread for dinner.

Dick took his seat on the edge of a sofa, and was tempted to rub his eyes to make sure that he was really awake. He could hardly believe that he was a guest in so fine a mansion.

Ida helped to put the boys at their ease.

"Do you like pictures?" she asked.

"Very much," answered Henry.

The little girl brought a book of handsome engravings, and, seating herself beside Dick, to whom she seemed to have taken a decided fancy, commenced showing them to him.

"There are the Pyramids of Egypt," she said, pointing to one engraving.

"What are they for?" asked Dick, puzzled. "I don't see any winders."

"No," said Ida, "I don't believe anybody lives there. Do they, papa?"

"No, my dear. They were used for the burial of the dead. The largest of them is said to be the loftiest building in the world with one exception. The spire of the Cathedral of Strasburg is twenty-four feet higher, if I remember rightly."

"Is Egypt near here?" asked Dick.

"Oh, no, it's ever so many miles off; about four or five hundred. Didn't you know?"

"No," said Dick. "I never heard."

"You don't appear to be very accurate in your information, Ida," said her mother. "Four or five thousand miles would be considerably nearer the truth."

After a little more conversation they sat down to dinner. Dick seated himself in an embarrassed way. He was very much afraid of doing or saying something which would be considered an impropriety, and had the uncomfortable feeling that everybody was looking at him, and watching his behavior.

"Where do you live, Dick?" asked Ida, familiarly.

"In Mott Street."

"Where is that?"

"More than a mile off."

"Is it a nice street?"

"Not very," said Dick. "Only poor folks live there."

"Are you poor?"

"Little girls should be seen and not heard," said her mother, gently.

"If you are," said Ida, "I'll give you the five-dollar gold-piece aunt gave me for a birthday present."

"Dick cannot be called poor, my child," said Mrs. Greyson, "since he earns his living by his own exertions."

"Do you earn your living?" asked Ida, who was a very inquisitive young lady, and not easily silenced. "What do you do?"

Dick blushed violently. At such a table, and in presence of the servant who was standing at that moment behind his chair, he did not like to say that he was a shoe-black, although he well knew that there was nothing dishonorable in the occupation.

Mr. Greyson perceived his feelings, and to spare them, said, "You are too inquisitive, Ida. Some time Dick may tell you, but you know we don't talk of business on Sundays."

Dick in his embarrassment had swallowed a large spoonful of hot soup, which made him turn red in the face. For the second time, in spite of the prospect of the best dinner he had ever eaten, he wished himself back in Mott Street. Henry Fosdick was more easy and unembarrassed than Dick, not having led such a vagabond and neglected life. But it was to Dick that Ida chiefly directed her conversation, having apparently taken a fancy to his frank and handsome face. I believe I have already said that Dick was a very good-looking boy, especially now since he kept his face clean. He had a frank, honest expression, which generally won its way to the favor of those with whom he came in contact.

Dick got along pretty well at the table by dint of noticing how the rest acted, but there was one thing he could not manage, eating with his fork, which, by the way, he thought a very singular arrangement.

At length they arose from the table, somewhat to Dick's relief. Again Ida devoted herself to the boys, and exhibited a profusely illustrated Bible for their entertainment. Dick was interested in looking at the pictures, though he knew very little of their subjects. Henry Fosdick was much better informed, as might have been expected.

When the boys were about to leave the house with Mr. Greyson for the Sunday school, Ida placed her hand in Dick's, and said persuasively. "You'll come again, Dick, won't you?"

"Thank you," said Dick, "I'd like to," and he could not help thinking Ida the nicest girl he had ever seen.

"Yes," said Mrs. Greyson, hospitably, "we shall be glad to see you both here again."

"Thank you very much," said Henry Fosdick, gratefully. "We shall like very much to come."

I will not dwell upon the hour spent in Sunday school, nor upon the remarks of Mr. Greyson to his class. He found Dick's ignorance of religious subjects so great that he was obliged to begin at the beginning with him. Dick was interested in hearing the children sing, and readily promised to come again the next Sunday.

When the service was over Dick and Henry walked homewards. Dick could not help letting his thoughts rest on the sweet little girl who had given him so cordial a welcome, and hoping that he might meet her again.

"Mr. Greyson is a nice man,—isn't he, Dick?" asked Henry, as they were turning into Mott Street, and were already in sight of their lodging-house.

"Aint he, though?" said Dick. "He treated us just as if we were young gentlemen."

"Ida seemed to take a great fancy to you."

"She's a tip-top girl," said Dick, "but she asked so many questions that I didn't know what to say."

He had scarcely finished speaking, when a stone whizzed by his head, and, turning quickly, he saw Micky Maguire running round the corner of the street which they had just passed.

Chapter 18

Micky Maguire's Second Defeat

DICK WAS no coward. Nor was he in the habit of submitting passively to an insult. When, therefore, he recognized Micky Maguire as his assailant, he instantly turned and gave chase. Micky anticipated pursuit, and ran at his utmost speed. It is doubtful if Dick would have overtaken him, but Micky had the ill luck to trip just as he had entered a narrow alley, and, falling with some violence, received a sharp blow from the hard stones, which made him scream with pain.

"Ow!" he whined. "Don't you hit a feller when he's down."

"What made you fire that stone at me?" demanded our hero, looking down at the fallen bully.

"Just for fun," said Micky.

"It would have been a very agreeable s'prise if it had hit me," said Dick. "S'posin' I fire 'a rock at you jest for fun."

"Don't!" exclaimed Micky, in alarm.

"It seems you don't like agreeable s'prises," said Dick, "any more'n the man did what got hooked by a cow one mornin, before breakfast. It didn't improve his appetite much."

"I've most broke my arm," said Micky, ruefully, rubbing the affected limb.

"If it's broke you can't fire no more stones, which is

a very cheerin' reflection," said Dick. "Ef you haven't money enough to buy a wooden one I'll lend you a quarter. There's one good thing about wooden ones, they aint liable to get cold in winter, which is another cheerin' reflection."

"I don't want none of yer cheerin' reflections," said Micky, sullenly. "Yer company aint wanted here."

"Thank you for your polite invitation to leave," said Dick, bowing ceremoniously. "I'm willin' to go, but ef you throw any more stones at me, Micky Maguire, I'll hurt you worse than the stones did."

The only answer made to this warning was a scowl from his fallen opponent. It was quite evident that Dick had the best of it, and he thought it prudent to say nothing.

"As I've got a friend waitin' outside, I shall have to tear myself away," said Dick. "You'd better not throw any more stones, Micky Maguire, for it don't seem to agree with your constitution."

Micky muttered something which Dick did not stay to hear. He backed out of the alley, keeping a watchful eye on his fallen foe, and rejoined Henry Fosdick, who was awaiting his return.

"Who was it, Dick?" he asked.

"A partic'lar friend of mine, Micky Maguire," said Dick. "He playfully fired a rock at my head as a mark of his 'fection. He loves me like a brother, Micky does."

"Rather a dangerous kind of a friend, I should think," said Fosdick. "He might have killed you."

"I've warned him not to be so 'fectionate another time," said Dick.

"I know him," said Henry Fosdick. "He's at the head of a gang of boys living at the Five-Points. He threatened to whip me once because a gentleman employed me to black his boots instead of him."

"He's been at the Island two or three times for stealing," said Dick. "I guess he won't touch me again. He'd rather get hold of small boys. If he ever does anything to you, Fosdick, just let me know, and I'll give him a thrashing."

Dick was right. Micky Maguire was a bully, and like most bullies did not fancy tackling boys whose strength was equal or superior to his own. Although he hated Dick more than ever, because he thought our hero was putting on airs, he had too lively a remembrance of his strength and courage to venture upon another open attack. He contented himself, therefore, whenever he met Dick, with scowling at him. Dick took this very philosophically, remarking that, "if it was soothin' to Micky's feelings, he might go ahead, as it didn't hurt him much."

It will not be necessary to chronicle the events of the next few weeks. A new life had commenced for Dick. He no longer haunted the gallery of the Old Bowery; and even Tony Pastor's hospitable doors had lost their old attractions. He spent two hours every evening in study. His progress was astonishingly rapid. He was gifted with a natural quickness; and he was stimulated by the desire to acquire a fair education as a means of "growin' up 'spectable," as he termed it. Much was due also to the patience and perseverance of Henry Fosdick, who made a capital teacher.

"You're improving wonderfully, Dick," said his friend, one evening, when Dick had read an entire paragraph without a mistake.

"Am I?" said Dick, with satisfaction.

"Yes. If you'll buy a writing-book to-morrow, we can begin writing to-morrow evening."

"What else do you know, Henry?" asked Dick.

"Arithmetic, and geography, and grammar."

"What a lot you know!" said Dick, admiringly.

"I don't *know* any of them," said Fosdick. "I've only studied them. I wish I knew a great deal more."

"I'll be satisfied when I know as much as you," said Dick.

"It seems a great deal to you now, Dick, but in a few months you'll think differently. The more you know, the more you'll want to know."

"Then there aint any end to learnin'?" said Dick.

"No."

"Well," said Dick, "I guess I'll be as much as sixty before I know everything."

"Yes; as old as that, probably," said Fosdick, laughing.

"Anyway, you know too much to be blackin' boots. Leave that to ignorant chaps like me."

"You won't be ignorant long, Dick."

"You'd ought to get into some office or countin'-room."

"I wish I could," said Fosdick, earnestly. "I don't succeed very well at blacking boots. You make a great deal more than I do."

"That's cause I aint troubled with bashfulness," said Dick. "Bashfulness aint as natural to me as it is to you. I'm always on hand, as the cat said to the milk. You'd better give up shines, Fosdick, and give your 'tention to mercantile pursuits."

"I've thought of trying to get a place," said Fosdick; "but no one would take me with these clothes;" and he directed his glance to his well-worn suit, which he kept as neat as he could, but which, in spite of all his care, began to show decided marks of use. There was also here and there a stain of blacking upon it, which, though an advertisement of his profession, scarcely added to its good appearance.

"I almost wanted to stay at home from Sunday school last Sunday," he continued, "because I thought everybody would notice how dirty and worn my clothes had got to be."

"If my clothes wasn't two sizes too big for you," said Dick, generously, "I'd change. You'd look as if you'd got into your great-uncle's suit by mistake."

"You're very kind, Dick, to think of changing," said Fosdick, "for your suit is much better than mine; but I don't think that mine would suit you very well. The pants would show a little more of your ankles than is the fashion, and you couldn't eat a very hearty dinner without bursting the buttons off the vest."

"That wouldn't be very convenient," said Dick. "I aint fond of lacin' to show my elegant figger. But I say," he added with a sudden thought, "how much money have we got in the savings bank?"

Fosdick took a key from his pocket, and went to the drawer in which the bank-books were kept, and, opening it, brought them out for inspection.

It was found that Dick had the sum of eighteen dollars and ninety cents placed to his credit, while Fosdick had six dollars and forty-five cents. To explain the large difference, it must be remembered that Dick had deposited five dollars before Henry deposited anything, being the amount he had received as a gift from Mr. Whitney.

"How much does that make, the lot of it?" asked Dick. "I aint much on figgers yet, you know."

"It makes twenty-five dollars and thirty-five cents, Dick," said his companion, who did not understand the thought which suggested the question.

"Take it, and buy some clothes, Henry," said Dick, shortly.

"What, your money too?"

"In course."

"No, Dick; you are too generous. I couldn't think of it. Almost three-quarters of the money is yours. You must spend it on yourself."

"I don't need it," said Dick.

"You may not need it now, but you will some time."

"I shall have some more then."

"That may be; but it wouldn't be fair for me to use your money, Dick. I thank you all the same for your kindness."

"Well, I'll lend it to you, then," persisted Dick, "and you can pay me when you get to be a rich merchant."

"But it isn't likely I ever shall be one."

"How d'you know? I went to a fortun' teller once, and she told me I was born under a lucky star with a hard name, and I should have a rich man for my particular friend, who would make my fortun'. I guess you are going to be the rich man."

Fosdick laughed, and steadily refused for some time to avail himself of Dick's generous proposal; but at length, perceiving that our hero seemed much disappointed, and would be really glad if his offer were accepted, he agreed to use as much as might be needful.

This at once brought back Dick's good-humor, and he entered with great enthusiasm into his friend's plans.

The next day they withdrew the money from the bank, and, when business got a little slack, in the afternoon, set out in search of a clothing store. Dick knew enough of the city to be able to find a place where a good bargain could be obtained. He was determined that Fosdick should have a good serviceable suit, even if it took all the money they had. The result of their search was that for twenty-three dollars Fosdick obtained a very neat outfit, including a couple of shirts, a hat, and a pair of shoes, besides a dark mixed suit, which appeared stout and of good quality.

"Shall I sent the bundle home?" asked the salesman, impressed by the off-hand manner in which Dick drew out the money in payment for the clothes.

"Thank you," said Dick, "you're very kind, but I'll take it home myself, and you can allow me something for my trouble."

"All right," said the clerk, laughing; "I'll allow it on your next purchase."

Proceeding to their apartment in Mott Street, Fosdick at once tried on his new suit, and it was found to be an excellent fit. Dick surveyed his new friend with much satisfaction.

"You look like a young gentleman of fortun'," he said, "and do credit to your governor."

"I suppose that means you, Dick," said Fosdick, laughing.

"In course it does."

"You should say *of* course," said Fosdick, who, in virtue of his position as Dick's tutor, ventured to correct his language from time to time.

"How dare you correct your gov'nor?" said Dick, with comic indignation. "I'll cut you off with a shillin', you young dog,' as the Markis says to his nephew in the play at the Old Bowery."

Chapter 19

Fosdick Changes His Business

FOSDICK DID NOT venture to wear his new clothes while engaged in his business. This he felt would have been wasteful extravagance. About ten o'clock in the morning, when business slackened, he went home, and, dressing himself, went to a hotel where he could see copies of the "Morning Herald" and "Sun," and, noting down the places where a boy was wanted, went on a round of applications. But he found it no easy thing to obtain a place. Swarms of boys seemed to be out of employment, and it was not unusual to find from fifty to a hundred applicants for a single place.

There was another difficulty. It was generally desired that the boy wanted should reside with his parents. When Fosdick, on being questioned, revealed the fact of his having no parents, and being a boy of the street, this was generally sufficient of itself to insure a refusal. Merchants were afraid to trust one who had led such a vagabond life. Dick, who was always ready for an emergency, suggested borrowing a white wig, and passing himself off for Fosdick's father or grandfather. But Henry thought this might be rather a difficult character for our hero to sustain. After fifty applications and as many failures, Fosdick began to get discouraged. There seemed to be no way out of his present business, for which he felt unfitted.

"I don't know but I shall have to black boots all my life," he said, one day, despondently, to Dick.

"Keep a stiff upper lip," said Dick. "By the time you

get to be a gray-headed veteran, you may get a chance to run errands for some big firm on the Bowery, which is a very cheerin' reflection."

So Dick by his drollery and perpetual good spirits kept up Fosdick's courage.

"As for me," said Dick, "I expect by that time to lay up a colossal fortun' out of shines, and live in princely style on the Avenoo."

But one morning, Fosdick, straying into French's Hotel, discovered the following advertisement in the columns of "The Herald,"—

"WANTED—A smart, capable boy to run errands, and make himself generally useful in a hat and cap store. Salary three dollars a week at first. Inquire at No.—Broadway, after ten o'clock, A.M."

He determined to make application, and, as the City Hall clock just then struck the hour indicated, lost no time in proceeding to the store, which was only a few blocks distant from the Astor House. It was easy to find the store, as from a dozen to twenty boys were already assembled in front of it. They surveyed each other askance, feeling that they were rivals, and mentally calculating each other's chances.

"There isn't much chance for me," said Fosdick to Dick, who had accompanied him. "Look at all these boys. Most of them have good homes, I suppose, and good recommendations, while I have nobody to refer to."

"Go ahead," said Dick. "Your chance is as good as anybody's."

While this was passing between Dick and his companion, one of the boys, a rather supercilious-looking young gentleman, genteelly dressed, and evidently having a very high opinion of his dress and himself, turned suddenly to Dick, and remarked,—

"I've seen you before."

"Oh, have you?" said Dick, whirling round; "then p'r'aps you'd like to see me behind."

At this unexpected answer all the boys burst into a laugh with the exception of the questioner, who, evidently considered that Dick had been disrespectful.

"I've seen you somewhere," he said, in a surly tone, correcting himself.

"Most likely you have," said Dick. "That's where I generally keep myself."

There was another laugh at the expense of Roswell Crawford, for that was the name of the young aristocrat. But he had his revenge ready. No boy relishes being an object of ridicule, and it was with a feeling of satisfaction that he retorted,—

"I know you for all your impudence. You're nothing but a boot-black."

This information took the boys who were standing around by surprise, for Dick was well-dressed, and had none of the implements of his profession with him.

"S'pose I be," said Dick. "Have you got any objection?"

"Not at all," said Roswell, curling his lip; "only you'd better stick to blacking boots, and not try to get into a store."

"Thank you for your kind advice," said Dick. "Is it gratooitous, or do you expect to be paid for it?"

"You're an impudent fellow."

"That's a very cheerin' reflection," said Dick, good-naturedly.

"Do you expect to get this place when there's gentlemen's sons applying for it? A boot-black in a store!. That would be a good joke."

Boys as well as men are selfish, and, looking upon Dick as a possible rival, the boys who listened seemed disposed to take the same view of the situation.

"That's what I say," said one of them, taking sides with Roswell.

"Don't trouble yourselves," said Dick. "I aint agoin' to cut you out. I can't afford to give up a independent and loocrative purfession for a salary of three dollars a week."

"Hear him talk!" said Roswell Crawford, with an unpleasant sneer. "If you are not trying to get the place, what are you here for?"

"I came with a friend of mine," said Dick, indicating Fosdick, "who's goin' in for the situation."

"Is he a boot-black, too?" demanded Roswell, super-ciliously.

"He!" retorted Dick, loftily. "Didn't you know his father was a member of Congress, and intimately acquainted with all the biggest men in the State?"

The boys surveyed Fosdick as if they did not quite know whether to credit this statement, which, for the credit of Dick's veracity, it will be observed he did not assert, but only propounded in the form of a question. There was no time for comment, however, as just then the proprietor of the store came to the door, and, casting his eyes over the waiting group, singled out Roswell Crawford, and asked him to enter.

"Well, my lad, how old are you?"

"Fourteen years old," said Roswell, consequentially.

"Are your parents living?"

"Only my mother. My father is dead. He was a gentleman," he added, complacently.

"Oh, was he?" said the shop-keeper. "Do you live in the city?"

"Yes, sir. In Clinton Place."

"Have you ever been in a situation before?"

"Yes, sir," said Roswell, a little reluctantly.

"Where was it?"

"In an office on Dey Street."

"How long were you there?"

"A week."

"It seems to me that was a short time. Why did you not stay longer?"

"Because," said Roswell, loftily, "the man wanted me to get to the office at eight o'clock, and make the fire. I'm a gentleman's son, and am not used to such dirty work."

"Indeed!" said the shop-keeper. "Well, young gentleman, you may step aside a few minutes. I will speak with some of the other boys before making my selection."

Several other boys were called in and questioned. Roswell stood by and listened with an air of complacency. He could not help thinking his chances the best. "The man can see I'm a gentleman, and will do credit to his store," he thought.

At length it came to Fosdick's turn. He entered with no very sanguine anticipations of success. Unlike Roswell, he set a very low estimate upon his qualifications when compared with those of other applicants. But his modest bearing, and quiet, gentlemanly manner, entirely free from pretension, prepossessed the shop-keeper, who was a sensible man, in his favor.

"Do you reside in the city?" he asked.

"Yes, sir," said Henry.

"What is your age?"

"Twelve."

"Have you ever been in any situation?"

"No, sir."

"I should like to see a specimen of your handwriting. Here, take the pen and write your name."

Henry Fosdick had a very handsome handwriting for a boy of his age, while Roswell, who had submitted to the same test, could do little more than scrawl.

"Do you reside with your parents?"

"No, sir, they are dead."

"Where do you live, then?"

"In Mott Street."

Roswell curled his lip when this name was pronounced, for Mott Street, as my New York readers know, is in the immediate neighborhood of the Five-Points, and very far from a fashionable locality.

"Have you any testimonials to present?" asked Mr. Henderson, for that was his name.

Fosdick hesitated. This was the question which he had foreseen would give him trouble.

But at this moment it happened most opportunely that Mr. Greyson entered the shop with the intention of buying a hat.

"Yes," said Fosdick, promptly; "I will refer to this gentleman."

"How do you do, Fosdick!" asked Mr. Greyson, noticing him for the first time. "How do you happen to be here?"

"I am applying for a place, sir," said Fosdick. "May I refer the gentleman to you?"

"Certainly, I shall be glad to speak a good word for you. Mr. Henderson, this is a member of my Sunday-school class, of whose good qualities and good abilities I can speak confidently."

"That will be sufficient," said the shop-keeper, who knew Mr. Greyson's high character and position. "He could have no better recommendation. You may come to the store to-morrow morning at half past seven o'clock. The pay will be three dollars a week for the first six months. If I am satisfied with you, I shall then raise it to five dollars."

The other boys looked disappointed, but none more so than Roswell Crawford. He would have cared less if any one else had obtained the situation; but for a boy who lived in Mott Street to be preferred to him, a gentleman's son, he considered indeed humiliating. In a spirit of petty spite, he was tempted to say, "He's a boot-black. Ask him if he isn't."

"He's an honest and intelligent lad," said Mr. Greyson. "As for you, young man, I only hope you have one-half his good qualities."

Roswell Crawford left the store in disgust, and the other unsuccessful applicants with him.

"What luck, Fosdick?" asked Dick, eagerly, as his friend came out of the store.

"I've got the place," said Fosdick, in accents of satisfaction; "but it was only because Mr. Greyson spoke up for me."

"He's a trump," said Dick, enthusiastically.

The gentleman, so denominated, came out before the boys went away, and spoke with them kindly.

Both Dick and Henry were highly pleased at the success of the application. The pay would indeed be small, but, expended economically, Fosdick thought he could get along on it, receiving his room-rent, as before, in return for his services as Dick's private tutor. Dick determined, as soon as his education would permit, to follow his companion's example.

"I don't know as you'll be willin' to room with a boot-black," he said, to Henry, "now you're goin' into business."

"I couldn't room with a better friend, Dick," said Fosdick, affectionately, throwing his arm round our hero. "When we part, it'll be because you wish it."

So Fosdick entered upon a new career.

Chapter 20

Nine Months Later

THE NEXT MORNING Fosdick rose early, put on his new suit, and, after getting breakfast, set out for the Broadway store in which he had obtained a position. He left his little blacking-box in the room.

"It'll do to brush my own shoes," he said. "Who knows but I may have to come back to it again?"

"No danger," said Dick; "I'll take care of the feet, and you'll have to look after the heads, now you're in a hat-store."

"I wish you had a place too," said Fosdick.

"I don't know enough yet," said Dick. "Wait till I've gradooated."

"And can put A.B. after your name."

"What's that?"

"It stands for Bachelor of Arts. It's a degree that students get when they graduate from college."

"Oh," said Dick, "I didn't know but it meant A Bootblack. I can put that after my name now. Wouldn't Dick Hunter, A.B., sound tip-top?"

"I must be going," said Fosdick. "It won't do for me to be late the very first morning."

"That's the difference between you and me," said Dick. "I'm my own boss, and there aint no one to find fault with me if I'm late. But I might as well be goin' too. There's a gent as comes down to his store pretty early that generally wants a shine."

The two boys parted at the Park. Fosdick crossed it,

and proceeded to the hat-store, while Dick, hitching up his pants, began to look about him for a customer. It was seldom that Dick had to wait long. He was always on the alert, and if there was any business to do he was always sure to get his share of it. He had now a stronger inducement than ever to attend strictly to business; his little stock of money in the savings bank having been nearly exhausted by his liberality to his roommate. He determined to be as economical as possible, and moreover to study as hard as he could, that he might be able to follow Fosdick's example, and obtain a place in a store or counting-room. As there were no striking incidents occurring in our hero's history within the next nine months, I propose to pass over that period, and recount the progress he made in that time.

Fosdick was still at the hat-store, having succeeded in giving perfect satisfaction to Mr. Henderson. His wages had just been raised to five dollars a week. He and Dick still kept house together at Mrs. Mooney's lodging-house, and lived very frugally, so that both were able to save up money. Dick had been unusually successful in business. He had several regular patrons, who had been drawn to him by his ready wit, and quick humor, and from two of them he had received presents of clothing, which had saved him an expense on that score. His income had averaged quite seven dollars a week in addition to this. Of this amount he was now obliged to pay one dollar weekly for the room which he and Fosdick occupied, but he was still able to save half the remainder. At the end of nine months therefore, or thirty-nine weeks, it will be seen that he had accumulated no less a sum than one hundred and seventeen dollars. Dick may be excused for feeling like a capitalist when he looked at the long row of deposits in his little bankbook. There were other boys in the same business who had earned as much money, but they had had little care for the future, and spent as they went along, so that few could boast a bank-account, however small.

"You'll be a rich man some time, Dick," said Henry Fosdick, one evening.

"And live on Fifth Avenoo," said Dick.

"Perhaps so. Stranger things have happened."

"Well," said Dick, "if such a misfortin' should come upon me I should bear it like a man. When you see a Fifth Avenoo manshun for sale for a hundred and seventeen dollars, just let me know and I'll buy it as an investment."

"Two hundred and fifty years ago you might have bought one for that price, probably. Real estate wasn't very high among the Indians."

"Just my luck," said Dick; "I was born too late. I'd orter have been an Indian, and lived in splendor on my present capital."

"I'm afraid you'd have found your present business rather unprofitable at that time."

But Dick had gained something more valuable than money. He had studied regularly every evening, and his improvement had been marvellous. He could now read well, write a fair hand, and had studied arithmetic as far as Interest. Besides this he had obtained some knowledge of grammar and geography. If some of my boy readers, who have been studying for years, and got no farther than this, should think it incredible that Dick, in less than a year, and studying evenings only, should have accomplished it, they must remember that our hero was very much in earnest in his desire to improve. He knew that, in order to grow up respectable, he must be well advanced, and he was willing to work. But then the reader must not forget that Dick was naturally a smart boy. His street education had sharpened his faculties, and taught him to rely upon himself. He knew that it would take him a long time to reach the goal which he had set before him, and he had patience to keep on trying. He knew that he had only himself to depend upon, and he determined to make the most of himself,—a resolution which is the secret of success in nine cases out of ten.

"Dick," said Fosdick, one evening, after they had completed their studies, "I think you'll have to get another teacher soon."

"Why?" asked Dick, in some surprise. "Have you been offered a more loocrative position?"

"No," said Fosdick, "but I find I have taught you all I know myself. You are now as good a scholar as I am."

"Is that true?" said Dick, eagerly, a flush of gratification coloring his brown cheek.

"Yes," said Fosdick. "You've made wonderful progress. I propose, now that evening schools have begun, that we join one, and study together through the winter."

"All right," said Dick. "I'd be willin' to go now; but when I first began to study I was ashamed to have anybody know that I was so ignorant. Do you really mean, Fosdick, that I know as much as you?"

"Yes, Dick, it's true."

"Then I've got you to thank for it," said Dick, earnestly. "You've made me what I am."

"And haven't you paid me, Dick?"

"By payin' the room-rent," said Dick, impulsively. "What's that? It isn't half enough. I wish you'd take half my money; you deserve it."

"Thank you, Dick, but you're too generous. You've more than paid me. Who was it took my part when all the other boys imposed upon me? And who gave me money to buy clothes, and so got me my situation?"

"Oh, that's nothing!" said Dick.

"It's a great deal, Dick. I shall never forget it. But now it seems to me you might try to get a situation yourself."

"Do I know enough?"

"You know as much as I do."

"Then I'll try," said Dick, decidedly.

"I wish there was a place in our store," said Fosdick. "It would be pleasant for us to be together."

"Never mind," said Dick; "there'll be plenty of chances. P'r'aps A.T. Stewart might like a partner. I wouldn't ask more'n a quarter of the profits."

"Which would be a very liberal proposal on your part," said Fosdick, smiling. "But perhaps Mr. Stewart might object to a partner living on Mott Street."

"I'd just as lieves move to Fifth Avenoo," said Dick.

Soft - hearted

"I aint got no prejudices in favor of Mott Street."

"Nor I," said Fosdick, "and in fact I have been thinking it might be a good plan for us to move as soon as we could afford. Mrs. Mooney doesn't keep the room quite so neat as she might."

"No," said Dick. "She aint got no prejudices against dirt. Look at that towel."

Dick held up the article indicated, which had now seen service nearly a week, and hard service at that, —Dick's avocation causing him to be rather hard on towels.

"Yes," said Fosdick, "I've got about tired of it. I guess we can find some better place without having to pay much more. When we move, you must let me pay my share of the rent."

"We'll see about that," said Dick. "Do you propose to move to Fifth Avenoo?"

"Not just at present, but to some more agreeable neighborhood than this. We'll wait till you get a situation, and then we can decide."

A few days later, as Dick was looking about for customers in the neighborhood of the Park, his attention was drawn to a fellow boot-black, a boy about a year younger than himself, who appeared to have been crying.

"What's the matter, Tom?" asked Dick. "Haven't you had luck to-day?"

"Pretty good," said the boy; "but we're havin' hard times at home. Mother fell last week and broke her arm, and to-morrow we've got to pay the rent, and if we don't the landlord says he'll turn us out."

"Haven't you got anything except what you earn?" asked Dick.

"No," said Tom, "not now. Mother used to earn three or four dollars a week; but she can't do nothin' now, and my little sister and brother are too young."

Dick had quick sympathies. He had been so poor himself, and obliged to submit to so many privations, that he knew from personal experience how hard it was. Tom Wilkins he knew as an excellent boy, who never squandered his money, but faithfully carried it home to his mother. In the days of his own extravagance and shiftlessness he had once or twice asked Tom to accompany him to the Old Bowery or Tony Pastor's, but Tom had always steadily refused.

"I'm sorry for you, Tom," he said. "How much do you owe for rent?"

"Two weeks now," said Tom.

"How much is it a week?"

"Two dollar a week—that makes four."

"Have you got anything towards it?"

"No; I've had to spend all my money for food for mother and the rest of us. I've had pretty hard work to do that. I don't know what we'll do. I haven't any place to go to, and I'm afraid mother'll get cold in her arm."

"Can't you borrow the money somewhere?" asked Dick.

Tom shook his head despondingly.

"All the people I know are as poor as I am," said he. "They'd help me if they could, but it's hard work for them to get along themselves."

"I'll tell you what, Tom," said Dick, impulsively, "I'll stand your friend."

"Have you got any money?" asked Tom, doubtfully.

"Got any money!" repeated Dick. "Don't you know that I run a bank on my own account? How much is it you need?"

"Four dollars," said Tom. "If we don't pay that before to-morrow night, out we go. You haven't got as much as that, have you?"

"Here are three dollars," said Dick, drawing out his pocket-book. "I'll let you have the rest to-morrow, and maybe a little more."

"You're a right down good fellow, Dick," said Tom; "but won't you want it yourself?"

"Oh, I've got some more," said Dick.

"Maybe I'll never be able to pay you."

" 'Spose you don't," said Dick; "I guess I won't fail."

philanthropic

"I won't forget it, Dick. I hope I'll be able to do somethin' for you sometime."

"All right," said Dick. "I'd ought to help you. I haven't got no mother to look out for. I wish I had."

There was a tinge of sadness in his tone, as he pronounced the last four words; but Dick's temperament was sanguine, and he never gave way to unavailing sadness. Accordingly he began to whistle as he turned away, only adding, "I'll see you to-morrow, Tom."

The three dollars which Dick had handed to Tom Wilkins were his savings for the present week. It was now Thursday afternoon. His rent, which amounted to a dollar, he expected to save out of the earnings of Friday and Saturday. In order to give Tom the additional assistance he had promised, Dick would be obliged to have recourse to his bank-savings. He would not have ventured to trench upon it for any other reason but this. But he felt that it would be selfish to allow Tom and his mother to suffer when he had it in his power to relieve them. But Dick was destined to be surprised, and that in a disagreeable manner, when he reached home.

Chapter 21

Dick Loses His Bank-Book

IT WAS hinted at the close of the last chapter that Dick was destined to be disagreeably surprised on reaching home.

Having agreed to give further assistance to Tom Wilkins, he was naturally led to go to the drawer where he and Fosdick kept their bank-books. To his surprise and uneasiness *the drawer proved to be empty!*

"Come here a minute, Fosdick," he said.

"What's the matter, Dick?"

"I can't find my bank-book, nor yours either. What's 'come of them?"

"I took mine with me this morning, thinking I might want to put in a little more money. I've got it in my pocket, now."

"But where's mine?" asked Dick, perplexed.

"I don't know. I saw it in the drawer when I took mine this morning."

"Are you sure?"

"Yes, positive, for I looked into it to see how much you had got."

"Did you lock it again?" asked Dick.

"Yes; didn't you have to unlock it just now?"

"So I did," said Dick. "But it's gone now. Somebody opened it with a key that fitted the lock, and then locked it ag'in."

"That must have been the way."

"It's rather hard on a feller," said Dick, who, for the first time since we became acquainted with him, began to feel down-hearted.

"Don't give it up, Dick. You haven't lost the money, only the bank-book."

"Aint that the same thing?"

"No. You can go to the bank to-morrow morning, as soon as it opens, and tell them you have lost the book, and ask them not to pay the money to any one except yourself."

"So I can," said Dick, brightening up. "That is, if the thief hasn't been to the bank to-day."

"If he has, they might detect him by his hand writing."

"I'd like to get hold of the one that stole it," said Dick, indignantly. "I'd give him a good lickin'."

"It must have been somebody in the house. Suppose we go and see Mrs. Mooney. She may know whether anybody came into our room to-day."

The two boys went downstairs, and knocked at the door of a little back sitting-room where Mrs. Mooney generally spent her evenings. It was a shabby little room, with a threadbare carpet on the floor, the walls covered with a certain large-figured paper, patches of which had been stripped off here and there, exposing the plaster, the remainder being defaced by dirt and grease. But Mrs. Mooney had one of those comfortable temperaments which are tolerant of dirt, and didn't mind it in the least. She was seated beside a small pine work-table, industriously engaged in mending stockings.

"Good-evening, Mrs. Mooney," said Fosdick, politely.

"Good-evening," said the landlady. "Sit down, if you can find chairs. I'm hard at work as you see, but a pore lone widder can't afford to be idle."

"We can't stop long, Mrs. Mooney, but my friend here has had something taken from his room to-day, and we thought we'd come and see you about it."

"What is it?" asked the landlady. "You don't think I'd take anything? If I am poor, it's an honest name I've always had, as all my lodgers can testify."

"Certainly not, Mrs. Mooney; but there are others in

the house that may not be honest. My friend has lost his bank-book. It was safe in the drawer this morning, but to-night it is not to be found."

"How much money was there in it?" asked Mrs. Mooney.

"Over a hundred dollars," said Fosdick.

"It was my whole fortun'," said Dick. "I was goin' to buy a house next year."

Mrs. Mooney was evidently surprised to learn the extent of Dick's wealth, and was disposed to regard him with increased respect.

"Was the drawer locked?" she asked.

"Yes."

"Then it couldn't have been Bridget. I don't think she has any keys."

"She wouldn't know what a bank-book was," said Fosdick. "You didn't see any of the lodgers go into our room to-day, did you?"

"I shouldn't wonder if it was Jim Travis," said Mrs. Mooney, suddenly.

This James Travis was a bar-tender in a low groggery in Mulberry Street, and had been for a few weeks an inmate of Mrs. Mooney's lodging-house. He was a coarse-looking fellow who, from his appearance, evidently patronized liberally the liquor he dealt out to others. He occupied a room opposite Dick's, and was often heard by the two boys reeling upstairs in a state of intoxication, uttering shocking oaths.

This Travis had made several friendly overtures to Dick and his room-mate, and had invited them to call round at the bar-room where he tended, and take something. But this invitation had never been accepted, partly because the boys were better engaged in the evening, and partly because neither of them had taken a fancy to Mr. Travis; which certainly was not strange, for nature had not gifted him with many charms, either of personal appearance or manners. The rejection of his friendly proffers had caused him to take a dislike to Dick and Henry, whom he considered stiff and unsocial.

"What makes you think it was Travis?" asked Fosdick.

"He isn't at home in the daytime."

"But he was to-day. He said he had got a bad cold, and had to come home for a clean handkerchief."

"Did you see him?" asked Dick.

"Yes," said Mrs. Mooney. "Bridget was hanging out clothes, and I went to the door to let him in."

"I wonder if he had a key that would fit our drawer," said Fosdick.

"Yes," said Mrs. Mooney. "The bureaus in the two rooms are just alike. I got 'em at auction, and most likely the locks is the same."

"It must have been he," said Dick, looking towards Fosdick.

"Yes," said Fosdick, "it looks like it."

"What's to be done? That's what I'd like to know," said Dick. "Of course he'll say he hasn't got it; and he won't be such a fool as to leave it in his room."

"If he hasn't been to the bank, it's all right," said Fosdick. "You can go there the first thing to-morrow morning, and stop their paying any money on it."

"But I can't get any money on it myself," said Dick. "I told Tom Wilkins I'd let him have some more money to-morrow, or his sick mother'll have to turn out of their lodgin's."

"How much money were you going to give him?"

"I gave him three dollars to-day, and was goin' to give him two dollars to-morrow."

"I've got the money, Dick. I didn't go to the bank this morning."

"All right. I'll take it, and pay you back next week."

"No, Dick; if you've given three dollars, you must let me give two."

"No, Fosdick, I'd rather give the whole. You know I've got more money than you. No, I haven't, either," said Dick, the memory of his loss flashing upon him. "I thought I was rich this morning, but now I'm in destitoot circumstances."

"Cheer up, Dick; you'll get your money back."

"I hope so," said our hero, rather ruefully.

The fact was, that our friend Dick was beginning to feel what is so often experienced by men who do business of a more important character and on a larger scale than he, the bitterness of a reverse of circumstances. With one hundred dollars and over carefully laid away in the savings bank, he had felt quite independent. Wealth is comparative, and Dick probably felt as rich as many men who are worth a hundred thousand dollars. He was beginning to feel the advantages of his steady self-denial, and to experience the pleasures of property. Not that Dick was likely to be unduly attached to money. Let it be said to his credit that it had never given him so much satisfaction as when it enabled him to help Tom Wilkins in his trouble.

Besides this, there was another thought that troubled him. When he obtained a place he could not expect to receive as much as he was now making from blacking boots,—probably not more than three dollars a week,—while his expenses without clothing would amount to four dollars. To make up the deficiency he had confidently relied upon his savings, which would be sufficient to carry him along for a year, if necessary. If he should not recover his money, he would be compelled to continue a boot-black for at least six months longer; and this was rather a discouraging reflection. On the whole it is not to be wondered at that Dick felt unusually sober this evening, and that neither of the boys felt much like studying.

The two boys consulted as to whether it would be best to speak to Travis about it. It was not altogether easy to decide. Fosdick was opposed to it.

"It will only put him on his guard," said he, "and I don't see as it will do any good. Of course he will deny it. We'd better keep quiet, and watch him, and, by giving notice at the bank, we can make sure that he doesn't get any money on it. If he does present himself at the bank, they will know at once that he is a thief, and he can be arrested."

This view seemed reasonable, and Dick resolved to

adopt it. On the whole, he began to think prospects were brighter than he had at first supposed, and his spirits rose a little.

"How'd he know I had any bank-book? That's what I can't make out," he said.

"Don't you remember?" said Fosdick, after a moment's thought, "we were speaking of our savings, two or three evenings since?"

"Yes," said Dick.

"Our door was a little open at the time, and I heard somebody come upstairs, and stop a minute in front of it. It must have been Jim Travis. In that way he probably found out about your money, and took the opportunity to-day to get hold of it."

This might or might not be the correct explanation. At all events it seemed probable.

The boys were just on the point of going to bed, later in the evening, when a knock was heard at the door, and, to their no little surprise, their neighbor, Jim Travis, proved to be the caller. He was a sallow-complexioned young man, with dark hair and bloodshot eyes.

He darted a quick glance from one to the other as he entered, which did not escape the boys' notice.

"How are ye, to-night?" he said, sinking into one of the two chairs with which the room was scantily furnished.

"Jolly," said Dick. "How are you?"

"Tired as a dog," was the reply. "Hard work and poor pay; that's the way with me. I wanted to go to the theatre, to-night, but I was hard up, and couldn't raise the cash."

Here he darted another quick glance at the boys; but neither betrayed anything.

"You don't go out much, do you?" he said.

"Not much," said Fosdick. "We spend our evenings in study."

"That's precious slow," said Travis, rather contemptuously. "What's the use of studying so much? You don't expect to be a lawyer, do you, or anything of that sort?"

"Maybe," said Dick. "I haven't made up my mind yet.

If my feller-citizens should want me to go to Congress some time, I shouldn't want to disapp'int 'em; and then readin' and writin' might come handy."

"Well," said Travis, rather abruptly, "I'm tired, and I guess I'll turn in."

"Good-night," said Fosdick.

The boys looked at each other as their visitor left the room.

"He came in to see if we'd missed the bank-book," said Dick.

"And to turn off suspicion from himself, by letting us know he had no money," added Fosdick.

"That's so," said Dick. "I'd like to have searched them pockets of his."

Chapter 22

Tracking the Thief

FOSDICK WAS right in supposing that Jim Travis had
stolen his bank-book. He was also right in supposing
that that worthy young man had come to the knowledge
of Dick's savings by what he had accidentally over-
heard. Now, Travis, like a very large number of young
men of his class, was able to dispose of a larger amount
of money than he was able to earn. Moreover, he had
no great fancy for work at all, and would have been
glad to find some other way of obtaining money enough
to pay his expenses. He had recently received a letter
from an old companion, who had strayed out to California, and going at once to the mines had been lucky
enough to get possession of a very remunerative claim.
He wrote to Travis that he had already realized two
thousand dollars from it, and expected to make his
fortune within six months.

Two thousand dollars! This seemed to Travis a very
large sum, and quite dazzled his imagination. He was
at once inflamed with the desire to go out to California
and try his luck. In his present situation he only
received thirty dollars a month, which was probably all
that his services were worth, but went a very little
way towards gratifying his expensive tastes. Accordingly
he determined to take the next steamer to the land of
gold, if he could possibly manage to get money enough
to pay the passage.

The price of a steerage passage at that time was

seventy-five dollars,—not a large sum, certainly,—but it might as well have been seventy-five hundred for any chance James Travis had of raising the amount at present. His available funds consisted of precisely two dollars and a quarter; of which sum, one dollar and a half was due to his washerwoman. This, however, would not have troubled Travis much, and he would conveniently have forgotten all about it; but, even leaving this debt unpaid, the sum at his command would not help him materially towards paying his passage money.

Travis applied for help to two or three of his companions; but they were all of that kind who never keep an account with savings banks, but carry all their spare cash about with them. One of these friends offered to lend him thirty-seven cents, and another a dollar; but neither of these offers seemed to encourage him much. He was about giving up his project in despair, when he learned, accidentally, as we have already said, the extent of Dick's savings.

One hundred and seventeen dollars! Why, that would not only pay his passage, but carry him up to the mines, after he had arrived in San Francisco. He could not help thinking it over, and the result of this thinking was that he determined to borrow it of Dick without leave. Knowing that neither of the boys were in their room in the daytime, he came back in the course of the morning, and, being admitted by Mrs. Mooney herself, said, by way of accounting for his presence, that he had a cold, and had come back for a handkerchief. The landlady suspected nothing, and, returning at once to her work in the kitchen, left the coast clear.

Travis at once entered Dick's room, and, as there seemed to be no other place for depositing money, tried the bureau-drawers. They were all readily opened, except one, which proved to be locked. This he naturally concluded must contain the money, and going back to his own chamber for the key of the bureau, tried it on his return, and found to his satisfaction that it would fit. When he discovered the bank-book, his joy was mingled with disappointment. He had expected to find bank-bills instead. This would have saved all further trouble, and would have been immediately available. Obtaining money at the savings bank would involve fresh risk. Travis hesitated whether to take it or not; but finally decided that it would be worth the trouble and hazard.

He accordingly slipped the book into his pocket, locked the drawer again, and, forgetting all about the handkerchief for which he had come home, went downstairs, and into the street.

There would have been time to go the savings bank that day, but Travis had already been absent from his place of business some time, and did not venture to take the additional time required. Besides, not being very much used to savings banks, never having had occasion to use them, he thought it would be more prudent to look over the rules and regulations, and see if he could not get some information as to the way he ought to proceed. So the day passed, and Dick's money was left in safety at the bank.

In the evening, it occurred to Travis that it might be well to find out whether Dick had discovered his loss. This reflection it was that induced the visit which is recorded at the close of the last chapter. The result was that he was misled by the boys' silence on the subject, and concluded that nothing had yet been discovered.

"Good!" thought Travis, with satisfaction. "If they don't find out for twenty-four hours, it'll be too late, then, and I shall be all right."

There being a possibility of the loss being discovered before the boys went out in the morning, Travis determined to see them at that time, and judge whether such was the case. He waited, therefore, until he heard the boys come out, and then opened his own door.

"Morning, gents," said he, sociably. "Going to business?"

"Yes," said Dick. "I'm afraid my clerks'll be lazy if I aint on hand."

"Good joke!" said Travis. "If you pay good wages, I'd like to speak for a place."

"I pay all I get myself," said Dick. "How's business with you?"

"So so. Why don't you call round, some time?"

"All my evenin's is devoted to literatoor and science," said Dick. "Thank you all the same."

"Where do you hang out?" inquired Travis, in choice language, addressing Fosdick.

"At Henderson's hat and cap store, on Broadway."

"I'll look in upon you some time when I want a tile," said Travis. "I suppose you sell cheaper to your friends."

"I'll be as reasonable as I can," said Fosdick, not very cordially; for he did not much fancy having it supposed by his employer that such a disreputable-looking person as Travis was a friend of his.

However, Travis had no idea of showing himself at the Broadway store, and only said this by way of making conversation, and encouraging the boys to be social.

"You haven't any of you gents seen a pearl-handled knife, have you?" he asked.

"No," said Fosdick; "have you lost one?"

"Yes," said Travis, with unblushing falsehood. "I left it on my bureau a day or two since. I've missed one or two other little matters. Bridget don't look to me any too honest. Likely she's got 'em."

"What are you goin' to do about it?" said Dick.

"I'll keep mum unless I lose something more, and then I'll kick up a row, and haul her over the coals. Have you missed anything?"

"No," said Fosdick, answering for himself, as he could do without violating the truth.

There was a gleam of satisfaction in the eyes of Travis, as he heard this.

"They haven't found it out yet," he thought. "I'll bag the money to-day, and then they may whistle for it."

Having no further object to serve in accompanying the boys, he bade them good-morning, and turned down another street.

"He's mighty friendly all of a sudden," said Dick.

"Yes," said Fosdick; "it's very evident what it all means. He wants to find out whether you have discovered your loss or not."

"But he didn't find out."

"No; we've put him on the wrong track. He means to get his money to-day, no doubt."

"My money," suggested Dick.

"I accept the correction," said Fosdick.

"Of course, Dick, you'll be on hand as soon as the bank opens."

"In course I shall. Jim Travis'll find he's walked into the wrong shop."

"The bank opens at ten o'clock, you know."

"I'll be there on time."

The two boys separated.

"Good luck, Dick," said Fosdick, as he parted from him. "It'll all come out right, I think."

"I hope 'twill," said Dick.

He had recovered from his temporary depression, and made up his mind that the money would be recovered. He had no idea of allowing himself to be outwitted by Jim Travis, and enjoyed already, in anticipation, the pleasure of defeating his rascality.

It wanted two hours and a half yet to ten o'clock, and this time to Dick was too precious to be wasted. It was the time of his greatest harvest. He accordingly repaired to his usual place of business, and succeeded in obtaining six customers, which yielded him sixty cents. He then went to a restaurant, and got some breakfast. It was now half-past nine, and Dick, feeling that it wouldn't do to be late, left his box in charge of Johnny Nolan, and made his way to the bank.

The officers had not yet arrived, and Dick lingered on the outside, waiting till they should come. He was not without a little uneasiness, fearing that Travis might be as prompt as himself, and finding him there, might suspect something, and so escape the snare. But, though looking cautiously up and down the street, he could discover no traces of the supposed thief. In due time ten o'clock struck, and immediately afterwards the doors of the bank were thrown open, and our hero entered.

As Dick had been in the habit of making a weekly visit for the last nine months, the cashier had come to know him by sight.

"You're early, this morning, my lad," he said, pleasantly. "Have you got some more money to deposit? You'll be getting rich, soon."

"I don't know about that," said Dick. "My bank-book's been stole."

"Stolen!" echoed the cashier. "That's unfortunate. Not so bad as it might be, though. The thief can't collect the money."

"That's what I came to see about," said Dick. "I was afraid he might have got it already."

"He hasn't been here yet. Even if he had, I remember you, and should have detected him. When was it taken?"

"Yesterday," said Dick. "I missed it in the evenin' when I got home."

"Have you any suspicion as to the person who took it?" asked the cashier.

Dick thereupon told all he knew as to the general character and suspicious conduct of Jim Travis, and the cashier agreed with him that he was probably the thief. Dick also gave his reason for thinking that he would visit the bank that morning, to withdraw the funds.

"Very good," said the cashier. "We'll be ready for him. What is the number of your book?"

"No. 5,678," said Dick.

"Now give me a little description of this Travis whom you suspect."

Dick accordingly furnished a brief outline sketch of Travis, not particularly complimentary to the latter.

"That will answer. I think I shall know him," said the cashier. "You may depend upon it that he shall receive no money on your account."

"Thank you," said Dick.

Considerably relieved in mind, our hero turned towards the door, thinking that there would be nothing gained by his remaining longer, while he would of course lose time.

He had just reached the doors, which were of glass, when through them he perceived James Travis himself just crossing the street, and apparently coming towards the bank. It would not do, of course, for him to be seen.

"Here he is," he exclaimed, hurrying back. "Can't you hide me somewhere? I don't want to be seen."

The cashier understood at once how the land lay. He quickly opened a little door, and admitted Dick behind the counter.

"Stoop down," he said, "so as not to be seen."

Dick had hardly done so when Jim Travis opened the outer door, and, looking about him in a little uncertainty, walked up to the cashier's desk.

Chapter 23

Travis Is Arrested

JIM TRAVIS advanced into the bank with a doubtful step, knowing well that he was on a dishonest errand, and heartily wishing that he were well out of it. After a little hesitation, he approached the paying-teller, and, exhibiting the bank-book, said, "I want to get my money out."

The bank-officer took the book, and, after looking at it a moment, said, "How much do you want?"

"The whole of it," said Travis.

"You can draw out any part of it, but to draw out the whole requires a week's notice."

"Then I'll take a hundred dollars."

"Are you the person to whom the book belongs?"

"Yes, sir," said Travis, without hesitation.

"Your name is—"

"Hunter."

The bank-clerk went to a large folio volume, containing the names of depositors, and began to turn over the leaves. While he was doing this, he managed to send out a young man connected with the bank for a policeman. Travis did not perceive this, or did not suspect that it had anything to do with himself. Not being used to savings banks, he supposed the delay only what was usual. After a search, which was only intended to gain time that a policeman might be summoned, the cashier came back, and, sliding out a piece of paper to Travis, said, "It will be necessary for you to write an order for the money."

Travis took a pen, which he found on the ledge outside, and wrote the order, signing his name "Dick Hunter," having observed that name on the outside of the book.

"Your name is Dick Hunter, then?" said the cashier, taking the paper, and looking at the thief over his spectacles.

"Yes," said Travis, promptly.

"But," continued the cashier, "I find Hunter's age is put down on the bank-book as fourteen. Surely you must be more than that."

Travis would gladly have declared that he was only fourteen; but, being in reality twenty-three, and possessing a luxuriant pair of whiskers, this was not to be thought of. He began to feel uneasy.

"Dick Hunter's my younger brother," he said. "I'm getting out the money for him."

"I thought you said your own name was Dick Hunter," said the cashier.

"I said my name was Hunter," said Travis, ingeniously. "I didn't understand you."

"But you've signed the name of Dick Hunter to this order. How is that?" questioned the troublesome cashier.

Travis saw that he was getting himself into a tight place; but his self-possession did not desert him.

"I thought I must give my brother's name," he answered.

"What is your own name?"

"Henry Hunter."

"Can you bring any one to testify that the statement you are making is correct?"

"Yes, a dozen if you like," said Travis, boldly. "Give me the book, and I'll come back this afternoon. I didn't think there'd be such a fuss about getting out a little money."

"Wait a moment. Why don't your brother come himself?"

"Because he's sick. He's down with the measles," said Travis.

Here the cashier signed to Dick to rise and show himself. Our hero accordingly did so.

forgiving

"You will be glad to find that he has recovered," said the cashier, pointing to Dick.

With an exclamation of anger and dismay, Travis, who saw the game was up, started for the door, feeling that safety made such a course prudent. But he was too late. He found himself confronted by a burly policeman, who seized him by the arm, saying, "Not so fast, my man. I want you."

"Let me go," exclaimed Travis, struggling to free himself.

"I'm sorry I can't oblige you," said the officer. "You'd better not make a fuss, or I may have to hurt you a little."

Travis sullenly resigned himself to his fate, darting a look of rage at Dick, whom he considered the author of his present misfortune.

"This is your book," said the cashier, handing back his rightful property to our hero. "Do you wish to draw out any money?"

"Two dollars," said Dick.

"Very well. Write an order for the amount."

Before doing so, Dick, who now that he saw Travis in the power of the law began to pity him, went up to the officer, and said,—

"Won't you let him go? I've got my bank-book back, and I don't want anything done to him."

"Sorry I can't oblige you," said the officer; "but I'm not allowed to do it. He'll have to stand his trial."

"I'm sorry for you, Travis," said Dick. "I didn't want you arrested. I only wanted my bank-book back."

"Curse you!" said Travis, scowling vindictively. "Wait till I get free. See if I don't fix you."

"You needn't pity him too much," said the officer. "I know him now. He's been to the Island before."

"It's a lie," said Travis, violently.

"Don't be too noisy, my friend," said the officer. "If you've got no more business here, we'll be going."

He withdrew with the prisoner in charge, and Dick, having drawn his two dollars, left the bank. Notwithstanding the violent words the prisoner had used towards himself, and his attempted robbery, he could not help feeling sorry that he had been instrumental in causing his arrest.

"I'll keep my book a little safer hereafter," thought Dick. "Now I must go and see Tom Wilkins."

Before dismissing the subject of Travis and his theft, it may be remarked that he was duly tried, and, his guilt being clear, was sent to Blackwell's Island for nine months. At the end of that time, on his release, he got a chance to work his passage on a ship to San Francisco, where he probably arrived in due time. At any rate, nothing more has been heard of him, and probably his threat of vengeance against Dick will never be carried into effect.

Returning to the City Hall Park, Dick soon fell in with Tom Wilkins.

"How are you, Tom?" he said. "How's your mother?"

"She's better, Dick, thank you. She felt worried about bein' turned out into the street; but I gave her that money from you, and now she feels a good deal easier."

"I've got some more for you, Tom," said Dick, producing a two-dollar bill from his pocket.

"I ought not to take it from you, Dick."

"Oh, it's all right, Tom. Don't be afraid."

"But you may need it yourself."

"There's plenty more where that came from."

"Any way, one dollar will be enough. With that we can pay the rent."

"You'll want the other to buy something to eat."

"You're very kind, Dick."

"I'd ought to be. I've only got myself to take care of."

"Well, I'll take it for my mother's sake. When you want anything done just call on Tom Wilkins."

"All right. Next week, if your mother doesn't get better, I'll give you some more."

Tom thanked our hero very gratefully, and Dick walked away, feeling the self-approval which always accompanies a generous and disinterested action. He was generous by nature, and, before the period at which he is introduced to the reader's notice, he frequently treated his friends to cigars and oyster-stews. Sometimes he invited them to accompany him to the theatre at his expense. But he never derived from these acts of liberality the same degree of satisfaction as from this timely gift to Tom Wilkins. He felt that his money was well bestowed, and would save an entire family from privation and discomfort. Five dollars would, to be sure, make something of a difference in the amount of his savings. It was more than he was able to save up in a week. But Dick felt fully repaid for what he had done, and he felt prepared to give as much more, if Tom's mother should continue to be sick, and should appear to him to need it.

Besides all this, Dick felt a justifiable pride in his financial ability to afford so handsome a gift. A year before, however much he might have desired to give, it would have been quite out of his power to give five dollars. His cash balance never reached that amount. It was seldom, indeed, that it equalled one dollar. In more ways than one Dick was beginning to reap the advantage of his self-denial and judicious economy.

It will be remembered that when Mr. Whitney at parting with Dick presented him with five dollars, he told him that he might repay it to some other boy who was struggling upward. Dick thought of this, and it occurred to him that after all he was only paying up an old debt.

When Fosdick came home in the evening, Dick announced his success in recovering his lost money, and described the manner in which it had been brought about.

"You're in luck, Dick," said Fosdick. "I guess we'd better not trust the bureau-drawer again."

"I mean to carry my book round with me," said Dick.

"So shall I, as long as we stay at Mrs. Mooney's. I wish we were in a better place."

"I must go down and tell her she needn't expect Travis back. Poor chap, I pity him!"

Travis was never more seen in Mrs. Mooney's establishment. He was owing that lady for a fortnight's rent of his room, which prevented her feeling much compassion for him. The room was soon after let to a more creditable tenant, who proved a less troublesome neighbor than his predecessor.

Chapter 24

Dick Receives a Letter

IT WAS about a week after Dick's recovery of his bankbook, that Fosdick brought home with him in the evening a copy of the "Daily Sun."

"Would you like to see your name in print, Dick?" he asked.

"Yes," said Dick, who was busy at the wash-stand, endeavoring to efface the marks which his day's work had left upon his hands. "They haven't put me up for mayor, have they? 'Cause if they have, I shan't accept. It would interfere too much with my private business."

"No," said Fosdick, "they haven't put you up for office yet, though that may happen sometime. But if you want to see your name in print, here it is."

Dick was rather incredulous, but, having dried his hands on the towel, took the paper, and following the directions of Fosdick's finger, observed in the list of advertised letters the name of "RAGGED DICK."

"By gracious, so it is," said he. "Do you s'pose it means me?"

"I don't know of any other Ragged Dick,—do you?"

"No," said Dick, reflectively; "it must be me. But I don't know of anybody that would be likely to write to me."

"Perhaps it is Frank Whitney," suggested Fosdick, after a little reflection. "Didn't he promise to write to you?"

"Yes," said Dick, "and he wanted me to write to him."

"Where is he now?"

"He was going to a boarding-school in Connecticut, he said. The name of the town was Barnton."

"Very likely the letter is from him."

"I hope it is. Frank was a tip-top boy, and he was the first that made me ashamed of bein' so ignorant and dirty."

"You had better go to the post-office to-morrow morning, and ask for the letter."

"P'r'aps they won't give it to me."

"Suppose you wear the old clothes you used to a year ago, when Frank first saw you? They won't have any doubt of your being Ragged Dick then."

"I guess I will. I'll be sort of ashamed to be seen in 'em though," said Dick, who had considerable more pride in a neat personal appearance than when we were first introduced to him.

"It will be only for one day, or one morning," said Fosdick.

"I'd do more'n that for the sake of gettin' a letter from Frank. I'd like to see him."

The next morning, in accordance with the suggestion of Fosdick, Dick arrayed himself in the long disused Washington coat and Napoleon pants, which he had carefully preserved, for what reason he could hardly explain.

When fairly equipped, Dick surveyed himself in the mirror,—if the little seven-by-nine-inch looking-glass, with which the room was furnished, deserved the name. The result of the survey was not on the whole a pleasing one. To tell the truth, Dick was quite ashamed of his appearance, and, on opening the chamber-door, looked around to see that the coast was clear, not being willing to have any of his fellow-boarders see him in his present attire.

He managed to slip out into the street unobserved, and, after attending to two or three regular customers who came down-town early in the morning, he made his way down Nassau Street to the post-office. He passed along until he came to a compartment on which he read

ADVERTISED LETTERS, and, stepping up to the little window, said,—

"There's a letter for me. I saw it advertised in the 'Sun' yesterday."

"What name?" demanded the clerk.

"Ragged Dick," answered our hero.

"That's a queer name," said the clerk, surveying him a little curiously. "Are you Ragged Dick?"

"If you don't believe me, look at my clo'es," said Dick.

"That's pretty good proof, certainly," said the clerk, laughing. "If that isn't your name, it deserves to be."

"I believe in dressin' up to your name," said Dick.

"Do you know any one in Barnton, Connecticut?" asked the clerk, who had by this time found the letter.

"Yes," said Dick. "I know a chap that's at boardin'-school there."

"It appears to be in a boy's hand. I think it must be yours."

The letter was handed to Dick through the window. He received it eagerly, and drawing back so as not to be in the way of the throng who were constantly applying for letters, or slipping them into the boxes provided for them, hastily opened it, and began to read. As the reader may be interested in the contents of the letter as well as Dick, we transcribe it below.

It was dated Barnton, Conn., and commenced thus,—

"DEAR DICK,—You must excuse my addressing this letter to 'Ragged Dick;' but the fact is, I don't know what your last name is, nor where you live. I am afraid there is not much chance of your getting this letter; but I hope you will. I have thought of you very often, and wondered how you were getting along, and I should have written to you before if I had known where to direct.

"Let me tell you a little about myself. Barnton is a very pretty country town, only about six miles from Hartford. The boarding-school which I attend is under the charge of Ezekiel Munroe, A. M. He is a man of about fifty, a graduate of Yale College, and has always been a teacher. It is a large two-story house, with an addition containing a good many small bed-chambers for the boys. There are about twenty of us, and there is one assistant teacher who teaches the English branches. Mr. Munroe, or Old Zeke, as we call him behind his back, teaches Latin and Greek. I am studying both these languages, because father wants me to go to college.

"But you won't be interested in hearing about our studies. I will tell you how we amuse ourselves. There are about fifty acres of land belonging to Mr. Munroe; so that we have plenty of room for play. About a quarter of a mile from the house there is a good-sized pond. There is a large, round-bottomed boat, which is stout and strong. Every Wednesday and Saturday afternoon, when the weather is good, we go out rowing on the pond. Mr. Barton, the assistant teacher, goes with us, to look after us. In the summer we are allowed to go in bathing. In the winter there is splendid skating on the pond.

"Besides this, we play ball a good deal, and we have various other plays. So we have a pretty good time, although we study pretty hard too. I am getting on very well in my studies. Father has not decided yet where he will send me to college.

"I wish you were here, Dick. I should enjoy your company, and besides I should like to feel that you were getting an education. I think you are naturally a pretty smart boy; but I suppose, as you have to earn your own living, you don't get much chance to learn. I only wish I had a few hundred dollars of my own. I would have you come up here, and attend school with us. If I ever have a chance to help you in any way, you may be sure that I will.

"I shall have to wind up my letter now, as I have to hand in a composition to-morrow, on the life and character of Washington. I might say that I have a friend who wears a coat that once belonged to the general. But I suppose that coat must be worn out by this time. I don't much like writing compositions. I would a good deal rather write letters.

"I have written a longer letter than I meant to. I hope you will get it, though I am afraid not. If you do, you must be sure to answer it, as soon as possible. You needn't mind if your writing does look like 'hens-tracks,' as you told me once.

"Good-by, Dick. You must always think of me, as your very true friend,

"FRANK WHITNEY"

Dick read this letter with much satisfaction. It is always pleasant to be remembered, and Dick had so few friends that it was more to him than to boys who are better provided. Again, he felt a new sense of importance in having a letter addressed to him. It was the first letter he had ever received. If it had been sent to him a year before, he would not have been able to read it. But now, thanks to Fosdick's instructions, he could not only read writing, but he could write a very good hand himself.

There was one passage in the letter which pleased Dick. It was where Frank said that if he had the money he would pay for his education himself.

"He's a tip-top feller," said Dick. "I wish I could see him ag'in."

There were two reasons why Dick would like to have seen Frank. One was, the natural pleasure he would have in meeting a friend; but he felt also that he would like to have Frank witness the improvement he had made in his studies and mode of life.

"He'd find me a little more 'spectable than when he first saw me," thought Dick.

Dick had by this time got up to Printing House Square. Standing on Spruce Street, near the "Tribune" office, was his old enemy, Micky Maguire.

It has already been said that Micky felt a natural enmity towards those in his own condition in life who wore better clothes than himself. For the last nine months, Dick's neat appearance had excited the ire of the young Philistine. To appear in neat attire and with a clean face Micky felt was a piece of presumption, and an assumption of superiority on the part of our hero, and he termed it "tryin' to be a swell."

Now his astonished eyes rested on Dick in his ancient attire, which was very similar to his own. It was a moment of triumph to him. He felt that "pride had had a fall," and he could not forbear reminding Dick of it.

"Them's nice clo'es you've got on," said he, sarcastically, as Dick came up.

"Yes," said Dick, promptly. "I've been employin' your tailor. If my face was only dirty we'd be taken for twin brothers."

"So you've give up tryin' to be a swell?"

"Only for this partic'lar occasion," said Dick. "I wanted to make a fashionable call, so I put on my regimentals."

"I don't b'lieve you've got any better clo'es," said Micky.

"All right," said Dick, "I won't charge you nothin' for what you believe."

Here a customer presented himself for Micky, and Dick went back to his room to change his clothes, before resuming business.

Chapter 25

Dick Writes His First Letter

WHEN FOSDICK reached home in the evening, Dick displayed his letter with some pride.

"It's a nice letter," said Fosdick, after reading it. "I should like to know Frank."

"I'll bet you would," said Dick. "He's a trump."

"When are you going to answer it?"

"I don't know," said Dick, dubiously. "I never writ a letter."

"That's no reason why you shouldn't. There's always a first time, you know."

"I don't know what to say," said Dick.

"Get some paper and sit down to it, and you'll find enough to say. You can do that this evening instead of studying."

"If you'll look it over afterwards, and shine it up a little."

"Yes, if it needs it; but I rather think Frank would like it best just as you wrote it."

Dick decided to adopt Fosdick's suggestion. He had very serious doubts as to his ability to write a letter. Like a good many other boys, he looked upon it as a very serious job, not reflecting that, after all, letter-writing is nothing but talking upon paper. Still, in spite of his misgivings, he felt that the letter ought to be answered, and he wished Frank to hear from him. After various preparations, he at last got settled down to his task, and, before the evening was over, a letter was written. As the first letter which Dick had ever produced, and because it was characteristic of him, my readers may like to read it.

Here it is,—

"DEAR FRANK,—I got your letter this mornin', and was very glad to hear you hadn't forgotten Ragged Dick. I aint so ragged as I was. Openwork coats and trowsers has gone out of fashion. I put on the Washington coat and Napoleon pants to go to the post-office, for fear they wouldn't think I was the boy that was meant. On my way back I received the congratulations of my intimate friend, Micky Maguire, on my improved appearance.

"I've give up sleepin' in boxes, and old wagons, findin' it didn't agree with my constitution. I've hired a room in Mott Street, and have got a private tooter, who rooms with me and looks after my studies in the evenin'. Mott Street aint very fashionable; but my manshun on Fifth Avenoo isn't finished yet, and I'm afraid it won't be till I'm a gray-haired veteran. I've got a hundred dollars towards it, which I've saved up from my earnin's. I haven't forgot what you and your uncle said to me, and I'm tryin' to grow up 'spectable. I haven't been to Tony Pastor's, or the Old Bowery, for ever so long. I'd rather save up my money to support me in my old age. When my hair gets gray, I'm goin' to knock off blackin' boots, and go into some light, genteel employment, such as keepin' an apple-stand, or disseminatin' peanuts among the people.

"I've got so as to read pretty well, so my tooter says. I've been studyin' geography and grammar also. I've made such astonishin' progress that I can tell a noun from a conjunction as far away as I can see 'em. Tell Mr. Munroe that if he wants an accomplished teacher in his school, he can send for me, and I'll come on by the very next train. Or, if he wants to sell out for a hundred dollars, I'll buy the whole concern, and agree to teach the scholars all I know myself in less than six months. Is teachin' as good business, generally speakin', as blackin' boots? My private tooter combines both, and is makin' a fortun' with great rapidity. He'll be as rich as Astor some time, *if he only lives long enough.*

"I should think you'd have a bully time at your school. I should like to go out in the boat, or play ball with you. When are you comin' to the city? I wish you'd write and let me know when you do, and I'll call and see you. I'll leave my business in the hands of my numerous clerks, and go round with you. There's lots of things you didn't see when you was here before. They're getting on fast at the Central Park. It looks better than it did a year ago.

"I aint much used to writin' letters. As this is the first one I ever wrote, I hope you'll excuse the mistakes. I hope you'll write to me again soon. I can't write so good a letter as you; but I'll do my best, as the man said when he was asked if he could swim over to Brooklyn backwards. Good-by, Frank. Thank you for all your kindness. Direct your next letter to No. — Mott Street.

> "Your true friend,
>
> "DICK HUNTER."

When Dick had written the last word, he leaned back in his chair, and surveyed the letter with much satisfaction.

"I didn't think I could have wrote such a long letter, Fosdick," said he.

"Written would be more grammatical, Dick," suggested his friend.

"I guess there's plenty of mistakes in it," said Dick. "Just look at it, and see."

Fosdick took the letter, and read it over carefully.

"Yes, there are some mistakes," he said; "but it sounds so much like you that I think it would be better to let it go just as it is. It will be more likely to remind Frank of what you were when he first saw you."

"Is it good enough to send?" asked Dick, anxiously.

"Yes; it seems to me to be quite a good letter. It is

written just as you talk. Nobody but you could have written such a letter, Dick. I think Frank will be amused at your proposal to come up there as teacher."

"P'r'aps it would be a good idea for us to open a seleck school here in Mott Street," said Dick, humorously. "We could call it 'Professor Fosdick and Hunter's Mott Street Seminary.' Boot-blackin' taught by Professor Hunter."

The evening was so far advanced that Dick decided to postpone copying his letter till the next evening. By this time he had come to have a very fair handwriting, so that when the letter was complete it really looked quite creditable, and no one would have suspected that it was Dick's first attempt in this line. Our hero surveyed it with no little complacency. In fact, he felt rather proud of it, since it reminded him of the great progress he had made. He carried it down to the post-office, and deposited it with his own hands in the proper box. Just on the steps of the building, as as he was coming out, he met Johnny Nolan, who had been sent on an errand to Wall Street by some gentleman, and was just returning.

"What are you doin' down here, Dick?" asked Johnny.

"I've been mailin' a letter."

"Who sent you?"

"Nobody."

"I mean, who writ the letter?"

"I wrote it myself."

"Can you write letters?" asked Johnny, in amazement.

"Why shouldn't I?"

"I didn't know you could write. I can't."

"Then you ought to learn."

"I went to school once; but it was too hard work, so I give it up."

"You're lazy, Johnny,—that's what's the matter. How'd you ever expect to know anything, if you don't try?"

"I can't learn."

"You can, if you want to."

Johnny Nolan was evidently of a different opinion.

He was a good-natured boy, large of his age, with
nothing particularly bad about him, but utterly lacking
in that energy, ambition, and natural sharpness, for
which Dick was distinguished. He was not adapted to
succeed in the life which circumstances had forced upon
him; for in the street-life of the metropolis a boy needs
to be on the alert, and have all his wits about him,
or he will find himself wholly distanced by his more
enterprising competitors for popular favor. To succeed in
his profession, humble as it is, a boot-black must depend
upon the same qualities which gain success in higher
walks in life. It was easy to see that Johnny, unless very
much favored by circumstances, would never rise much
above his present level. For Dick, we cannot help hoping
much better things.

Chapter 26

An Exciting Adventure

DICK NOW began to look about for a position in a store or counting-room. Until he should obtain one he determined to devote half the day to blacking boots, not being willing to break in upon his small capital. He found that he could earn enough in half a day to pay all his necessary expenses, including the entire rent of the room. Fosdick desired to pay his half; but Dick steadily refused, insisting upon paying so much as compensation for his friend's services as instructor.

It should be added that Dick's peculiar way of speaking and use of slang terms had been somewhat modified by his education and his intimacy with Henry Fosdick. Still he continued to indulge in them to some extent, especially when he felt like joking, and it was natural to Dick to joke, as my readers have probably found out by this time. Still his manners were considerably improved, so that he was more likely to obtain a situation than when first introduced to our notice.

Just now, however, business was very dull, and merchants, instead of hiring new assistants, were disposed to part with those already in their employ. After making several ineffectual applications, Dick began to think he should be obliged to stick to his profession until the next season. But about this time something occurred which considerably improved his chances of preferment.

This is the way it happened.

As Dick, with a balance of more than a hundred dollars in the savings bank, might fairly consider himself a young man of property, he thought himself justified in occasionally taking a half holiday from business, and going on an excursion. On Wednesday afternoon Henry Fosdick was sent by his employer on an errand to that part of Brooklyn near Greenwood Cemetery. Dick hastily dressed himself in his best, and determined to accompany him.

The two boys walked down to the South Ferry, and, paying their two cents each, entered the ferry-boat. They remained at the stern, and stood by the railing, watching the great city, with its crowded wharves, receding from view. Beside them was a gentleman with two children,— a girl of eight and a little boy of six. The children were talking gayly to their father. While he was pointing out some object of interest to the little girl, the boy managed to creep, unobserved, beneath the chain that extends across the boat, for the protection of passengers, and, stepping incautiously to the edge of the boat, fell over into the foaming water.

At the child's scream, the father looked up, and, with a cry of horror, sprang to the edge of the boat. He would have plunged in, but, being unable to swim, would only have endangered his own life, without being able to save his child.

"My child!" he exclaimed in anguish,—"who will save my child? A thousand—ten thousand dollars to any one who will save him!"

There chanced to be but few passengers on board at the time, and nearly all these were either in the cabins or standing forward. Among the few who saw the child fall was our hero.

Now Dick was an expert swimmer. It was an accomplishment which he had possessed for years, and he no sooner saw the boy fall than he resolved to rescue him. His determination was formed before he heard the liberal offer made by the boy's father. Indeed, I must do Dick the justice to say that, in the excitement of the moment, he did not hear it at all, nor would it have stimulated the alacrity with which he sprang to the rescue of the little boy.

Little Johnny had already risen once, and gone under for the second time, when our hero plunged in. He was obliged to strike out for the boy, and this took time. He reached him none too soon. Just as he was sinking for the third and last time, he caught him by the jacket. Dick was stout and strong, but Johnny clung to him so tightly, that it was with great difficulty he was able to sustain himself.

"Put your arms round my neck," said Dick.

The little boy mechanically obeyed, and clung with a grasp strengthened by his terror. In this position Dick could bear his weight better. But the ferry-boat was receding fast. It was quite impossible to reach it. The father, his face pale with terror and anguish, and his hands clasped in suspense, saw the brave boy's struggles, and prayed with agonizing fervor that he might be successful. But it is probable, for they were now midway of the river, that both Dick and the little boy whom he had bravely undertaken to rescue would have been drowned, had not a row-boat been fortunately near. The two men who were in it witnessed the accident, and hastened to the rescue of our hero.

"Keep up a little longer," they shouted, bending to their oars, "and we will save you."

Dick heard the shout, and it put fresh strength into him. He battled manfully with the treacherous sea, his eyes fixed longingly upon the approaching boat.

"Hold on tight, little boy," he said. "There's a boat coming."

The little boy did not see the boat. His eyes were closed to shut out the fearful water, but he clung the closer to his young preserver. Six long, steady strokes, and the boat dashed along side. Strong hands seized Dick and his youthful burden, and drew them into the boat, both dripping with water.

"God be thanked!" exclaimed the father, as from the steamer he saw the child's rescue. "That brave boy shall be rewarded, if I sacrifice my whole fortune to compass it."

"You've had a pretty narrow escape, young chap," said one of the boatmen to Dick. "It was a pretty tough job you undertook."

"Yes," said Dick. "That's what I thought when I was in the water. If it hadn't been for you, I don't know what would have 'come of us."

"Anyhow you're a plucky boy, or you wouldn't have dared to jump into the water after this little chap. It was a risky thing to do."

"I'm used to the water," said Dick, modestly. "I didn't stop to think of the danger, but I wasn't going to see that little fellow drown without tryin' to save him."

The boat at once headed for the ferry wharf on the Brooklyn side. The captain of the ferry-boat, seeing the rescue, did not think it necessary to stop his boat, but kept on his way. The whole occurrence took place in less time than I have occupied in telling it.

The father was waiting on the wharf to receive his little boy, with what feeling of gratitude and joy can be easily understood. With a burst of happy tears he clasped him to his arms. Dick was about to withdraw modestly, but the gentleman perceived the movement, and, putting down the child, came forward, and, clasping his hand, said with emotion, "My brave boy, I owe you a debt I can never repay. But for your timely service I should now be plunged into an anguish which I cannot think of without a shudder."

Our hero was ready enough to speak on most occasions, but always felt awkward when he was praised. "It wasn't any trouble," he said, modestly. "I can swim like a top."

"But not many boys would have risked their lives for a stranger," said the gentleman. "But," he added with a sudden thought, as his glance rested on Dick's dripping garments, "both you and my little boy will take cold in wet clothes. Fortunately I have a friend living close at hand, at whose house you will have an opportunity of taking off your clothes, and having them dried."

Dick protested that he never took cold; but Fosdick, who had now joined them, and who, it is needless to say, had been greatly alarmed at Dick's danger, joined in urging compliance with the gentleman's proposal, and in the end our hero had to yield. His new friend secured a hack, the driver of which agreed for extra recompense to receive the dripping boys into his carriage, and they were whirled rapidly to a pleasant house in a side street, where matters were quickly explained, and both boys were put to bed.

"I aint used to goin' to bed quite so early," thought Dick. "This is the queerest excursion I ever took."

Like most active boys Dick did not enjoy the prospect of spending half a day in bed; but his confinement did not last as long as he anticipated.

In about an hour the door of his chamber was opened, and a servant appeared, bringing a new and handsome suit of clothes throughout.

"You are to put on these," said the servant to Dick; "but you needn't get up till you feel like it."

"Whose clothes are they?" asked Dick.

"They are yours."

"Mine! Where did they come from?"

"Mr. Rockwell sent out and bought them for you. They are the same size as your wet ones."

"Is he here now?"

"No. He bought another suit for the little boy, and has gone back to New York. Here's a note he asked me to give you."

Dick opened the paper, and read as follows,—

"Please accept this outfit of clothes as the first instalment of a debt which I can never repay. I have asked to have your wet suit dried, when you can reclaim it. Will you oblige me by calling to-morrow at my counting room, No.—, Pearl Street.

"Your friend,

"JAMES ROCKWELL."

Chapter 27

Conclusion

WHEN DICK was dressed in his new suit, he surveyed his figure with pardonable complacency. It was the best he had ever worn, and fitted him as well as if it had been made expressly for him.

"He's done the handsome thing," said Dick to himself; "but there wasn't no 'casion for his givin' me these clothes. My lucky stars are shinin' pretty bright now. Jumpin' into the water pays better than shinin' boots; but I don't think I'd like to try it more'n once a week."

About eleven o'clock the next morning Dick repaired to Mr. Rockwell's counting-room on Pearl Street. He found himself in front of a large and handsome warehouse. The counting-room was on the lower floor. Our hero entered, and found Mr. Rockwell sitting at a desk. No sooner did that gentleman see him than he arose, and, advancing, shook Dick by the hand in the most friendly manner.

"My young friend," he said, "you have done me so great a service that I wish to be of some service to you in return. Tell me about yourself, and what plans or wishes you have formed for the future."

Dick frankly related his past history, and told Mr. Rockwell of his desire to get into a store or counting-room, and of the failure of all his applications thus far. The merchant listened attentively to Dick's statement, and, when he had finished, placed a sheet of paper before him, and, handing him a pen, said, "Will you write your name on this piece of paper?"

Dick wrote, in a free, bold hand, the name Richard Hunter. He had very much improved his penmanship, as has already been mentioned, and now had no cause to be ashamed of it.

Mr. Rockwell surveyed it approvingly.

"How would you like to enter my counting-room as clerk, Richard?" he asked.

Dick was about to say "Bully," when he recollected himself, and answered, "Very much."

"I suppose you know something of arithmetic, do you not?"

"Yes, sir."

"Then you may consider yourself engaged at a salary of ten dollars a week. You may come next Monday morning."

"Ten dollars!" repeated Dick, thinking he must have misunderstood.

"Yes; will that be sufficient?"

"It's more than I can earn," said Dick, honestly.

"Perhaps it is at first," said Mr. Rockwell, smiling; "but I am willing to pay you that. I will besides advance you as fast as your progress will justify it."

Dick was so elated that he hardly restrained himself from some demonstration which would have astonished the merchant; but he exercised self-control, and only said, "I'll try to serve you so faithfully, sir, that you won't repent having taken me into your service."

"And I think you will succeed," said Mr. Rockwell, encouragingly. "I will not detain you any longer, for I have some important business to attend to. I shall expect to see you on Monday morning."

Dick left the counting-room, hardly knowing whether he stood on his head or his heels, so overjoyed was he at the sudden change in his fortunes. Ten dollars a week was to him a fortune, and three times as much as he had expected to obtain at first. Indeed he would have been glad, only the day before, to get a place at three dollars a week. He reflected that with the stock of clothes which he had now on hand, he could save up at least half of it, and even then live better than he had been accustomed to do; so that his little fund in the savings bank, instead of being diminished, would be steadily increasing. Then he was to be advanced if he deserved it. It was indeed a bright prospect for a boy who, only a year before, could neither read nor write, and depended for a night's lodging upon the chance hospitality of an alley-way or old wagon. Dick's great ambition to "grow up 'spectable" seemed likely to be accomplished after all.

"I wish Fosdick was as well off as I am," he thought generously. But he determined to help his less fortunate friend, and assist him up the ladder as he advanced himself.

When Dick entered his room on Mott Street, he discovered that some one else had been there before him, and two articles of wearing apparel had disappeared.

"By gracious!" he exclaimed; "somebody's stole my Washington coat and Napoleon pants. Maybe it's an agent of Barnum's, who expects to make a fortun' by exhibitin' the valooable wardrobe of a gentleman of fashion."

Dick did not shed many tears over his loss, as, in his present circumstances, he never expected to have any further use for the well-worn garments. It may be stated that he afterwards saw them adorning the figure of Micky Maguire; but whether that estimable young man stole them himself, he never ascertained. As to the loss, Dick was rather pleased that it had occurred. It seemed to cut him off from the old vagabond life which he hoped never to resume. Henceforward he meant to press onward, and rise as high as possible.

Although it was yet only noon, Dick did not go out again with his brush. He felt that it was time to retire from business. He would leave his share of the public patronage to other boys less fortunate than himself. That evening Dick and Fosdick had a long conversation. Fosdick rejoiced heartily in his friend's success, and on his side had the pleasant news to communicate that his pay had been advanced to six dollars a week.

"I think we can afford to leave Mott Street now." he continued. "This house isn't as neat as it might be, and I should like to live in a nicer quarter of the city."

"All right," said Dick. "We'll hunt up a new room tomorrow. I shall have plenty of time, having retired from business. I'll try to get my reg'lar customers to take Johnny Nolan in my place. That boy hasn't any enterprise. He needs somebody to look out for him."

"You might give him your box and brush, too, Dick."

"No," said Dick; "I'll give him some new ones, but mine I want to keep, to remind me of the hard times I've had, when I was an ignorant boot-black, and never expected to be anything better."

"When, in short, you were 'Ragged Dick.' You must drop that name, and think of yourself now as"—

"Richard Hunter, Esq.," said our hero, smiling.

"A young gentleman on the way to fame and fortune," added Fosdick.

MARK, THE MATCH BOY

Chapter 1

Richard Hunter at Home

"FOSDICK," said Richard Hunter, "what was the name of that man who owed your father two thousand dollars, which he never paid him?"

"Hiram Bates," answered Fosdick, in some surprise. "What made you think of him?"

"I thought I remembered the name. He moved out West, didn't he?"

"So I heard at the time."

"Do you happen to remember where? Out West is a very large place."

"I do not know exactly, but I think it was Milwaukie."

"Indeed!" exclaimed Richard Hunter, in visible excitement. "Well, Fosdick, why don't you try to get the debt paid?"

"Of what use would it be? How do I know he is living in Milwaukie now? If I should write him a letter, there isn't much chance of my ever getting an answer."

"Call and see him."

"What, go out to Milwaukie on such a wild-goose chase as that? I can't think what you are driving at, Dick."

"Then I'll tell you, Fosdick. Hiram Bates is now in New York."

"How do you know?" asked Fosdick, with an expression of mingled amazement and incredulity.

"I'll show you."

Richard Hunter pointed to the list of hotel arrivals in the "Evening Express," which he held in his hand. Among the arrivals at the Astor House occurred the name of Hiram Bates, from Milwaukie.

"If I am not mistaken," he said, "that is the name of your father's debtor."

"I don't know but you are right," said Fosdick, thoughtfully.

"He must be prosperous if he stops at a high-priced hotel like the Astor."

"Yes, I suppose so. How much good that money would have done my poor father," he added, with a sigh.

"How much good it will do you, Fosdick."

Fosdick shook his head. "I would sell out my chance of getting it for ten dollars," he said.

"I would buy it at that price if I wanted to make money out of you; but I don't. I advise you to attend to this matter at once."

"What can I do?" asked Fosdick, who seemed at a loss to understand his companion's meaning.

"There is only one thing to do," said Dick, promptly. "Call on Mr. Bates this evening at the hotel. Tell him who you are, and hint that you should like the money."

"I haven't got your confidence, Dick. I shouldn't know how to go about it. Do you really think it would do any good? He might think I was impertinent."

"Impertinent to ask payment of a just debt! I don't see it in that light. I think I shall have to go with you."

"I wish you would,—that is, if you really think there is any use in going."

"You mustn't be so bashful if you want to get on in the world, Fosdick. As long as there's a chance of getting even a part of it, I advise you to make the attempt."

"Well, Dick, I'll be guided by your advice."

"Two thousand dollars would be a pretty good wind-fall for you."

"That's true enough, considering that I only get eight dollars a week."

"I wish you got more."

"So do I, for one particular reason."

"What is that?"

"I don't feel satisfied to have you pay ten dollars a week towards our board, while I pay only six."

"Didn't you promise not to say anything more about that?" said Dick, reproachfully.

"But I can't help *thinking* about it. If we had stayed at our old boarding-house in Bleecker Street, I could have paid my full share."

"But this is a nicer room."

"Much nicer. If I only paid my half, I should be glad of the chance."

"Well, I'll promise you one thing. If Mr. Bates pays you the two thousand dollars, you may pay your half of the expenses."

"Not much chance of that, Dick."

"We can tell better after calling at the Astor House. Get on your coat and we'll start."

While the boys,—for the elder of the two is but eighteen—are making preparations to go out, a few explanations may be required by the reader. Those who have read "Ragged Dick" and "Fame and Fortune,"— the preceding volumes of this series,—will understand that less than three years before Richard Hunter was an ignorant and ragged bootblack about the streets, and Fosdick, though possessing a better education, was in the same business. By a series of upward steps, partly due to good fortune, but largely to his own determination to improve, and hopeful energy, Dick had now become a book-keeper in the establishment of Rockwell & Cooper, on Pearl Street, and possessed the confidence and good wishes of the firm in a high degree.

Fosdick was two years younger, and, though an excellent boy, was less confident, and not so well fitted as his friend to contend with the difficulties of life, and fight his way upward. He was employed in Henderson's hat and cap store on Broadway, and was at present earning a salary of eight dollars a week. As the two paid sixteen dollars weekly for their board, Fosdick would have had nothing left if he had paid his full share. But Richard Hunter at first insisted on paying eleven dollars out of the sixteen, leaving his friend but five to pay. To this Fosdick would not agree, and was with difficulty prevailed upon at last to allow Richard to pay ten; but he had always felt a delicacy about this, although he well knew how gladly his friend did it.

The room which they now occupied was situated in St. Mark's Place, which forms the eastern portion of Eighth Street. It was a front room on the third floor, and was handsomely furnished. There was a thick carpet, of tasteful figure, on the floor. Between the two front windows was a handsome bureau, surmounted by a large mirror. There was a comfortable sofa, chairs covered with hair-cloth, a centre-table covered with books, crimson curtains, which gave a warm and cosey look to the room when lighted up in the evening, and all the accessories of a well-furnished room which is used at the same time as parlor and chamber. This, with an excellent table, afforded a very agreeable home to the boys,—a home which, in these days, would cost considerably more, but for which, at the time of which I write, sixteen dollars was a fair price.

It may be thought that, considering how recently Richard Hunter had been a ragged bootblack, content to sleep in boxes and sheltered doorways, and live at the cheapest restaurants, he had become very luxurious in his tastes. Why did he not get a cheaper boarding-place, and save up the difference in price? No doubt this consideration will readily suggest itself to the minds of some of my young readers.

As Richard Hunter had a philosophy of his own on this subject, I may as well explain it here. He had observed that those young men who out of economy contented themselves with small and cheerless rooms, in which there was no provision for a fire, were driven in the evening to the streets, theatres, and hotels, for the comfort which they could not find at home. Here they felt obliged to spend money to an extent of which they probably were not themselves fully aware, and in the end wasted considerably more than the two or three dollars a week extra which would have provided them with a comfortable home. But this was not all. In the roamings spent outside many laid the foundation of wrong habits, which eventually led to ruin or shortened their lives. They lost all the chances of improvement which they might have secured by study at home in the long winter evenings, and which in the end might have qualified them for posts of higher responsibility, and with a larger compensation.

Richard Hunter was ambitious. He wanted to rise to an honorable place in the community, and he meant to earn it by hard study. So Fosdick and he were in the habit of spending a portion of every evening in improving reading or study. Occasionally he went to some place of amusement, but he enjoyed thoroughly the many evenings when, before a cheerful fire, with books in their hands, his room-mate and himself were adding to their stock of knowledge. The boys had for over a year taken lessons in French and mathematics, and were now able to read the French language with considerable ease.

"What's the use of moping every evening in your room?" asked a young clerk who occupied a hall bedroom adjoining.

"I don't call it moping. I enjoy it," was the reply.

"You don't go to a place of amusement once a month."

"I go as often as I like."

"Well, you're a queer chap. You pay such a thundering price for board. You could go to the theatre four times a week without its costing you any more, if you would take a room like mine."

"I know it; but I'd rather have a nice, comfortable room to come home to."

"Are you studying for a college professor?" asked the other, with a sneer.

"I don't know," said Dick, good-humoredly; "but I'm open to proposals, as the oyster remarked. If you know any first-class institution that would like a dignified professor, of extensive acquirements, just mention me, will you?"

So Richard Hunter kept on his way, indifferent to the criticisms which his conduct excited in the minds of young men of his own age. He looked farther than they, and knew that if he wanted to succeed in life, and win the respect of his fellow-men, he must do something else than attend theatres, and spend his evenings in billiard saloons. Fosdick, who was a quiet, studious boy, fully agreed with his friend in his views of life, and by his companionship did much to strengthen and confirm Richard in his resolution. He was less ambitious than Dick, and perhaps loved study more for its own sake.

With these explanations we shall now be able to start fairly in our story.

Chapter 2

At the Astor House

THE TWO friends started from their room about seven o'clock, and walked up to Third Avenue, where they jumped on board a horse-car, and within half an hour were landed at the foot of the City Hall Park, opposite Beekman Street. From this point it was necessary only to cross the street to the Astor House.

The Astor House is a massive pile of gray stone, and has a solid look, as if it might stand for hundreds of years. When it was first erected, a little more than thirty years since, it was considered far up town, but now it is far down town, so rapid has been the growth of the city.

Richard Hunter ascended the stone steps with a firm step, but Henry Fosdick lingered behind.

"Do you think we had better go up, Dick?" he said irresolutely.

"Why not?"

"I feel awkward about it."

"There is no reason why you should. The money belongs to you rightfully, as the representative of your father, and it is worth trying for."

"I suppose you are right, but I shan't know what to say."

"I'll help you along if I find you need it. Come along."

Those who possess energy and a strong will generally gain their point, and it was so with Richard Hunter.

They entered the hotel, and, ascending some stone steps, found themselves on the main floor, where the reading-room, clerk's office, and dining-room are located.

Dick, to adopt the familiar name by which his companion addressed him, stepped up to the desk, and drew towards him the book of arrivals. After a brief search he found the name of "Hiram Bates, Milwaukie, Wis.," toward the top of the left-hand page.

"Is Mr. Bates in?" he inquired of the clerk, pointing to the name.

"I will send and inquire, if you will write your name on this card."

Dick thought it would be best to send his own name, as that of Fosdick might lead Mr. Bates to guess the business on which they had come.

He accordingly wrote the name,

RICHARD HUNTER,

in his handsomest handwriting, and handed it to the clerk.

That functionary touched a bell. The summons was answered by a servant.

"James, go to No. 147, and see if Mr. Bates is in. If he is, give him this card."

The messenger departed at once, and returned quickly.

"The gentleman is in, and would be glad to have Mr. Hunter walk up."

"Come along, Fosdick," said Dick, in a low voice.

Fosdick obeyed, feeling very nervous. Following the servant upstairs, they soon stood before No. 147.

James knocked.

"Come in," was heard from the inside, and the two friends entered.

They found themselves in a comfortably furnished room. A man of fifty-five, rather stout in build, and with iron-gray hair, rose from his chair before the fire, and looked rather inquiringly. He seemed rather surprised to find that there were two visitors, as well as at the evident youth of both.

"Mr. Hunter?" he said, inquiringly, looking from one to the other.

"That is my name," said Dick, promptly.

"Have I met you before? If so, my memory is at fault."

"No, sir, we have never met."

"I presume you have business with me. Be seated, if you please."

"First," said Dick, "let me introduce my friend Henry Fosdick."

"Fosdick!" repeated Hiram Bates, with a slight tinge of color.

"I think you knew my father," said Fosdick, nervously.

"Your father was a printer,—was he not?" inquired Mr. Bates.

"Yes, sir."

"I do remember him. Do you come from him?"

Fosdick shook his head.

"He has been dead for two years," he said sadly.

"Dead!" repeated Hiram Bates, as if shocked. "Indeed I am sorry to hear it."

He spoke with evident regret, and Henry Fosdick, whose feelings towards his father's debtor had not been very friendly, noticed this, and was softened by it.

"Did he die in poverty, may I ask?" inquired Mr. Bates, after a pause.

"He was poor," said Fosdick; "that is, he had nothing laid-up; but his wages were enough to support him and myself comfortably."

"Did he have any other family?"

"No sir; my mother died six years since, and I had no brothers or sisters."

"He left no property then?"

"No, sir."

"Then I suppose he was able to make no provision for you?"

"No, sir."

"But you probably had some relatives who came forward and provided for you?"

"No, sir; I had no relatives in New York."

"What then did you do? Excuse my questions, but I have a motive in asking."

"My father died suddenly, having fallen from a Brooklyn ferry-boat and drowned. He left nothing, and I knew of nothing better to do than to go into the streets as a boot-black."

"Surely you are not in that business now?" said Mr. Bates, glacing at Fosdick's neat dress.

"No, sir; I was fortunate enough to find a friend,"— here Fosdick glanced at Dick,—"who helped me along, and encouraged me to apply for a place in a Broadway store. I have been there now for a year and a half."

"What wages do you get? Excuse my curiosity, but your story interests me."

"Eight dollars a week."

"And do you find you can live comfortably on that?"

"Yes, sir; that is, with the assistance of my friend here."

"I am glad you have a friend who is able and willing to help you."

"It is not worth mentioning," said Dick, modestly. "I have received as much help from him as he has from me."

"I see at any rate that you are good friends, and a good friend is worth having. May I ask, Mr. Fosdick, whether you ever heard your father refer to me in any way?"

"Yes, sir."

"You are aware, then, that there were some money arrangements between us?"

"I have heard him say that you had two thousand dollars of his, but that you failed, and that it was lost."

"He informed you rightly. I will tell you the particulars, if you are not already aware of them."

"I should be very glad to hear them, sir. My father died so suddenly that I never knew anything more than that you owed him two thousand dollars."

"Five years since," commenced Mr. Bates, "I was a broker in Wall Street. As from my business I was expected to know the best investments, some persons brought me money to keep for them, and I either agreed to pay them a certain rate of interest, or gave them an interest in my speculations. Among the persons was your father. The way in which I got acquainted with him was this: Having occasion to get some prospectuses of a new company printed, I went to the office with which he was connected. There was some error in the printing, and he was sent to my office to speak with me about it. When our business was concluded, he waited a moment, and then said, 'Mr. Bates, I have saved up two thousand dollars in the last ten years, but I don't know much about investments, and I should consider it a favor if you would advise me.'

" 'I will do so with pleasure,' I said. 'If you desire it I will take charge of it for you, and either allow you six per cent. interest, or give you a share of the profits I may make from investing it.'

"Your father said that he should be glad to have me take the money for him, but he would prefer regular interest to uncertain profits. The next day he brought the money, and put it in my hands. To confess the truth I was glad to have him do so, for I was engaged in extensive speculations, and thought I could make use of it to advantage. For a year I paid him the interest regularly. Then there came a great catastrophe, and I found my brilliant speculations were but bubbles, which broke and left me but a mere pittance, instead of the hundred thousand dollars which I considered myself worth. Of course those who had placed money in my hands suffered, and among them your father. I confess that I regretted his loss as much as that of any one, for I liked his straightforward manner, and was touched by his evident confidence in me."

Mr. Bates paused a moment and then resumed:—

"I left New York, and went to Milwaukie. Here I was obliged to begin life anew, or nearly so, for I only carried a thousand dollars out with me. But I have been greatly prospered since then. I took warning by my past failures, and have succeeded, by care and good fortune, in accumulating nearly as large a fortune as the one of which I once thought myself possessed. When fortune began to smile upon me I thought of your father, and tried through an agent to find him out. But he reported to me that his name was not to be found either in the New York or Brooklyn Directory, and I was too busily engaged to come on myself, and make inquiries. But I am glad to find that his son is living, and that I yet have it in my power to make restitution."

Fosdick could hardly believe his ears. Was he after all to receive the money which he had supposed irrevocably lost?

As for Dick it is not too much to say that he felt even more pleased at the prospective good fortune of his friend than if it had fallen to himself.

Chapter 3

Fosdick's Fortune

MR. BATES took from his pocket a memorandum book, and jotted down a few figures in it.

"As nearly as I can remember," he said, "it is four years since I ceased paying interest on the money which your father entrusted to me. The rate I agreed to pay was six per cent. How much will that amount to?"

"Principal and interest two thousand four hundred and eighty dollars," said Dick, promptly.

Fosdick's breath was almost taken away as he heard this sum mentioned. Could it be possible that Mr. Bates intended to pay him as much as this? Why, it would be a fortune.

"Your figures would be quite correct, Mr. Hunter," said Mr. Bates, "but for one consideration. You forget that your friend is entitled to compound interest, as no interest has been paid for four years. Now, as you are no doubt used to figures, I will leave you to make the necessary correction."

Mr. Bates tore a leaf from his memorandum book as he spoke, and handed it with a pencil to Richard Hunter.

Dick made a rapid calculation, and reported two thousand five hundred and twenty-four dollars.

"It seems, then, Mr. Fosdick," said Mr. Bates, "that I am your debtor to a very considerable amount."

"You are very kind, sir," said Fosdick; "but I shall be quite satisfied with the two thousand dollars without any interest."

"Thank you for offering to relinquish the interest; but it is only right that I should pay it. I have had the use of the money, and I certainly would not wish to defraud you of a penny of the sum which it took your father ten years of industry to accumulate. I wish he were living now to see justice done his son."

"So do I," said Fosdick, earnestly. "I beg your pardon, sir," he said, after a moment's pause.

"Why?" asked Mr. Bates in a tone of surprise.

"Because," said Fosdick, "I have done you injustice. I thought you failed in order to make money, and intended to cheat my father out of his savings. That made me feel hard towards you."

"You were justified in feeling so," said Mr. Bates. "Such cases are so common that I am not surprised at your opinion of me. I ought to have explained my position to your father, and promised to make restitution whenever it should be in my power. But at the time I was discouraged, and could not foresee the favorable turn which my affairs have since taken. Now," he added, with a change of voice, "we will arrange about the payment of this money."

"Do not pay it until it is convenient, Mr. Bates," said Fosdick.

"Your proposal is kind, but scarcely business-like, Mr. Fosdick," said Mr. Bates. "Fortunately it will occasion me no inconvenience to pay you at once. I have not the ready money with me as you may suppose, but I will give you a cheque for the amount upon the Broadway Bank, with which I have an account; and it will be duly honored on presentation to-morrow. You may in return make out a receipt in full for the debt and interest. Wait a moment. I will ring for writing materials."

These were soon brought by a servant of the hotel, and Mr. Bates filled in a cheque for the sum specified above, while Fosdick, scarcely knowing whether he was awake or dreaming, made out a receipt to which he attached his name.

"Now," said Mr. Bates, "we will exchange documents."

Fosdick took the cheque, and deposited it carefully in his pocket-book.

"It is possible that payment might be refused to a boy like you, especially as the amount is so large. At what time will you be disengaged to-morrow?"

"I am absent from the store from twelve to one for dinner."

"Very well, come to the hotel as soon as you are free, and I will accompany you to the bank, and get the money for you. I advise you, however, to leave it there on deposit until you have a chance to invest it."

"How would you advise me to invest it, sir?" asked Fosdick.

"Perhaps you cannot do better than buy shares of some good bank. You will then have no care except to collect your dividends twice a year."

"That is what I should like to do," said Fosdick. "What bank would you advise?"

"The Broadway, Park, or Bank of Commerce, are all good banks. I will attend to the matter for you, if you desire it."

"I should be very glad if you would, sir."

"Then that matter is settled," said Mr. Bates. "I wish I could as easily settle another matter which has brought me to New York at this time, and which, I confess, occasions me considerable perplexity."

The boys remained respectfully silent, though not without curiosity as to what this matter might be.

Mr. Bates seemed plunged in thought for a short time. Then speaking, as if to himself, he said, in a low voice, "Why should I not tell them? Perhaps they may help me."

"I believe," he said, "I will take you into my confidence. You may be able to render me some assistance in my perplexing business."

"I shall be very glad to help you if I can," said Dick.

"And I also," said Fosdick.

"I have come to New York in search of my grandson," said Mr. Bates.

"Did he run away from home?" asked Dick.

"No, he has never lived with me. Indeed, I may add that I have never seen him since he was an infant."

The boys looked surprised.

"How old is he now?" asked Fosdick.

"He must be about ten years old. But I see that I must give you the whole story of what is a painful passage in my life, or you will be in no position to help me.

"You must know, then, that twelve years since I considered myself rich, and lived in a handsome house up town. My wife was dead, but I had an only daughter, who I believe was generally considered attractive, if not beautiful. I had set my heart upon her making an advantageous marriage; that is, marrying a man of wealth and social position. I had in my employ a clerk, of excellent business abilities, and of good personal appearance, whom I sometimes invited to my house when I entertained company. His name was John Talbot. I never suspected that there was any danger of my daughter's falling in love with the young man, until one day he came to me, and overwhelmed me with surprise by asking her hand in marriage.

"You can imagine that I was very angry, whether justly or not I will not pretend to say. I dismissed the young man from my employ, and informed him that never, under any circumstances, would I consent to his marrying Irene. He was a high-spirited young man, and, though he did not answer me, I saw by the expression of his face that he meant to persevere in his suit.

"A week later my daughter was missing. She left behind a letter stating that she could not give up John Talbot, and by the time I read the letter she would be his wife. Two days later a Philadelphia paper was sent me containing a printed notice of their marriage, and the same mail brought me a joint letter from both, asking my forgiveness.

"I had no objections to John Talbot except his poverty; but my ambitious hopes were disappointed, and I felt the blow severely. I returned the letter to the address given, accompanied by a brief line to Irene, to the effect that I disowned her, and would never more acknowledge her as my daughter.

"I saw her only once after that. Two years after, she appeared suddenly in my library, having been admitted by the servant, with a child in her arms. But I hardened my heart against her, and though she besought my forgiveness, I refused it, and requested her to leave the house. I cannot forgive myself when I think of my unfeeling severity. But it is too late to redeem the past. As far as I can I would like to atone for it.

"A month since I heard that both Irene and her husband were dead, the latter five years since, but that the child, a boy, is still living, probably in deep poverty. He is my only descendant, and I seek to find him, hoping that he may be a joy and solace to me in the old age which will soon be upon me. It is for the purpose of tracing him that I have come to New York. When you," turning to Fosdick, "referred to your being compelled to resort to the streets, and the hard life of a boot-black, the thought came to me that my grandson may be reduced to a similar extremity. It would be hard indeed that he should grow up ignorant, neglected, and subject to every privation, when a comfortable and even luxurious home awaits him, if he can only be found."

"What is his name?" inquired Dick.

"My impression is, that he was named after his father, John Talbot. Indeed, I am quite sure that my daughter wrote me to this effect in a letter which I returned after reading."

"Have you reason to think he is in New York?"

"My information is, that his mother died here a year since. It is not likely that he has been able to leave the city."

"He is about ten years old?"

"I used to know most of the boot-blacks and newsboys when I was in the business," said Dick, reflectively; "but I cannot recall that name."

"Were you ever in the business, Mr. Hunter?" asked Mr. Bates, in surprise.

"Yes," said Richard Hunter, smiling; "I used to be

one of the most ragged boot-blacks in the city. Don't you remember my Washington coat, and Napoleon pants, Fosdick?"

"Surely that was many years ago?"

"I remember them well."

"It is not yet two years since I gave up blacking boots."

"You surprise me Mr. Hunter," said Mr. Bates. "I congratulate you on your advance in life. Such a rise shows remarkable energy on your part."

"I was lucky," said Dick, modestly. "I found some good friends who helped me along. But about your grandson: I have quite a number of friends among the street-boys, and I can inquire of them whether any boy named John Talbot has joined their ranks since my time."

"I shall be greatly obliged to you if you will," said Mr. Bates. "But it is quite possible that circumstances may have led to a change of name, so that it will not do to trust too much to this. Even if no boy bearing that name is found, I shall feel that there is this possibility in my favor."

"That is true," said Dick. "It is very common for boys to change their name. Some can't remember whether they ever had any names, and pick one out to suit themselves, or perhaps get one from those they go with. There was one boy I knew named 'Horace Greeley.' Then there were 'Fat Jack,' 'Pickle Nose,' 'Cranky Jim,' 'Tickle-me-foot,' and plenty of others.* You knew some of them, didn't you, Fosdick?"

"I knew 'Fat Jack' and 'Tickle-me-Foot,'" answered Fosdick.

"This of course increases the difficulty of finding and identifying the boy," said Mr. Bates. "Here," he said, taking a card photograph from his pocket, "is a picture of my daughter at the time of her marriage. I have had these taken from a portrait in my possession."

---

* See sketches of the Formation of the Newsboys' Lodging-house, by C. L. Brace, Secretary of the Children's Aid Society.

"Can you spare me one?" asked Dick. "It may help me to find the boy."

"I will give one to each of you. I need not say that I shall feel most grateful for any service you may be able to render me, and will gladly reimburse any expenses you may incur, besides paying you liberally for your time. It will be better perhaps for me to leave fifty dollars with each of you to defray any expenses you may be at."

"Thank you," said Dick; "but I am well supplied with money, and will advance whatever is needful, and if I succeed I will hand in my bill."

Fosdick expressed himself in a similar way, and after some further conversation he and Dick rose to go.

"I congratulate you on your wealth, Fosdick," said Dick, when they were outside. "You're richer than I am now."

"I never should have got this money but for you, Dick. I wish you'd take some of it."

"Well, I will. You may pay my fare home on the horse-cars."

"But really I wish you would."

But this Dick positively refused to do, as might have been expected. He was himself the owner of two up-town lots, which he eventually sold for five thousand dollars, though they only cost him one, and had three hundred dollars besides in the bank. He agreed, however, to let Fosdick henceforth bear his share of the expenses of board, and this added two dollars a week to the sum he was able to lay up.

Chapter 4

A Difficult Commission

IT NEED hardly be said that Fosdick was punctual to his appointment at the Astor House on the following day.

He found Mr. Bates in the reading-room, looking over a Milwaukie paper.

"Good-morning, Mr. Fosdick," he said, extending his hand. "I suppose your time is limited, therefore it will be best for us to go at once to the bank."

"You are very kind, sir, to take so much trouble on my account," said Fosdick.

"We ought all to help each other," said Mr. Bates. "I believe in that doctrine, though I have not always lived up to it. On second thoughts," he added, as they got out in front of the hotel, "if you approve of my suggestions about the purchase of bank shares, it may not be necessary to go to the bank, as you can take this cheque in payment."

"Just as you think best, sir. I can depend upon your judgment, as you know much more of such things than I."

"Then we will go at once to the office of Mr. Ferguson, a Wall Street broker, and an old friend of mine. There we will give an order for some bank shares."

Together the two walked down Broadway until they reached Trinity Church, which fronts the entrance to Wall Street. Here then they crossed the street, and soon reached the office of Mr. Ferguson.

Mr. Ferguson, a pleasant-looking man with sandy hair

and whiskers, came forward and shook Mr. Bates cordially by the hand.

"Glad to see you, Mr. Bates," he said. "Where have you been for the last four years?"

"In Milwaukie. I see you are at the old place."

"Yes, plodding along as usual. How do you like the West?"

"I have found it a good place for business, though I am not sure whether I like it as well to live in as New York."

"Shan't you come back to New York some time?"

Mr. Bates shook his head.

"My business ties me to Milwaukie," he said. I doubt if I shall ever return."

"Who is this young man?" said the broker, looking at Fosdick. "He is not a son of yours, I think?"

"No; I am not fortunate enough to have a son. He is a young friend who wants a little business done in your line and I have accordingly brought him to you."

"We will do our best for him. What is it?"

"He wants to purchase twenty shares in some good city bank. I used to know all about such matters when I lived in the city, but I am out of the way of such knowledge now."

"Twenty shares, you said?"

"Yes."

"It happens quite oddly that a party brought in only fifteen minutes since twenty shares in the — Bank to dispose of. It is a good bank, and I don't know that he can do any better than take them."

"Yes, it is a good bank. What interest does it pay now?"

"Eight per cent."*

"That is good. What is the market value of the stock?"

"It is selling this morning at one hundred and twenty."

"Twenty shares then will amount to twenty-four hundred dollars."

"Precisely."

---

* This was before the war. Now most of the National Banks in New York pay ten per cent., and some even higher.

"Well, perhaps we had better take them. What do you say, Mr. Fosdick?"

"If you advise it, sir, I shall be very glad to do so."

"Then the business can be accomplished at once, as the party left us his signature, authorizing the transfer."

The transfer was rapidly effected. The broker's commission of twenty-five cents per share amounted to five dollars. It was found on paying this, added to the purchase money, that one hundred and nineteen dollars remained,—the cheque being for two thousand five hundred and twenty-four dollars.

The broker took the cheque, and returned this sum, which Mr. Bates handed to Fosdick.

"You may need this for a reserve fund," he said, "to draw upon if needful until your dividend comes due. The bank shares will pay you probably one hundred and sixty dollars per year."

"One hundred and sixty dollars!" repeated Fosdick, in surprise. "That is a little more than three dollars a week."

"Yes."

"It will be very acceptable, as my salary at the store is not enough to pay my expenses."

"I would advise you not to break in upon your capital if you can avoid it," said Mr. Bates. "By and by, if your salary increases, you may be able to add the interest yearly to the principal, so that it may be accumulating till you are a man, when you may find it of use in setting you up in business."

"Yes, sir; I will remember that. But I can hardly realize that I am really the owner of twenty bank shares."

"No doubt it seems sudden to you. Don't let it make you extravagant. Most boys of your age would need a guardian, but you have had so much experience in taking care of yourself, that I think you can get along without one."

"I have my friend Dick to advise me," said Fosdick.

"Mr. Hunter seems quite a remarkable young man," said Mr. Bates. "I can hardly believe that his past history has been as he gave it."

"It is strictly true, sir. Three years ago he could not read or write."

"If he continues to display the same energy, I can predict for him a prominent position in the future."

"I am glad to hear you say so, sir. Dick is a very dear friend of mine."

"Now, Mr. Fosdick, it is time you were thinking of dinner. I believe this is your dinner hour?"

"Yes, sir."

"And it is nearly over. You must be my guest to-day. I know of a quiet little lunch room near by, which I used to frequent some years ago when I was in business on this street. We will drop in there, and I think you will be able to get through in time."

Fosdick could not well decline the invitation, but accompanied Mr. Bates to the place referred to, where he had a better meal than he was accustomed to. It was finished in time, for as the clock on the city hall struck one, he reached the door of Henderson's store.

Fosdick could not very well banish from his mind the thoughts of his extraordinary change of fortune, and I am obliged to confess that he did not discharge his duties quite as faithfully as usual that afternoon. I will mention one rather amusing instance of his preoccupation of mind.

A lady entered the store, leading by the hand her son Edwin, a little boy of seven.

"Have you any hats that will fit my little boy?" she said.

"Yes, ma'am," said Fosdick, absently, and brought forward a large-sized man's hat, of the kind popularly known as "stove-pipe."

"How will this do?" asked Fosdick.

"I don't want to wear such an ugly hat as that," said Edwin, in dismay.

The lady looked at Fosdick as if she had very strong doubts of his sanity. He saw his mistake, and, coloring deeply, said, in a hurried tone, "Excuse me; I was thinking of something else."

The next selection proved more satisfactory, and Edwin went out of the store feeling quite proud of his new hat.

Towards the close of the afternoon, Fosdick was surprised at the entrance of Mr. Bates. He came up to the counter where he was standing, and said, "I am glad I have found you in. I was not quite sure if this was the place where you were employed."

"I am glad to see you, sir," said Fosdick.

"I have just received a telegram from Milwaukie," said Mr. Bates, "summoning me home immediately on matters connected with business. I shall not therefore be able to remain here to follow up the search upon which I had entered. As you and your friend have kindly offered your assistance, I am going to leave the matter in your hands, and will authorize you to incur any expenses you may deem advisable, and I will gladly reimburse you whether you succeed or not."

Fosdick assured him that they would spare no efforts, and Mr. Bates, after briefly thanking him, and giving him his address, hurried away, as he had determined to start on his return home that very night.

Chapter 5

Introduces Mark, the Match Boy

IT WAS growing dark, though yet scarcely six o'clock, for the day was one of the shortest in the year, when a small boy, thinly clad, turned down Frankfort Street on the corner opposite French's Hotel. He had come up Nassau Street, passing the "Tribune" Office and the old Tammany Hall, now superseded by the substantial new "Sun" building.

He had a box of matches under his arm, of which very few seemed to have been sold. He had a weary, spiritless air, and walked as if quite tired. He had been on his feet all day, and was faint with hunger, having eaten nothing but an apple to sustain his strength. The thought that he was near his journey's end did not seem to cheer him much. Why this should be so will speedily appear.

He crossed William Street, passed Gold Street, and turned down Vandewater Street, leading out of Frankfort's Street on the left. It is in the form of a short curve, connecting with that most crooked of all New York avenues, Pearl Street. He paused in front of a shabby house, and went upstairs. The door of a room on the third floor was standing ajar. He pushed it open, and entered, not without a kind of shrinking.

A coarse-looking woman was seated before a scanty fire. She had just thrust a bottle into her pocket after taking a copious draught therefrom, and her flushed face showed that this had long been a habit with her.

"Well, Mark, what luck to-night?" she said, in a husky voice.

"I didn't sell much," said the boy.

"Didn't sell much? Come here," said the woman, sharply.

Mark came up to her side, and she snatched the box from him, angrily.

"Only three boxes gone?" she repeated. "What have you been doing all day?"

She added to the question a coarse epithet which I shall not repeat.

"I tried to sell them, indeed I did, Mother Watson, indeed I did," said the boy, earnestly, "but everybody had bought them already."

"You didn't try," said the woman addressed as Mother Watson. "You're too lazy, that's what's the matter. You don't earn your salt. Now give me the money."

Mark drew from his pocket a few pennies, and handed to her.

She counted them over, and then, looking up sharply, said, with a frown, "There's a penny short. Where is it?"

"I was so hungry," pleaded Mark, "that I bought an apple,—only a little one."

"You bought an apple, did you?" said the woman, menacingly. "So that's the way you spend my money, you little thief?"

"I was so faint and hungry," again pleaded the boy.

"What business had you to be hungry? Didn't you have some breakfast this morning?"

"I had a piece of bread."

"That's more than you earned. You'll eat me out of house and home, you little thief! But I'll pay you off. I'll give you something to take away your appetite. You won't be hungry any more, I reckon."

She dove her flabby hand into her pocket, and produced a strap, at which the boy gazed with a frightened look.

"Don't beat me, Mother Watson," he said, imploringly.

"I'll beat the laziness out of you," said the woman, vindictively. "See if I don't."

She clutched Mark by the collar, and was about to bring the strap down forcibly upon his back, ill protected by his thin jacket, when a visitor entered the room.

"What's the matter, Mrs. Watson?" asked the intruder.

"Oh, it's you, Mrs. Flanagan?" said the woman, holding the strap suspended in the air. "I'll tell you what's the matter. This little thief has come home, after selling only three boxes of matches the whole day, and I find he's stole a penny to buy an apple with. It's for that I'm goin' to beat him."

"Oh, let him alone, the poor lad," said Mrs. Flanagan, who was a warm-hearted Irish woman. "Maybe he was hungry."

"Then why didn't he work? Them that work can eat."

"Maybe people didn't want to buy."

"Well, I can't afford to keep him in his idleness," said Mrs. Watson. "He may go to bed without his supper."

"If he can't sell his matches, maybe people would give him something."

Mrs. Watson evidently thought favorably of this suggestion, for, turning to Mark, she said, "Go out again, you little thief, and mind you don't come in again till you've got twenty-five cents to bring to me. Do you mind that?"

Mark listened, but stood irresolute.

"I don't like to beg," he said.

"Don't like to beg!" screamed Mrs. Watson. "Do you mind that, now, Mrs. Flanagan? He's too proud to beg."

"Mother told me never to beg if I could help it," said Mark.

"Well, you can't help it," said the woman, flourishing the strap in a threatening manner. "Do you see this?"

"Yes."

"Well, you'll feel it too, if you don't do as I tell you. Go out now."

"I'm so hungry," said Mark; "won't you give me a piece of bread?"

"Not a mouthful till you bring back twenty-five cents. Start now, or you'll feel the strap."

The boy left the room with a slow step, and wearily

descended the stairs. I hope my young readers will never know the hungry craving after food which tormented the poor little boy as he made his way towards the street. But he had hardly reached the foot of the first staircase when he heard a low voice behind him, and, turning, beheld Mrs. Flanagan, who had hastily followed after him.

"Are you very hungry?" she asked.

"Yes, I'm faint with hunger."

"Poor boy!" she said, compassionately; "come in here a minute."

She opened the door of her own room, which was just at the foot of the staircase, and gently pushed him in.

It was a room of the same general appearance as the one above, but was much neater looking.

"Biddy Flanagan isn't the woman to let a poor motherless child go hungry when she's a bit of bread or meat by her. Here, Mark, lad, sit down, and I'll soon bring you something that'll warm up your poor stomach."

She opened a cupboard, and brought out a plate containing a small quantity of cold beef, and two slices of bread.

"There's some better mate than you'll get of Mother Watson. "It's cold, but it's good."

"She never gives me any meat at all," said Mark, gazing with a look of eager anticipation at the plate which to his famished eye looked so inviting.

"I'll be bound she don't," said Mrs. Flanagan. "Talk of you being lazy! What does she do herself but sit all day doing nothin' except drink whiskey from the black bottle! She might get washin' to do, as I do, if she wanted to, but she won't work. She expects you to get money enough for both of you."

Meanwhile Mrs. Flanagan had poured out a cup of tea from an old tin teapot that stood on the stove.

"There, drink that, Mark dear," she said. "It'll warm you up, and you'll need it this cold night, I'm thinkin'."

The tea was not of the best quality, and the cup was cracked and discolored; but to Mark it was grateful and refreshing, and he eagerly drank it.

"Is it good?" asked the sympathizing woman, observ-

ing with satisfaction the eagerness with which it was
drunk.

"Yes, it makes me feel warm," said Mark.

"It's better nor the whiskey Mother Watson drinks,"
said Mrs. Flanagan. "It won't make your nose red like
hers. It would be a sight better for her if she'd throw
away the whiskey, and take to the tea."

"You are very kind, Mrs. Flanagan," said Mark, rising
from the table, feeling fifty per cent. better than when
he sat down.

"Oh bother now, don't say a word about it! Shure
you're welcome to the bit you've eaten, and the little sup
of tea. Come in again when you feel hungry, and Bridget
Flanagan won't be the woman to send you off hungry if
she's got anything in the cupboard."

"I wish Mother Watson was as good as you are," said
Mark.

"I aint so good as I might be," said Mrs. Flanagan;
"but I wouldn't be guilty of tratin' a poor boy as that
woman trates you, more shame to her! How came you
with her any way? She aint your mother, is she."

"No," said Mark, shuddering at the bare idea. "My
mother was a good woman, and worked hard. She didn't
drink whiskey. Mother was always kind to me. I wish she
was alive now."

"When did she die, Mark dear?"

"It's going on a year since she died. I didn't know what
to do, but Mother Watson told me to come and live with
her, and she'd take care of me."

"Sorra a bit of kindness there was in that," commented
Mrs. Flanagan. "She wanted you to take care of her.
Well, and what did she make you do?"

"She sent me out to earn what I could. Sometimes I
would run on errands, but lately I have sold matches."

"Is it hard work sellin' them?"

"Sometimes I do pretty well, but some days it seems as
if nobody wanted any. To-day I went round to a great
many offices, but they all had as many as they wanted,
and I didn't sell but three boxes. I tried to sell more, indeed I did, but I couldn't."

"No doubt you did Mark dear. It's cold you must be in that thin jacket of yours this cold weather. I've got a shawl you may wear if you like. You'll not lose it, I know."

But Mark had a boy's natural dislike to being dressed as a girl, knowing, moreover, that his appearance in the street with Mrs. Flanagan's shawl would subject him to the jeers of the street boys. So he declined the offer with thanks, and, buttoning up his thin jacket, descended the remaining staircase, and went out again into the chilling and uninviting street. A chilly, drizzling rain had just set in, and this made it even more dreary than it had been during the day.

Chapter 6

Ben Gibson

BUT IT WAS not so much the storm or the cold weather that Mark cared for. He had become used to these, so far as one can become used to what is very disagreeable. If after a hard day's work he had had a good home to come back to, or a kind and sympathizing friend, he would have had that thought to cheer him up. But Mother Watson cared nothing for him, except for the money he brought her, and Mark found it impossible either to cherish love or respect for the coarse woman whom he generally found more or less affected by whiskey.

Cold and hungry as he had been oftentimes, he had always shrunk from begging. It seemed to lower him in his own thoughts to ask charity of others. Mother Watson had suggested it to him once or twice, but had never actually commanded it before. Now he was required to bring home twenty-five cents. He knew very well what would be the result if he failed to do this. Mother Watson would apply the leather strap with merciless fury, and he knew that his strength was as nothing compared to hers. So, for the first time in his life, he felt that he must make up his mind to beg.

He retraced his steps to the head of Frankfort Street, and walked slowly down Nassau Street. The rain was falling, as I have said, and those who could remained under shelter. Besides, business hours were over. The thousands who during the day made the lower part of the city a busy hive had gone to their homes in the upper portion of the island, or across the river to Brooklyn or the towns on the Jersey shore. So, however willing he might be to beg, there did not seem to be much chance at present.

The rain increased, and Mark in his thin clothes was soon drenched to the skin. He felt damp, cold, and uncomfortable. But there was no rest for him. The only home he had was shut to him, unless he should bring home twenty-five cents, and of this there seemed very little prospect.

At the corner of Fulton Street he fell in with a boy of twelve, short and sturdy in frame, dressed in a coat whose tails nearly reached the sidewalk. Though scarcely in the fashion, it was warmer than Mark's, and the proprietor troubled himself very little about the looks.

This boy, whom Mark recognized as Ben Gibson, had a clay pipe in his mouth, which he seemed to be smoking with evident enjoyment.

"Where you goin'?" he asked, halting in front of Mark.

"I don't know," said Mark.

"Don't know!" repeated Ben, taking his pipe from his mouth, and spitting. "Where's your matches?"

"I left them at home."

"Then what'd you come out for in this storm?"

"The woman I live with won't let me come home till I've brought her twenty-five cents."

"How'd you expect to get it?"

"She wants me to beg."

"That's a good way," said Ben, approvingly; "when you get hold of a soft chap, or a lady. Them's the ones to shell out."

"I don't like it," said Mark. "I don't want people to think me a beggar."

"What's the odds?" said Ben, philosophically. "You're just the chap to make a good beggar."

"What do you mean by that, Ben?" said Mark, who was far from considering this much of a compliment.

"Why you're a thin, pale little chap, that people will

pity easy. Now I aint the right cut for a beggar. I tried it once, but it was no go."

"Why not?" asked Mark, who began to be interested in spite of himself.

"You see," said Ben, again puffing out a volume of smoke, "I look too tough, as if I could take care of myself. People don't pity me. I tried it one night when I was hard up. I hadn't got but six cents, and I wanted to go to the Old Bowery bad. So I went up to a gent as was comin' up Wall Street from the Ferry, and said, 'Won't you give a poor boy a few pennies to save him from starvin'?'

" 'So you're almost starvin', are you, my lad?' says he.

" 'Yes, sir,' said I, as faint as I could.

" 'Well, starvin' seems to agree with you,' says he, laughin'. 'You're the healthiest-lookin' beggar I've seen in a good while.'

"I tried it again on another gent, and he told me he guessed I was lazy; that a good stout boy like me ought to work. So I didn't make much beggin', and had to give up goin' to the Old Bowery that night, which I was precious sorry for, for there was a great benefit that evenin'. Been there often?"

"No, I never went."

"Never went to the Old Bowery!" ejaculated Ben, whistling in his amazement. "Where were you raised, I'd like to know? I should think you was a country greeny, I should."

"I never had a chance," said Mark, who began to feel a little ashamed of the confession.

"Won't your old woman let you go?"

"I never have any money to go."

"If I was flush I'd take you myself. It's only fifteen cents," said Ben. "But I haven't got money enough only for one ticket. I'm goin' to-night."

"Are you?" asked Mark, a little enviously.

"Yes, it's a good way to pass a rainy evenin'. You've got a warm room to be in, let alone the play, which is splendid. Now, if you could only beg fifteen cents from some charitable cove, you might go along of me."

"If I get any money I've got to carry it home."

"Suppose you don't, will the old woman cut up rough?"

"She'll beat me with a strap," said Mark, shuddering.

"What makes you let her do it?" demanded Ben, rather disdainfully.

"I can't help it."

"She wouldn't beat me," said Ben, decidedly.

"What would you do?" asked Mark, with interest.

"What would I do?" retorted Ben. "I'd kick, and bite, and give her one for herself between the eyes. That's what I'd do. She'd find me a hard case, I reckon."

"It wouldn't be any use for me to try that," said Mark. "She's too strong."

"It don't take much to handle you," said Ben, taking a critical survey of the physical points of Mark. "You're most light enough to blow away."

"I'm only ten years old," said Mark, apologetically. "I shall be bigger some time."

"Maybe," said Ben, dubiously; "but you don't look as if you'd ever be tough like me."

"There," he added, after a pause, "I've smoked all my 'baccy. I wish I'd got some more."

"Do you like to smoke?" asked Mark.

"It warms a feller up," said Ben. "It's jest the thing for a cold, wet day like this. Didn't you ever try it?"

"No."

"If I'd got some 'baccy here, I'd give you a whiff; but I think it would make you sick the first time."

"I don't think I should like it," said Mark, who had never felt any desire to smoke, though he knew plenty of boys who indulged in the habit.

"That's because you don't know nothin' about it," remarked Ben. "I didn't like it at first till I got learned."

"Do you smoke often?"

"Every day after I get through blackin' boots; that is, when I ain't hard up, and can't raise the stamps to pay for the 'baccy. But I guess I'll be goin' up to the Old Bowery. It's most time for the doors to open. Where you goin'?"

"I don't know where to go," said Mark, helplessly.

"I'll tell you where you'd better go. You won't find nobody round here. Besides it aint comfortable lettin' the rain fall on you and wet you through." (While this conversation was going on, the boys had sheltered themselves in a doorway.) "Just you go down to Fulton Market. There you'll be out of the wet, and you'll see plenty of people passin' through when the boats come in. Maybe some of 'em will give you somethin'. Then ag'in, there's the boats. Some nights I sleep aboard the boats."

"You do? Will they let you?"

"They don't notice. I just pay my two cents, and go aboard, and snuggle up in a corner and go to sleep. So I ride to Brooklyn and back all night. That's cheaper'n the Newsboys' Lodgin' House, for it only costs two cents. One night a gentleman came to me, and woke me up, and said, 'We've got to Brooklyn, my lad. If you don't get up they'll carry you back again.'

"I jumped up and told him I was much obliged, as I didn't know what my family would say if I didn't get home by eleven o'clock. Then, just as soon as his back was turned, I sat down again and went to sleep. It aint so bad sleepin' aboard the boat, 'specially in a cold night. They keep the cabin warm, and though the seat isn't partic'larly soft its better'n bein' out in the street. If you don't get your twenty-five cents, and are afraid of a lickin', you'd better sleep aboard the boat."

"Perhaps I will," said Mark, to whom the idea was not unwelcome, for it would at all events save him for that night from the beating which would be his portion if he came home without the required sum.

"Well, good-night," said Ben; "I'll be goin' along."

"Good-night, Ben," said Mark, "I guess I'll go to Fulton Market."

Accordingly Mark turned down Fulton Street, while Ben steered in the direction of Chatham Street, through which it was necessary to pass in order to reach the theatre, which is situated on the Bowery, not far from its junction with Chatham Street.

Ben Gibson is a type of a numerous class of improvident boys, who live on from day to day, careless of appearances, spending their evenings where they can, at the theatre when their means admit, and sometimes at gambling saloons. Not naturally bad, they drift into bad habits from the force of outward circumstances. They early learn to smoke or chew, finding in tobacco some comfort during the cold and wet days, either ignorant of or indifferent to the harm which the insidious weed will do to their constitution. So their growth is checked, or their blood is impoverished, as is shown by their pale faces.

As for Ben, he was gifted with a sturdy frame and an excellent constitution, and appeared as yet to exhibit none of the baneful effects of this habit. But no growing boy can smoke without ultimately being affected by it, and such will no doubt be the case with Ben.

Chapter 7

Fulton Market

JUST ACROSS from Fulton Ferry stands Fulton Market. It is nearly fifty years old, having been built in 1821, on ground formerly occupied by unsightly wooden buildings, which were, perhaps fortunately, swept away by fire. It covers the block bounded by Fulton, South, Beekman, and Front Streets, and was erected at a cost of about a quarter of a million of dollars.

This is the chief of the great city markets, and an immense business is done here. There is hardly an hour in the twenty-four in which there is an entire lull in the business of the place. Some of the outside shops and booths are kept open all night, while the supplies of fish, meats, and vegetables for the market proper are brought at a very early hour, almost before it can be called morning.

Besides the market proper the surrounding sidewalks are roofed over, and lined with shops and booths of the most diverse character, at which almost every conceivable article can be purchased. Most numerous, perhaps, are the chief restaurants, the counters loaded with cakes and pies, with a steaming vessel of coffee smoking at one end. The floors are sanded, and the accommodations are far from elegant or luxurious; but it is said that the viands are by no means to be despised. Then there are fruit-stalls with tempting heaps of oranges, apples, and in their season the fruits of summer, presided over for the most part by old women, who scan shrewdly the faces of passers-by, and are ready on the smallest provocation to vaunt the merits of their wares. There are candy and cocoanut cakes for those who have a sweet tooth, and many a shop-boy invests in these on his way to or from Brooklyn to the New York store where he is employed; or the father of a family, on his way to his Brooklyn home, thinks of the little ones awaiting him, and indulges in a purchase of what he knows will be sure to be acceptable to them.

But it is not only the wants of the body that are provided for at Fulton Market. On the Fulton Street side may be found extensive booths, at which are displayed for sale a tempting array of papers, magazines, and books, as well as stationery, photograph albums, etc., generally at prices twenty or thirty per cent. lower than is demanded for them in the more pretentious Broadway or Fulton Avenue stores.

Even at night. therefore. the outer portion of the market presents a bright and cheerful shelter from the inclement weather, being securely roofed over, and well lighted. while some of the booths are kept open, however late the hour.

Ben Gibson, therefore, was right in directing Mark to Fulton Market, as probably the most comfortable place to be found in the pouring rain which made the thoroughfares dismal and dreary. Mark, of course, had been in Fulton Market often. and saw at once the wisdom of the advice. He ran down Fulton Street as fast as he could, and arrived there panting and wet to the skin. Uncomfortable as he was. the change from the wet streets to the bright and comparatively warm shelter of the market made him at once more cheerful. In fact, it compared favorably with the cold and uninviting room which he shared with Mother Watson.

As Mark looked around him. he could not help wishing that he tended in one of the little restaurants that looked so bright and inviting to him. Those who are accustomed to lunch at Delmonico's, or at some of the large and stylish hotels, or have their meals served by attentive servants in brown stone dwellings in the more fashionable quarters of the city, would be likely to turn up their noses at his humble taste, and would feel it an infliction to take a meal amid such plebeian surroundings. But then Mark knew nothing about the fare at Delmonico's, and was far enough from living in a brown stone front, and so his ideas of happiness and luxury were not very exalted, or he would scarcely have envied a stout butcher boy whem he saw sitting at an unpainted wooden table, partaking of a repast which was more abundant than choice.

But from the surrounding comfort Mark's thoughts were brought back to the disagreeable business which brought him here. He was to solicit charity from some one of the passers-by, and with a sigh he began to look about him to select some compassionate face.

"If there was only somebody here that wanted an errand done," he thought, "and would pay me twenty-five cents for doing it, I wouldn't have to beg. I'd rather work two hours for the money than beg it."

But there seemed little chance of this. In the busy portion of the day there might have been some chance, though this would be uncertain; but now it was very improbable. If he wanted to get twenty-five cents that night he must get it from charity.

A beginning must be made, however disagreeable. So Mark went up to a young man who was passing along on his way to the boat, and in a shamefaced manner said, "Will you give me a few pennies, please?"

The young man looked good-natured, and it was that which gave Mark confidence to address him.

"You want some pennies, do you?" he said, with a smile, pausing in his walk.

"If you please, sir."

"I suppose your wife and family are starving, eh?"

"I haven't got any wife or family, sir," said Mark.

"But you've got a sick mother, or some brothers or sisters that are starving, haven't you?"

"No, sir."

"Then I'm afraid you're not up to your business. How long have you been round begging?"

"Never before," said Mark, rather indignantly.

"Ah, that accounts for it. You haven't learned the business yet. After a few weeks you'll have a sick mother starving at home. They all do, you know."

"My mother is dead," said Mark; "I shan't tell a lie to get money."

"Come, you're rather a remarkable boy," said the young man, who was a reporter on a daily paper, going over to attend a meeting in Brooklyn, to write an account of it to appear in one of the city dailies in the morning. "I don't generally give money in such cases, but I must make an exception in your case."

He drew a dime from his vest-pocket and handed it to Mark.

Mark took it with a blush of mortification at the necessity.

"I wouldn't beg if I could help it," he said, desiring to justify himself in the eyes of the good-natured young man.

"I'm glad to hear that, Johnny." (Johnny is a common name applied to boys whose names are unknown.) "It isn't a very creditable business. What makes you beg, then?"

"I shall be beaten if I don't," said Mark.

"That's bad. Who will beat you?"

"Mother Watson."

"Tell Mother Watson, with my compliments, that she's a wicked old tyrant. I'll tell you what, my lad, you must grow as fast as you can, and by and by you'll get too large for that motherly old woman to whip. But there goes the bell. I must be getting aboard."

This was the result of Mark's first begging appeal. He looked at the money, and wished he had got it in any other way. If it had been the reward of an hour's work he would have gazed at it with much greater satisfaction.

Well, he had made a beginning. He had got ten cents. But there still remained fifteen cents to obtain, and without that he did not feel safe in going back.

So he looked about him for another person to address. This time he thought he would ask a lady. Accordingly he went up to one, who was walking with her son, a boy of sixteen, to judge from appearance, and asked for a few pennies.

"Get out of my way, you little beggar!" she said, in a disagreeable tone. "Aint you ashamed of yourself, going round begging, instead of earning money like honest people?"

"I've been trying to earn money all day," said Mark, rather indignant at this attack.

"Oh no doubt," sneered the woman. "I don't think you'll hurt yourself with work."

"I was round the streets all day trying to sell matches," said Mark.

"You mustn't believe what he says, mother," said the boy. "They're all a set of humbugs, and will lie as fast as they can talk."

"I've no doubt of it, Roswell," said Mrs. Crawford. "Such little impostors never get anything out of me. I've got other uses for my money."

Mark was a gentle, peaceful boy, but such attacks naturally made him indignant.

"I am not an impostor, and I neither lie nor steal," he said, looking alternately from the mother to the son.

"Oh, you're a fine young man, I've no doubt," said Roswell, with a sneer. "But we'd better be getting on, mother, unless you mean to stop in Fulton Market all night."

So mother and son passed on, leaving Mark with a sense of mortification and injury. He would have given the ten cents he had, not to have asked charity of this woman who had answered him so unpleasantly.

Those of my readers who have read the two preceding volumes of this series will recognize in Roswell Crawford and his mother old acquaintances who played an important part in the former stories. As, however, I may have some new readers, it may be as well to explain that Roswell was a self-conceited boy, who prided himself on being "the son of a gentleman," and whose great desire was to find a place where the pay would be large and the duties very small. Unfortunately for his pride, his father had failed in business shortly before he died, and his mother had been compelled to keep a boarding-house. She, too, was troubled with a pride very similar to that of her son, and chafed inwardly at her position, instead of reconciling herself to it, as many better persons have done.

Roswell was not very fortunate in retaining the positions he obtained, being generally averse to doing anything except what he was absolutely obliged to do. He had lost a situation in a dry-goods store in Sixth Avenue, because he objected to carrying bundles, considering it beneath the dignity of a gentleman's son. Some months before he had tried to get Richard Hunter discharged from his situation in the hope of succeeding him in it; but this plot proved utterly unsuccessful, as is fully described in "Fame and Fortune."

We shall have more to do with Roswell Crawford in the course of the present story. At present he was employed in a retail bookstore up town, on a salary of six dollars a week.

Chapter 8

On The Ferry-Boat

MARK HAD made two applications for charity, and still had but ten cents. The manner in which Mrs. Crawford met his appeal made the business seem more disagreeable than ever. Besides, he was getting tired. It was not more than eight o'clock, but he had been up early, and had been on his feet all day. He leaned against one of the stalls, but in so doing he aroused the suspicions of the vigilant old woman who presided over it.

"Just stand away there," she said. "You're watchin' for a chance to steal one of them apples."

"No, I'm not," said Mark, indignantly. "I never steal."

"Don't tell me," said the old woman, who had a hearty aversion to boys, some of whom, it must be confessed, had in times past played mean tricks on her; "don't tell me! Them that beg will steal, and I see you beggin' just now."

To this Mark had no reply to make. He saw that he was already classed with the young street beggars, many of whom, as the old woman implied, had no particular objection to stealing, if they got a chance. Altogether he was so disgusted with his new business, that he felt it impossible for him to beg any more that night. But then came up the consideration that this would prevent his returning home. He very well knew what kind of a reception Mother Watson would give him, and he had a very unpleasant recollection and terror of the leather strap.

But where should he go? He must pass the night somewhere, and he already felt drowsy. Why should he not follow Ben Gibson's suggestions, and sleep on the Fulton ferry-boat? It would only cost two cents to get on board, and he might ride all night. Fortunately he had more than money enough for that, though he did not like to think how he came by the ten cents.

When Mark had made up his mind, he passed out of one of the entrances of the market, and, crossing the street, presented his ten cents at the wicket, where stood the fare-taker.

Without a look towards him, that functionary took the money, and pushed back eight cents. These Mark took, and passed round into the large room of the ferry-house.

The boat was not in, but he already saw it halfway across the river, speeding towards its pier.

There were a few persons waiting besides himself, but the great rush of travel was diminished for a short time. It would set in again about eleven o'clock when those who had passed the evening at some place of amusement in New York would be on their way home.

Mark with the rest waited till the boat reached its wharf. There was the usual bump, then the chain rattled, the wheel went round, and the passengers began to pour out upon the wharf. Mark passed into the boat, and went at once to the "gentlemen's cabin," situated on the left-hand side of the boat. Generally, however, gentlemen rather unfairly crowd into the ladies' cabin, sometimes compelling the ladies, to whom it of right belongs, to stand, while they complacently monopolize the seats. The gentlemen's cabin, so called, is occupied by those who have a little more regard to the rights of ladies, and by the smokers, who are at liberty to indulge in their favorite comfort here.

When Mark entered, the air was redolent with tobacco-smoke, generally emitted from clay pipes and cheap cigars, and therefore not so agreeable as under other circumstances it might have been. But it was warm and comfortable, and that was a good deal.

In the corner Mark espied a wide seat nearly double the

size of an ordinary seat, and this he decided would make the most comfortable niche for him.

He settled himself down there as well as he could. The seat was hard, and not so comfortable as it might have been; but then Mark was not accustomed to beds of down, and he was so weary that his eyes closed and he was soon in the land of dreams.

He was dimly conscious of the arrival at the Brooklyn side, and the ensuing hurried exit of passengers from that part of the cabin in which he was; but it was only a slight interruption, and when the boat, having set out on its homeward trip, reached the New York side, he was fast asleep.

"Poor little fellow!" thought more than one, with a hasty glance at the sleeping boy. "He is taking his comfort where he can."

But there was no good Samaritan to take him by the hand, and inquire into his hardships, and provide for his necessities, or rather there was one, and that one well known to us.

Richard Hunter and his friend Henry Fosdick had been to Brooklyn that evening to attend an instructive lecture which they had seen announced in one of the daily papers. The lecture concluded at half-past nine, and they took the ten o'clock boat over the Fulton ferry.

They seated themselves in the first cabin, towards the Brooklyn side, and did not, therefore, see Mark until they passed through the other cabin on the arrival of the boat at New York.

"Look there, Fosdick," said Richard Hunter. "See that poor little chap asleep in the corner. Doesn't it remind you of the times we used to have, when we were as badly off as he?"

"Yes, Dick, but I don't think I ever slept on a ferry-boat."

"That's because you were not on the streets long. I took care of myself eight years, and more than once took a cheap bed for two cents on a boat like this. Most likely I've slept in that very corner."

"It was a hard life, Dick."

"Yes, and a hard bed too; but there's a good many that are no better off now. I always feel like doing something to help along those like this little chap here."

"I wonder what he is,—a boot-black?"

"He hasn't got any brush or box with him. Perhaps he's a newsboy. I think I'll give him a surprise."

"Wake him up, do you mean?"

"No, poor little chap! Let him sleep. I'll put fifty cents in his pocket, and when he wakes up he won't know where it came from."

"That's a good idea, Dick. I'll do the same. All right. Here's the money. Put mine in with yours. Don't wake him up."

Dick walked softly up to the match-boy, and gently inserted the money—one dollar—in one of the pockets of his ragged vest.

Mark was so fast asleep that he was entirely unconscious of the benevolent act.

"That'll make him open his eyes in the morning," he said.

"Unless somebody relieves him of the money during his sleep."

"Not much chance of that. Pickpockets won't be very apt to meddle with such a ragged little chap as that, unless it's in a fit of temporary aberration of mind."

"You're right, Dick. But we must hurry out now, or we shall be carried back to Brooklyn."

"And so get more than our money's worth. I wouldn't want to cheat the corporation so extensively as that."

So the two friends passed out of the boat, and left the match boy asleep in the cabin, quite unconscious that good fortune had hovered over him, and made him richer by a dollar, while he slept.

While we are waiting for him to awake, we may as well follow Richard Hunter and his friend home.

Fosdick's good fortune, which we recorded in the earlier chapters of this volume, had made no particular change in their arrangements. They were already living in better style than was usual among youths situated as they were. There was this difference, however, that whereas formerly Dick paid the greater part of the joint expense it was now divided equally. It will be remembered that Fosdick's interest on the twenty bank shares purchased in his name amounted to one hundred and sixty dollars annually, and this just about enabled him to pay his own way, though not leaving him a large surplus for clothing and incidental expenses. It could not be long, however, before his pay would be increased at the store, probably by two dollars a week. Until that time he could economize a little; for upon one thing he had made up his mind,—not to trench upon his principal except in case of sickness or absolute necessity.

The boys had not forgotten or neglected the commission which they had undertaken for Mr. Hiram Bates. They had visited, on the evening after he left, the Newsboys' Lodging House, then located at the corner of Fulton and Nassau Streets, in the upper part of the "Sun" building, and had consulted Mr. O'Connor, the efficient superintendent, as to the boy of whom they were in search. But he had no information to supply them with. He promised to inquire among the boys who frequented the lodge, as it was possible that there might be some among them who might have fallen in with a boy named Talbot.

Richard Hunter also sought out some of his old acquaintances, who were still engaged in blacking boots, or selling newspapers, and offered a reward of five dollars for the discovery of a boy of ten, named Talbot, or John Talbot.

As the result of this offer a red-haired boy was brought round to the counting-room one day, who stoutly asserted that his name was John Talbot, and his guide in consequence claimed the reward. Dick, however, had considerable doubt as to the genuineness of his claim, and called the errand-boy, known to the readers of earlier volumes, as Micky Maguire.

"Micky," said Richard, "this boy says he is John Talbot. Do you know him?"

"Know him!" repeated Micky; "I've knowed him ever

since he was so high. He's no more John Talbot than I am. His name is Tim Hogan, and I'll defy him to say it isn't."

Tim looked guilty, and his companion gave up the attempt to obtain the promised reward. He had hired Tim by the promise of a dollar to say he was John Talbot, hoping by the means to clear four dollars for himself.

"That boy'll rise to a seat in the Common Council if he lives long enough," said Dick. "He's an unusually promising specimen."

Chapter 9

A Pleasant Discovery

THE NIGHT wore away, and still Mark, the match boy, continued to sleep soundly in the corner of the cabin where he had established himself. One of the boat hands passing through noticed him, and was on the point of waking him, but, observing his weary look and thin attire, refrained from an impulse of compassion. He had a boy of about the same age, and the thought came to him that some time his boy might be placed in the same situation, and this warmed his heart towards the little vagrant.

"I suppose I ought to wake him up," he reflected, "but he isn't doing any harm there, and he may as well have his sleep out."

So Mark slept on,—a merciful sleep, in which he forgot his poverty and friendless condition; a sleep which brought new strength and refreshment to his limbs.

When he woke up it was six o'clock in the morning. But it was quite dark still, for it was in December, and, so far as appearances went, it might have been midnight. But already sleepy men and boys were on their way to the great city to their daily work. Some were employed a considerable distance up town, and must be at their posts at seven. Others were employed in the markets and must be stirring at an early hour. There were keepers of street-stands, who liked to be ready for the first wave in the tide of daily travel that was to sweep without interruption through the city streets until late at night. So, altogether, even at this early hour there was quite a number of passengers.

Mark rubbed his eyes, not quite sure where he was, or how he got there. He half expected to hear the harsh voice of Mother Watson, which usually aroused him to his daily toil. But there was no Mother Watson to be seen, only sleepy, gaping men and boys, clad in working dress.

Mark sat up and looked around him.

"Well, young chap, you've had a nap, haven't you?" said a man at his side, who appeared, from a strong smell of paint about his clothes, to be a journeyman painter.

"Yes," said Mark. "Is it morning?"

"To be sure it is. What did you expect it was?"

"Then I've been sleeping all night," said the match boy, in surprise.

"Where?"

"Here."

"In that corner?" asked the painter.

"Yes," said Mark; "I came aboard last night, and fell asleep, and that's the last I remember."

"It must be rather hard to the bones," said the painter. "I think that I should prefer a regular bed."

"I do feel rather sore," said the match boy; "but I slept bully."

"A little chap like you can curl up anywhere. I don't think I could sleep very well on these seats. Haven't you got any home?"

"Yes," said Mark, "a sort of a home."

"Then why didn't you sleep at home?"

"I knew I should get a beating if I went home without twenty-five cents."

"Well, that's hard luck. I wonder how I should feel," he continued, laughing, "if my wife gave me a beating when I came home short of funds."

But here the usual bump indicated the arrival of the boat at the slip, and all the passengers, the painter included, rose, and hurried to the edge of the boat.

With the rest went Mark. He had no particular object

in going thus early; but his sleep was over, and there was no inducement to remain longer in the boat.

The rain was over also. The streets were still wet from the effects of the quantity that had fallen, but there was no prospect of any more. Mark's wet clothes had dried in the warm, dry atmosphere of the cabin, and he felt considerably better than on the evening previous.

Now, however, he could not help wondering what Mother Watson had thought of his absence.

"She'll be mad, I know," he thought. "I suppose she'll whip me when I get back."

This certainly was not a pleasant thought. The leather strap was an old enemy of his, which he dreaded, and with good reason. He was afraid that he would get a more severe beating, for not having returned the night before, at the hands of the angry old woman.

"I wish I didn't live with Mother Watson," he thought.

Straight upon this thought came another. "Why should he?"

Mother Watson had no claim upon him. Upon his mother's death she had assumed the charge of him, but, as it turned out, rather for her own advantage than his. She had taken all his earnings, and given him in return a share of her miserable apartment, a crust of bread or two, daily seasoned with occasional assaults with the leather strap. It had never occurred to Mark before, but now for the first time it dawned upon him that he had the worst of the bargain. He could live more comfortably by retaining his earnings, and spending them upon himself.

Mark was rather a timid, mild-mannered boy, or he would sooner have rebelled against the tyranny and abuse of Mother Watson. But he had had little confidence in himself, and wanted somebody to lean on. In selecting the old woman, who had acted thus far as his guardian, he had leaned upon a broken reed. The last night's experience gave him a little courage. He reflected that he could sleep in the Newsboys' Lodging House for five cents, or on the ferry-boat again for two, while the fare at his old home was hardly so sumptuous but that he could obtain the same without very large expense.

So Mark thought seriously of breaking his yoke and declaring himself free and independent. A discovery which he made confirmed him in his half-formed resolution.

He remembered that after paying his toll he had eight cents left, which he had placed in his vest-pocket. He thought that these would enable him to get some breakfast, and drew them out. To his astonishment there were two silver half-dollars mingled with the coppers. Mark opened his eyes wide in astonishment. Where could they have come from? Was it possible that the tollman had given him them by mistake for pennies? That could not be, for two reasons: First, he remembered looking at the change as it was handed him, and he knew that there were no half-dollars among them. Again, the eight pennies were all there, the silver coins making the number ten.

It was certainly very strange and surprising, and puzzled Mark not a little. We, who know all about it, find the explanation very easy, but to the little match boy it was an unfathomable mystery.

The surprise, however, was of an agreeable character. With so much money in his possession, Mark felt like a man with a handsome balance at his banker's, and with the usual elasticity of youth he did not look forward to the time when this supply would be exhausted.

"I won't go back to Mother Watson," he determined. "She's beaten me times enough. I'll take care of myself."

While these thoughts were passing through his mind, he had walked up Fulton Street, and reached the corner of Nassau. Here he met his friend of the night before, Ben Gibson.

Ben looked rather sleepy. He had been at the Old Bowery Theatre the night before until twelve o'clock, and, having no money left to invest in a night's lodging, he had crept into a corner of the "Times" printing office, and slept, but had not quite slept off his fatigue.

"Hallo, young 'un!" said he. "Where did you come from?"

"From Fulton Ferry," said Mark. "I slept on the boat."

"Did you? How'd you like it?"

"Pretty good," said Mark. "It was rather hard."

"How'd you make out begging?"

"Not very well. I got ten cents."

"So you didn't dare to go home to the old woman?"

"I shan't go home there any more," said the match boy.

"Do you mean it?"

"Yes, I do."

"Bully for you! I like your pluck. I wouldn't go back and get a licking, if I were you. What'll Mother Watson say?"

"She'll be mad, I expect," said Mark.

"Keep a sharp lookout for her. I'll tell you what you can do: stay near me, and if she comes prowlin' round I'll manage her."

"Could you?" said Mark, quickly, who, from certain recollections, had considerable fear of his stout tyrant.

"You may just bet on that. What you goin' to do?"

"I think I shall go and get some breakfast," said Mark.

"So would I, if I had any tin; but I'm dead broke,—spent my last cent goin' to the Old Bowery. I'll have to wait till I've had one or two shines before I can eat breakfast."

"Are you hungry?"

"I'll bet I am."

"Because," said Mark, hesitating, "I'll lend you money enough for breakfast, and you can pay me when you earn it."

"You lend me money!" exclaimed Ben, in astonishment. "Why, you haven't got but eight cents."

"Yes, I have," said Mark, producing the two half-dollars.

"Where'd you get them?" asked the boot-black, in unfeigned surprise, looking at Mark as if he had all at once developed into an Astor or a Stewart.

"You haven't been begging this morning, have you?"

"No," said the match boy, "and I don't mean to beg again if I can help it."

"Then where'd you get the money?"

"I don't know."

"Don't know! You haven't been stealin', have you?"

Mark disclaimed the imputation indignantly.

"Then you found a pocket-book?"

"No, I didn't."

"Then where did you get the money?"

"I don't know any more than you do. When I went to sleep on the boat I didn't have it, but this morning when I felt in my pocket it was there."

"That's mighty queer," said Ben, whistling.

"So I think."

"It's good money, aint it?"

"Try it and see."

Ben tossed up one of the coins. It fell with a clear, ringing sound on the sidewalk.

"Yes, that's good," he said. "I just wish somebody'd treat me that way. Maybe it's the vest. If 'tis I'd like to buy it."

"I don't think it's that," said Mark, laughing.

"Anyway you've got the money. I'll borrow twenty cents of you, and we'll go and get some breakfast."

Chapter 10

On the War Path

BEN LED the way to a cheap restaurant, where for eighteen cents each of the boys got a breakfast, which to their not very fastidious tastes proved very satisfactory.

"There," said Ben, with a sigh of satisfaction, as they rose from the table, "now I feel like work; I'll pay up that money afore night."

"All right," said Mark.

"What are you goin' to do?"

"I don't know," said Mark, irresolutely.

"You're a match boy,—aint you?"

"Yes."

"Where's your matches?"

"In Mother Watson's room."

"You might go and get 'em when she's out."

"No," said Mark, shaking his head, "I won't do that."

"Why not? You aint afraid to go round there,—be you?"

"It isn't that,—but the matches are hers, not mine."

"What's the odds?"

"I won't take anything of hers."

"Well, you can buy some of your own, then. You've got money enough."

"So I will," said Mark. "It's lucky that money came to me in my sleep."

"That's a lucky boat. I guess I'll go there and sleep to-night."

Mark did as he proposed. With the money he had he was able to purchase a good supply of matches, and when it became light enough he began to vend them.

Hitherto he had not been very fortunate in the disposal of his wares, being timid and bashful; but then he was working for Mother Watson, and expected to derive very little advantage for himself from his labors. Now he was working for himself, and this seemed to put new spirit and courage into him. Then again he felt that he had shaken off the hateful thraldom in which Mother Watson had held him, and this gave him a hopefulness which he had not before possessed.

The consequence was that at noon he found that he had earned forty cents in addition to his investment. At that time, too, Ben was ready to pay him his loan, so that Mark found himself twenty-two cents better off than he had been in the morning, having a capital of a dollar and thirty cents, out of which, however, he must purchase his dinner.

While he is getting on in such an encouraging manner we must go back to Mother Watson.

When Mark did not return the night before she grumbled considerably; but no thought of his intentional desertion dawned upon her. Indeed, she counted upon his timidity and lack of courage, knowing well that a more spirited boy would have broken her chain long before. She only thought, therefore, that he had not got the twenty-five cents, and did not dare to come back, especially as she had forbidden him to do so.

So, determining to give him a taste of the leather strap in the morning, she went to bed, first taking a fresh potation from the whiskey bottle, which was her constant companion.

Late in the morning Mother Watson woke, feeling as usual, at that hour of the day, cross and uncomfortable, and with a strong desire to make some one else uncomfortable. But Mark, whom she usually made to bear the burden of her temper, was still away. For the first time the old woman began to feel a little apprehensive that he had deserted her. This was far from suiting her, as she found his earnings very convenient, and found it besides pleasant to have somebody to scold.

She hastily dressed, without paying much attention to her toilet. Indeed, to do Mother Watson justice, her mind was far from being filled with the vanity of dress, and if she erred on that subject it was in the opposite extreme.

When her simple toilet was accomplished she went downstairs, and knocked at Mrs. Flanagan's door.

"Come in!" said a hearty voice.

Mrs. Flanagan was hard at work at her wash-tub, and had been for a good couple of hours. She raised her good-natured face as the old woman entered.

"The top of the morning to you, Mother Watson," she said. "I hope you're in fine health this morning, mum."

"Then you'll be disappointed," said Mrs. Watson. "I've got a bad feeling at my stomach, and have it most every morning."

"It's the whiskey," thought Mrs. Flanagan; but she thought it best not to intimate as much, as it might lead to hostilities.

"Better take a cup of tea," said she.

"I haven't got any," said the old woman. "I wouldn't mind a cup if you've got some handy."

"Sit down then," said Mrs. Flanagan, hospitably. "I've got some left from breakfast, only it's cold, but if you'll wait a bit, I'll warm it over for you."

Nothing loth, Mother Watson sank into a chair, and began to give a full account of her ailments to her neighbor, who tried hard to sympathize with her, though, knowing the cause of the ailments, she found this rather difficult.

"Have you seen anything of my boy this morning?" she asked after a while.

"What, Mark?" said Mrs. Flanagan. "Didn't he come home last night?"

"No," said the old woman, "and he isn't home yet. When he does come I'll give him a dose of the strap. He's a bad, lazy, shiftless boy, and worries my life out."

"You're hard on the poor boy, Mother Watson. You must remember he's but a wisp of a lad, and hasn't much strength."

"He's strong enough," muttered Mother Watson. "It's lazy he is. Just let him come home, that's all!"

"You told him not to come home unless he had twenty-five cents to bring with him."

"So I did, and why didn't he do it?"

"He couldn't get the money, it's likely, and he's afraid of bein' bate."

"Well, he will be bate then, Mrs. Flanagan, you may be sure of that," said the old woman, diving her hand into her pocket to see that the strap was safe.

"Then you're a bad, cruel woman, to bate that poor motherless child," said Mrs. Flanagan, with spirit.

"Say that again, Mrs. Flanagan," ejaculated Mother Watson, irefully. "My hearin' isn't as good as it was, and maybe I didn't hear you right."

"No wonder your hearin' isn't good," said Mrs. Flanagan, who now broke bounds completely. "I shouldn't think you'd have any sense left with the whiskey you drink."

"Perhaps you mean to insult me," said the old woman, glaring at her hostess with one of the frowns which used to send terror to the heart of poor Mark.

"Take it as you please, mum," said Mrs. Flanagan, intrepidly. "I'm entirely willin'. I've been wanting to spake my mind a long while, and now I've spoke it."

Mother Watson clutched the end of the strap in her pocket, and eyed her hostess with a half wish that it would do to treat her as she had treated Mark so often; but Mrs. Flanagan with her strong arms and sturdy frame looked like an antagonist not very easily overcome, and Mrs. Watson forbore, though unwillingly.

Meanwhile the tea was beginning to emit quite a savory odor, and the wily old woman thought it best to change her tactics.

Accordingly she burst into tears, and, rocking backward and forward, declared that she was a miserable old woman, and hadn't a friend in the world, and succeeded in getting up such a display of misery that the soft heart of Mrs. Flanagan was touched, and she apologized for the unpleasant personal observations she had made, and hoped Mother Watson would take the tea.

To this Mother Watson finally agreed, and intimating that she was faint, Mrs. Flanagan made some toast for her, of which the cunning old woman partook with exceeding relish, notwithstanding her state of unhappiness.

"Come in any time, Mother Watson," said Mrs. Flanagan, "when you want a sip of tea, and I'll be glad to have you take some with me."

"Thank you, Mrs. Flanagan; maybe I'll look in once in a while. A sip of tea goes to the right spot when I feel bad at my stomach."

"Must you be goin', Mother Watson?"

"Yes," said the old woman; "I'm goin' out on a little walk, to see my sister that keeps a candy-stand by the Park railins. If Mark comes in, will you tell him he'll find the matches upstairs?"

This Mrs. Flanagan promised to do, and the old woman went downstairs, and into the street.

But she had not stated her object quite correctly. It was true that she had a sister, who was in the confectionery and apple line, presiding over one of the stalls beside the Park railings. But the two sisters were not on very good terms, chiefly because the candy merchant, who was more industrious and correct in her habits than her sister, declined to lend money to Mother Watson,— a refusal which led to a perfect coolness between them. It was not therefore to see her that the old woman went out. She wanted to find Mark. She did not mean to lose her hold upon him, if there was any chance of retaining it, and she therefore made up her mind to visit the places where he was commonly to be found, and, when found, to bring him home, by violence, if necessary.

So with an old plaid cloak depending from her broad shoulders, and her hand grasping the strap in her pocket, she made her way to the square, peering about on all sides with her ferret-like eyes in the hope of discovering the missing boy.

Chapter 11

Mark's Victory

MEANWHILE MARK, rejoicing in his new-found freedom, had started on a business walk among the stores and offices at the lower part of Nassau Street, and among the law and banking offices of Wall Street. Fortunately for Mark there had been a rise in stocks, and Wall Street was in a good-humor. So a few of the crumbs from the tables of the prosperous bankers and brokers fell in his way. One man, who had just realized ten thousand dollars on a rise in some railway securities, handed Mark fifty cents, but declined to take any of his wares. So this was all clear profit and quite a windfall for the little match boy. Again, in one or two cases he received double price for some of his matches, and the result was that he found himself by eleven o'clock the possessor of two dollars and a quarter, with a few boxes of matches still left.

Mark could hardly realize his own good fortune. Somehow it seemed a great deal more profitable as well as more agreeable to be in business for himself, than to be acting as the agent of Mother Watson. Mark determined that he would never go back to her unless he was actually obliged to do so.

He wanted somebody to sympathize with him in his good fortune, and, as he had nearly sold out, he determined to hunt up Ben Gibson, and inform him of his run of luck.

Ben, as he knew, was generally to be found on Nassau

Street, somewhere near the corner of Spruce Street. He therefore turned up Nassau Street from Wall, and in five minutes he reached the business stand of his friend Ben.

Ben had just finished up a job as Mark came up. His patron was a young man of verdant appearance, who, it was quite evident, hailed from the country. He wore a blue coat with brass buttons, and a tall hat in the style of ten years before, with an immense top. He gazed with complacency at the fine polish which Ben had imparted to his boots,—a pair of stout cowhides,—and inquired with an assumption of indifference:—

"Well, boy, what's the tax?"

"Twenty-five cents," said Ben, coolly.

"Twenty-five cents!" ejaculated the customer, with a gasp of amazement. "Come now, you're jokin'."

"No, I aint," said Ben.

"You don't mean to say you charge twenty-five cents for five minutes' work?"

"Reg'lar price," said Ben.

"Why I don't get but twelve and a half cents an hour when I work out hayin'," said the young man in a tone expressive of his sense of the unfairness of the comparative compensation.

"Maybe you don't have to pay a big license," said Ben.

"A license for blackin' boots?" ejaculated the countryman, in surprise.

"In course. I have to deposit five hundred dollars, more or less, in the city treasury, before I can black boots."

"Five—hundred—dollars!" repeated the customer, opening his eyes wide at the information.

"In course," said Ben. "If I didn't they'd put me in jail for a year."

"And does he pay a license too?" asked the countryman, pointing to Mark, who had just come up.

"He only has to pay two hundred and fifty dollars," said Ben. "They aint so hard on him as on us."

The young man drew out his wallet reluctantly, and managed to raise twenty-three cents, which he handed to Ben.

"I wouldn't have had my boots blacked, if I'd known the price," he said. "I could have blacked 'em myself at home. They didn't cost but three dollars, and it don't pay to give twenty-five cents to have 'em blacked."

"It'll make 'em last twice as long," said Ben. "My blackin' is the superiorest kind, and keeps boots from wearin' out."

"I haven't got the other two cents," said the young man. "Aint that near enough?"

"It'll do," said Ben, magnanimously, "seein' you didn't know the price."

The victimized customer walked away, gratified to have saved the two cents, but hardly reconciled to have expended almost quarter of a dollar on a piece of work which he might have done himself before leaving home.

"Well, what luck, Mark?" said Ben. "I took in that chap neat, didn't I?"

"But you didn't tell the truth," said Mark. "You don't have to buy a license."

"Oh, what's the odds?" said Ben, whose ideas on the subject of truth were far from being strict. "It's all fair in business. Didn't that chap open his eyes when I told him about payin' five hundred dollars?"

"I don't think it's right, Ben," said Mark, seriously.

"Don't you go to preachin', Mark," said Ben, not altogether pleased. "You've been tied to an old woman's apron-string too long,—that's what's the matter with you."

"Mother Watson didn't teach me the truth," said Mark. "She don't care whether I tell it or not except to her. It was my mother that told me I ought always to tell the truth."

"Women don't know anything about business," said Ben. "Nobody in business speaks the truth. Do you see that sign?"

Mark looked across the street, and saw a large placard, setting forth that a stock of books and stationery was selling off at less than cost.

"Do you believe that?" asked Ben.

"Perhaps it's true," said Mark.

"Then you're jolly green, that's all I've got to say," said Ben. "But you haven't told me how much you've made."

"See here," said Mark, and he drew out his stock of money.

"Whew!" whistled Ben, in amazement. "You're in luck. I guess you've been speculatin' on your license too."

"No," said Mark; "one gentleman gave me fifty cents, and two others paid me double price."

"Why, you're gettin' rich!" said Ben. "Aint you glad you've left the old woman?"

But just then Mark lifted up his eyes, and saw a sight that blanched his cheek. There, bearing down upon him, and already but a few feet distant, was Mother Watson! She was getting over the ground as fast as her stoutness would allow. She had already caught sight of Mark, and her inflamed eyes were sparkling with triumphant joy. Mark saw with terror that her hand was already feeling in the pocket where she kept the leather strap. Much as he always feared the strap, the idea of having it applied to him in the public street made it even more distasteful.

"What shall I do, Ben?" he said, clutching the arm of his companion.

"What are you afraid of? Do you see a copp after you?"

A "copp" is the street-boy's name for a policeman.

"No," said Mark; "there's Mother Watson coming after me. Don't you see her?"

"That's Mother Watson, is it?" asked Ben, surveying the old body with a critical eye. "She's a beauty, she is!"

"What shall I do, Ben? She'll beat me."

"No, she won't," said Ben. "You just keep quiet, and leave her to me. Don't be afraid. She shan't touch you."

"She might strike you," said Mark, apprehensively.

"She'd better not!" said Ben, very decidedly; "not unless she wants to be landed in the middle of next week at very short notice."

By this time Mother Watson came up, puffing and panting with the extraordinary efforts she had made. She

could not speak at first, but stood and glared at the match
boy in a vindictive way.

"What's the matter with you, old lady?" asked Ben,
coolly. "You ain't sick, be you? I'd offer to support your
delicate form, but I'm afraid you'd be too much for me."

"What do you mean by runnin' away from home, you
little thief?" said the old woman, at length regaining her
breath. Of course her remark was addressed to Mark.

"You're very polite, old lady," said Ben; "but I've
adopted that boy, and he's goin' to live with me now."

"I aint speakin' to you, you vagabone!" said Mother
Watson, "so you needn't give me no more of your impertinence. I'm a-speakin' to him."

"I'm not going to live with you any more," said Mark,
gaining a little courage from the coolness of his friend,
the boot-black.

"Aint a goin' to live with me?" gasped the old woman,
who could hardly believe she heard aright. "Come right
away, sir, or I'll drag you home."

"Don't you stir, Mark," said Ben.

Mother Watson drew out her strap, and tried to get at
the match boy, but Ben put himself persistently in her
way.

"Clear out, you vagabone!" said the old lady, "or I'll
give you something to make you quiet."

"You'd better keep quiet yourself," said Ben, not in
the least frightened. "Don't you be afraid, Mark. If she
kicks up a rumpus, I'll give her over to a copp. He'll settle her."

Mother Watson by this time was very much incensed.
She pulled out her strap, and tried to get at Mark, but
the boot-black foiled her efforts constantly.

Carried away with anger, she struck Ben with the
strap.

"Look here, old lady," said Ben, "that's goin' a little
too far. You won't use that strap again;" and with a
dexterous and vigorous grasp he pulled it out of her hand.

"Give me that strap, you vagabone!" screamed the old
woman, furiously.

"Look here, old lady, what are you up to?" demanded the voice of one having authority.

Mother Watson, turning round, saw an object for which she never had much partiality,—a policeman.

"O sir," said she, bursting into maudlin tears, "it's my bad boy that I want to come home, and he won't come."

"Which is your boy,—that one?" asked the policeman, pointing to Ben Gibson.

"No, not that vagabone!" said the old woman, spitefully. "I wouldn't own him. It's the other boy."

"Do you belong to her?" asked the officer, addressing Mark.

"No, sir," said the match boy.

"He does," vociferated the old woman.

"Is he your son?"

"No," she said, after a moment's hesitation.

"Is he any relation of yours?"

"Yes, he's my nephew," said Mother Watson, making up her mind to a falsehood as the only means of recovering Mark.

"Is this true?" asked the officer.

"No, it isn't," said Mark. "She's no relation to me, but when my mother died she offered to take care of me. Instead of that she's half starved me, and beaten me with a strap when I didn't bring home as much money as she wanted."

"Then you don't want to go back with her?"

"No, I'm going to take care of myself."

"Is there anybody that will prove the truth of what you say?"

"Yes," said Mark, "I'll call Mrs. Flanagan."

"Who is she?"

"She lives in the same house with us."

"Shall he call her, or will you give him up?" asked the officer. "By the way, I think you're the same woman I saw drunk in the street last week."

Mother Watson took alarm at this remark, and, muttering that it was hard upon a poor widder woman to take her only nephew from her, shuffled off, leaving Mark and Ben in full possession of the field, with the terrible strap thrown in as a trophy of the victory they had won.

"I know her of old," said the policeman. "I guess you'll do as well without her as with her."

Satisfied that there would be no more trouble, he resumed his walk, and Mark felt that now in truth he was free and independent.

As Mother Watson will not reappear in this story, it may be said that only a fortnight later she was arrested for an assault upon her sister, the proprietor of the apple-stand, from whom she had endeavored in vain to extort a loan, and was sentenced to the Island for a period of three months, during which she ceased to grace metropolitan society.

Chapter 12

The Newsboys' Lodging House

WHEN MOTHER WATSON had turned the corner, Mark breathed a sigh of relief.

"Don't you think she'll come back again?" he asked anxiously of Ben Gibson.

"No," said Ben, "she's scared of the copp. If she ever catches you alone, and tries to come any of her games, just call a copp, and she'll be in a hurry to leave."

"Well," said Mark, "I guess I'll try to sell the rest of my matches. I haven't got but a few."

"All right; I'll try for another shine, and then we'll go and have some dinner. I'd like to get hold of another greeny."

Mark started with his few remaining matches. The feeling that he was his own master, and had a little hoard of money for present expenses, gave him courage, and he was no longer deterred by his usual timidity. In an hour he had succeeded in getting rid of all his matches, and he was now the possessor of two dollars and seventy-five cents, including the money Ben Gibson owed him. Ben also was lucky enough to get two ten-cent customers, which helped his receipts by twenty cents. Ben, it may be remarked, was not an advocate of the one-price system. He blacked boots for five cents when he could get no more. When he thought there was a reasonable prospect of getting ten cents, that was his price. Sometimes, as in the case of the young man from the rural districts, he advanced his fee to twenty-five cents. I don't approve Ben's system for my part. I think it savors considerably of sharp practice, and that fair prices in the long run are the best for all parties.

The boys met again at one o'clock, and adjourned to a cheap underground restaurant on Nassau Street, where they obtained what seemed to them a luxurious meal of beefsteak, with a potato, a small plate of bread, and a cup of what went by the name of coffee. The steak was not quite up to the same article at Delmonico's, and there might be some reasonable doubts as to whether the coffee was a genuine article; but as neither of the boys knew the difference, we may quote Ben's familiar phrase, and say, "What's the odds?"

Indeed, the free and easy manner in which Ben threw himself back in his chair, and the condescending manner in which he assured the waiter that the steak was "a prime article," could hardly have been surpassed in the most aristocratic circles.

"Well, Mark, have you had enough?" asked Ben.

"Yes," said Mark.

"Well, I haven't," said Ben. "I guess I'll have some puddin'. Look here, Johnny," to the colored waiter, "just bring a feller a plate of apple dump with both kinds of sauce."

After giving this liberal order Ben tilted his chair back, and began to pick his teeth with his fork. He devoted himself with assiduity to the consumption of the pudding, and concluded his expensive repast by the purchase of a two-cent cigar, with which he ascended to the street.

"Better have a cigar, Mark," he said.

"No, thank you," said the match boy. "I think I'd rather not."

"Oh, you're feared of being sick. You'll come to it in time. All business men smoke."

It is unnecessary to dwell upon the events of the afternoon. Mark was satisfied with the result of his morning's work, and waited about with Ben till the close of the afternoon, when the question came up, as to where the night should be passed.

"I guess we'd better go to the Lodge," said Ben. "Were you ever there?"

"No," said Mark.

"Well, come along. They'll give us a jolly bed, all for six cents, and there's a good, warm room to stay in. Then we can get breakfast in the mornin' for six cents more."

"All right," said Mark. "We'll go."

The down-town Newsboys' Lodging House was at that time located at the corner of Fulton and Nassau Streets. It occupied the fifth and sixth stories of the building then known as the "Sun" building, owned by Moses S. Beach, the publisher of that journal. In the year 1868 circumstances rendered it expedient to remove the Lodge to a building in Park Place. It is to be hoped that at some day not far distant the Children's Aid Society, who carry on this beneficent institution, will be able to erect a building of their own in some eligible locality, which can be permanently devoted to a purpose so praiseworthy.

Ben and Mark soon reached the entrance to the Lodge on Fulton Street. They ascended several flights of narrow stairs till they reached the top story. Then, opening a door at the left, they found themselves in the main room of the Lodge. It was a low-studded room of considerable dimensions, amply supplied with windows, looking out on Fulton and Nassau Streets. At the side nearest the door was a low platform, separated from the rest of the room by a railing. On this platform were a table and two or three chairs. This was the place for the superintendent, and for gentlemen who from time to time address the boys.

The superintendent at that time was Mr. Charles O'Connor, who still retains the office. Probably no one could be found better adapted to the difficult task of managing the class of boys who avail themselves of the good offices of the Newsboys' Home. His mild yet firm manner, and more than all the conviction that he is their friend, and feels a hearty interest in their welfare, secure a degree of decorum and good behavior which could hardly be anticipated. Oaths and vulgar speech, however common in the street, are rarely heard here, or, if heard, meet with instant rebuke.

The superintendent was in the room when Ben and Mark entered.

"Well. Ben, what luck have you had to-day?" said Mr. O'Connor.

"Pretty good," said Ben.

"And who is that with you?"

"Mother Watson's nephew," said Ben, with a grimace.

"He's only joking, sir," said Mark. "My name is Mark Manton."

"I am glad to see you. Mark," said the superintendent. "What is your business?"

"I sell matches, sir."

"Have you parents living?"

"No, sir; they are both dead."

"Where have you been living?"

"In Vandewater Street."

"With any one?"

"Yes, with a woman they call Mother Watson."

"Is she a relation of yours?"

"No, sir," said Mark, hastily.

"What sort of a woman is she?"

"Bad enough, sir. She gets drunk about every day, and used to beat me with a strap when I did not bring home as much money as she expected."

"So you have left her?"

"Yes, sir."

"Have you ever been up here before?"

"No, sir."

"I suppose you know the rules of the place."

"Yes, sir; Ben has told me."

"You had better go and wash. We shall have supper pretty quick. Have you any money?"

"Yes, sir."

Mark took out his hoard of money, and showed it to the superintendent, who was surprised at the amount.

"How did you get so much?" he asked.

"Part of it was given me," said Mark.

"What are you going to do with it? You don't need it all?"

"Will you keep it for me, sir?"

"I will put as much of it as you can spare into the bank for you. This is our bank."

He pointed to a table beside the railing on the outside. The top of it was pierced with narrow slits, each having a number attached. Each compartment was assigned to any boy who desired it, and his daily earnings were dropped in at the end of the day. Once a month the bank was opened, and the depositor was at liberty to withdraw his savings if he desired it. This is an excellent arrangement, as it has a tendency to teach frugal habits to the young patrons of the Lodge. Extravagance is one of their besetting sins. Many average a dollar and over as daily earnings, yet are always ragged and out at elbows, and often are unsupplied with the small price of a night's lodging at the Home. The money is squandered on gambling, cigars, and theatre-going, while the same sum would make them comfortable and independent of charity. The disposition to save is generally the first encouraging symptom in a street boy, and shows that he has really a desire to rise above his circumstances, and gain a respectable position in the world.

Ben, who had long frequented the Lodging House off and on, led the way to the washing-room, where Mark, to his satisfaction, was able to cleanse himself from the dust and impurity of the street. At Mother Watson's he had had no accommodations of the kind, as the old lady was not partial to water either internally or externally. He was forced to snatch such opportunities as he could find.

"Now," said Ben, "we'll go into the gymnasium."

A room opposite the main room had been fitted up with a few of the principal appliances of a gymnasium, and these were already in use by quite a number of boys.

Mark looked on, but did not participate, partly from bashfulness, and partly because he did not very well understand the use of the different appliances.

"How do you like it?" asked Ben.

"Very much," said Mark, with satisfaction. "I'm glad you brought me here."

"I'll show you the beds by and by," said Ben.

The rooms on the floor below are used for lodging. Tiers of neat beds, some like those in a steamboat or a hospital, filled a large room. They were very neat in appearance, and looked comfortable. In order to insure their continuing neat, the superintendent requires such as need it to wash their feet before retiring to bed.

The supper was of course plain, but of good quality and sufficient quantity.

About nine o'clock Mark got into the neat bed which was assigned him, and felt that it was more satisfactory even than the cabin of a Brooklyn ferry-boat. He slept peacefully except towards morning, when he dreamed that his old persecutor, Mother Watson, was about to apply the dreaded strap. He woke up terrified, but soon realized with deep satisfaction that he was no longer in her clutches.

Chapter 13

What Befell the Match Boy

DURING THE NEXT three months Mark made his home at the Lodging House. He was easily able to meet the small charges of the Lodge for bed and breakfast, and saved up ten dollars besides in the bank. Ben Gibson began to look upon him as quite a capitalist.

"I don't see how you save up so much money, Mark," he said. "You don't earn more'n half as much as I do."

"It's because you spend so much, Ben. It costs you considerable for cigars and such things, you know, and then you go to the Old Bowery pretty often."

"A feller must have some fun," said Ben. "They've got a tearin' old play at the Bowery now. You'd better come to-night."

Mark shook his head.

"I feel pretty tired when it comes night," he said. "I'd rather stay at home."

"You aint so tough as I am," said Ben.

"No," said Mark, "I don't feel very strong. I think something's the matter with me."

"Nothin' aint ever the matter with me," said Ben, complacently; "but you're a puny little chap, that look as if you might blow away some day."

It was now April, and the weather was of that mild character that saps the strength and produces a feeling of weakness and debility. Mark had been exposed during the winter to the severity of stormy weather, and more than once got thoroughly drenched. It was an exposure that Ben would only have laughed at, but Mark was slightly built, without much strength of constitution, and he had been feeling very languid for a few days, so that it was with an effort that he dragged himself round during the day with his little bundle of matches.

This conversation with Ben took place in the morning just as both boys were going to work.

They separated at the City Hall Park, Ben finding a customer in front of the "Times" building, while Mark, after a little deliberation, decided to go on to Pearl Street with his matches. He had visited the offices in most of the lower streets, but this was a new region to him, and he thought he might meet with better success there. So he kept on his way.

The warm sun and the sluggish air made his head ache, and he felt little disposition to offer his wares for sale. He called at one or two offices, but effected no sales. At length he reached a large warehouse with these names displayed on the sign over the door:—

"ROCKWELL & COOPER."

This, as the reader will remember, was the establishment in which Richard Hunter, formerly Ragged Dick, was now book-keeper.

At this point a sudden faintness came over Mark, and he sank to the ground insensible.

A moment before Richard Hunter handed a couple of letters to the office boy,—known to the readers of the earlier volumes in this series as Micky Maguire,—and said, "Michael, I should like to have you carry these at once to the post-office. On the way you may stop at Trescott & Wayne's, and get this bill cashed, if possible."

"All right. Mr. Hunter," said Michael, respectfully.

Richard Hunter and Micky Maguire had been bootblacks together, and had had more than one contest for the supremacy. They had been sworn enemies, and Micky had done his utmost to injure Richard, but the latter, by his magnanimity, had finally wholly overcome the antipathy of his former foe, and, when opportunity offered, had lifted him to a position in the office where he was himself employed. In return, Micky had become an enthusiastic admirer of Richard, and, so far from taking advantage of their former relations, had voluntarily taken up the habit of addressing him as Mr. Hunter.

Michael went out on his errand, but just outside the door came near stepping upon the prostrate form of the little match boy.

"Get up here!" he said, roughly, supposing at first that Mark had thrown himself down out of laziness and gone to sleep.

Mark didn't answer, and Micky, bending over, saw his fixed expression and waxen pallor.

"Maybe the little chap's dead," he thought, startled, and, without more ado, took him up in his strong arms, and carried him into the counting-room.

"Who have you got there, Michael?" asked Richard Hunter, turning round in surprise.

"A little match boy that was lyin' just outside the door. He looks as if he might be dead."

Richard jumped at once from his stool, and, approaching the boy, looked earnestly in his face.

"He has fainted away," he said, after a pause. "Bring some water, quick!"

Micky brought a glass of water, which was thrown in the face of Mark. The match boy gave a little shiver, and, opening his eyes, fixed them upon Richard Hunter.

"Where am I?" he asked, vacantly.

"You are with friends," said Richard, gently. "You were found at our door faint. Do you feel sick?"

"I feel weak," said Mark.

"Have you been well lately?"

"No, I've felt tired and weak."

"Are you a match boy?"

"Yes."

"Have you parents living?"

"No," said Mark.

"Poor fellow!" said Richard. "I know how to pity you. I have no parents either."

"But you have got money," said Mark. "You don't have to live in the street."

"I was once a street boy like you."

"You!" repeated the match boy, in surprise.

"Yes. But where do you sleep?"

"At the Lodging House."

"It is a good place. Michael, you had better go to the post-office now.

Mark looked about him a little anxiously.

"Where are my matches?" he asked.

"Just outside; I'll get them," said Michael, promptly. He brought them in, and then departed on his errand.

"I guess I'd better be going," said Mark, rising feebly.

"No," said Richard. "You are not able. Come here and sit down. You will feel stronger by and by. Did you eat any breakfast this morning?"

"A little," said Mark, "but I was not very hungry."

"Do you think you could eat anything now?"

Mark shook his head.

"No," he said, "I don't feel hungry. I only feel tired."

"Would you like to rest?"

"Yes. That's all I want."

"Come here then, and I will see what I can do for you."

Mark followed his new friend into the warehouse, where Richard found a soft bale of cotton, and told Mark he might lie down upon it. This the poor boy was glad enough to do. In his weakness he was disposed to sleep, and soon closed his eyes in slumber. Several times Richard went out to look at him, but found him dozing, and was unwilling to interrupt him.

The day wore away, and afternoon came.

Mark got up from his cotton bale, and with unsteady steps came to the door of the counting-room.

"I'm going," he said.

Richard turned round.

"Where are you going?"

"I'm going to the Lodge. I think I won't sell any more matches to-day."

"I'll take all you've left," said Richard. "Don't trouble yourself about them. But you are not going to the Lodge."

Mark looked at him in surprise.

"I shall take you home with me to-night," he said. "You are not well, and I will look after you. At the Lodge there will be a crowd of boys, and the noise will do you harm."

"You are very kind," said Mark; "but I'm afraid I'll trouble you."

"No," said Richard, "I shan't count it a trouble. I was once a poor boy like you, and I found friends. I'll be your friend. Go back and lie down again, and in about an hour I shall be ready to take you with me."

It seemed strange to Mark to think that there was somebody who proposed to protect and look after him. In many of the offices which he visited he met with rough treatment, and was ordered out of the way, as if he were a dog, and without human feelings. Many who treated him in this way were really kind-hearted men who had at home children whom they loved, but they appeared to forget that these neglected children of the street had feelings and wants as well as their own, who were tenderly nurtured. They did not remember that they were somebody's children, and that cold, and harshness, and want were as hard for them to bear as for those in a higher rank of life. But Mark was in that state of weakness when it seemed sweet to throw off all care or thought for the future, and to sink back upon the soft bale with the thought that he had nothing to do but to rest.

"That boy is going to be sick," thought Richard Hunter to himself. "I think he is going to have a fever."

It was because of this thought that he decided to carry him home. He had a kind heart, and he knew how terrible a thing sickness is to these little street waifs, who have no mother or sister to smooth their pillows, or cheer them with gentle words. The friendless condition of the little match boy touched his heart, and he resolved that, as he had the means of taking care of him, he would do so.

"Michael," he said, at the close of business hours, "I wish you would call a hack."

"What, to come here?" asked Micky, surprised.

"Yes. I am going to take that little boy home with me. I think he is going to be sick, and I am afraid he would have a hard time of it if I sent him back into the street."

"Bully for you, Mr. Hunter!" said Micky, who, though rough in his outward manners, was yet capable of appreciating kindness in others. There were times indeed in the past when he had treated smaller boys brutally, but it was under the influence of passion. He had improved greatly since, and his better nature was beginning to show itself.

Micky went out, and soon returned in state inside a hack. He was leaning back, thinking it would be a very good thing if he had a carriage of his own to ride in. But I am afraid that day will never come. Micky has already turned out much better than was expected, but he is hardly likely to rise much higher than the subordinate position he now occupies. In capacity and education he is far inferior to his old associate, Richard Hunter, who is destined to rise much higher than at present.

Richard Hunter went to the rear of the warehouse where Mark still lay on his bale.

"Come," he said; "we'll go home now."

Mark rose from his recumbent position, and walked to the door. He saw with surprise the carriage, the door of which Micky Maguire held open.

"Are we going to ride in that?" he asked.

"Yes," said Richard Hunter. "Let me help you in."

The little match boy sank back in the soft seat in vague surprise at his good luck. He could not help wondering what Ben Gibson would say if he could see him now.

Richard Hunter sat beside him, and supported Mark's head. The driver whipped up his horse, and they were speedily on their way up the Bowery to St. Mark's Place.

Chapter 14

Richard Hunter's Ward

IT WAS about half-past five o'clock in the afternoon when the carriage containing Richard Hunter and the match boy stopped in front of his boarding-place in St. Mark's Place. Richard helped the little boy out, saying, cheerfully, "Well, we've got home."

"Is this where you live?" asked Mark faintly.

"Yes. How do you like it?"

"It's a nice place. I am afraid you are taking too much trouble about me."

"Don't think of that. Come in."

Richard had ascended the front steps, after paying the hackman, and taking out his night-key opened the outside door.

"Come upstairs," he said.

They ascended two flights of stairs, and Richard threw open the door of his room. A fire was already burning in the grate, and it looked bright and cheerful.

"Do you feel tired?" asked Richard.

"Yes, a little."

"Then lie right down on the bed. You are hungry too, —are you not?"

"A little."

"I will have something sent up to you."

Just then Fosdick, who, it will be remembered, was Richard Hunter's room-mate, entered the room. He looked with surprise at Mark, and then inquiringly at Richard.

"It is a little match boy," explained the latter, "who

fell in a fainting-fit in front of our office. I think the poor fellow is going to be sick, so I brought him home, and mean to take care of him till he is well."

"You must let me share the expense, Dick," said Fosdick.

"No, but I'll let you share the care of him. That will do just as well."

"But I would rather share the expense. He reminds me of the way I was situated when I fell in with you. What is your name?"

"Mark Manton," said the match boy.

"I've certainly seen him somewhere before," said Fosdick, reflectively. "His face looks familiar to me."

"So it does to me. Perhaps I've seen him about the streets somewhere."

"I have it," said Fosdick, suddenly; "don't you remember the boy we saw sleeping in the cabin of the Fulton Ferry-boat?"

"Yes."

"I think he is the one. Mark," he continued, turning to the match boy, "didn't you sleep one night on a Brooklyn ferry-boat about three months ago?"

"Yes," said Mark.

"And did you find anything in your vest-pocket in the morning?"

"Yes," said the match boy with interest. "I found a dollar, and didn't know where it came from. Was it you that put it in?"

"He had a hand in it," said Fosdick, pointing with a smile to his room-mate.

"I was very glad to get it," said Mark. "I only had eight cents besides, and that gave me enough to buy some matches. That was at the time I ran away."

"Who did you run away from?"

"From Mother Watson."

"Mother Watson?" repeated Dick. "I wonder if I don't know her. She is a very handsome old lady, with a fine red complexion, particularly about the nose."

"Yes," said Mark, with a smile.

"And she takes whiskey when she can get it?"

"Yes."

"How did you fall in with her?"

"She promised to take care of me when my mother died, but instead of that she wanted me to earn money for her."

"Yes, she was always a very disinterested old lady. So it appears you didn't like her as a guardian?"

"No."

"Then suppose you take me. Would you like to be my ward?"

"I think I would, but I don't know what it means," said Mark.

"It means that I'm to look after you," said Dick, "just as if I was your uncle or grandfather. You may call me grandfather if you want to."

"Oh, you're too young," said Mark, amused in spite of his weakness.

"Then we won't decide just at present about the name. But I forgot all about your being hungry."

"I'm not very hungry."

"At any rate you haven't had anything to eat since morning, and need something. I'll go down and see Mrs. Wilson about it."

Richard Hunter soon explained matters to Mrs. Wilson, to whom he offered to pay an extra weekly sum for Mark, and arranged that a small single bed should be placed in one corner of the room temporarily in which the match boy should sleep. He speedily reappeared with a bowl of broth, a cup of tea, and some dry toast. The sight of these caused the match boy's eyes to brighten, and he was able to do very good justice to all.

"Now," said Richard Hunter, "I will call in a doctor, and find out what is the matter with my little ward."

In the course of the evening Dr. Pemberton, a young dispensary physician, whose acquaintance Richard had casually made, called at his request and looked at the patient.

"He is not seriously sick," he pronounced. "It is chiefly debility that troubles him, brought on probably by exposure, and over-exertion in this languid spring weather."

"Then you don't think he is going to have a fever?" said Dick.

"No, not if he remains under your care. Had he continued in the street, I think he would not have escaped one."

"What shall we do for him?"

"Rest is most important of all. That, with nourishing food and freedom from exposure, will soon bring him round again."

"He shall have all these."

"I suppose you know him, as you take so much interest in him?"

"No, I never saw him but once before to-day, but I am able to befriend him, and he has no other friends."

"There are not many young men who would take all this trouble about a poor match boy," said the doctor.

"It's because they don't know how hard it is to be friendless and neglected," said Dick. "I've known that feeling, and it makes me pity those who are in the same condition I once was."

"I wish there were more like you, Mr. Hunter," said Dr. Pemberton. "There would be less suffering in the world. As to our little patient here, I have no doubt he will do well, and soon be on his legs again."

Indeed Mark was already looking better and feeling better. The rest which he had obtained during the day, and the refreshment he had just taken, were precisely what he needed. He soon fell asleep, and Richard and Fosdick, lighting the gas lamp on the centre-table, sat down to their evening studies.

In a few days Mark was decidedly better, but it was thought best that he should still keep the room. He liked it very well in the evening when Dick and Fosdick were at home, but he felt rather lonesome in the daytime. Richard Hunter thought of this one day, and said, "Can you read, Mark?"

"Yes," said the match boy.

"Who taught you? Not Mother Watson, surely."

"No, she couldn't read herself. It was my mother who taught me."

"I think I must get you two or three books of stories to read while we are away in the daytime."

"You are spending too much money for me, Mr. Hunter."

"Remember I am your guardian, and it is my duty to take care of you."

The next morning on his way down town, Richard Hunter stepped into a retail bookstore on Broadway. As he entered, a boy, if indeed it be allowable to apply such a term to a personage so consequential in his manners, came forward.

"What, Roswell Crawford, are you here?" asked Richard Hunter, in surprise.

Roswell, who has already been mentioned in this story, and who figured considerably in previous volumes of this series, answered rather stiffly to this salutation.

"Yes," he said. "I am here for a short time. I came in to oblige Mr. Baker."

"You were always very obliging, Roswell," said Richard, good-humoredly.

Roswell did not appear to appreciate this compliment. He probably thought it savored of irony.

"Do you want to buy anything this morning?" he said, shortly.

"Yes; I would like to look at some books of fairy stories."

"For your own reading, I suppose," said Roswell.

"I may read them, but I am getting them for my ward."

"Is he a boot-black?" sneered Roswell, who knew all about Dick's early career.

"No," said Richard, "he's a match boy; so if you've got any books that you can warrant to be just the thing for match boys, I should like to see them."

"We don't have many customers of that class," said Roswell, unpleasantly. "They generally go to cheaper establishments, when they are able to read."

"Do they?" said Dick. "I'm glad you've got into a place where you only meet the cream of society," and Dick glanced significantly at a red-nosed man who came in to buy a couple of sheets of note-paper.

Roswell colored.

"There are some exceptions," he said, and glanced pointedly at Richard Hunter himself.

"Well," said Dick, after looking over a collection of juvenile books, "I'll take these two."

He drew out his pocket-book, and handed Roswell a ten-dollar bill. Roswell changed it with a feeling of jealousy and envy. He was the "son of a gentleman," as he often boasted, but he never had a ten-dollar bill in his pocket. Indeed, he was now working for six dollars a week, and glad to get that, after having been out of a situation for several months.

Just then Mr. Gladden, of the large down-town firm of Gladden & Co., came into the store, and, seeing Richard, saluted him cordially.

"How are you this morning, Mr. Hunter?" he said. "Are you on your way down town?"

"Yes, sir," said Richard.

"Come with me. We will take an omnibus together;" and the two walked out of the store in familiar conversation.

"I shouldn't think such a man as Mr. Gladden would notice a low boot-black," said Roswell, bitterly.

The rest of the day he was made unhappy by the thought of Dick's prosperity, and his own hard fate, in being merely a clerk in a bookstore with a salary of six dollars a week.

Chapter 15

Mark Gets A Place

IN A WEEK from the purchase of the books, Mark felt that he was fully recovered. He never had much color, but the unhealthy pallor had left his cheeks, and he had an excellent appetite.

"Well, Mark, how do you feel to-night?" asked Richard, on his return from the store one evening.

"I'm all right, now, Mr. Hunter. I think I will go to work to-morrow morning."

"What sort of work?"

"Selling matches."

"Do you like to sell matches?"

"I like it better than selling papers, or blacking boots."

"But wouldn't you like better to be in a store?"

"I couldn't get a place," said Mark.

"Why not?"

"My clothes are ragged," said the match boy with some hesitation. "Besides I haven't got anybody to refer to."

"Can't you refer to your guardian?" asked Richard Hunter, smiling.

"Do you think I had better try to get a place in a store, Mr. Hunter?" asked Mark.

"Yes, I think it would be much better for you than to sell matches on the street. You are not a strong boy, and the exposure is not good for you. As to your clothes, we'll see if we cannot supply you with something better than you have on."

"But," said Mark. "I want to pay for my clothes myself. I have got ten dollars in the bank at the Newsboys' Lodge."

"Very well. You can go down to-morrow morning and get it. But we needn't wait for that. I will go and get you some clothes before I go to business."

In the morning Richard Hunter went out with the match boy, and for twenty dollars obtained for him a very neat gray suit, besides a supply of under-clothing. Mark put them on at once, and felt not a little pleased with the improvement in his appearance.

"You can carry your old clothes to Mr. O'Connor," said Richard. "They are not very good, but they are better than none, and he may have an opportunity of giving them away."

"You have been very kind to me, Mr. Hunter," said Mark, gratefully. "Good-by."

"Good-by? What makes you say that?"

"Because I am going now to the Newsboys' Lodge."

"Yes, but you are coming back again."

"But I think I had better go there to live now. It will be much cheaper, and I ought not to put you to so much expense."

"You're a good boy, Mark, but you must remember that I am your guardian, and am to be obeyed as such. You're not going back to the Lodge to live. I have arranged to have you stay with me at my boarding-place. As soon as you have got a place you will work in the daytime, and every Saturday night you will bring me your money. In the evening I shall have you study a little, for I don't want you to grow up as ignorant as I was at your age."

"Were you ignorant, Mr. Hunter?" asked Mark, with interest.

"Yes, I was," said Richard. "When I was fourteen, I couldn't read nor write."

"I can hardly believe that, Mr. Hunter," said Mark. "You're such a fine scholar."

"Am I?" asked Richard, smiling, yet well pleased with the compliment.

"Why, you can read French as fast as I can read English, and write beautifully."

"Well, I had to work hard to do it," said Richard Hunter. "But I feel paid for all the time I've spent in trying to improve myself. Sometimes I've thought I should like to spend the evening at some place of amusement rather than in study; but if I had, there'd be nothing to show for it now. Take my advice, Mark, and study all you can, and you'll grow up respectable and respected."

"Now," he added, after a pause, "I'll tell you what you may do. You may look in my 'Herald' every morning, and whenever you see a boy advertised for you can call, or whenever, in going along the street, you see a notice 'Boy wanted,' you may call in, and sooner or later you'll get something. If they ask for references, you may refer to Richard Hunter, book-keeper for Rockwell & Cooper."

"Thank you, Mr. Hunter," said Mark. "I will do so."

On parting with his guardian the match boy went down town to the Lodging House. The superintendent received him kindly.

"I didn't know what had become of you, Mark," he said. "If it had been some of the boys, I should have been afraid they had got into a scrape, and gone to the Island. But I didn't think that of you."

"I hope you'll never hear that of me, Mr. O'Connor," said Mark.

"I hope not. I'm always sorry to hear of any boy's going astray. But you seem to have been doing well since I saw you;" and the superintendent glanced at Mark's new clothes.

"I've met with some kind friends," said the match boy. "I have been sick, and they took care of me."

"And now you have come back to the Lodge."

"Yes, but not to stay. I came for the money that I have saved up in the bank. It is going for these clothes."

"Very well. You shall have it. What is the name of the friend who has taken care of you?"

"Richard Hunter."

"I know him," said the superintendent. "He is an excellent young man. You could not be in better hands."

On leaving the Lodge Mark felt a desire to find his old ally, Ben Gibson, who, though rather a rough character, had been kind to him.

Ben was not difficult to find. During business hours he was generally posted on Nassau Street, somewhere between Fulton Street and Spruce Street.

He was just polishing off a customer's boots when Mark came up, and touched him lightly on the shoulder. Ben looked up, but did not at first recognize the match boy in the neatly dressed figure before him.

"Shine yer boots!" he asked, in a professional tone.

"Why, Ben, don't you know me?" asked Mark, laughing.

"My eyes, if it aint Mark, the match boy!" exclaimed Ben, in surprise. "Where've you been all this while, Mark?"

"I've been sick, Ben."

"I'd like to be sick too, if that's the way you got them clo'es. I didn't know what had 'come of you."

"I found some good friends," said Mark.

"If your friends have got any more good clo'es they want to get rid of," said Ben, "tell 'em you know a chap that can take care of a few. Are you in the match business now?"

"I haven't been doing anything for three weeks," said Mark.

"Goin' to sell matches again?"

"No."

"Sellin' papers?"

"No, I'm trying to find a place in a store."

"I don't think I'd like to be in a store," said Ben, reflectively. "I'm afraid my delicate constitution couldn't stand the confinement. Besides, I'm my own boss now, and don't have nobody to order me round."

"But you don't expect to black boots all your life, Ben, do you?"

"I dunno," said Ben. "Maybe when I'm married, I'll choose some other business. It would be rather hard to support a family at five cents a shine. Are you comin' to the Lodge to-night?"

"No," said Mark, "I'm boarding up at St. Mark's Place."

"Mother Watson hasn't opened a fashionable boardin' house up there, has she?"

"I guess not," said Mark, smiling. "I can't think what has become of her. I haven't seen her since the day she tried to carry me off."

"I've heard of her," said Ben. "She's stoppin' with some friends at the Island. They won't let her come away on account of likin' her company so much."

"I hope I shall never see her again," said Mark, with a shudder. "She is a wicked old woman. But I must be going, Ben."

"I s'pose you'll come and see a feller now and then."

"Yes, Ben, when I get time. But I hope to get a place soon."

Mark walked leisurely up Broadway. Having been confined to the house for three weeks, he enjoyed the excitement of being out in the street once more. The shop windows looked brighter and gayer than before, and the little match boy felt that the world was a very pleasant place after all.

He had passed Eighth Street before he was fairly aware of the distance he had traversed. He found himself looking into the window of a bookstore. While examining the articles in the window his eye suddenly caught the notice pasted in the middle of the glass on a piece of white paper:—

"BOY WANTED"

"Perhaps they'll take me," thought Mark, suddenly. "At any rate I'll go in and see."

Accordingly he entered the store, and looked about him a little undecidedly.

"Well, sonny, what do you want?" asked a clerk.

"I see that you want a boy," said Mark.

"Yes. Do you want a place?"

"I am trying to get one."

"Well, go and see that gentleman about it."

He pointed to a gentleman who was seated at a desk in the corner of the store.

"Please, sir, do you want a boy?" he asked.

"Yes," said the gentleman. "How old are you?"

"Ten years old."

"You are rather young. Have you been in any place before?"

"No, sir."

"Do you know your way about the city pretty well?"

"Yes, sir."

"I want a boy to deliver papers and magazines, and carry small parcels of books. Do you think you could do that?"

"Yes, sir."

"Without stopping to play on the way?"

"Yes, sir."

"I have just discharged one boy, because he was gone an hour and a half on an errand to Twentieth Street. You are the first boy that has answered my advertisement. I'll try you on a salary of three dollars a week, if you can go to work at once. What is your name?

"Mark Manton."

"Very well, Mark. Go to Mr. Jones, behind the counter there, and he will give you a parcel to carry to West Twenty-first Street."

"I'm in luck," thought Mark. "I didn't expect to get a place so easily."

Chapter 16

Mark's First Impressions

PROBABLY MY READERS already understand that the bookstore in which Mark has secured a place is the same in which Roswell Crawford is employed. This circumstance, if Mark had only known it. was likely to make his position considerably less desirable than it would otherwise have been. Mr. Baker, the proprietor of the store, was very considerate in his treatment of those in his employ, and Mr. Jones, his chief clerk, was good-natured and pleasant. But Roswell was very apt to be insolent and disagreeable to those who were, or whom he considered to be, in an inferior position to himself. while his lofty ideas of his own dignity and social position as the "son of a gentleman" made him not very desirable as a clerk. Still he had learned something from his bad luck thus far. He had been so long in getting his present place, that he felt it prudent to sacrifice his pride to some extent for the sake of retaining it. But if he could neglect his duties without attracting attention, he resolved to do it, feeling that six dollars was a beggarly salary for a young gentleman of his position and capacity. It was unfortunate for him, and a source of considerable annoyance, that he could get no one except his mother to assent to his own estimate of his abilities. Even his Cousin Gilbert, who had been Rockwell & Cooper's book-keeper before Richard Hunter succeeded to the position, did not conceal his poor opinion of Roswell; but this the latter attributed to prejudice, being persuaded in his own mind that his cousin was somewhat inclined to be envious of his superior abilities.

At the time that Mark was so suddenly engaged by Mr. Baker, Roswell had gone out to dinner. When he returned, Mark had gone out with the parcel to West Twenty-first Street. So they missed each other just at first.

"Well, Crawford," said Mr. Jones, as Roswell re-entered the store, "Mr. Baker has engaged a new boy."

"Has he? What sort of a fellow is he?"

"A little fellow. He doesn't look as if he was more than ten years old."

"Where is he?"

"Mr. Baker sent him on an errand to Twenty-first Street."

"Humph!" said Roswell, a little discontented, "I was going to recommend a friend of mine."

"There may be a chance yet. This boy may not suit."

In about five minutes Mr. Baker and Mr. Jones both went out to dinner. It was the middle of the day, when there is very little business, and it would not be difficult for Roswell to attend to any customers who might call.

As soon as he was left alone, Roswell got an interesting book from the shelves, and, sitting down in his employer's chair, began to read, though this was against the rules in business hours. To see the pompous air with which Roswell threw himself back in his chair, it might have been supposed that he was the proprietor of the establishment, though I believe it is true, as a general rule, that employers are not in the habit of putting on so many airs, unless the position is a new one and they have not yet got over the new feeling of importance which it is apt to inspire at first.

While Roswell was thus engaged Mark returned from his errand.

He looked about him in some uncertainty on entering the store, not seeing either Mr. Baker or the chief clerk.

"Come here," said Roswell, in a tone of authority.

Mark walked up to the desk.

"So you are the new boy?" said Roswell, after a close scrutiny.

"Yes."

"It would be a little more polite to say 'Yes sir.' "

"Yes, sir."

"What is your age?"

"Ten years."

"Humph! You are rather young. If I had been consulted I should have said 'Get a boy of twelve years old.' "

"I hope I shall suit," said Mark.

"I hope so," said Roswell, patronizingly. "You will find us very easy to get along with if you do your duty. We were obliged to send away a boy this morning because he played instead of going on his errands at once."

Mark could not help wondering what was Roswell's position in the establishment. He talked as if he were one of the proprietors; but his youthful appearance made it difficult to suppose that.

"What is your name?" continued Roswell.

"Mark Manton."

"Have you been in any place before?"

"No, sir."

"Do you live with your parents?"

"My parents are dead."

"Then whom do you live with?"

"With my guardian."

"So you have a guardian?" said Roswell, a little surprised. "What is his name?"

"Mr. Hunter."

"Hunter!" repeated Roswell, hastily. "What is his first name?"

"Richard I believe."

"Dick Hunter!" exclaimed Roswell, scornfully. "Do you mean to say that he has charge of you?"

"Yes," said Mark, firmly, for he perceived the tone in which his friend was referred to, and resented it. Moreover the new expression which came over Roswell's face brought back to his recollection the evening when, for the first time in his life, he had begged in Fulton Market, and been scornfully repulsed by Roswell and his mother. Roswell's face had at first seemed familiar to him, but it was only now that he recognized him. Roswell, on the other hand, was not likely to identify the neatly dressed boy before him with the shivering little beggar of the market. But it recurred to him all at once that Dick had referred to his ward as a match boy.

"You were a match boy?" he said, in the manner of one making a grave accusation.

"Yes, sir."

"Then why didn't you keep on selling matches, and not try to get a place in a respectable store?"

"Because Mr. Hunter thought it better for me to go into a store."

"Mr. Hunter! Perhaps you don't know that your guardian, as you call him, used to be a bootblack."

"Yes, he told me so."

"They called him 'Ragged Dick' then," said Roswell, turning up his nose. "He couldn't read or write, I believe."

"He's a good scholar now," said Mark.

"Humph! I suppose he told you so. But you mustn't believe all he tells you."

"He wouldn't tell anything but the truth," said Mark, who was bolder in behalf of his friend than he would have been for himself.

"So he did tell you he was a good scholar? I thought so."

"No, he told me nothing about it; but since I have lived with him I've heard him read French as well as English."

"Perhaps that isn't saying much," said Roswell, with a sneer. "Can you read yourself?"

"Yes."

"That is more than I expected. What induced Mr. Baker to take a boy from the street is more than I can tell."

"I suppose I can run errands just as well, if I was once a match boy," said Mark, who did not fancy the tone which Roswell assumed towards him, and began to doubt whether he was a person of as much importance as he at first supposed.

"We shall see," said Roswell, loftily. "But there's one thing I'll advise you, young man, and that is, to treat me with proper respect. You'll find it best to keep friends with me. I can get you turned away any time."

Mark hardly knew whether to believe this or not. He already began to suspect that Roswell was something of a humbug, and though it was not in his nature to form a causeless dislike, he certainly did not feel disposed to like Roswell. He did not care so much for any slighting remarks upon himself, as for the scorn with which Roswell saw fit to speak of his friend, Richard Hunter, who by his good offices had won the little boy's lasting gratitude. Mark did not reply to the threat contained in these last words of Roswell.

"Is there anything for me to do?" he asked.

"Yes, you may dust off those books on the counter. There's the duster hanging up."

This was really Roswell's business, and he ought to have been at work in this way instead of reading; but it was characteristic of him to shift his duties upon others. He was not aware of how much time had passed, and supposed that Mark would be through before Mr. Barker returned. But that gentleman came in while Roswell was busily engaged in reading.

"Is that the way you do your work, Roswell?" asked his employer.

Roswell jumped to his feet in some confusion.

"I thought I had better set the new boy to work," he said.

"Dusting the books is your work, not his."

"He was doing nothing, sir."

"He will have plenty to do in carrying out parcels. Besides, I don't know that it is any worse for him to be idle than you. You were reading also, which you know is against the rules of the store."

Roswell made no reply, but it hurt his pride considerably to be censured thus in presence of Mark, to whom he had spoken with such an assumption of power and patronage.

"I wish I had a store of my own," he thought, discontentedly. "Then I could do as I pleased without having anybody to interfere with me."

But Roswell did not understand, and there are plenty of boys in the same state of ignorance, that those who fill subordinate positions acceptably are most likely to rise to stations where they will themselves have control over others.

"I suppose you have not been to dinner," said Mr. Baker, turning to Mark.

"No, sir."

"You board in St. Mark's Place, I think you said?"

"Yes, sir."

"Very well, here is a parcel to go to East Ninth Street. You may call and leave that at the address marked upon it, and may stay out long enough for dinner. But don't be gone more than an hour in all."

"No, sir."

"I am glad that boy isn't my employer," though Mark, referring of course to Roswell Crawford, who, by the way, would have been indignant at such an appellation. "I like Mr. Baker a great deal better."

Mark was punctual to his appointment, and in a little less than an hour reported himself at the store again for duty.

Chapter 17

Bad Advice

ROSWELL PURSUED his way home with a general sense of discontent. Why should he be so much worse off than Richard Hunter, who had only been a ragged bootblack three years before? The whole world seemed to be in a conspiracy to advance Richard, and to keep him down. To think he should be only earning six dollars a week, while Dick, whom he considered so far beneath him, was receiving twenty, was really outrageous. And now he had pushed a low dependent of his into Baker's store where Roswell was obliged to associate with him!

Certainly Roswell's grievances were numerous. But there was one thing he did not understand, that the greatest obstacle to his advancement was himself. If he had entered any situation with the determination to make his services valuable, and discharge his duties, whatever they might be, with conscientious fidelity, he would have found his relations with his employer much more agreeable and satisfactory.

Mrs. Crawford still kept the house in Clinton Place, letting nearly all the rooms to lodgers. In this way she succeeded in making both ends meet, though with considerable difficulty, so that she had not the means to supply Roswell with the spending-money he desired. Her nephew, James Gilbert, Richard Hunter's predecessor as book-keeper, still boarded with her. It will be remembered by the readers of "Fame and Fortune," that this Gilbert, on being questioned by Mr. Rockwell as to his share in the plot against Dick, had angrily resigned his position, thinking, probably, that he should lose it at any rate.

It so happened that business was generally depressed at this time, and it was three months before he succeeded in obtaining another place, and then he was compelled to work for eight hundred dollars, or two hundred less than he had formerly received. This was a great disappointment to him, and did not help his temper much, which had never been very sweet. He felt quite exasperated against Dick, whom, very much against his wishes, he had been the means of promoting to his own place. Indeed, on this point, he sympathized heartily with Roswell, whose dislike to Richard Hunter has already been shown.

"Well, mother," said Roswell, as he entered Mrs. Crawford's presence, "I'm getting tired of Baker's store."

"Don't say so, Roswell," said his mother, in alarm. "Remember how long it took you to get the place."

"I have to work like a dog for six dollars a week," said Roswell.

"Yes," said his cousin, with a sneer, "that's precisely the way you work. Dogs spend their time running around the street doing nothing."

"Well, I have to work hard enough," said Roswell, "but I wouldn't mind that so much, if I didn't have to associate with low match boys."

"What do you mean, Roswell?" asked his mother, who did not understand the allusion.

"Baker hired a new boy to-day, and who do you think he turns out to be?"

"Not that boy, Ragged Dick?"

"No, you don't think he would give up Cousin James' place, where he gets a thousand dollars a year, to go into Baker's as boy?"

"Who was it, then?"

"He used to be a ragged match boy about the street. Dick Hunter picked him up somewhere, and got him a situation in our store, on purpose to spite me, I expect."

As the reader is aware, Roswell was mistaken in his

supposition, as Mark obtained the place on his own responsibility.

"The boot-black seems to be putting on airs," said Mrs. Crawford.

"Yes, he pretends to be the guardian of this match boy."

"What's the boy's name?"

"Mark Manton."

"If I were Mr. Baker," said Mrs. Crawford, "I should be afraid to take a street boy into my employ. Very likely he isn't honest."

"I wish he would steal something," said Roswell, not very charitably. "Then we could get rid of him, and the boot-black would be pretty well mortified about it."

"He'll be found out sooner or later," said Mrs. Crawford. "You may depend on that. You'd better keep a sharp lookout for him, Roswell. If you catch him in stealing, it will help you with Mr. Baker, or ought to."

This would have comforted Roswell more, but that he was privately of the opinion that Mark was honest, and would not be likely to give him any chance of detecting him in stealing. Still, by a little management on his part, he might cause him to fall under suspicion. It would of course be miserably mean on his part to implicate a little boy in a false charge; but Roswell *was* a mean boy, and he was not scrupulous where his dislike was concerned. He privately decided to think over this new plan for getting Mark into trouble.

"Isn't dinner ready, mother?" he asked, rather impatiently.

"It will be in about ten minutes."

"I'm as hungry as a bear."

"You can always do your part at the table," said his cousin unpleasantly.

"I don't know why I shouldn't. I have to work hard enough."

"You are always talking about your hard work. My belief is that you don't earn your wages."

"I should think it was a pity if I didn't earn six dollars a week," said Roswell.

"Come, James, you're always hard on Roswell," said Mrs. Crawford. "I am sure he has hard times enough without his own relations turning against him."

James Gilbert did not reply. He was naturally of a sarcastic turn, and, seeing Roswell's faults, was not inclined to spare them. He might have pointed them out, however, in a kindly manner, and then his young cousin might possibly been benefited; but Gilbert felt very little interest in Roswell.

Immediately after dinner Roswell took up his cap. His mother observed this, and inquired, "Where are you going, Roswell?"

"I'm going out to walk."

"Why don't you go with your cousin?"

James Gilbert had also taken his hat.

"He don't want to be bothered with me," said Roswell, and this statement Gilbert did not take the trouble to contradict.

"Why can't you stay in and read?"

"I haven't got anything to read. Besides I've been cooped up in the store all day, and I want to breathe a little fresh air."

There was reason in this, and his mother did not gainsay it, but still she felt that it was not quite safe for a boy to spend his evenings out in a large city, without any one to look after him.

Roswell crossed Broadway, and, proceeding down Eighth Street, met a boy of about his own age in front of the Cooper Institute.

"How long have you been waiting, Ralph?" he asked.

"Not long. I only just came up."

"I couldn't get away as soon as I expected. Dinner was rather late."

"Have a cigar, Roswell?" asked Ralph.

"Yes," said Roswell, "I don't mind."

"You'll find these cigars pretty good. I paid ten cents apiece."

"I don't see how you can afford it," said Roswell. "Your cigars must cost you considerable."

"I don't always buy ten-centers. Generally I pay only five cents."

"Well, that mounts up when you smoke three or four in a day. Let me see. what wages do you get?"

"Seven dollars a week."

"That's only a dollar more than I get," said Roswell.

"I know one thing. it's miserably small," said Ralph. "We ought to get twice what we do."

"These shop-keepers are awfully mean," said Roswell, beginning to puff away at his cigar.

"That's so."

"But still you always seem to have plenty of money. That's what puzzles me," said Roswell. "I'm always pinched. I have to pay my mother all my wages but a dollar a week. And what's a dollar?" he repeated, scornfully.

"Well," said Ralph, "my board costs me all but a dollar. So we are about even there."

"Do you pay your board out of your earnings?"

"I have to. My governor won't foot the bills, so I have to."

"Still you seem to have plenty of money," persisted Roswell.

"Yes, I look out for that," said Ralph Graham, significantly.

"But I don't see how you manage. I might look out all day, and I wouldn't be any the better off."

"Perhaps you don't go the right way to work," said his companion, taking the cigar from his mouth, and knocking off the ashes.

"Then I wish you'd tell me the right way."

"Why, the fact is," said Ralph, slowly, "I make my employer pay me higher wages than he thinks he does."

"I don't see how you can do that," said Roswell, who didn't yet understand.

Ralph took the cigar, now nearly smoked out, from his mouth, and threw it on the pavement. He bent towards Roswell, and whispered something in his ear. Roswell started and turned pale.

"But," he said, "that's dishonest."

"Hush!" said Ralph, "don't speak so loud. Oughtn't employers to pay fair wages,—tell me that?"

"Certainly."

"But if they don't and won't, what then?"

"I don't know."

"Well, I do. We must help ourselves, that is all."

"But, " said Roswell, "what would be thought of you if it were found out?"

"There's plenty of clerks that do it. Bless you, it's expected. I heard a man say once that he expected to lose about so much by his clerks."

"But I think it would be better to pay good wages."

"So do I, only you see they won't do it."

"How much do you—do you make outside of your salary?" asked Roswell.

"From three to five dollars a week."

"I should think they'd find you out."

"I don't let them. I'm pretty careful. Well, what shall we do this evening? There's a pretty good play at Niblo's. Suppose we go there."

"I haven't got money enough," said Roswell.

"Well, I'll pay for both to-night. You can pay another time."

"All right!" said Roswell, though he did not know when he should have money enough to return the favor. They crossed to Broadway, and walked leisurely to Niblo's Garden. The performance lasted till late, and it was after eleven when Roswell Crawford got into bed.

Chapter 18

The First Step

To DO Roswell Crawford justice, the idea of taking money from his employer had never occurred to him until the day when it was suggested to him by Ralph Graham. The suggestion came to him at an unfortunate time. He had always felt with a sense of bitter injustice that his services were poorly compensated, and that his employer was making money out of him. Yet he knew very well that there was no chance of an advance. Besides, he really felt the need of more money to keep up appearances equal to Ralph Graham, and some other not very creditable acquaintances that he had managed to pick up. So Roswell allowed Ralph's suggestion to recur to his mind with dangerous frequency. He was getting familiar with what had at first startled and shocked him.

But it was not at once that he brought his mind to the point. He was not possessed of much courage, and could not help fearing that he would get himself into a scrape. It needed a little more urging on the part of Ralph.

"Well, Roswell," said Ralph, a few evenings after the conversation recorded in the last chapter, "when are you going to take me to the theatre?"

"I didn't know I was going to take you at all," said Roswell.

"Come, there's no use in crawling off that way. Didn't I take you to Niblo's last week?"

"Yes."

"And didn't you promise to take me some night in return?"

"I should like to do it well enough," said Roswell, "but I never have any money."

"You might have some if you chose."

"The way you mentioned?"

"Yes."

"I don't like to try it."

"Then you are foolish. It's what half the clerks do. They have to."

"Do you think many do it?" said Roswell, irresolutely.

"To be sure they do," said Ralph, confidently.

"But I am sure it would be found out."

"Not if you're careful."

"I shouldn't know how to go about it."

"Then I'll tell you. You're in the store alone some of the time, I suppose."

"Yes, when Mr. Baker and Mr. Jones are gone to dinner."

"Where is the money kept?"

"There are two drawers. The one that has the most money in it is kept locked, and Mr. Baker carries away the key with him. He leaves a few dollars in another drawer, but nothing could be taken from that drawer without being missed."

"Does he keep much money in the first drawer?"

"I expect so."

"Then," said Ralph, promptly, "you must manage to get into that."

"But how am I to do it?" asked Roswell. "Didn't I tell you that it was kept locked, and that Mr. Baker took the key?"

"I can't say you are very smart, Roswell," said Ralph, a little contemptuously.

"Tell me what you mean, then."

"What is easier than to get a key made that will fit the drawer? All you'll have to do, is to take an impression of the lock with sealing-wax, and carry it to a locksmith. He'll make you a key for two shillings."

"I don't know," said Roswell, undecidedly. "I don't quite like to do it."

"Do just as you please," said Ralph; "only if I carry you to the theatre I expect you to return the compliment."

"Well, I'll think of it," said Roswell.

"There is another way you can do," suggested Ralph, who was full of evil suggestions, and was perhaps the most dangerous counsellor that Roswell could have had at this time.

"What is it?"

"If you make any sales while you are alone you might forget to put the money into the drawer."

"Yes, I might do that."

"And ten to one Baker would never suspect. Of course he doesn't know every book he has in his store, or the exact amount of stationery he keeps on hand."

"No, I suppose not."

"You might begin that way. There couldn't be any danger of detection."

This suggestion struck Roswell more favorably than the first, as it seemed safer. Without giving any decided answer, he suffered the thought to sink into his mind, and occupy his thoughts.

The next day when about the middle of the day Roswell found himself alone, a customer came in and bought a package of envelopes, paying twenty-five cents.

With a half-guilty feeling Roswell put this sum into his pocket.

"Mr. Baker will never miss a package of envelopes," he thought.

He sold two or three articles, but the money received for these he put into the drawer. He did not dare to take too much at first. Indeed, he took a little credit to himself, so strangely had his ideas of honesty got warped, for not taking more when he might have done so as well as not.

Mr. Baker returned, and nothing was said. As might have been expected, he did not miss the small sum which Roswell had appropriated.

That evening Roswell bought a couple of cigars with the money he had stolen (we might as well call things by their right names), and treated Ralph to one.

"There's a splendid play on at Wallack's," said he, suggestively.

"Perhaps we'll go to-morrow evening," said Roswell.

"That's the way to talk," said Ralph, looking keenly at Roswell. "Is there anything new with you?"

"Not particularly," said Roswell, coloring a little, for he did not care to own what he had done to his companion, though it was from him that he had received the advice.

The next day when Roswell was again alone, a lady entered the shop.

"Have you got La Fontaine's Fables in English?" she asked. "I have asked at half a dozen stores, but I can't find it. I am afraid it is out of print."

"Yes, I believe we have it," said Roswell.

He remembered one day when he was looking for a book he wanted to read, that he had come across a shop-worn copy of La Fontaine's Fables. It was on a back shelf, in an out-of-the-way place. He looked for it, and found his memory had served him correctly.

"Here it is," he said, handing it down.

"I am very glad to get it," said the lady. How much will it be?"

"The regular price is a dollar and a quarter, but as this is a little shop-worn you may have it for a dollar."

"Very well."

The lady drew out a dollar bill from her purse, and handed it to Roswell.

He held it in his hand till she was fairly out of the door. Then the thought came into his mind, "Why should I not keep this money? Mr. Baker would never know. Probably he has quite forgotten that such a book was in his stock."

Besides, as the price of a ticket to the family circle at Wallack's was only thirty cents, this sum would carry in him and his friend, and there would be enough left for an ice-cream after they had got through.

The temptation was too much for poor Roswell. I call him poor, because I pity any boy who foolishly yields to such a temptation for the sake of a temporary gratification.

Roswell put the money into his vest-pocket, and shortly afterwards Mr. Baker returned to the store.

"Have you sold anything, Roswell?" he inquired, on entering.

"Yes, sir. I have sold a slate, a quire of notepaper, and one of Oliver Optic's books."

Roswell showed Mr. Baker the slate, on which, as required by his employer, he had kept a record of sales.

Mr. Baker made no remark, but appeared to think all was right.

So the afternoon passed away without any incident worthy of mention.

In the evening Roswell met Ralph Graham, as he had got into the habit of doing.

"Well, Roswell, I feel just like going to the theatre to-night," were his first words of salutation.

"Well, we'll go," said Roswell.

"Good! You've got money to buy the tickets, then?"

"Yes," said Roswell, with an air of importance. "What's the play?"

"It's a London play that's had a great run. Tom Hastings tells me it is splendid. You take me there to-night, and I'll take you to the New York Circus some evening next week."

This arrangement was very satisfactory to Roswell, who had never visited the circus, and had a great desire to do so. At an early hour the boys went to the theatre, and succeeded in obtaining front seats in the family circle. Roswell managed to enjoy the play, although unpleasant thoughts of how the money was obtained by which the tickets were procured, would occasionally intrude upon him. But the fascination of the stage kept them from troubling him much.

When the performance was over, he suggested an ice-cream.

"With all my heart," said Ralph. "I feel warm and thirsty, and an ice-cream will cool my throat."

So they adjourned to a confectionery establishment nearly opposite, and Roswell, with an air of importance, called for the creams. They sat leisurely over them, and it was nearly half past eleven when Roswell got home.

"What keeps you out so late, Roswell?" asked his mother, anxiously, for she was still up.

"I was at the theatre." said Roswell.

"Where did you get the money?"

"It's only thirty cents to the family circle," said Roswell, carelessly. "I'm tired, and will go right up to bed."

So he closed the discussion, not caring to answer many inquiries as to his evening's amusement. His outlay for tickets and for the ice-cream afterwards had just used up the money he had stolen, and all that he had to compensate for the loss of his integrity was a headache, occasioned by late hours, and the warm and confined atmosphere at the theatre.

Chapter 19

Richard Hunter Is Promoted

IT WAS with eager importance that Mark awaited the return of Richard Hunter, to communicate to him his good luck in securing a place. The thought that he had secured it by his own exertions gave him great satisfaction.

"I've got a place," were his first words, as Richard entered the house.

"Already?" asked Richard Hunter. "You have been quite smart, Mark. How did you manage to obtain it?"

Mark gave the particulars, which need not be repeated.

"What kind of a store is it?"

"A bookstore."

"What is the name of your employer?"

"Baker."

"Baker's bookstore!" repeated Richard, turning to Fosdick. "That is where our particular friend, Roswell Crawford, is employed."

"Yes," said Mark; "there's a boy there about sixteen or seventeen. I believe that is his name."

"I am not sure whether his being there will make it pleasant to you. Does he know that you are a friend of mine?"

"Yes," said Mark; "he inquired particularly about you, Mr. Hunter."

"He's very fond of me," said Dick; "I suppose he sent me his love."

"No," said Mark, smiling; "he didn't speak as if he loved you very much."

"He doesn't like me very much. I am afraid when he gets to be president I shan't stand much chance of an office. He didn't try to bully you,—did he?"

"He said he could get me sent off if I wasn't careful to please him."

"That sounds like Roswell."

"He talked as if he was one of the firm," said Mark; "but when Mr. Baker came in, he began to scold him for not dusting the books. After that I didn't think so much of what he said."

"It's a way he has," said Fosdick. "He don't like me much either, as I got a place that he was trying for."

"If he bullies you, just let me know," said Richard. "Perhaps I can stop it."

"I am not afraid," said Mark. "Mr. Baker is there most of the time, and he wouldn't dare to bully me before him."

Sunday morning came,—a day when the noisy streets were hushed, and the hum of business was stilled. Richard Hunter and Fosdick still attended the Sunday school, to which they had now belonged for over two years. They were still members of Mr. Greyson's class, and were much better informed in religious matters than formerly. Frequently—for they were favorite scholars with Mr. Greyson—he invited them home to dine at his handsome residence. Both boys were now perfectly self-possessed on such occasions. They knew how to behave at the table with perfect decorum, and no one would have judged from their dress, manners, or conversation, that they had not always been accustomed to the same style of living.

Mr. and Mrs. Greyson noticed with pleasure the great improvement in their protegés, and always welcomed them with kind hospitality. But there was another member of the family who always looked forward with pleasure to seeing them. This was Ida, now a young lady of thirteen, who had from the first taken an especial fancy to Dick, as she always called him.

"Well, Mark," said Richard Hunter, on Sunday morning, "wouldn't you like to go to Sunday school with me?"

"Yes," said Mark. "Mother always wanted me to go to Sunday school, but she was so poor that she could not dress me in suitable clothes."

"There is nothing to prevent your going now. We shall be ready in about half an hour."

At the appointed time the three set out. The distance was not great, the church being situated four blocks farther up town on Fifth Avenue. They chanced to meet Mr. Greyson on the church steps.

"Good-morning, Richard. Good-morning, Henry," he said. Then, glancing at Mark, "Who is your young friend?"

"His name is Mark Manton," said Richard. "He is my ward."

"Indeed! I had not thought of you in the character of a guardian," said Mr. Greyson, smiling.

"I should like to have him enter one of the younger classes," said Richard.

"Certainly, I will gladly find a place for him. Perhaps you can take him in your class."

"In my class!" repeated Richard, in surprise.

"Yes, I thought I had mentioned to you that Mr. Benton was about to leave the city, and is obliged to give up his class. I would like to have you take it."

"But am I qualified to be a teacher?" asked Richard, who had never before thought of being invited to take a class.

"I think you have excellent qualifications for such a position. It speaks well for you, however, that you should feel a modest hesitation on the subject."

"I think Fosdick would make a better teacher than I."

"Oh, I intend to draft him into the service also. I shall ask him to take the next vacancy."

The class assigned to our friend Dick (we are sometimes tempted to call him by his old, familiar name) consisted of boys of from ten to eleven years of age. Among these Mark was placed. Although he had never before attended a Sunday school, his mother, who was an excellent woman, had given him considerable religious instruction, so that he was about as well advanced as the rest of the class.

Richard easily adapted himself to the new situation in which he was placed. He illustrated the lesson in a familiar and oftentimes quaint manner, so that he easily commanded the attention of the boys, who were surprised when the time came for the lesson to close.

"I am glad you are my teacher, Mr. Hunter," said one of the boys at the close of the service.

"Thank you," said Richard, who felt gratified at the compliment. "It's new business to me, but I hope I shall be able to interest you."

"Won't you come and dine with us?" asked Mr. Greyson, as they were leaving the church.

Richard Hunter hesitated.

"I don't know if Mark can find his way home," he said with hesitation.

"Yes, I can, Mr. Hunter," said Mark. "Don't trouble yourself about me."

"But I mean to have him come too," said Mr. Greyson. "Our table is a large one, as you know, and we can accommodate three as well as two."

"Do come, Dick," said Ida Greyson.

Richard was seldom able to resist a request preferred by Ida, and surrendered at discretion. So, as usual, Fosdick walked on with Mr. Greyson, this time with Mark beside him, while Richard walked with Ida.

"Who is that little boy, Dick?" asked the young lady.

"That's my ward, Miss Ida," said Richard.

"You don't mean to say you are his guardian, Dick?"

"Yes, I believe I am."

"Why," said the lively young lady, "I always thought guardians were old, and cross, and bald-headed."

"I don't know but that description will suit me after a while," said Dick. "My hair has been coming out lately."

"Has it, really?" said Ida, who took this seriously. "I hope you won't be bald, I don't think you would look well."

"But I might wear a wig."

"I don't like wigs," said the young lady, decidedly. "If you were a lady now, you might wear a cap. How funny you'd look in a cap!" and she burst out into a peal of merry laughter.

"I think a cap would be more becoming to you," said Richard.

"Do you ever scold your ward?" asked Ida.

"No, he's a pretty good boy. He don't need it."

"Where did you get acquainted with him? Have you known him long?"

"He was taken sick at the door of our office one day. So I had him carried to my boarding-place, and took care of him till he got well."

"That was very good of you," said Ida, approvingly. "What did he use to do?"

"He was a match boy."

"Does he sell matches now?"

"No; he has got a place in a bookstore."

"What did you say his name was?"

"Mark."

"That a pretty good name, but I don't like it so well as Dick."

"Thank you," said Richard. "I am glad you like my name."

At this moment they were passing the Fifth Avenue Hotel. Standing on the steps were two acquaintances of ours, Roswell Crawford and Ralph Graham. They had cigars in their mouths, and there was a swaggering air about them, which was not likely to prepossess any sensible person in their favor. They had not been to church, but had spent the morning in sauntering about the city, finally bringing up at the Fifth Avenue Hotel, where, posting themselves conspicuously on the steps, they watched the people passing by on their way from church.

Richard Hunter bowed to Roswell, as it was his rule never to be found wanting in politeness. Roswell was ill-mannered enough not to return the salutation.

"Who is that, Roswell?" asked Ralph Graham.

"It's a bootblack," said Roswell, sneeringly.

"What do you mean? I am speaking of that nice-looking young fellow that bowed to you just now."

"His name is Hunter. He used to be a bootblack, as I told you; but he's got up in the world, and now he's putting on airs."

"He seems to have got into good company, at any rate. He is walking with the daughter of Mr. Greyson, a rich merchant down town."

"He's got impudence enough for anything," said Roswell, with a feeling of bitter envy which he could not conceal. "It really makes me sick to see him strutting about as if he were a gentleman's son."

"Like you," suggested Ralph, slyly; for he had already been informed by Roswell, on various occasions, that he was "a gentleman's son."

"Yes," said Roswell, "I'm a gentleman's son, if I'm not so lucky as some people. Did you see that small boy in front?"

"Walking with Mr. Greyson?"

"Yes, I suppose so."

"What of him?"

"That's our errand boy."

"Is it?" asked Ralph, in some surprise. "He seems to be one of the lucky kind too."

"He sold matches about the streets till a few weeks ago," said Roswell, spitefully.

"He sold them to some purpose, it seems, for he's evidently going home to dine with Mr. Greyson."

"Mr. Greyson seems to be very fond of low company. That's all I can say."

"When you and I get to be as rich as he is, we can choose our own company."

"I hope I shall choose better than he."

"Well, let's drop them," said Ralph, who was getting tired of the subject. "I must be getting home to dinner."

"So must I."

"Come round to my room, after dinner, and we'll have another smoke."

"Yes, I'll come round. I suppose mother'll be wanting me to go to church with her, but I've got tired of going to church."

Chapter 20

The Madison Club

Two DAYS afterwards, when Roswell as usual met his friend Ralph, the latter said, with an air of importance:—

"I've got news for you, Roswell."

"What is it?" inquired Roswell.

"You've been unanimously elected a member of our club."

"Your club?"

"Yes; didn't I ever mention it to you?"

"No."

"Well, I believe I didn't. You see I intended to propose your name as a member, and not feeling certain whether you would be elected, I thought I had better not mention it to you."

"What is the name of the club?" asked Roswell, eagerly.

"The Madison Club."

"What made you call it that?"

"Why, you see, there's one fellow in the club that lives on Madison Avenue, and we thought that would be an aristocratic name, so we chose it."

Roswell liked whatever was aristocratic, and the name pleased him.

"Did you say I was unanimously elected, Ralph?" he asked.

"Yes; I proposed your name at our meeting last night. It was on account of that, that I couldn't meet

337

you as usual. But hereafter we can go together to the meetings."

"How many fellows belong?"

"Twenty. We don't mean to have more than twenty-five. We are quite particular whom we elect."

"Of course," said Roswell, in a tone of importance. "You wouldn't want a set of low fellows like that Dick Hunter."

"No. By the way, I've got somewhere your notification from the secretary. Here it is."

He drew from his pocket a note adorned with a large and elaborate seal, which Roswell, opening, found read as follows:—

"MADISON CLUB.

"Mr. ROSWELL CRAWFORD.

"Sir:—I have the honor of informing you that at the last regular meeting of the Madison Club you were unanimously elected a member.

"Yours respectfully,
"JAMES TRACY"

This document Roswell read with much satisfaction. It sounded well to say that he was a member of the Madison Club, and his unanimous election could only be regarded as a high compliment.

"I will join," he said, pompously. "When is the next meeting?"

"Next Tuesday evening."

"Where does the society meet?"

"In a room on Fourth Avenue. You can come round early, and we will go together."

"All right. What do you do at the meetings?"

"Well, we smoke, and tell stories, and have a good time. Generally there are some eatables provided. However, you'll know all about it, when you join. Oh, by the way, there's one thing I forgot to tell you," added Ralph. "There's an initiation fee of five dollars."

"A fee of five dollars!" repeated Roswell, soberly.

"Yes."

"What is it for?"

"To defray expenses, of course. There's the rent, and lights, and stationery, and the eatables. They always, I think, have an initiation fee at clubs."

"Are there any other expenses?"

"Not much. There's only a dollar a month. That isn't much."

"I don't know how I'm going to raise the five dollars," said Roswell, soberly. "I could manage the dollar a month afterwards."

"Oh, you'll think of some way," said Ralph.

"My mother wouldn't give it to me, so there's no use asking her."

"Why can't you pay it out of your extra wages?" said Ralph significantly.

"I shouldn't dare to take such a large sum," said Roswell. "They would find me out."

"Not if you're careful."

"They don't keep but a few dollars in the drawer at one time."

"But didn't you tell me there was another drawer?"

"Yes; but that is always kept locked."

"Open it then."

"I have no key."

"Get one that will fit it then."

"I don't like to do that."

"Well, it's nothing to me," said Ralph, "only I should like to have you belong to the club, and you can't unless you are able to pay the initiation fee."

"I would like very much to belong," said Roswell, irresolutely.

"I know you would enjoy it. We have splendid times."

"I'll see what I can do to raise the money," said Roswell.

"That's the way to talk. You'll manage to get it some way."

It was a great temptation to Roswell. The more he thought of it, the more he thought he should like to say that he was a member of the Madison Club. He had a weak love of gentility, and he was persuaded that it would improve his social standing. But he did not wish to adopt the course recommended by Ralph if there was any other way of getting the money. He determined, therefore, first to make the effort to obtain the money from his mother on some pretext or other. By the time he reached home, which was at an earlier hour than usual, he had arranged his pretext.

"I am glad you are home early," said Mrs. Crawford,

"Yes, I thought I'd come home early to-night. Mother, I wish you'd let me have four dollars."

"What for, Roswell?"

"I want to buy a new hat. This one is getting shabby."

Roswell's plan was, if he could obtain the four dollars from his mother, to make up the extra dollar out of sales unaccounted for. As to the failure to buy the hat, he could tell his mother that he had lost the money or make some other excuse. That thought did not trouble him much. But he was not destined to succeed.

"I am sorry you are dissatisfied with your hat, Roswell," said Mrs. Crawford, "for I cannot possibly spare you the money now."

"So you always say," grumbled Roswell.

"But it's true," said his mother. "I'm very short just now. The rent comes due in a few days, and I am trying hard to get together money enough to pay it."

"I thought you had money coming in from your lodgers."

"There's Mr. Bancroft hasn't paid me for six weeks, and I'm afraid I am going to lose his room-rent. It's hard work for a woman to get along. Everybody takes advantage of her," said Mrs. Crawford, sighing.

"Can't you possibly let me have the money by Saturday, mother?"

"No, Roswell. Perhaps in a few weeks I can. But I don't think your hat looks bad. You can go and get it pressed if you wish."

But Roswell declared that wouldn't do, and left the room in an ill-humor. Instead of feeling for his mother, and wishing to help her, he was intent only upon his own selfish gratifications.

So much, then, was plain,—in his efforts to raise the

money for the initiation fee at the club, he could not expect any help from his mother. He must rely upon other means.

Gradually Roswell came to the determination to follow the dangerous advice which had been proffered him by Ralph Graham. He could not bear to give up the project of belonging to the club, and was willing to commit a dishonest act rather than forego the opportunity.

He began to think now of the manner in which he could accomplish what he had in view. The next day when noon came he went round to the locked drawer, and, lighting a piece of sealing-wax which he had taken from one of the cases, he obtained a clear impression of the lock.

"I think that will do," thought Roswell.

At that moment a customer entered the store, and he hurried the stick of sealing-wax into his pocket.

When the store closed, Roswell went round to a locksmith, whose sign he remembered to have seen in Third Avenue.

He entered the shop with a guilty feeling at his heart, though he had a plausible story arranged for the occasion.

"I want a key made," he said, in a business-like manner; "one that will fit this lock."

Here he displayed the wax impression.

"What sort of a lock is it?" asked the locksmith, looking at it.

"It is a bureau drawer," said Roswell. "We have lost the key, and can't open it. So I took the impression in wax. How soon can you let me have it?"

"Are you in a hurry for it?"

"Yes; didn't I tell you we couldn't open the drawer?"

"Well, I'll try to let you have it by to-morrow night."

"That will do," said Roswell.

He left the locksmith's shop with mixed feelings of satisfaction and shame at the thought of the use to which he was intending to put the key. It was a great price he had determined to pay for the honor of belonging to the Madison Club.

Chapter 21

Roswell Joins the Madison Club

IT WAS not until Saturday night that Roswell obtained the key. The locksmith. like tradesmen and mechanics in general, kept putting him off, to Roswell's great annoyance.

As he did not get the key till Saturday night. of course there would be no opportunity of using it till Monday. The only time then was the hour in which Mr. Baker and Mr. Jones were absent, and Roswell was left alone. But to his great vexation, an old gentleman came in directly after Mr. Baker went out, and inquired for him.

"He's gone to dinner." said Roswell.

"I think I'll wait till he returns," said the visitor, coolly sitting down in Mr. Baker's arm-chair.

Roswell was in dismay, for this would of course prevent his using the key which he had taken so much trouble to obtain.

"Mr. Baker is always out a good while," said Roswell.

"Never mind, I can wait for him. I came in from the country this morning, and shall not need to start back till four."

"Perhaps," suggested Roswell, "you could go out and do the rest of your errands, and come back at two o'clock. Mr. Baker will be sure to be back then."

"Who told you I had any more errands to do?" asked the old gentleman, sharply.

"I thought you might have," said Roswell, somewhat confused.

"You are very considerate; but, as my business is over

for the day, I will ask your permission to remain till my nephew returns."

So this was Mr. Baker's uncle, a shrewd old gentleman, if he did live in the country.

"Certainly," said Roswell, but not with a very good grace, adding to himself; "there'll be no chance for me to get the money to-day. I hope the old fellow won't come round again to-morrow."

The next day was Tuesday. In the evening the club was to meet, so there was no time to lose.

Fortunately, as Roswell thought, the coast was clear.

"Suppose the key won't fit?" he thought with uneasiness.

It would have been lucky for Roswell if the key had not fitted. But it proved to fit exactly. Turning it in the lock, the drawer opened, and before him lay a pile of bills.

How much or how little there might be Roswell did not stop to examine. He knew that a customer might come in at any time, and he must do at once what he meant to do. At the top of the pile there was a five-dollar bill. He took it, slipped it hastily into his vest-pocket, relocked the drawer, and, walking away from it, began to dust the books upon the counter.

He felt that he had taken the decisive step. He was supplied with the necessary money to pay the initiation fee. The question was, would Mr. Baker find it out?

Suppose he should, how would it be possible to evade suspicion, or to throw it upon some one else?

"If I could make him think it was the match boy," thought Roswell, "I should be killing two birds with one stone. I must see what can be done."

When Mr. Baker returned, Roswell feared he would go to the drawer, but he did not seem inclined to do this.

He just entered the store, and said, "Mr. Jones, I am obliged to go over to Brooklyn on a little business, and I may not be back this afternoon."

"Very well, sir," said Mr. Jones.

Roswell breathed freer after he had left the shop. It

had occurred to him as possible that if the money were missed, he might be searched, in which case the key and the bill in his pocket would be enough to convict him. Now he should not see Mr. Baker again till the next day probably, when the money would be disposed of.

Mr. Baker, as he anticipated, did not return from Brooklyn before Roswell left the store.

Roswell snatched a hasty supper, and went over to his friend Ralph Graham's room, immediately afterwards.

"Glad to see you, Roswell," said Ralph; "are you coming to the club with me to-night?"

"Yes," said Roswell.

"Have you got the five dollars?"

"Yes."

"How did you manage it?"

"Oh, I contrived to get it," said Roswell, who did not like to confess in what way he had secured possession of the money.

"Well, it's all right, as long as you've got it. I was afraid you wouldn't succeed."

"So was I," said Roswell. "I had hard work of it. What time do the club meetings begin?" he asked.

"At eight o'clock, but I generally go round about half an hour before. Generally, some of the fellows are there, and we can have a social chat. I guess we'll go round at half-past seven, and that will give me a chance to introduce you to some of the members before the meeting begins."

"I should like that," said Roswell.

In a short time the boys set out. They paused before a small house on Fourth Avenue, and rang the bell. The summons was answered by a colored man.

"Any members of the club upstairs?" inquired Ralph.

"Yes, sir," said the attendant. "There's Mr. Tracy, Mr. Wilmot, and Mr. Burgess."

"Very well, I'll go up."

"Jackson," said Ralph, "this gentleman is Mr. Crawford, a new member."

"Glad to make your acquaintance, sir," said Jackson.

"Thank you," said Roswell.

"Jackson takes care of the club-room," explained Ralph, "and is in attendance to admit the members on club nights. Now let us go upstairs."

They went up one flight of stairs, and opened the door of a back room.

It was not a very imposing-looking apartment, being only about twenty feet square, the floor covered with a faded carpet, while the furniture was not particularly sumptuous. At one end of the room was a table, behind which were two arm-chairs.

"That is where the president and secretary sit," said Ralph.

There were already three or four youths in the room. One of them came forward and offered his hand to Ralph.

"How are you, Graham?" he said.

"How are you, Tracy?" returned Ralph. "This is Mr. Crawford, who was elected a member at our last meeting. Roswell, this is Mr. Tracy, our secretary."

"I am glad to see you, Mr. Crawford," said Tracy. "I hope you received the notification of your election which I sent you."

"Yes," said Roswell. "I am much obliged to you."

"I hope you intend to accept."

"It will give me great pleasure," said Roswell. "You must have very pleasant meetings."

"I hope you will find them pleasant. By the way, here is our president, Mr. Brandon. Brandon, let me introduce you to a new member of our society, Mr. Crawford."

The president, who was a tall young man of eighteen, bowed graciously to Roswell.

"Mr. Crawford," said he, "allow me, in the name of the society, to bid you welcome to our gay and festive meetings. We are a band of good fellows, who like to meet together and have a social time. We are proud to receive you into our ranks."

"And I am very glad to belong," said Roswell, who felt highly pleased at the cordial manner in which he was received.

"You'd better go to the secretary, and enter your name in the books of the club," suggested Ralph. "You can pay him the five dollars at the same time. Here, Tracy, Mr. Crawford wants to enroll his name."

"All right," said Tracy; "walk this way if you please, Mr. Crawford."

Roswell wrote down his name, residence, and the store where he was employed.

"I see, Mr. Crawford, you are engaged in literary pursuits," said the secretary.

"Yes, for the present," said Roswell. "I don't think I shall remain long, as the book business doesn't give me scope enough; but I shall not leave at present, as it might inconvenience Mr. Baker. What is your initiation fee?"

"Five dollars."

"I happen to have the money with me, I believe," said Roswell. "Here it is."

"Thank you; that is right. I will enter you as paid. The monthly assessments are one dollar, as perhaps Graham told you."

"Yes, I think he mentioned it. It is quite reasonable, I think," said Roswell, in a tone which seemed to indicate that he was never at a loss for money.

"Yes, I think so, considering our expenses. You see we have to pay for the room; then we pay Jackson's wages, and there are cigars, etc., for the use of the members. Have you ever before belonged to a club?"

"No," said Roswell. "I have always declined hitherto (he had never before received an invitation); but I was so much pleased with what I heard of the Madison Club from my friend Graham, that I determined to join. I am glad that you are particular whom you admit as members of the club."

"Oh, yes, we are very exclusive," said Tracy. "We are not willing to admit anybody and everybody."

Meanwhile there had been numerous arrivals, until probably nearly all the members of the club were present.

"Order, gentlemen!" said the president, assuming the chair, and striking the table at the same time. "The club will please come to order."

There was a momentary confusion, but at length the members settled into their seats, and silence prevailed. Roswell Crawford took a seat beside Ralph Graham.

Chapter 22

A Club Night

"THE SECRETARY will read the journal of the last meeting," said President Brandon.

Tracy rose, and read a brief report, which was accepted, according to form.

"Is there any business to come before the club?" inquired the president.

"I would like to nominate a friend of mine as a member of the club," said Burgess.

"What's his name?" inquired a member.

"Henry Drayton."

"Will Mr. Burgess give some account of his friend, so that the members can vote intelligently on his election?" requested Brandon.

"He's a jolly sort of fellow, and a good singer," said Burgess. "He'll help make our meetings lively. He's about my age—"

"In his second childhood," suggested Wilmot.

This produced a laugh at the expense of Burgess, who took it good-naturedly.

"Has he got five dollars?" inquired another member.

"His father is a rich man," said Burgess. "There will be no fear about his not paying his assessments."

"That's the principal thing," said Wilmot. "I second the nomination."

A vote was taken which was unanimously affirmative.

"Mr. Drayton is unanimously elected a member of the Madison Club," announced the president. "Notification will be duly sent him by the secretary. Is there any other business to come before the club?"

As there appeared to be none, Brandon added, "Then we will proceed to the more agreeable duties which have brought us hither."

He rang a small bell.

Jackson answered the summons.

"Jackson, is the punch ready?" inquired the president.

"Yes, sir," said Jackson.

"Then bring it in. I appoint Wilmot and Burgess to lend you the necessary aid."

A large flagon of hot whiskey punch was brought in and placed on a table. Glasses were produced from a closet in the corner of the room, and it was served out to the members.

"How do you like it, Roswell?" inquired Ralph Graham.

"It's—rather strong," said Roswell, coughing.

"Oh, you'll soon be used to it. The fellows will begin to be jolly after they've drunk a glass or two."

"Do they ever get tight?" whispered Roswell.

"A little lively,—that all."

The effect predicted soon followed.

"Wilmot, give us a song," said Burgess.

"What will you have?" said Wilmot, whose flushed face showed that the punch had begun to affect him.

"Oh, you can give us an air from one of the operas."

"Villikens and his Dinah?" suggested Tracy.

"Very good," said Wilmot.

Wilmot was one of those, who, with no voice or musical ear, are under the delusion that they are admirable singers. He executed the song in his usual style, and was rewarded with vociferous applause, which appeared to gratify him.

"Gentlemen," he said, laying his hand upon his heart, "I am deeply grateful for your kind appreciation of my—"

"Admirable singing," suggested Dunbar.

"Of my admirable singing," repeated Wilmot, gravely.

This speech was naturally followed by an outburst of laughter. Wilmot looked around him in grave surprise.

"I don't see what you fellows are laughing at," he said, "unless you're all drunk."

He sat down amid a round of applause, evidently puzzled to understand the effect of his words.

After this, David Green arose, and rehearsed amid great applause a stump speech which he had heard at some minstrel entertainment which he had attended.

"How do you like it, Roswell?" again inquired Ralph Graham.

"It's splendid," said Roswell, enthusiastically.

"Are you glad you joined?"

"Yes; I wouldn't have missed it for a good deal."

"I knew you'd say so. Have your glass filled. Here, Jackson, fill this gentleman's glass."

Roswell was beginning to feel a little light-headed; but the punch had excited him, and he had become in a degree reckless of consequences. So he made no opposition to the proposal, but held out his glass, which was soon returned to him filled to the brim.

"Speech from the new member!" called Dunbar, after a while.

"Yes, speech, speech!"

All eyes were turned towards Roswell.

"You'd better say something," said Ralph.

Roswell rose to his feet, but found it necessary to hold on to his chair for support.

"Mr. President," commenced Roswell, gazing about him in a vacant way, "this is a great occasion."

"Of course it is," said Burgess.

"We are assembled to-night—"

"So we are. Bright boy!" said David Green.

"I am a gentleman's son," continued Roswell.

"What's the gentleman's name?" interrupted Wilmot.

"And I think it's a shame that I should only be paid six dollars a week for my services."

"Bring your employer here, and we'll lynch him," said Tracy. "Such mean treatment of a member of the

Madison Club should meet with the severest punishment. Go ahead."

"I don't think I've got anything more to say," said Roswell. "As my head doesn't feel just right, I'll sit down."

There was a round of applause, and Wilmot arose.

"Mr. President," he said, gravely, "I have been very much impressed with the remarks of the gentleman who has just sat down. They do equal credit to his head and his heart. His reference to his salary was most touching. If you will allow me, I will pause a moment and wipe away an unbidden tear." (Here amid laughter and applause, Wilmot made an imposing demonstration with a large handkerchief. He then proceeded.) "Excuse my emotion, gentlemen. I merely arose to make the motion that the gentleman should furnish us a copy of his remarks, that they may be engrossed on parchment, and a copy sent to the principal libraries in Europe and America."

Roswell was hardly in a condition to understand that fun was being made of him, but listened soberly, sipping from time to time from his glass.

"The motion is not in order," said Brandon. "The hour for business has gone by."

The punch was now removed, and cards were produced. The remainder of the evening was spent in playing euchre and other games. Roswell took a hand, but found he was too dizzy to play correctly, and for the remainder of the evening contented himself with looking on. Small sums were staked among some of the players, and thus a taste for gambling was fostered which might hereafter lead to moral shipwreck and ruin.

This was the way in which the members of the Madison Club spent their evenings,—a very poor way, as my young readers will readily acknowledge. I heartily approve of societies organized by young people for debate and mutual improvement. They are oftentimes productive of great good. Some of our distinguished men date their first impulse to improve and advance themselves to their connection with such a society. But the Madison Club had no salutary object in view. It was adapted to inspire a taste for gambling and drinking, and the money spent by the members to sustain it was worse than wasted.

Roswell, however, who would have found nothing to interest or attract him in a Debating Society, was very favorably impressed by what he had seen of the Madison Club. He got an erroneous impression that it was likely to introduce him into the society of gentlemen, and his aristocratic predilections were, as we know, one of Roswell's hobbies.

It was about eleven when the club broke up its meeting. Previous to this there was a personal difficulty between Wilmot and Tracy, which resulted in a rough-and-tumble fight, in which Wilmot got the worst of it. How the quarrel arose no one could remember,—the principals least of all. At last they were reconciled, and were persuaded to shake hands.

They issued into the street, a noisy throng. Roswell's head ached, the punch, to which he was not accustomed, having affected him in this way. Besides this he felt a little dizzy.

"I wish you'd come home with me, Ralph," he said to his friend. "I don't feel quite right."

"Oh, you'll feel all right to-morrow. Your head will become as strong as mine after a while. I'm as cool as a cucumber."

"It's rather late, isn't it?" asked Roswell.

"Hark, there's the clock striking. I'll count the strokes. Eleven o'clock!" he said, after counting. "That isn't very late."

Ralph accompanied Roswell to the door of his mother's house in Clinton Place.

"Good-night, old fellow!" he said. "You'll be all right in the morning."

"Good-night," said Roswell.

He crept up to bed, but his brain was excited by the punch he had drank, and it was only after tossing about for two hours that he at length sank into a troubled sleep.

Chapter 23

Who Was the Thief?

WHEN ROSWELL rose the next morning he felt cross and out of sorts. His head still ached a little, and he wished he were not obliged to go to the store. But it was out of the question to remain at home, so he started about half an hour after the usual time, and of course arrived late.

"You are late this morning," said Mr. Baker. "You must be more particular about being here in good season."

Roswell muttered something about not feeling quite well.

Putting his hand into his pocket by chance, his fingers came in contact with the key which he had made to open the cash drawer. Just as he was passing Mark, he drew it out and let it drop into the side-pocket of his jacket. So, if suspicion were excited, the key would be found on Mark, not on him.

The critical moment came sooner than he had anticipated.

A Mr. Gay, one of the regular customers of the bookstore, entered a few minutes later.

"Good-morning, Mr. Baker," he said. "Have you got a 'Tribune' this morning?"

"Yes, here is one. By the way, you are just the man I wanted to see."

"Indeed, I feel complimented."

355

"Wait till you hear what I am going to say. You bought a copy of 'Corinne' here on Monday?"

"Yes."

"And handed me a five-dollar bill on the Park Bank?"

"Yes."

"Well, I find the bill was a skilfully executed counterfeit."

"Indeed! I didn't examine it very closely. But I know where I took it, and will give you a good bill in exchange for it."

"I locked it up lest it should get out," said Mr. Baker.

He went to the drawer which Roswell had opened. Roswell listened to this conversation with dismay. He realized that he was in a tight place, for it was undoubtedly the five-dollar counterfeit which he had taken, and paid to the Secretary of the Madison Club. He awaited nervously the result of Mr. Baker's examination.

"Don't you find it?" asked Mr. Gay.

"It is very strange," said Mr. Baker. "I placed it at the top of a pile of bills, and now it is gone."

"Look through the pile. Perhaps your memory is at fault," said Mr. Gay.

Mr. Baker did so.

"No," he said, "the bill has disappeared."

"Do you miss anything else?"

"No. The money is just five dollars short."

"Perhaps you forgot yourself, and paid it away to a customer."

"Impossible; I always make change out of this drawer."

"Well, when you find it, I will make it right. I am in a hurry this morning."

Mr. Gay went out.

"Has any one been to this drawer?" inquired Mr. Baker, abruptly.

"You always keep it locked,—do you not?" said Mr. Jones.

"And keep the key myself. Yes."

"Then I don't see how it could have been opened."

"There was nothing peculiar about the lock. There might easily be another key to fit it."

"I hope you don't suspect me, Mr. Baker?"

"No, Mr. Jones, you have been with me five years, and I have perfect confidence in you."

"Thank you, sir."

"I hope you don't suspect me, sir," said Roswell, boldly. "I am willing to turn my pockets inside-out, to show that I have no key that will fit the lock."

"Very well. You may do so."

Roswell turned his pockets inside-out, but of course no key was found.

"How lucky I got rid of it!" he thought.

"Now it's your turn, Mark," he said.

"I'm perfectly willing," said Mark, promptly.

He put his hand into his pocket, and, to his unutterable astonishment and dismay, drew out a key.

"I didn't know I had this in my pocket," he said, startled.

"Hand me that key," said Mr. Baker, sternly.

Mark handed it to him mechanically.

Mr. Baker went behind the counter, and fitted the key in the lock. It proved to open the drawer with ease.

"Where did you get this key?" he said.

"I didn't know I had it, sir," said Mark, earnestly. "I hope you will believe me."

"I don't understand how you can hope anything of the kind. It seems very clear that you have been at my drawer, and taken the missing money. When did you take it?"

"I have never opened the drawer, nor taken your money," said Mark, in a firm voice, though his cheek was pale, and his look was troubled.

"I am sorry to say that I do not believe you," said Mr. Baker, coldly. "Once more, when did you take the five dollars?"

"I did not take it at all, sir."

"Have you lent the key to any one?"

"No, sir. I did not know I had it."

"I don't know what to do in the matter," said the bookseller, turning to Mr. Jones, his assistant. "It seems clear to me that the boy took the missing bill."

"I am afraid so," said Jones, who was a kind-hearted man, and pitied Mark. "But I don't know when he could have had the chance. He is never left alone in the store."

"Roswell," said Mr. Baker, "have you left Mark alone in the store at any time within two or three days?"

Roswell saw the point of the inquiry, and determined, as a measure of safety, to add falsehood to his former offence.

"Yes, sir," he said, in an apologetic tone, "I left him in the store for two or three minutes yesterday."

"Why did you leave him? Did you go out of the store?"

"Yes, sir. A friend was passing, and I went out to speak to him. I don't think I stayed more than two or three minutes."

"And Mark was left alone in the store?"

"Yes, sir. I had no idea that any harm would come of it."

Mark looked intently at Roswell when he uttered this falsehood.

"You had better confess, Mark, that you took the money when Roswell was out of the store," said his employer. "If you make a full confession, I will be as lenient with you as I can, considering your youth."

"Mr. Baker," said Mark, quietly, more at his ease now, since he began to understand that there was a plot against him, "I cannot confess what is not true. I don't know what Roswell means by what he has just said, but I was not left alone in the store for a moment all day yesterday, nor did Roswell go out to speak to a friend while I was about."

"There seems to be a conflict of evidence here," said Mr. Baker.

"I hope the word of a gentleman's son is worth more than that of a match boy," said Roswell, haughtily.

"To whom do you refer, when you speak of a match boy?"

"To *him*," said Roswell, pointing to Mark. "He used to be a vagabond boy about the streets, selling matches, and sleeping anywhere he could. No wonder he steals."

"I never stole in my life," said Mark, indignantly. "It is true that I sold matches about the streets, and I should have been doing it now, if it had not been for my meeting with kind friends."

"As to his having been a match boy, that has no bearing upon the question," said Mr. Baker. "It is the discovery of the key in his pocket that throws the gravest suspicion upon him. I must see his friends, and inquire into the matter."

"Of course they will stand by him," said Roswell.

"We may get some light thrown upon his possession of the key, at any rate, and can judge for ourselves."

"I shall keep you employed until this matter is investigated," said Mr. Baker to Mark. "Here is a parcel of books to be carried to Twenty-Seventh Street. Come back as soon as they are delivered."

Mark went out with a heavy heart, for it troubled him to think he was under suspicion. Theft, too, he had always despised. He wondered if Richard Hunter would believe him guilty. He could not bear to think that so kind a friend should think so ill of him.

But Mark's vindication was not long in coming. He had been out scarcely ten minutes when Roswell, on looking up, saw to his dismay Tracy, the secretary of the Madison Club, entering the store. His heart misgave him as to the nature of the business on which he had probably come.

He went forward hastily to meet him.

"How are you, Crawford?" said Tracy.

"Pretty well. I am very busy now. I will see you, after the store closes, anywhere you please."

"Oh," said Tracy, in a voice loud enough for Mr. Baker to hear, "It won't take a minute. The bill you gave me last night was a bad one. Of course you didn't know it."

Roswell turned red and pale, and hoped Mr. Baker did not hear. But Mr. Baker had caught the words, and came forward.

"Show me the bill, if you please, young gentleman," he said. "I have a good reason for asking."

"Certainly, sir," said Tracy, rather surprised. "Here it is."

A moment's glance satisfied Mr. Baker that it was the missing bill.

"Did Roswell pay you this bill?" he asked.

"Yes, sir."

"For what did he owe it?"

"I am the secretary of the Madison Club, and this was paid as the entrance fee."

"I recognize the bill," said Mr. Baker. "I will take it, if you please, and you can look to him for another."

"Very well," said Tracy puzzled by the words, the motive of which he did not understand.

"Perhaps you will explain this," said Mr. Baker, turning to Roswell. "It seems that you took this bill."

Roswell's confidence deserted him, and he stood pale and downcast.

"The key I presume, belonged to you."

"Yes, sir," he ejaculated, with difficulty.

"And you dropped it into Mark's pocket,—thus meanly trying to implicate him in a theft which you had yourself committed."

Roswell was silent.

"Have you taken money before?"

"I never opened the drawer but once."

"That was not my question. Make a full confession, and I will not have you arrested, but shall require you to make restitution of all the sums you have stolen. I shall not include this bill, as it is now returned to my possession. Here is a piece of paper. Write down the items."

Roswell did so. They footed up a little over six dollars. Mr. Baker examined it.

"Is this all?" he said.

"Yes, sir."

"Half a week's wages are due you, I will therefore deduct three dollars from this amount. The remainder I shall expect you to refund. I shall have no further occasion for your services."

Roswell took his cap, and was about to leave the store.

"Wait a few minutes. You have tried to implicate Mark in your theft. You must wait till his return, and apologize to him for what you have attempted to do."

"Must I do this?" asked Roswell, ruefully.

"You must," said Mr. Baker, firmly.

When Mark came in, and was told how he had been cleared of suspicion, he felt very happy. Roswell made the apology dictated to him, with a very bad grace, and then was permitted to leave the store.

At home he tried to hide the circumstances attending his discharge from his mother and his cousin; but the necessity of refunding the money made that impossible.

It was only a few days afterwards that Mrs. Crawford received a letter, informing her of the death of a brother in Illinois, and that he had left her a small house and farm. She had found it so hard a struggle for a livelihood in the city, that she decided to remove thither, greatly to Roswell's disgust, who did not wish to be immured in the country. But his wishes could not be gratified, and, sulky and discontented, he was obliged to leave the choice society of the Madison Club, and the attractions of New York, for the quiet of a country town. Let us hope that, away from the influences of the city, his character may be improved, and become more manly and self-reliant. It is only just to say that he was led to appropriate what did not belong to him, by the desire to gratify his vanity, and through the influence of a bad adviser. If he can ever forget that he is "the son of a gentleman," I shall have some hopes for him.

Chapter 24

An Excursion to Fort Hamilton

TOWARDS THE CLOSE of May there was a general holiday, occasioned by the arrival of a distinguished stranger
in the city. All the stores were to be closed, there was
to be a turnout of the military, and a long procession.
Among those released from duty were our three friends,
Fosdick, Richard Hunter, and his ward Mark.

"Well, Dick, what are you going to do to-morrow?"
inquired Fosdick, on the evening previous.

"I was expecting an invitation to ride in a barouche
with the mayor," said Richard; "but probably he forgot
my address and couldn't send it. On the whole I'm glad
of it, being rather bashful and not used to popular
enthusiasm."

"Shall you go out and see the procession?" continued
Fosdick.

"No," said Dick; "I have been thinking of another
plan, which I think will be pleasanter."

"What is it?"

"It's a good while since we took an excursion. Suppose
we go to Fort Hamilton to-morrow."

"I should like that," said Fosdick. "I was never there.
How do we get there?"

"Cross over Fulton Ferry to Brooklyn, and there we
might take the cars to Fort Hamilton. It's seven or
eight miles out there."

"Why do you say 'might' take the cars?"

"Because the cars will be crowded with excursionists, and I have been thinking we might hire a carriage on the Brooklyn side, and ride out there in style. It'll cost more money, but we don't often take a holiday, and we can afford it for once. What you do say, Mark?"

"Do you mean me to go?" asked Mark, eagerly.

"Of course I do. Do you think your guardian would trust you to remain in the city alone?"

"I go in for your plan, Dick," said Fosdick. "What time do you want to start?"

"About half-past nine o'clock. That will give us plenty of time to go. Then, after exploring the fort, we can get dinner at the hotel, and drive where we please afterwards. I suppose there is sea-bathing near by."

Dick's idea was unanimously approved, and by no one more than by Mark. Holidays had been few and far between with him, and he anticipated the excursion with the most eager delight. He was only afraid that the weather would prove unpropitious. He was up at four, looking out of the window; but the skies were clear, and soon the sun came out with full radiance, dissipating the night-shadows, and promising a glorious day.

Breakfast was later than usual, as people like to indulge themselves in a little longer sleep on Sundays and holidays; but it was over by half-past eight, and within a few minutes from that time the three had taken the cars to Fulton Ferry.

In about half an hour the ferry was reached, and, passing through, the party went on board the boat. They had scarcely done so, when an exclamation of surprise was heard, proceeding from feminine lips, and Dick heard himself called by name.

"Why, Mr. Hunter, this is an unexpected pleasure. I am *so* glad to have met you."

Turning his head, Dick recognized Mr. and Mrs. Clifton. Both had been fellow-boarders with him in Bleecker Street. The latter will be rememberd by the readers of "Fame and Fortune" as Miss Peyton. When close upon the verge of old-maidenhood, she had been married, for the sake of a few thousand dollars which she possessed, by Mr. Clifton, a clerk on a small salary, in constant pecuniary difficulties. With a portion of his wife's money he had purchased a partnership in a dry-goods store on Eighth Avenue; but the remainder of her money Mrs. Clifton had been prudent enough to have settled upon herself.

Mrs. Clifton still wore the same ringlets, and exhibited the same youthful vivacity which had characterized her when an inmate of Mrs. Browning's boarding-house, and only owned to being twenty-four, though she looked full ten years older.

"How d'e do, Hunter?" drawled Mr. Clifton, upon whose arm his wife was leaning.

"Very well, thank you," said Dick. "I see Mrs. Clifton is as fascinating as ever."

"O you wicked flatterer!" said Mrs. Clifton, shaking her ringlets, and tapping Dick on the shoulder with her fan. "And here is Mr. Fosdick too, I declare. How do you do, Mr. Fosdick?"

"Quite well, thank you, Mrs. Clifton."

"I declare I've a great mind to scold you for not coming round to see us. I should so much like to hear you sing again."

"My friend hasn't sung since your marriage, Mrs. Clifton," said Dick. "He took it very much to heart. I don't think he has forgiven Clifton yet for cutting him out."

"Mr. Hunter is speaking for himself," said Fosdick, smiling. "He has sung as little as I have."

"Yes, but for another reason," said Dick. "I did not think it right to run the risk of driving away the boarders; so, out of regard to my landlady, I repressed my natural tendency to warble."

"I see you're just as bad as ever," said Mrs. Clifton, in excellent spirits. "But really you must come round and see us. We are boarding in West Sixteenth Street, between Eighth and Ninth Avenues."

"If your husband will promise not to be jealous," said Dick.

"I'm not subject to that complaint," said Clifton, coolly. "Got a cigar about you, Hunter?"

"No, I don't smoke."

"No, don't you though? I couldn't get along without it. It's my great comfort."

"Yes, he's always smoking," said Mrs. Clifton, with some asperity. "Our rooms are so full of tobacco smoke, that I don't know but some of my friends will begin to think I smoke myself."

"A man must have some pleasure," said Clifton, not appearing to be much discomposed by his wife's remarks.

It may be mentioned that although Mrs. Clifton was always gay and vivacious in company, there were times when she could display considerable ill-temper, as her husband frequently had occasion to know. Among the sources of difficulty and disagreement was that portion of Mrs. Clifton's fortune which had been settled upon herself, and of which she was never willing to allow her husband the use of a single dollar. In this, however, she had some justification, as he was naturally a spendthrift, and, if placed in his hands, it would soon have melted away.

"Where are you going, Mr. Hunter?" inquired Mrs. Clifton, after a pause.

"Fosdick and I have planned to take a carriage and ride to Fort Hamilton."

"Delightful!" said Mrs. Clifton. "Why can't we go too, Mr. Clifton?"

"Why, to tell the plain truth," said her husband, "I haven't got money enough with me. If you'll pay for the carriage, I'm willing to go."

Mrs. Clifton hesitated. She had money enough with her, but was not inclined to spend it. Still the prospect of making a joint excursion with Richard Hunter and Fosdick was attractive, and she inquired:—

"How much will it cost?"

"About five dollars probably."

"Then I think we'll go," she said, "that is, if our company would not be disagreeable to Mr. Hunter."

"On the contrary," said Dick. "We will get separate

carriages, but I will invite you both to dine with us after visiting the fort."

Mr. Clifton brightened up at this, and straightway became more social and cheerful.

"Mrs. Clifton," said Richard Hunter, "I believe I haven't yet introduced you to my ward."

"Is that your ward?" inquired the lady, looking towards Mark. "What is his name?"

"Mark Manton."

"How do you like your guardian?" inquired Mrs. Clifton.

"Very much," said Mark, smiling.

"Then I won't expose him," said Mrs. Clifton. "We used to be great friends before I married."

"Since that sad event I have never recovered my spirits," said Dick. "Mark will tell you what a poor appetite I have."

"Is that true, Mark?" asked the lady.

"I don't think it's *very* poor," said Mark, with a smile.

Probably my readers will not consider this conversation very brilliant; but Mrs. Clifton was a silly woman, who was fond of attention, and was incapable of talking sensibly. Richard would have preferred not to have her husband or herself in the company, but, finding it inevitable, submitted to it with as good a grace as possible.

Carriages were secured at a neighboring stable, and the two parties started. The drive was found to be very pleasant, particularly the latter portion, when a fresh breeze from the sea made the air delightfully cool. As they drove up beside the fort, they heard the band within, playing a march, and, giving their horses in charge, they were soon exploring the interior. The view from the ramparts proved to be fine, commanding a good view of the harbor and the city of New York, nearly eight miles distant to the north.

"It is a charming view," said Mrs. Clifton, with girlish enthusiasm.

"I know what will be more charming," said her husband.

"What is it?"

"A prospect of the dinner-table. I feel awfully hungry."

"Mr. Clifton never thinks of anything but eating," said his wife.

"By Jove! you can do your share at that," retorted her husband not very gallantly. "You'd ought to see her eat, Hunter."

"I don't eat more than a little bird," said Mrs. Clifton, affectedly. "I appeal to Mr. Hunter."

"If any little bird ate as much as you, he'd be sure to die of *dyspepsy*," said her husband. If the word in italics is incorrectly spelled, I am not responsible, as that is the way Mr. Clifton pronounced it.

"I confess the ride has given me an appetite also," said Dick. "Suppose we go round to the hotel, and order dinner."

They were soon seated round a bountifully spread dinner-table, to which the whole party, not excepting Mrs. Clifton, did excellent justice. It will not be necessary or profitable to repeat the conversation which seasoned the repast, as, out of deference to Mrs. Clifton's taste, none of the party ventured upon any sensible remarks.

After dinner they extended their drive, and then parted, as Mr. and Mrs. Clifton decided to make a call upon some friends living in the neighborhood.

About four o'clock Richard Hunter and his friends started on their return home. They had about reached the Brooklyn Broadway line, when Fosdick suddenly exclaimed:—

"Dick, there's a carriage overturned a little ways ahead of us. Do you see it?"

Looking in the direction indicated, Dick saw that Fosdick was correct.

"Let us hurry on," he said. "Perhaps we may be able to render some assistance."

Coming up, they found that a wheel had come off, and a gentleman of middle age was leaning against a tree with an expression of pain upon his features, while a boy of about seventeen was holding the horse.

"Frank Whitney!" exclaimed Dick.

To Frank Whitney Dick was indebted for the original impulse which led him to resolve upon gaining a respectable position in society, as will be remembered by the readers of "Ragged Dick;" and for this he had always felt grateful.

"Dick!" exclaimed Frank, in equal surprise. "I am really glad to see you. You are a friend in need."

"Tell me what has happened."

"The wheel of our carriage came off, as you see, and my uncle was pitched out with considerable violence, and has sprained his ankle badly. I was wondering what to do, when luckily you came up."

"Tell me how I can help you," said Dick, promptly, "and I will do so."

"We are stopping at the house of a friend in Brooklyn. If you will give my uncle a seat in your carryall, for he is unable to walk, and carry him there, it will be a great favor. I will remain and attend to the horse and carriage."

"With pleasure, Frank. Are you going to remain in this neighborhood long?"

"I shall try to gain admission to the sophomore class of Columbia College this summer, and shall then live in New York, where I hope to see you often. I intended to enter last year, but decided for some reasons to delay a year. However, if I am admitted to advanced standing, I shall lose nothing. Give me your address, and I will call on you very soon."

"I am afraid I shall inconvenience you," said Mr. Whitney.

"Not at all," said Dick, promptly. "We have plenty of room, and I shall be glad to have an opportunity of obliging one to whom I am indebted for past kindness."

Mr. Whitney was assisted into the carriage, and they resumed their drive, deviating from their course somewhat, in order to leave him at the house of the friend with whom he was stopping.

"I am very glad to have met Frank again," thought Dick; "I always liked him."

Chapter 25

An Important Discovery

MARK REMAINED in the bookstore on the same footing as before. He was not old enough to succeed to Roswell's vacant place, but Mr. Baker, as a mark of his satisfaction with him, and partly also to compensate for the temporary suspicions which he had entertained of his honesty, advanced his wages a dollar a week. He therefore now received four dollars, which yielded him no little satisfaction, as it enabled him to pay a larger share of his expenses.

They were all seated in Richard Hunter's pleasant room in St. Mark's Place one evening, when Dick said, suddenly:—

"Oh, by the way, Fosdick, I forgot to tell you that I had a letter from Mr. Bates to-day."

"Did you? What does he say?"

"I will read it to you."

Richard drew the letter from the envelope, and read as follows: —

"MY DEAR MR. HUNTER:—I have received your letter, reporting that you have as yet obtained no trace of my unfortunate grandson, John Talbot. I thank you sincerely for your kind and persistent efforts. I fear that he may have left New York, possibly in the care of persons unfit to take charge of him. It is a great source of anxiety to me lest he should be suffering privation and bad treatment at this moment, when I, his grandfather, have abundance of worldly means, and have it in my power to

371

rear him handsomely. I cannot help feeling that it is a fitting punishment for the cruel harshness with which I treated his mother. Now I am amassing wealth but I have no one to leave it to. I feel that I have small object in living. Yet I cannot give up the thought that my grandson is still living. I cannot help indulging the hope that some day, by the kind favor of Providence, he may be given back to me.

"If it will not be too much trouble to you and Mr. Fosdick, I shall feel indebted if you will still continue on the watch for the lost boy. Any expenses which you may incur, as I have already assured you, will be most cheerfully paid by your obliged friend and servant,

"HIRAM BATES."

While Richard was reading this letter, Mark listened attentively. Looking up, Richard observed this.

"Did you ever meet with a boy named John Talbot, Mark?" he inquired.

"No," said Mark, "not *John* Talbot."

"Did you ever meet any boy named Talbot? It is not certain that the name is John."

"Talbot used to be my name," said Mark.

"Used to be your name!" exclaimed Richard, in surprise. "I thought it was Manton."

"Some of the boys gave me that name because there was a story came out in one of the story papers about Mark Manton. After a while I got to calling myself so, but my real name is Mark Talbot."

"It would be strange if he should turn out to be the right boy after all, Dick," said Fosdick. "Where is the photograph? That will soon settle the question."

Richard Hunter opened his desk, and took out the card photograph which Mr. Bates had left with him.

"Mark," he said, "did you ever see any one who looked like that picture?"

Mark took the picture in his hand. No sooner did his eyes rest upon it than they filled with tears.

"That is my mother," he said. "Where did you get it?"

"Your mother! Are you sure?"

"Yes; I should know it anywhere, though it looks younger than she did."

"Do you know what her name was, before she was married?"

"Yes; she has told me often. It was Irene Bates."

"How strange!" exclaimed Richard and Fosdick together. "Mark," continued Richard, "I think you are the very boy I had been in search of for several months. I had succeeded without knowing it."

"Please tell me all about it," said Mark. "I don't understand."

"I have a great piece of good luck to announce to you, Mark. Your grandfather is a rich man, formerly in business in New York, but now a successful merchant in Milwaukie. He has no child, no descendant except yourself. He has been anxiously seeking for you, intending to give you all the advantages which his wealth can procure."

"Do you think I shall like him?" asked Mark, timidly.

"Yes; I think he will be very kind to you."

"But he was not kind to my mother. Although he was rich, he let her suffer."

"He has repented of this, and will try to make up to you his neglect to your mother."

Mark was still thoughtful. "If it had come sooner, my poor mother might still have been alive," he said.

"I think I had better telegraph to Mr. Bates tomorrow," said Richard. "The news will be so welcome that I don't like to keep it back a single day."

"Perhaps it will be better," said Fosdick. "You will have to give up your ward, Dick."

"Yes; but as it will be for his good, I will not object."

The next morning the following message was flashed over the wires to Milwaukie:—

"HIRAM BATES

"Your grandson is found. He is well, and in my charge.
"RICHARD HUNTER."

In the course of the forenoon, the following answer was received:—

"RICHARD HUNTER.

"How can I thank you? I take the next train for New York.

"HIRAM BATES."

On the afternoon succeeding, Mr. Bates entered Richard's counting-room. He clasped his hand with fervor.

"Mr. Hunter," he said, "I do not know how to thank you. Where is my boy?"

"I am just going up to the house," said Richard. "If you will accompany me, you shall soon see him."

"I am impatient to hear all the particulars," said Mr. Bates. "Remember, I know nothing as yet. I only received your telegram announcing his discovery. When did you find him?"

"That is the strangest part of it," said Richard. "I found him sick just outside the office door several weeks since. I took him home, and when he recovered let him get a place in a bookstore; but, having become interested in him, I was unwilling to lose sight of him, and still kept him with me. All this while I was searching for your grandson, and had not the least idea that he was already found."

"How did you discover this at last?"

"By his recognition of his mother's photograph. It was lucky you thought of leaving it with me."

"Is his name John?"

"He says his name is Mark, but for his last name he had adopted a different one, or I should have made the discovery sooner."

"How did he make a living before you found him? Poor boy!" said Mr. Bates, sighing. "I fear he must have suffered many privations."

"He was selling matches for some time,—what we call a match boy. He had suffered hardships; but I leave him to tell you his story himself."

"How does he feel about meeting me?" asked Mr. Bates.

"You are a stranger to him, and he naturally feels a

little timid, but he will soon be reassured when he gets acquainted with you."

Mark had already arrived. As they entered the room, Mr. Bates said with emotion, "Is that he?"

"Yes, sir."

"Come here, Mark," he said, in a tone which took away Mark's apprehension. "Do you know who I am?"

"Are you my grandfather?"

"Yes, I have come to take care of you, and to see that you suffer no more from poverty."

Mr. Bates stooped down and pressed a kiss upon the boy's forehead.

"I can see Irene's look in his eyes," he said. "It is all the proof I need that he is my grandchild."

It was arranged that in three days, for he had some business to transact, he should go back to Milwaukie carrying Mark with him. He went round to Mr. Baker's store the next morning with his grandson, and explained to him why he should be obliged to withdraw him from his employ.

"I am sorry to lose him," said Mr. Baker. "He is quick and attentive to his duties, and has given me excellent satisfaction; but I am glad of his good fortune."

"It gives me pleasure to hear so good an account of him," said Mr. Bates. "Though he will be under no necessity of taking another situation, but will for several years devote himself to study, the same good qualities for which you give him credit will insure his satisfactory progress in school."

Chapter 26

Conclusion

IT WAS not long before Mark felt quite at home with his grandfather. He no longer felt afraid of him, but began to look forward with pleasant anticipations to his journey West, and the life that was to open before him in Milwaukie. It was a relief to think that he would not now be obliged to take care of himself, but would have some one both able and willing to supply his wants, and provide him with a comfortable home.

He felt glad again that he was going to school. He remembered how anxious his poor mother had been that he should receive a good education, and now his grandfather had promised to send him to the best school in Milwaukie.

The next morning after their meeting, Mr. Bates took Mark to a large clothing establishment, and had him fitted out with new clothes in the most liberal manner. He even bought him a silver watch, of which Mark felt very proud.

"Now, Mark," said his grandfather, "if there is any one that was kind to you when you were a poor match boy, I should like to do something to show my gratitude for their kindness. Can you think of any one?"

"Yes," said Mark; "there's Ben Gibson."

"And who is Ben Gibson?"

"He blacks boots down on Nassau Street. When I ran away from Mother Watson, who treated me so badly,

377

he stood by me, and prevented her from getting hold of me again."

"Is there any one besides?"

"Yes," said Mark, after a pause; "there is Mrs. Flanagan. She lives in the same tenement-house where I used to. When I was almost starved she used to give me something to eat, though she was poor herself."

"I think we will call and see her first," said Mr. Bates. "I am going to let you give her a hundred dollars."

"She will be delighted," said Mark, his eyes sparkling with joy. "It will seem a fortune to her. Let us go at once."

"Very well," said his grandfather. "Afterwards we will try to find your friend Ben."

I forgot to mention that Mr. Bates was stopping at the Fifth Avenue Hotel.

They took the University Place cars, which landed them at the junction of Barclay Street and Broadway. From thence it was but a short distance to Vandewater Street, where Mark lived when first introduced to the reader.

They climbed the broken staircase, and paused in front of Mrs. Flanagan's door.

Mark knocked.

Mrs. Flanagan opened the door, and stared with some surprise at her visitors.

"Don't you know me, Mrs. Flanagan?" asked Mark.

"Why, surely it isn't Mark, the little match boy?" said Mrs. Flanagan, amazed.

"Yes, it is. So you didn't know me?"

"And it's rale delighted I am to see you lookin' so fine. And who is this gentleman?"

"It is my grandfather, Mrs. Flanagan. I'm going out West to live with him."

Mrs. Flanagan dropped a courtesy to Mr. Bates, who said, "My good woman, Mark tells me that you were kind to him when he stood in need of kindness."

"And did he say that?" said Mrs. Flanagan, her face beaming with pleasure. "Shure it was little I did for him, bein' poor myself; but that little he was heartily welcome to, and I'm delighted to think he's turned out so lucky. The ould woman trated him very bad. I used to feel as if I'd like to break her ould bones for her."

"Mark and I both want to thank you for your kindness to him, and he has a small gift to give you."

"Here it is," said Mark, drawing from his pocket a neat pocket-book, containing a roll of bills. "You'll find a hundred dollars inside, Mrs. Flanagan," he said. "I hope they will help you."

"A hundred dollars!" ejaculated Mrs. Flanagan, hardly believing her ears. "Does this good gentleman give me a hundred dollars!"

"No, it is Mark's gift to you," said Mr. Bates.

"It's rich I am with so much money," said the good woman. "May the saints bless you both! Now I can buy some clothes for the childer, and have plenty left beside. This is a happy day entirely. But won't you step in, and rest yourselves a bit? It's a poor room, but—"

"Thank you, Mrs. Flanagan," said Mr. Bates, "but we are in haste this morning. Whenever Mark comes to New York he shall come and see you."

They went downstairs, leaving Mrs. Flanagan so excited with her good fortune, that she left her work, and made a series of calls upon her neighbors, in which she detailed Mark's good fortune and her own.

"Now we'll go and find your friend, Ben Gibson," said Mr. Bates.

"I think we'll find him on Nassau Street," said Mark. He was right.

In walking down Nassau Street on the east side, Mr. Bates was accosted by Ben himself.

"Shine yer boots?"

"How are you, Ben?" said Mark.

Ben stared in surprise till he recognized his old companion.

"Blest if it aint Mark," he said. "How you're gettin' on!"

"Ben, this is my grandfather," said Mark.

"Well, you're a lucky chap," said Ben, enviously. "I wish I could find a rich grandfather. I don't believe I ever had a grandfather."

"How are you getting on, my lad?" inquired Mr. Bates.

"Middlin'," said Ben. "I haven't laid by a fortun' yet."

"No, I suppose not. How do you like blacking boots?"

"Well, there's other things I might like better," said Ben,—"such as bein' a rich merchant; but that takes rather more capital than blackin' boots."

"I see you are an original," said Mr. Bates, smiling.

"Am I?" said Ben. "Well, I'm glad of it, though I didn't know it before. I hope it aint anything very bad."

"Mark says you treated him kindly when he lived about the street."

"It wasn't much," said Ben.

"I want to do something for you. What shall I do?"

"Well," said Ben, "I should like a new brush. This is most worn out."

"How would you like to go to Milwaukie with Mark, if I will get you a place there?"

"Do you mean it?" said Ben, incredulously.

"Certainly."

"I haven't any money to pay for goin' out there."

"I will take care of that," said Mr. Bates.

"Then I'll go," said Ben, "and I'm much obliged to you. Mark, you're a brick, and so's your grandfather. I never expected to have such good luck."

"Then you must begin to make arrangements at once. Mark, here is some money. You may go with Ben, see that he takes a good bath, and then buy him some clothes. I am obliged to leave you to do it, as I must attend to some business in Wall Street. I shall expect to see you both at the Fifth Avenue Hotel at two o'clock."

At two o'clock, Mr. Bates found the two boys awaiting him. There was a great change in Ben's appearance. He had faithfully submitted to the bath, and bloomed out in a tasteful suit of clothes, selected by Mark. Mark had taken him besides to a barber's and had his long hair cut. So he now made quite a presentable appearance, though he felt very awkward in his new clothes.

"It don't seem natural to be clean," he confessed to Mark.

"You'll get used to it after a while," said Mark, laughing.

"Maybe I will; but I miss my old clothes. They seemed more comfortable."

The next day they were to start. Ben remained at the hotel with his friend Mark, feeling, it must be confessed, a curious sensation at his unusual position.

They went to make a farewell call on Richard Hunter.

"Mr. Hunter," said Mr. Bates, "money will not pay you for the service you have done me, but I shall be glad if you will accept this cheque."

Richard saw that it was a cheque for a thousand dollars.

"Thank you for your liberality, Mr. Bates," he said; "but I do not deserve it."

"Let me be the judge of that."

"I will accept it on one condition."

"Name it, Mr. Hunter."

"That you will allow me to give it to the Newsboys' Lodge, where I once found shelter, and where so many poor boys are now provided for."

"I will give an equal sum to that institution," said Mr. Bates, "and I thank you for reminding me of it. As for this money, oblige me by keeping it youself."

"Then," said Richard, "I will keep it as a charity fund, and whenever I have an opportunity of helping along a boy who is struggling upward as I once had to struggle, I will do it."

"A noble resolution, Mr. Hunter! You have found out the best use of money."

Mark is now at an excellent school in Milwaukie, pursuing his studies. He is the joy and solace of his grandfather's life, hitherto sad and lonely, and is winning the commendation of his teachers by his devotion to study. A place was found for Ben Gibson, where he had some advantages of education, and he is likely to do well. He has been persuaded by Mark to leave off smoking,—a habit which he had formed in the streets of New York. The shrewdness which his early experiences taught him will be likely to benefit him in the business career which lies before him.

Every year Mark sends a substantial present to Mrs. Flanagan, under his grandfather's direction, and thus makes the worthy woman's life much more comfortable and easy. From time to time Mark receives a letter from Richard Hunter, who has not lost his interest in the little match boy was was once his ward.

So the trials of Mark, the Match Boy, as far as they proceeded from poverty and privation, are at an end. He has found a comfortable and even luxurious home, and a relative whose great object in life is to study his happiness.